FATE
OF THE
SUN
KING

FATE OF THE SUN KING

NISHA J. TULI

FOREVER

New York Boston

Cover design by Miblart. Cover copyright © 2024 by Hachette Book Group, Inc.

Forever
Hachette Book Group
1290 Avenue of the Americas, New York, NY 10104
read-forever.com
@readforeverpub

First Edition: June 2024

Forever is an imprint of Grand Central Publishing. The Forever name and logo are registered trademarks of Hachette Book Group, Inc.

The publisher is not responsible for websites (or their content) that are not owned by the publisher.

The Hachette Speakers Bureau provides a wide range of authors for speaking events. To find out more, go to hachettespeakersbureau.com or email HachetteSpeakers@hbgusa.com.

Forever books may be purchased in bulk for business, educational, or promotional use. For information, please contact your local bookseller or the Hachette Book Group Special Markets Department at special.markets@hbgusa.com.

Library of Congress Cataloging-in-Publication Data

Names: Tuli, Nisha J., author.
Title: Fate of the Sun King / Nisha J. Tuli.
Description: First edition. | New York : Forever, 2024. | Series: Artefacts of Ouranos ; book 3 |
Identifiers: LCCN 2023054995 | ISBN 9781538767672 (trade paperback) | ISBN 9781538767689 (ebook)
Subjects: LCGFT: Fantasy fiction. | Romance fiction. | Novels.
Classification: LCC PR9199.4.T8347 F38 2024 | DDC 813/.6—dc23/eng/20231204
LC record available at https://lccn.loc.gov/2023054995

ISBNs: 978-1-5387-6767-2 (trade paperback); 978-1-5387-6768-9 (ebook)

Printed in the United States of America

LSC-C

Printing 3, 2025

For every reader who delights in the
delicious angst of a slow burn.
(Yes, I promise I let them do it in this one.
I couldn't take it anymore either.)

CELESTRIA

BELTZA MOUNTAINS

THE MANOR

TOR

NOSTRAZA

SIVA FOREST

ALLUVION

SINEN RIVER

ZELEN COVE

APHELION

THE SARGA WOODS

OURANOS

AUTHOR'S NOTE

Dear Readers,

Welcome back to Ouranos! I know that some of you have been waiting a very, very long time for this book and I am beyond thrilled to be finally sharing it with you. Thank you for all your patience, your enthusiasm, and your grace, as this book took a little longer to get into your hands.

Thank you to everyone who's found their way into my in-boxes and my mentions to tell me how much you've loved these stories. I cherish every single message, and they keep me striving to make my books the best they can be. This has been the hardest book yet in the series, but you all make it worth it.

Now it's finally here, and I am bursting to share *Fate of the Sun King* with you. In these pages, you will find the action and stakes you loved from *Trial*, as well as the tension, angst, and heat from *Rule*. I've poured my heart and my soul into these pages, and I hope you enjoy reading them as we continue our journey with Lor and her friends.

As always, I'm listing the content warnings before the text if you'd like to read them. Otherwise, skip to the glossary and then to Chapter 1, where we begin our story back in Aphelion.

Love,

Nisha

Content Warnings: *In this book, you'll find a lot of the same themes and topics as the rest of the series, including mentions of past sexual abuse, along with the usual bits of violence, death, torture, and blood. There's also swearing and on-page sex, as well as suicide ideation and alcohol abuse.*

Glossary of Characters

Lor: Our heroine and the main badass babe of our world, who needs no introduction. A prisoner inside Nostraza for twelve years. Competed in the Sun Queen Trials against her will. Has some secrets she's keeping close that might include being lost royalty. Will not get wrapped up in anyone's territorial Fae bullshit. Do NOT touch her soap.

Nadir: Prince of The Aurora. Kidnapped Lor from the Sun Palace in Aphelion after the Trials. Helped her find the Crown. Was saved by Lor's magic as they narrowly escaped his father. A *little* intense and suffering thanks to all the fee-fees he might have for our heroine.

Tristan: Lor's brother—oldest of the three Heart siblings. Also lived inside Nostraza and protected his sisters at every cost. He has some magic, and we're just getting to know him. But he has a story to tell.

Willow: Lor's older sister—middle child of the Heart siblings. The calm one. The one Lor and Tristan protected at every turn. The one who doesn't fall asleep to bloody fantasies of vengeance. Is getting to know a certain Aurora Princess.

Amya: Princess of the Aurora and Nadir's little sister. She's the nice one. Our goth princess with Aurora-colored highlights and a wardrobe we'd all kill for.

Mael: Captain of Nadir's guard. His best friend and comic relief.

Atlas: If you've forgotten who Atlas is ... No, there's no way you did. The Sun King. Master manipulator. Got Lor out of Nostraza to compete in the Trials for some mysterious reason that *maybe* you'll find out in this book. Not blond despite everyone comparing him to a certain High Lord of Spring (IYKYK).

Gabriel: You know him, you love him, and he's back. One of the Sun King's warders and Lor's babysitter during the Trials. He's grumpy but weirdly lovable. Has a chip to go with the wings on his shoulders, but maybe he has reasons. *He's* the blond.

Rion: The Aurora King. You might remember him from that time he locked up Lor and her siblings and then tormented her for a while. He's still after her. He's also after his son. Basically, everyone is on his shitlist right now.

Meora: Nadir and Amya's mother. The Aurora Queen whose only mistake was meeting Rion, who then punished her for getting pregnant with Nadir, all while *he* was trying to make his girlfriend jealous. She doesn't speak anymore, and we need to get rid of Rion so she can be free.

Serce: Lor's grandmother and the former Heart Queen who broke the world. Got a little too big for her britches. She's ding-dong dead.

Wolf: Lor's grandfather and former king of the Woodlands, who was along for Serce's ride. It's tough because he seemed like a nice guy, but he also just let her run amok, and he isn't blameless. Also ding-dong dead.

Daedra: Lor's great grandmother. Serce's mother. Former Heart Queen who did her best, but a mother's job is thankless, and sometimes your kids just don't turn out the way you'd hoped. Also . . . dead.

Cloris Payne: High Priestess of Zerra who was helping Serce and Wolf until she lost her mind thanks to the arcturite cuffs she was forced to wear. Look, I think you get it. Dead.

Apricia: Is alive, unfortunately. Really alive. Head bitch during the Sun Queen Trials. She won the thing, though, and now Aphelion gets her as their queen. Haven't they suffered enough?

Callias: Aphelion's most-coveted-stylist-with-a-very-long-cock. Not sure what else needs to be said.

Halo: Fallen Tribute. Befriended Lor during the Trials.

Marici: Another fallen Tribute. Halo's girlfriend and also Lor's friend. Okay, they weren't that nice to Lor at the beginning, but they all worked it out. Now Halo and Marici just want to be together.

Hylene: One of Nadir's friends. Long red hair and she takes no prisoners. You'll see more of her soon.

Etienne: Another one of Nadir's circle. He's quiet but he's useful. You'll see.

Zerra: God/goddess (we use these interchangeably because why not?) of Ouranos. Supreme being. The one who rules them all.

Cedar: King of the Woodlands, eastern kingdom of forest and tree magic. Lor and her siblings' great-uncle.

Elswyth: Queen of the Woodlands. The great-aunt.

Cyan: King of Alluvion, the water kingdom. He's got blue hair and light blue skin, and we don't know much about him yet. Currently looking for a bonded partner.

Bronte: Queen of Tor, the mountain queendom. Bonded to Yael.

D'Arcy: Queen of Celestria, the sky queendom. Has been through seven bonded partners. So far.

CHAPTER ONE

GABRIEL

APHELION: THE SUN PALACE

Pain throbs behind my left eye, reminding me of the time an angry lover twisted my balls in his grip after finding me buried between his sister's thighs. I told him jealousy wasn't a good look, and unsurprisingly, that only made things worse.

Another stab pulses in my temple as I jingle a ring of golden keys in my hand, hating the sound. They're too shiny and bright in this corridor's weak light. A mockery of what lives in this abandoned corner of the palace, carefully shielded by false curtains of shadow.

My footsteps ring sharply in the silence, like razors slicing into my eardrums, each more ominous than the last.

I both loathe and look forward to this task.

When I reach the door, I pause and drag in a deep, grounding breath before I insert the key and swivel the lock. The door drifts open on carefully oiled hinges, as silent as dust tumbling through a sunbeam. Though we're far from the curiosity of acutely tuned High Fae hearing, every layer of these buried secrets is carefully considered.

Thanks to his powers of illusion, Atlas ensures this corner garners little notice from passersby, their eyes slithering over the archway of the dimly lit hall. They swear they noticed something, but a moment later, it's gone, and surely they have better things to do.

A feat he's managed for nearly a hundred years.

On the far side of the door, a stone stairwell spirals up into the darkness. My dogged steps strike like nails against steel, winding the tight corner, suffocating me as I ascend. The top landing reveals another door—this one heavier and stronger, fortified with iron bands, bolts, and a barrier of protective magic for a dose of good measure. Even a full-grown Imperial Fae at the height of his strength would struggle to break it down.

I pick out another key from the ring and flip the lock before opening another door oiled into silence. The tower room is comfortably sized to suit its single discarded resident. Unlike the rest of the Sun Palace, it boasts none of the usual gilded trappings. No resplendent décor or surfaces polished to a high shine. Here are stone floors and walls, everything grey and faded, like a memory you're trying to forget.

Windows inset around the perimeter afford a breathtaking view of Aphelion from every side. The taunting blue of the ocean. The glittering domes of the city's buildings. The shadow of The Umbra lying to the south.

What I can't decide is whether the king offered this panorama as a kindness or as further penance for a sin that was never committed except in his own mind. I suspect it's the latter. To be confined to this space, forced to bear witness to the untouchable outside world, is a prison of its own sort.

Atlas's already shaky moral compass deserted him so many years ago I've forgotten he ever had one.

I take a moment to gather myself before my gaze wanders to the figure on the bed. Tyr lies on his side, his knees tucked up, his thin hands clutching the covers, his eyes distant and vacant. Once as bright and blue as the sea, decades of confinement have dimmed them to haunted hollows of muted grey shadows. His once shining blond hair is the same—muddied by time and torment and the years spent without the sun's warmth on his face.

I stride to his side and crouch on my haunches, putting me at eye level with the royal Fae, who was once a king. Who, by all rights, is *still* a king, but there are only eleven people left in the world who know that—ten of whom are magically bound to silence.

"How are you doing today?" I ask, though I'm not expecting an answer.

Tyr's eyes flick up, registering me before they flick away again. He listens when I speak, though he rarely responds. Sometimes he does, and those are the good days, if there is such a thing. But they happen less and less, and it's actually been weeks since he last said a word.

"Plans are underway for the bonding ceremony," I say as I push myself up and move about the room before unloading the bag slung over my shoulder and unpacking its contents onto the dresser pushed against the far wall.

Atlas can't place his trust in the palace servants, so Tyr's care has fallen to me and the other nine warders. But Tyr makes my brothers uncomfortable, so the duty lies mostly with me. It's one of the few tasks I approach without resentment, because I don't trust anyone else to do a proper job.

My haul includes the usual load of dried goods. Some loaves of bread. Hunks of cheese. Fruit and vegetables. Wine and beer and water. Though he'll wait until I leave, he'll eat it all. That knowledge offers some consolation. At least he's not starving himself, and I take my victories where they arise.

"The queen's guest list would probably wrap around the entire city," I continue, keeping up a stream of chatter. "Twice."

No one has ever accused me of being verbose, but I hate the silence that squats in the corners of this room when Tyr isn't in the mood for conversation. As a result, I find myself babbling into the vacancy like a fool.

"She's stirring up all kinds of shit about another delay."

As I ramble, I consider the circumstances of all that's transpired over the last several months. The many things I don't understand about Atlas's plan to bond. He isn't the Primary or an ascended king, so I'm not sure what he's hoping to accomplish. At the same time, I also don't understand what he's waiting for. He held the Trials to find a partner, or so I presume, and the Mirror chose Apricia. So this should all be over.

But Atlas continues deferring, and her shrill screeches can probably be heard all the way to The Aurora. The entire thing is wearing on every last one of my fucking nerves. I understand it has something to do with Lor, but after months of digging and questioning, I'm no closer to an answer.

Clearly, I've missed something important about the woman who made my life hell during the Trials, though I'll grudgingly admit she started growing on me in the end. Like an annoying little pet you can't bring yourself to abandon at the side of the road despite the fact it keeps chewing up your shoes.

I sense Tyr listening as I chatter about the kingdom and the latest news on the ground. Reports from The Umbra speak of increasing unrest stirring within its streets. The low fae demand the right to buy property within the twenty-four districts, but their bids for housing in the upper quarters are continually denied by the city council at Atlas's behest. Despite everything working against them, plenty have cobbled together enough wealth to afford a home in the districts, but their wishes fall on Atlas's unwilling ears.

I've never understood why they remain here rather than heading for The Woodlands or Alluvion, where they'd be free to live as equals. But I know all too well that abandoning the place you call home isn't as simple as it sounds. Besides, it's hardly fair they're the ones being pushed out.

In addition, the Aurora King's roving bands of poachers act as enough of a threat to keep them confined within our walls. They might hold few rights in Aphelion, but it's probably a marginally better fate than conscription to Rion's mines.

"Hungry?" I ask Tyr as I fix him a plate of food, slicing some of the cheese I know he likes and adding a few crackers, along with a cream puff that's his favorite treat. I also pour him a generous glass of the vintage whisky I bought—it cost nearly as much as an entire flat in one of the lower districts, but why shouldn't he be allowed to indulge whenever he can?

I set the food on the table next to the bed, glancing over, wondering if we're having a good day or a bad one. He's barely reacted to my presence, and that probably tells me the answer.

My gaze skits over the arcturite cuffs ringing his neck and wrists. The glowing blue stone, mined in the Beltza Mountains far to the north, has cut him off from his magic since the day Atlas confined him to this room.

Atlas used the warder's promise against me and my brothers, convincing Tyr to turn over the rule of Aphelion to Atlas. We were forced to capture Tyr against our will, bind him in the cuffs, and lock him away—possibly forever or until... something drastic changes.

The memory haunts me in my dreams and when I'm awake, but I had no choice. I still have no choice. Going against the king's command means suffering unimaginable amounts of pain and, eventually, death. More than once, I've considered it. Just allowing my insubordination to end it all. But then Tyr would be without me, and I can't rely on the others to protect him the way I can. At least this way I can do my part, as much as I despise myself for every second of it.

Tyr's gaze tracks my movements as I settle into the chair in the corner, picking up the book on the nearby table and flipping to where I marked our page two days ago. I've read hundreds of books to Tyr over the years. He refuses to read them independently, instead waiting for me to arrive. It's another small thing I can offer. Maybe it makes this miserable life just a little less miserable.

As I read, I watch him from the corner of my vision, noticing how his eyes move as though they're tracking the words on the page. I think he's listening to every syllable, but whenever he utters a word, I worry it will be the last time I hear his voice for good.

Sometimes he lies so still it's like he's already gone. Lately, I worry about his condition deteriorating faster than ever. I confirmed long ago that prolonged exposure to arcturite slowly erodes the sanity of High Fae minds. I don't know what Atlas plans. He can't kill Tyr: the Mirror would transfer the magic to the true Primary, and he'd lose everything he's been trying to gain for centuries.

After an hour, I close the book and stand, knowing I have a thousand other duties needing my attention.

Tyr, as usual, hasn't touched his food. I've never understood why he refuses to eat in my presence, but I don't press the matter. A man forced to live this threadbare existence is entitled to his eccentricities. At least he's eating. That must be enough for now.

I stand over him, wishing there was more I could do. I tuck back a lock of his hair, the strands dry and brittle to the touch. He'll need a trim soon, along with a shave of his thickening beard. I'll bring some scissors and a razor next time. For obvious reasons, I can't leave these items here. I note his tunic also looks a little ratty. It might be time for new clothes as well.

"I'll be back tomorrow," I say, trying not to sound quite as maudlin as I feel. "Eat up."

Tyr blinks, and I like to think it's because he's acknowledging me. I hope it is. I miss him and everything we almost were.

I check the room one more time, pausing when the floor starts to vibrate under my feet. Another tremor. These shifts started happening several weeks ago, but their origin remains a mystery.

Whatever. This isn't my concern. I have plenty of other things to worry about right now.

Once the rumbling subsides, I close the door gently behind me before I make my way back down the stairs and immediately head towards Atlas's apartments, brushing past his sentries outside.

After knocking on the door of the king's study, I call out, "Atlas?"

"Enter," comes the voice on the other side.

I find him standing at the window, cradling a mug of tea in his hand, staring out across the city.

"I've just been to see him," I say, keeping my voice low. The study is warded against eavesdropping, but I can't defy the insistent hush of the secrets I hold. It feels wrong to speak of them in a normal tone of voice. Like I'm normalizing shit that should never be normalized.

"Hmm," Atlas replies, still focused on the view outside.

Thankfully, he doesn't see the way my jaw clenches at his indifference. The way he behaves like he doesn't give a fuck about the brother from whom he's stolen everything makes me so furious red bleeds into the corners of my vision.

Finally, Atlas pushes himself from the window and walks over to settle on the shiny leather couch in the center of the room. He takes a long sip of his tea before he settles back and gives me a look that seems to ask *Is there anything else you need to bother me with?*

"He's getting worse," I push. "The cuffs—"

"Aren't going anywhere," Atlas says, his response chilled with the threat that he will not entertain this conversation again.

"But they're killing him."

Finally, Atlas arches a brow and pins me with a cold look. "What would you have me do? Take them off so he can kill me?"

The king glares with his piercing aquamarine gaze, daring me to break. We've known each other for a long time. Atlas might call us friends, but it's hard for me to consider our relationship in that light. When one side holds all the power, and you are merely a servant at his command, it's more complicated than *friendship.*

I resist the urge to unleash the truth that squats on the tip of my tongue, burning like acid. That *yes*, I'd love to see Tyr break free and pay Atlas back for everything he deserves.

"No," I say, my words clipped. "But this is killing *him.*"

I emphasize the last word, hoping that might rouse Atlas's attention at the very least. In the eyes of the Mirror, death by neglect amounts to the same outcome as slicing his throat with a dagger.

"If you don't do something..." I trail off, allowing the threat to dangle between us.

"Everything will be fine once I've bonded," Atlas says with a wave of his hand, and I want to demand an explanation for what *that* means.

"Speaking of which," I ask instead, even knowing he won't answer, "I've heard you've pushed the ceremony date again. If bonding will solve this, why do you keep delaying?"

What game is Atlas playing? He's refusing to bond to Apricia while simultaneously extolling the virtues of doing so. None of this makes any damn sense.

"I have my reasons," Atlas says, evasive as ever. "Do you have any leads on where Lor is yet?"

"This all has something to do with her," I say again. This is far from the first time we've had this conversation, and it definitely won't be the last. "Tell me what's going on. Why does she matter?"

Atlas rolls his shoulders before he takes a deep sip of his drink. "The less you know, the better, Gabriel. I'm doing this for your protection. I only ever have your best interests at heart."

I ignore the colossal absurdity of those last statements as I press him further.

"But if I knew, I might be better positioned to help you. I wouldn't be searching blindly."

It's the truth, but it's only partly why I want to know.

What I really want to understand is whose side I should be on.

Atlas exhales a drawn-out sigh as though *I'm* the one who's in the wrong here.

"Knowing why I need her won't help you find her. Do you have any leads on where the fuck she is?"

I shake my head. I have thoughts and theories about where she might be, but something is keeping me from sharing that information with Atlas. A deeply rooted premonition tells me this is the right move.

Nadir came to the Sun Queen Ball asking about a missing girl. Worried Atlas was doing something reckless with Lor, I revealed her to Nadir, or at least I tried. Did he see the tattoo on her shoulder before Atlas threw him out of the palace? Was Nadir the one who took her? Why would he care about her at all? Why do I care?

Despite everything, my duty is to protect Atlas, not for his sake but for Tyr's.

There were no clues left the night she disappeared, and I'm starting to wonder if she dissolved into mist. It wouldn't surprise me if she somehow got herself out. Almost from the beginning, I was positive she was hiding something. And she proved she was resourceful when she made it through the Trials, even with help.

"You need to find her," Atlas says. "The future of this kingdom depends on it."

"Why?" I try again. "Why? She was a prisoner from The Aurora. Why does she matter?"

"Come on, Gabriel. You know by now she's more than that."

I clench my teeth at the condescension in the king's tone. I'm *this* close to going over the edge and beating him to a bloody pulp. But that would be pointless. It would land me in the dungeons again, or worse. I shudder at the idea of Tyr's fate, locked in a tower, never able to roam free. Just the suggestion dredges up too many memories I'd rather forget.

Thankfully, I'm saved from my murderous impulses when the door to the study slams open.

"Atlas!" Apricia spits as she storms into the room. Her long dark hair is peppered with streaks of gold, and she wears an over-the-top golden gown that is completely ridiculous given the hour of the day. "I've just been told you postponed the bonding ceremony *again*!"

Her voice is high and fever pitched, shrill enough to shatter crystal. It complements her face, which flushes red. Her eyes shine like she's about to dissolve into a waterfall of raging tears. *Why* did she have to be the winner of the Trials? Literally any of the other Tributes would have been better.

"My darling," Atlas says, the words infused with false warmth. "It couldn't be helped."

"Don't 'darling' me," Apricia says, raising a finger. "My father is furious!"

"Hmm" is his reply as he places his mug on the table with a clink.

"Answer me!" she practically screams. "Why have you delayed again?"

Atlas uncrosses his long legs and stands, approaching Apricia. He's wearing his most charming smile, the one I know so well. I can practically feel Apricia's panties melting at the sight. I have no idea how she can possibly still be attracted to him.

Atlas cups her face in his hands.

"My queen. I want this bonding to be the most momentous. Most significant. Most memorable one to ever occur in Ouranos. I want them to strum ballads about it. Immortalize it in the history books. I want the story of our love and our joining to be one generations of High Fae tell their grandchildren centuries from now."

Apricia looks up at him with such tender hope in her eyes that I almost feel sorry for her. Almost.

"You do?" she whispers, clearly on the verge of blubbering and ruining her caked-on eyeliner.

"You know I do. I want everyone to understand how much my love burns for you, my queen. How much this means to me and to Aphelion. You will be the greatest queen they've ever known. And that, my love, takes time to get just right."

Atlas uses his thumb to wipe a tear escaping down her cheek. I've nearly bitten my tongue clean off from holding in a derisive scoff.

"I hope you can understand and give me a little more time to sort out every detail. I don't want to leave anything to chance. Hmm?"

He tilts his head with an imploring expression, and I watch in fascination, always amazed at how Atlas can talk anyone into doing anything for him, often to their personal detriment.

Including his own brother.

Including me.

When Lor lost her shit on him in the throne room after the fourth Trial, it was so satisfying to watch. I wanted to stand up and cheer. Finally, someone saw through his charm, even if it took her a little while to get there. It makes me even more suspicious about who or what she is.

"Okay," Apricia finally says with a sniff. "I understand. It's just that I want to bond with you so much."

"I know, my dear," comes his smooth reply. "And I do too. It's my greatest desire, but I refuse to proceed until everything is as perfect as you are. Understood?"

She nods slowly, and he releases her face before he plants a soft kiss on her cheek. "Head back to your rooms, and I'll come see you later. I've ordered some of those fancy pastries from Auren's for you."

Apricia's eyes light up. It's a little pathetic how easily she's bought.

"Okay," she says, somewhat mollified, wiping a tear from her cheek. "Will you have supper with me?"

"Of course," Atlas says. "I just need to finish talking with Gabriel and take care of a few tasks."

"And will you..." Apricia's eyes dart to me, but she must decide I'm not worth censoring herself for. "Stay the night with me?"

Atlas gives her another patient smile and taps the tip of her nose. "You know I want to, but we agreed to wait until after the bonding, didn't we? Please don't bring this up again."

She nods, her momentary buoyancy deflating like she's been stuck with a thousand tiny pins. "Of course. Right. I'm sorry."

With one last lingering look at the king, she turns to leave.

As the door falls closed, we both watch her.

Then Atlas whirls on me, a hard expression on his face.

"Find Lor, Gabriel. *Now.* I don't care what you must do. Find her, or I can't be held responsible for what happens next."

With that, he spins away and strides for the exit before he pauses and looks back at me.

"I've also received word that Erevan is stirring up shit in The Umbra again. Deal with it."

Then he slams the door behind him, leaving me staring after him alone.

Chapter Two

LOR

Aphelion: The Umbra

I slam the glass onto the filthy countertop, a slug of fire whisky burning down my throat. A random elbow digs into my spine, and I toss a glare over my shoulder. It goes entirely unnoticed. Far too many people are stuffed within these rickety walls, and it's so crowded that I can barely move or hear myself think. But the seedy, worn-out taverns of The Umbra are ideal for picking up the snippets of gossip and possible information we so desperately need.

A loose-knit cap disguises my hair, and generous clothing hides any hint of my curves. At a quick glance, I appear like a man barely old enough to grow a beard.

This place is a dump. A row of grimy windows filter in weak sunlight while a few feeble sconces attempt to make up the difference. The floor is so sticky that I'm considering burning these boots.

I signal to the bartender for another drink. He's low fae with silvery skin, a thatch of bright green hair, and a cocky smile. He wears nothing on top but a scant leather vest, revealing a chest stacked with glistening muscles. The view, at least, isn't the worst.

"Same again?" he asks with a lazy half smile, and I nod, feeling a set of eyes burn into the back of my neck from across the room. Looking over my shoulder, I glimpse Nadir sitting in the corner with his arms crossed so tightly I'm surprised he hasn't crushed a rib. Even under his hood, I sense the disapproving scowl on his too-beautiful face.

He's pissed the bartender is flirting with me, even though he's flirting with *everyone*, and I wish this High Fae prince would just calm the fuck down.

Has he become more possessive since that fateful night in the Heart Castle when I lost my calm and screamed that I'd never belong to him? The memory makes me wince every time it leaks into my thoughts. Which is a lot.

My magic lurches under my skin, reminding me of what it wants. Like I need the hint. Like Nadir doesn't already occupy my head and my heart and spirit, and I can't shake him loose. But I refuse to let on how much he continues to affect me.

Nor can I admit that maybe I regret drawing that line in the sand.

But I can't lose sight of my purpose, and I refuse to put up with his territorial Fae bullshit.

Under his cloak, he's dressed in his usual black, though he's opted for something a little less polished than his standard suits, with a tunic and casual pants. It doesn't do anything to make him look any less devastating.

I sigh, accepting the glass the bartender lays in front of me and tossing the contents back as I attempt to tune *out* Nadir's presence and tune *into* the surrounding conversations.

We all arrived in the city about a week ago and have been piecing together the current landscape in Aphelion, intending to infiltrate the Sun Palace without attracting attention from Atlas. While we expected this to be a simple matter of sneaking inside—relatively speaking, of course—it seems we've landed in a roiling pot thanks to the upcoming bonding ceremony combined with the unrest stirring in The Umbra. Nadir wants us to be careful and take our time before making any moves we can't take back.

Amya has eyes and ears everywhere, and they all confirm Atlas still has scouts and spies searching for something. Or someone, in this case. And that he's doing so with increasing regularity, becoming less and less discreet, suggesting he's growing more desperate. That knowledge could work for or against us, but we've yet to determine which. The one positive is that he appears so confident about his dominion over Aphelion that he isn't searching *within* its walls. Still, I tug down on my hat because I'm not taking any chances.

How I wish I could storm up to the palace and demand an explanation, but the Mirror has to be my first priority. That and getting my magic back.

My glass is empty again, and I stare at it. The tavern's

conversation focuses on increasing worries about the low haul counts from The Umbra's fishing nets and traps. Catching sea life is one of the few ways the low fae can pay for their needs, and their concern throbs through the atmosphere like a gathering storm.

Amya's spies have also determined that Atlas postponed the bonding ceremony yet again, but that news has little impact on The Umbra. I understand why. What difference does Atlas's bonding to Apricia make to any of them? The citizens of The Umbra's interests are centered on finding food and supplies while working around Atlas's oppressive laws.

As I wait for the bartender to notice my empty drink, warmth at the back of my neck has me casting another quick glance at Nadir. I try to resist but can't help how he draws me in. My locked magic has been going wild since I denied him, and it's furious with me.

He's watching me and doesn't try to hide it. Leaning back in his seat with his arms crossed, he's glaring at everyone around him while somehow making it feel like I'm the only one in the room he sees.

While no one appears to recognize him as the Aurora Prince, he carries himself in a way that definitely draws attention. This is no downtrodden citizen of The Umbra.

Thankfully, he's not the only noble who darkens these corners. Dozens of Aphelion High Fae nobles traverse the streets, eating at the restaurants, drinking at the bars, and frequenting the brothels.

I've heard that elves and pixies are an especially alluring delicacy for the High Fae, and it's not hard to see why. They're all stunning with their soft, pearlescent skin and curvaceous bodies. I'm not sure what their treatment is like, but I've been assured they're at least paid well for their services. Not that it matters when you're low fae in Aphelion, since living in one of the nicer, more affluent districts is forbidden for their kind.

I've thought constantly about the low fae I saw in The Aurora. Which is worse? Being conscripted to Rion's mines or living under an illusion of freedom, confined by Atlas's rules? I fume at the way Atlas lied to my face about this, too. He'd outright said the people of The Umbra were free to leave at any time, but conveniently failed to mention they aren't actually allowed to buy a house or property anywhere else in Aphelion.

Was anything he said to me real? What I wouldn't do to get in a room alone with him and force him to reveal every scheming, lying thought in his head.

I scan the bar, finding Tristan in another far corner, conversing with a group of dwarves. Amya and Willow are in another quarter of The Umbra, seeing what else they can pick up. I don't like Willow being so far away from us, but I know Amya will protect her.

"Lor?" comes a voice, and I flinch, my gaze sliding to the corner of my eye.

Callias, Aphelion's most-coveted-stylist-with-a-very-long-cock, stands a few feet away with his hand on the bar. "Is that you?"

Keeping my focus on the glass between my hands, I pretend to ignore him, hoping he'll think he's mistaken me for someone else.

"I know it's you," he says, coming closer. "That silly hat doesn't fool me."

Still gazing into the depth of my glass, I mumble, "I don't know what you're talking about."

He scoffs and then bends down so his mouth is next to my ear.

"Nice try, Tribute. What are you doing here?"

Finally, I glare at him. "Shhh. Keep your voice down."

He rolls his eyes and straightens up as I look away. While I continue staring into my glass with my shoulders hunched, hoping no one has noticed, I hear him ordering a drink for himself and another for me. A moment later, two more glasses thunk onto the counter.

We drink in silence. Nadir's eyes burn me from the other side of the room, and he's probably less than a second away from storming his royal Fae ass over.

"You going to talk soon?" Callias asks casually as he turns around to face the room and leans against the bar. He's just far enough away that anyone watching might not immediately pick up on the fact that he's addressing me. "Or should I go outside and get Gabriel?"

"What?" I ask, and then press my mouth shut. Shit. Gabriel is here, too?

"That got your attention," Callias says with a smirk.

"He's here? Why? Why are *you* here?"

"I saw him wandering around. He's hard to miss, with the wings and all. And can't a Fae come to The Umbra for a drink on his day off? It's very fashionable to do so, you know."

"Is it? Coming to slum it with the persecuted? How very . . . classy," I say, and Callias smiles.

"I've missed that attitude, Final Tribute. Where have you been?"

My gaze flickers across the room. Nadir is now sitting forward, watching me and Callias with all the intensity of a falcon stalking a mouse from the sky. I give him a pointed look that I hope sends the message that he's to stay where he is. Not that I really expect him to do anything I say.

Tristan is looking over as well, a line forming between his brows. He exchanges a look with Nadir in a rare show of camaraderie. I need to get all of us out of here.

"Doesn't matter," I say, pushing myself from the bar and hiking my collar around my neck. "Please forget you saw me."

It's not like Callias owes me anything, but we bonded during the Trials, and I'm hoping that's enough to stop him from ratting me out.

Keeping my eyes on my feet, I brush past, weaving through the increasingly drunken crowd, and burst outside. The Umbra isn't exactly what I imagined when I first heard about it. Yes, I'd expected it to be destitute, but the truth is more complicated than that.

Wealthy low fae who have been corralled within its boundaries have done their best to fix up the shabby, run-down buildings. I've been told The Umbra has always existed as an "unofficial" twenty-fifth district, though it's never been referred to that way. When Atlas took the crown a century ago, he forced the low fae to relocate within its borders, seizing whatever property they owned and redistributing it to the nobility.

What kind of monster would do that? Once again, I curse my absolute stupidity and naivety during the Trials. Atlas had me totally fooled.

In the past century, the once grand buildings have fallen into disrepair despite the best efforts of its citizens. Their king expends resources to maintain only the other twenty-four districts, leaving The Umbra to its inevitable erosion. I scowl at the building ahead made of faded sandstone. Frescoes and decorative scrolls surround the large windows, while the walls are carved with roses and vines, all dulled and chipped by time.

Here, the destitute rub elbows with the rich, but they all wrestle the same set of chains. There's so much disparity packed into this tight corner that it feels like a powder keg waiting to explode.

All along, I'd wondered how no one in the palace realized I wasn't from The Umbra during the Trials, but now I understand it's because they had no idea what was happening. They're forbidden from coming too close, and they certainly weren't allowed to attend the public events. They simply had to swallow what they were told.

That fact is evidenced inside the square where I find myself. A High Fae male stands on a platform with his fist raised towards the crowd gathering around him. They're all fed up with this treatment, and they've found a leader to rally for their cause. Someone who has a better chance of pulling the ear of the king in a way the low fae could never hope to.

"What happened?" asks a low voice to my left, and I don't have to turn around to know it's Nadir. Even if I didn't know his voice like my own heart, my magic jumps when he brushes against me. I adjust my position so we're no longer touching without trying to make it too obvious. I don't want to hurt him, but I'm attempting to keep some distance.

"Nothing," I say. "Just needed to get some air."

"Who were you talking to?"

"No one. Just someone who wanted to buy me a drink."

I ignore his low growl before I stalk away, trying to lose myself in the crowd and wondering where Tristan is. Our instructions are to always meet back at home base if we find ourselves separated. I don't have to turn around to know Nadir is on my heels. I feel him everywhere.

"For too long, the Sun King has treated you like second-class citizens!" booms the man currently stoking the crowd. His name is Erevan, and despite being High Fae, he's become the leader of their growing rebellion. He wears a simple brown suede tunic and vest, though they're clearly well-made. His wavy blond hair is tied at his nape, and his bright blue eyes sweep over the crowd, who admire him with a manic sense of adoring fervor.

He raises a fist to the sky, and hundreds more raise up to a chorus of passionate cheers. "He keeps you within these walls! He keeps you from living anywhere but these crumbling houses! He keeps you from doing business with the High Fae! He forbids you from using your magic. And why? Because he fears you! Because he fears what your magic can do!"

"Yah!" comes another chorus of agreement, and the charge in the air is turning frenzied. Erevan lists a ream of grievances done to their people, and each one just sounds worse and worse. I don't blame any of them for feeling this way and wonder how we can help while we're here. Of course, Nadir has said we need to stay out of it, but I don't plan on listening to him anytime soon.

That's when I notice a pair of white feathered wings, and I halt in my tracks. Nadir practically crashes into me because he's following so closely. Thankfully, it isn't Gabriel, but it is one of the other warders who could recognize me. I think his name is Jareth. I remember him interrupting my first dinner with Atlas during the Trials. As I scan the square, I see more milling about. What are they doing here? Are they here to stop Erevan?

Their postures are casual as they stroll through the square, listening to him rouse the crowd with impassive expressions.

A warning burns up the base of my spine. Has Erevan noticed their arrival? Shouldn't he stop this? It's one thing to revile the king openly but quite another to do it right in the presence of his most trusted servants.

Erevan shouts something else, and that's when I notice the slightest dip in his voice as the blush pales on his cheeks. He's just taken note of the warders, but he doesn't back down, continuing his tirade of crimes committed by the king, his voice pitching louder. His bravery is impressive. Or stupid.

Movement catches the corner of my eye as more bodies flood down alleyways towards the square—soldiers dressed in the Sun King's uniforms.

"Where's Tris?" I ask, spinning around. I pray he's still safely inside the bar.

"I'm not sure," Nadir says, "but we should get out of here. He'll meet us at the house."

His gaze follows the same path as mine, and it's clear he's noticed the same thing. Shit is about to go down.

Unfortunately, just as we're about to make our exit, said shit breaks out completely. There's barely a second of warning before the king's army spills into the plaza to a chorus of panicked screams. The crowd moves like a wall, shoving and pushing, as everyone scrambles to evacuate.

A body crashes into me, knocking me back so hard I nearly stumble, barely catching myself at the last moment. An unfamiliar crowd surrounds me, and I can't see where Nadir ended up. It doesn't matter, I remind myself. He can take care of himself. I need to get out of here and take cover before someone recognizes me.

Another surge of bodies drags me towards the center of the square, and I fight against it, elbows out, clawing my way in the opposite direction. Hoping I don't inflict too much damage on someone who doesn't deserve it, I battle against the crush.

It feels like it takes forever, the cacophony reaching ear-piercing levels. There are screams and the sounds of steel clashing on steel. "Rebels" are cut down without mercy to the thunk of bodies hitting stone and the sound of keening wails.

Another one of the king's rules prevents low fae from purchasing weapons, and thus, they have to rely on whatever relics they can find or whatever they can cobble together, leaving them mostly unarmed and outmatched.

I need to get out. I keep pushing and pushing until finally I burst through the edge of the crowd. A stream of people flows away from the square, trying to seek cover, but guards block every exit. It's absolute chaos. I spot an unmanned alley and approach it, trying to keep ahead of the river of Fae and humans. Tugging down my hat, I finally reach the exit, casting a look over my shoulder before I duck into the safety of the shadows.

Then I turn around and crash into a brick wall.

"Oof," I cry, stumbling back until an arm catches me, pulling me up.

It isn't a wall, after all.

It's a High Fae male.

With snowy white wings and golden armor. With angry blue eyes and wavy blond hair.

"What the *fuck* are you doing here, Final Tribute?" Gabriel snarls in my face.

CHAPTER THREE

*S*hit. *Shit. Shit.*

I attempt to twist myself from Gabriel's iron grip, but he's already dragging me deeper into the network of small alleys as the sounds of the fighting dim to a muffled hush.

"Let go of me," I demand, stumbling after him, failing to keep up with his long, furious strides. His grip only tightens, and I wince, sure he's leaving bruises on my skin.

Gods, I forgot what an asshole he is.

My time away from Aphelion softened my memories, reminding me of the slightly-better-than-the-rest parts. In my head, I'd painted Atlas as the chief villain in my story, but as I note the set of his hardened jaw and piercing stare, I remember Gabriel also had his role to play.

He ignores me and drags me further until we finally stop

at a deserted corner. What's he going to do? Murder me right out here in the open? Surely he's going to take me back to Atlas first?

He yanks me forward and shoves me against a stone wall, my hands slapping the rough surface to protect my nose from a painful collision. I whip around to face him with my chin lifted high. If this is the end, I'll try to go out with *some* dignity.

"What are you doing here?" he asks again, poisoning it with even more venom. "Do you have *any fucking* idea what will happen if Atlas finds out you're in Aphelion?"

"Of course I know!" I snap. "What are you doing here? You're supposed to be in your fancy palace."

Gabriel closes his eyes and sucks in a long breath as he begs for patience. "I'm *supposed* to be out here, Lor. But *you* are not. Where have you been?"

"It doesn't matter," I say. "What are you going to do with me?"

He presses his mouth together, conflict warring in his eyes. Nadir told me Gabriel is essentially a slave, unable to disobey Atlas's orders, existing with little agency of his own. At the time, it made me feel sorry for him.

"Are you going to take me to him?"

There's no need to elaborate on whom I mean.

"I should," he replies, but his words precede an unmistakable moment of hesitation.

"Do you have a choice?" I ask carefully, wondering how touchy he is about this subject. I can't really hold it against him if some magical oath forces him to obey Atlas. Not that I think he'd be inclined to protect me either way.

His fierce gaze slides to me, his eyes blazing with fury. Okay, definitely touchy.

"I have my ways of getting around his orders."

My breath hitches with surprise.

"Does that mean you'll let me go?" My question probably sounds more hopeful than it has a right to be.

He seems to consider my question, his blue eyes swirling with that blend of anger and irritation I remember so well.

"I want to know everything," he says finally. "Who are you? Why did I steal you from Nostraza? And how did you run away? Tell me everything, and I'll do what I can to keep you out of his hands for now. But I can't make that decision before knowing why he wants you and if you're a danger to him or Aphelion."

I try not to groan. What he's asking makes sense, but how many people will learn my less-secret-with-each-passing-day secret before all of this is over?

That's when a set of sharp footsteps draws our attention to a hooded figure ghosting down the alley. Someone else might find it ominous, but I know exactly who's prowling towards us.

Gabriel visibly reacts as Nadir pushes off his hood, first in surprise and then with resigned exhaustion as he drags a hand down his face.

"I should have known," he says.

Nadir smirks and then shrugs. "Probably."

"I take it you two know each other?" I ask, picking up on the familiarity between them.

"Unfortunately, yes," Gabriel says, and I don't know why

there's something nice about the fact that he's also irritated by Nadir's presence. At least it's not just me.

"What are you *both* doing here?" Gabriel asks, throwing up his hands. "Atlas banned you from Aphelion."

"Mmm," says Nadir. "You know I've never been very good at following orders. Especially where Atlas is concerned."

Gabriel once again runs a hand down his face and then through his hair, mussing the halo of his curls.

"I want an explanation. Start talking," he says to me. "Now."

"Not here." I shake my head. "Anyone might find us."

"Come on," Nadir says. "Follow us."

Nadir's gaze falls on me before he jerks his chin in command. I roll my eyes as I push myself from the wall. Zerra, he's so bossy.

Then he turns, and we both follow behind as we curve our way deeper and deeper into the twisting alleyways. As we continue, I listen for the sounds of the confrontation in the square, but either it's over or we've moved out of hearing range.

"Did you see what happened in the plaza?" I ask Nadir's back. The path narrows, forcing us to walk in single file.

"They arrested some of the low fae, but most simply scattered."

"Did they kill any?"

He peers over his shoulder at me. "Some. Yes."

I don't like that answer. "What was the point of that?" I look back at Gabriel now, continuing my line of questions.

"A message," Gabriel says. "Atlas can't take down Erevan

yet and risk a full-out riot, but it's a reminder that he won't tolerate these acts of aggression."

"Acts of aggression," I scoff. "As if their demands aren't perfectly legitimate."

Gabriel says nothing as I cast another look over my shoulder, but I catch a falter in his eyes, there for a moment and then gone.

We continue in silence as we wind our way through the alleys until we emerge on the far side of The Umbra. It's quieter here, where a small market sells fruit, fish, and other perishable goods. Food and other consumables are the only items low fae are permitted to trade and bargain for in the upper districts. So at least Atlas isn't technically forcing them to starve. He probably looks in the mirror and pats himself on the back for his generosity.

We cross the northwest boundary of The Umbra and turn down a wider boulevard. Our Aphelion hideout is carefully situated in the Eighth District, which just happens to maintain the furthest physical distance from the palace. The nondescript house is of middling variety, owned by a High Fae of the working class named Nerissa. Apparently, she's an old acquaintance of Nadir's, and I haven't entirely worked out their relationship.

Not that I care. It's definitely none of my business.

I sigh, knowing how ridiculous I sound, even in my own head.

We always enter the house from the back—Nadir's orders—so we make our way down another alley before we reach the gate that cordons off the rear of the property. I'm not sure if it's safe to be showing Gabriel where we're staying, but I'm trusting Nadir to know what he's doing. If he's known Gabriel for a while, maybe he understands his intentions better than I do.

We shove open the gate, ensuring the alley is clear before we file into the small backyard. The stone courtyard is surrounded by patches of green grass and flowerbeds stuffed with roses carefully tended daily and constantly by Nerissa, like they're her children. In fact, she's here right now, wearing her gardening apron, her chestnut hair piled in a messy knot on top of her head.

At our entrance, she looks over, a pair of clippers poised in midair. Her gaze skirts over me and Nadir and then lands on Gabriel.

"What happened?" she asks, dropping her tools into her basket and dusting off her apron. "Where's Tristan?"

She peers past us, looking for my brother, as my throat tightens with fear.

"You mean he's not back yet?"

Nerissa shakes her head, and I'm about to spin on my heel and head back towards the square when Nadir seizes my wrist.

"He'll be fine," Nadir says. "There's nothing you can do."

I grit my teeth, and my nostrils flare as I prepare to tell him I have no intention of abandoning my brother. But the gate creaks and a familiar head of black hair emerges through it. My chest expands in relief.

"Tris," I say as he pauses at the sight of Gabriel. He's definitely hard to mistake for a casual visitor, what with the wings, sun tattoo on his neck, and gleaming golden armor.

"Who's this?" Tristan asks, his gaze sweeping over him with mistrust.

"This is Gabriel," I say, and Tristan's eyes narrow. He remembers everything I shared about my warder during the Trials.

"Why is he here? And why did you leave the bar so abruptly?"

"Come on," I reply. "We'll explain everything."

Finally, we all filter into the house. I remove my hat and jacket and hang them on a hook against the wall. Gabriel follows me to the front sitting area, where we find Willow, along with Amya, Mael, and Hylene.

"I ran into someone who recognized me," I say to Tristan to explain my abrupt departure from the tavern. "That's why I left." Then I look at Gabriel. "It was Callias."

There's a collective exchange of wary looks around the room.

"I don't think he'll say anything," I say. "But I should probably try to find him."

"Leave it to me," Gabriel says, and my brow furrows with surprise. "As long as you keep up our end of the bargain."

"What bargain?" Willow asks, her tone sharp. She's also eyeing Gabriel with obvious misgivings, and after everything I told her about him, I don't blame her.

"He wants to know everything," I say.

"Oh great," Willow says, throwing up her hands. "Just what we need. Another witness to our crimes."

I nod at her words, which mirror my own thoughts.

"He said he'd consider not turning us in to Atlas if we tell him."

"Why did you bring him here?" Mael asks. "If he plans to turn Lor in, is showing him our hiding place the best idea?"

He aims the question at Nadir, who shrugs. "He knows we're in Aphelion now; finding us within its walls wouldn't take long."

Mael sighs and leans back in his chair, unconvinced but apparently resigned.

"Have a seat," I say to Gabriel. "We might as well start at the beginning, I guess."

Gabriel hesitates at first, then settles into one of the armchairs, perching on the edge and staring at me.

"This better be good, Final Tribute."

Over the next while, I fill Gabriel in on some of the particulars about my past, careful to carve around some of the more significant points. I don't know whose side he's on, but I reason I can share the same details Atlas must have. He can learn it from me or the Sun King. I keep the bits about my trapped magic and the Crown a secret. Nothing good would come of that information falling into the wrong hands.

I do tell him who I am.

That I'm the grandchild of Serce, the Heart Queen who tangled with forbidden magic and nearly ruined everything. That I'm the Primary of Heart. He's as shocked as Nadir and the others were when I told them the same thing weeks ago in The Aurora. He asks all the same questions. Makes the same comments.

The baby died. There were no heirs. All of it was a lie.

When I'm finally done, the room goes quiet as everyone watches my former warder, wondering what he'll do. Several emotions cross his face as he pieces these fragments together. I know what he's thinking. This finally explains Atlas's strange interest in me during the Trials. Why he was so intent on me winning, and why he lost his shit when the Mirror rejected me. It probably explains some things going on in the Sun Palace that I have no idea about.

Finally, after several moments of silence, Gabriel speaks. "But why are you here in Aphelion? You must know that being here puts you in danger." He looks around the room. "And who are all these people?"

"Oh, come on. I'm hurt," Mael says, pressing a hand to his chest. "Surely it hasn't been that long?"

"I don't mean *you*," Gabriel says, his voice rough. "You two." He squints at Willow and then at Tristan before looking at me. "These are your friends. From Nostraza."

"I . . . How did you know that?"

"I remember them from the fourth Trial."

"You saw that?"

"Yes," he says, his expression grim, but he doesn't elaborate further. "But it seems pretty obvious now that you're related."

"Yes, this is Tristan and Willow. My brother and sister. The prince helped me 'liberate' them from the prison."

He looks me up and down before he addresses Nadir. "The prince. And did the prince also 'liberate' you from the Sun Palace? I've been wondering how you managed it."

Nadir's mouth hooks up at the corner, a sparkle of glee in his eyes. "Gabe, don't pretend you didn't intentionally reveal who she was. You practically handed me an engraved invitation to steal her."

Gabriel's mouth presses into a flat line.

"What?" I ask. "What are you talking about?"

Nadir arches his brow. "During the Sun Queen Ball. Remember when he grabbed you? He very conveniently moved the shoulder of your dress so I could see the brand from Nostraza. It was only a second, but I'd bet money he did it on purpose."

I blink, remembering so many things from that night with stark clarity, but I hadn't realized that. I study Gabriel with increasing confusion.

"Or was that just a coincidence?" Nadir asks Gabriel, clearly goading him.

"I don't know what you're talking about. If that happened, it was pure chance."

"Hmm," Nadir says, leaning back and folding his hands behind his head like his point has been made.

Gabriel doesn't respond, instead looking around the room before his gaze lands on Hylene with a definite hint of admiration curving his mouth. "And you are?"

"Hylene," she says, returning his look of interest with one of her own.

"That's your name, but who are you?"

"That's for me to know and you to find out."

She winks, and it's obvious Gabriel isn't getting anything else out of her for now.

Finally, he returns his attention to me.

"What are you doing here, Lor? Why didn't you stay in The Aurora, as far away from Atlas as possible?"

I wrinkle my nose because I'm going to have to tell him this part.

"Well, we kind of have to get to the Mirror."

Gabriel lets out a long-suffering sigh and pinches the bridge of his nose like he can't believe what the fuck his life has come to.

"Why in the heavens of Zerra do you need to get to the Mirror?"

"Because it told me I had to return once I figured out who I am," I say, massaging the truth just enough to make it sound believable. I'm far too good at lying at this point in my life. I've been doing it for as long as I can remember.

"Why?"

"I don't know. That's what we need to find out."

"And how do you plan to get the Mirror?"

I can see what's written on his face. He wants to know but also doesn't want to hear the answer.

"Don't tell him anything else," Nadir says now, his earlier cool slipping away. "He said he wanted to know who you are, and now he knows. That is enough."

Nadir is right, but I harbor a strange old affection for Gabriel. He was kind of horrible to me during the Trials, but I think we understood one another by the end. At least a little. He said a tiny, infinitesimal part of him kind of liked me, and I know it's foolish to put much stock in that, but he also didn't run straight to Atlas today.

"Can I trust you?" I ask, ignoring Nadir, which feels better than it should.

Gabriel sighs. "I'm not sure."

He rolls his neck, trying to ease some tension, clearly distressed about so many things.

"Don't tell me," he says finally, shaking his head. "I don't want to know what your plans are. The less I know, the better."

I nod and look around the room, catching everyone's wary expressions as Gabriel stands.

"So?" I ask as I stand up too.

"So?" he asks.

"Was that enough? Are you going to tell Atlas I'm here?"

"What about the . . . thingy?" Mael asks, waving a hand at Gabriel.

"Thingy?" Gabriel replies, his voice dripping with disdain.

"You know." Mael fakes a noose around his neck, his tongue lolling out. "The thing where you can't lie to him, or you . . . die?"

Something flashes in Gabriel's eyes, and it's obviously a painful subject. I wish I'd known about this during the Trials. It might have made everything different between us.

"That's not how it works," Gabriel says, his tone sharp, and Mael holds up his hands in defense.

"Sorry, man. Just making sure."

"I have it under control. But I should go," Gabriel says before he tugs on the hem of his jacket and turns on his heel, heading down the front hallway.

"Gabriel," I call, following him before he stops, pausing for a second before he spins around.

"Will you tell him?"

He looks down at me, his mouth pressing together. I don't beg him to protect me. I don't ask. I already know that nothing I could say would change his mind.

He huffs out a breath, laden with exhaustion. "I'm not sure yet."

Then he spins around again, and before I can say anything else, he opens the door and slams it behind him.

Chapter Four

Nadir

I brush past Lor, flinging open the door and descending the steps onto the busy street. I'm breaking my rule about using the front entrance, but I need to catch up with Gabriel.

"Gabe!" I call, spying his blond head weaving through the crowd. His shoulders stiffen as he attempts to ignore me, so I pick up my pace, shoving through the throng. "Gabriel, please! Stop."

He comes to a halt, spinning around to face me. People surround us on all sides, and I'd prefer we didn't have this conversation here in the open. I jerk my chin, asking him to join me inside a busy coffee shop, where we find a secluded corner table.

After ordering a round of drinks from the human server, I get to the point.

"Don't fuck with me. Are you going to tell him we're here?"

Atlas has been turning over Ouranos searching for Lor, but I'm counting on the fact that he hasn't yet considered she's in the last place he'd think to look. If Gabriel discloses our presence, our window of opportunity erodes away to nothing.

Atlas *will* eventually become aware of us, and I'm not foolish enough to think we can remain here undetected forever. Still, I'm hoping we'll have accomplished everything we need to by then.

"You heard me. I told Lor I haven't decided yet."

"But what does that mean? Do you have to tell him?"

Gabriel blinks, studying me, while the server returns with our drinks before scurrying off. He picks up his spoon and stirs his coffee, avoiding the full force of my scrutiny.

"Gabriel. Do you have to tell him? Should we run?"

His spoon clinks on the walls of his mug, but eventually, he peers up, a flicker darkening his expression.

"He told me to find her and bring her to him."

He pauses on a sharp breath, and my shoulders tighten across my back. It's as I feared. He doesn't have a choice. I move to stand, prepared to give the order to pack up because we're leaving immediately. We'll have to figure out a new plan. "But—" Gabriel says, placing a hand on my forearm and stilling me. "I didn't find her. She found me."

A heartbeat passes before his meaning settles between us, and I sink back into my seat, giving him a quizzical look. "How much does your king know about these loopholes of yours?"

"Enough," Gabriel says, his expression grim. "But Atlas doesn't concern himself with details he'd rather not consider."

Gabriel lifts his mug to his lips, blowing on the surface as his gaze slides to me. He doesn't have to finish the rest of his thought—he uses that fact to his advantage whenever possible.

"So you'll stay quiet then."

"For now," he says. "But I can stretch the limits of my leash for only so long. He doesn't have to give a direct order for me to believe you might be acting against his best interests, which is at the heart of everything I'm compelled to protect."

I nod, understanding his position. I know he has no choice. "What if I swore to you that nothing we're doing here is intended to hurt Atlas? This has nothing to do with him. Or Aphelion, for that matter."

"That helps," he says. "I might be able to give you more time then."

I blow out a breath of relief. "Thank you."

"Consider it a debt repaid. After all this time." He gives me a significant look, and I nod again. "Besides, I'm not entirely sure whose side I'm on at the present moment."

Those words slip out like he hadn't really meant to give them voice as he stares out the window. We both fall into silence, enveloped by the chatter of the afternoon patrons.

A rumble vibrates under my feet as the ground shifts. Gabriel and I cling to the table, protecting our coffee cups from bouncing off the surface as the café falls silent, bracing against the quake. It lasts only a few seconds before it stops, everyone pausing in surprise for several beats before the conversation rushes back.

Reports have been filing in through Aphelion and from

the rest of Ouranos of strange happenings just like this. The earth trembling, and stars falling from the sky. Of diminishing resources in the lakes and rivers and forests. Of unusual temperatures. Snow falling in deserts and avalanches roaring through mountains. It's all become a source of gossip and speculation.

It reminds me a bit of the unrest we experienced after we lost our magic all those years ago and similar things occurred. But our magic seems fine, and I'm sure it's just the cycle of nature and its quirks, though it also feels like it's come on rather suddenly.

"Why are *you* here with Lor?" Gabriel asks after another moment.

"You know I can't tell you that."

"Yeah. I figured," he says, picking up his coffee and taking a sip. "You were a bit weird about her, though. What was that about?"

"Weird?" I ask, attempting to keep my tone innocent, knowing that when it comes to Lor, I'm about as opaque as glass.

Gabriel sits back and eyes me up and down, seeing right through my transparent brick wall. He's always been an observant asshole. It's what makes him such a good soldier.

"Oh fuck. Don't tell me that you two are . . ." He curls his lip.

"Watch it," I snarl, and Gabriel's eyebrows shoot up.

"Don't you find her a little feral? Abrasive? Mouthy?"

I lean back, crossing my legs, offering him a lazy grin.

She's feral and difficult and makes me want to tear my hair out sometimes. All the time. It's what makes me so insane.

"Yes. Very."

Gabriel snorts. "It's your funeral, I guess."

"I guess."

I look around the café, noting the steady stream of Fae and humans coming in and out.

Gabriel is watching me, his keen eyes missing nothing.

"What?" I ask.

"You're hiding something. What is she to you? Really."

He narrows his gaze, once again noticing details anyone else might miss.

"I'm not sure yet."

"What do you mean by *yet*?"

I shrug my shoulders, suddenly unable to meet his inquisitive gaze. I've suspected the truth for a while, but for some reason, it's hard to say out loud. I've never in all my years heard of it happening. And what are the odds that this woman my father stole, tortured, and tossed into Nostraza is my mate?

They're basically zero. And yet, I can't ignore the way she makes me feel.

The word has been cycling through my thoughts for weeks, twisting me up until I barely recognize myself. But in the best possible way.

Gabriel doesn't press further, and I'd rather not tell him anyway. As much as I do trust him not to screw me over intentionally, I must always consider that what he does isn't always his choice.

"What happened there in the square? With the low fae," I ask, deliberately changing the subject.

Gabriel blows out a sigh as he takes the hint. "Things are

getting worse. They keep pushing, and the harder they do, the more Atlas digs in his heels. Erevan keeps trying to get him to listen, but Atlas won't hear it."

"What is his problem?" I ask, having never really understood why Atlas treats them with so little humanity. At least with my father, his disdain for the low fae has nothing to do with how he actually feels but rather what he can use them for. He simply doesn't see them as anything but tools to achieve his own ends.

Gabriel shakes his head. "I don't know, but it's all going to blow up soon. I'm worried about what will happen if something doesn't change."

"Have you considered getting them out?" I ask.

"Of course I have. But where would they go?"

"To the other realms."

"This is their home, and they don't want to leave. Besides, too many of them are afraid to wander the countryside . . ."

He drops off, leaving the thought unfinished.

"Because of my father."

He nods. "While this situation isn't ideal, it's better than being enslaved and forced to work to death in the mines, or so I have to believe."

I grind my teeth, thinking of the shame my father brings to The Aurora. We're an embarrassment. Monsters living under the guise of gilded royalty.

"Anyway," Gabriel says, polishing off his coffee and standing up. "I should get going."

"You won't say anything," I confirm again, and he nods.

"For now."

"Thank you." I hold out my hand. We grip forearms before he releases me and stalks out, his wings pulled tight to ease his way through the stream of bodies. Leaving my coffee untouched, I toss a few coins on the table and exit the café, heading towards our home base.

Entering through the back, I find the main floor vacant.

As I head towards the stairs, my stomach lurches, knowing Lor is nearby. I can't help the way I'm drawn towards her. I've been trying to give her the space that she needs, but fuck, it's so hard. Everything about her calls to me. Pulls me in.

Does she understand what a mate bond means? She grew up sheltered from the ways of our people, and I suspect she has no idea. She must feel what I feel, though. She has to know it means something, if only she'd stop fighting it so hard.

At the top of the stairs, I find her door open. She's sitting on her bed with her legs crossed and eyes closed, wearing the Heart Crown. She keeps trying to speak to it, hoping it will wake up and release her magic.

I watch as her eyebrows draw together, taking this rare opportunity to just study her. She has no idea how beautiful she is. How I feel so lost when I'm around her. I scared her that night inside Heart when I pushed her too hard. I need to figure out how to get her to open up again.

The tension in her shoulders and neck tells me the Crown remains frustratingly quiet.

"You can come in," she says, her eyes still closed. Of course she must feel my presence, just like I'm constantly aware of hers.

"No luck?" I ask as her lids slide open, and I stop to lean

against the bedpost. Her gaze drifts over me, and I feel it like a touch against my skin. She quickly looks away and pulls the Crown off her head, tossing it onto the bedspread.

"Nothing."

I give her a chance to collect her thoughts.

"You talked to Gabriel?" she asks.

"I did."

"And he'll keep quiet for now? He can?"

"He'll do what he's able to to give us time."

She nods with a dip of her chin. "Why wouldn't he tell Atlas right away?"

"Honestly, I'm not sure. I get the sense that something is brewing between them. Besides, he owes me one."

She narrows her gaze. "How does he owe you?"

"Can I try again?" I ask, deflecting her question. That story is Gabriel's to tell. "With my magic? It's been a while."

She hesitates, and I think I understand why. It's hard not to recall the last time I funneled my magic into her, when the tension between us became too much. Every thought and sensation sharpened to excruciating clarity. It was too intimate and too raw, but it might be the only way through.

"Sure," she finally says. "Thank you."

She's different since I took her to Heart. Or rather, not different, but there's something new underneath her confidence and impulsiveness. Something layered with that anger and bravado that's often her own worst enemy. It's a thread of vulnerability I don't think she's ever allowed herself to fully experience.

She was obviously shaken by that experience in Heart with

my father when he nearly captured us both, and it's changed parts of her. There are so many layers to this woman that I want to peel apart and understand.

As I settle on the edge of the bed, I brace myself for her to shuffle away. Thankfully, she stays where she is, so close but so far, which is a relief because I'm pretty sure that would rip out my heart. Again.

Our gazes meet, and every nerve in my body ignites with fire. My hands fist into the blanket, resisting the urge to reach out. My magic is going wild—more and more so with each passing day—like someone is hurling a steel ball at bricks lining my limbs. Ever since she put the hammer down on anything physical between us, my magic has been feral. I don't know what happens to those who deny the mate bond—I wonder if it's ever happened. I have to give her the space and the time she needs. But how is this not driving her insane?

"I'm ready," she says, her throat bobbing on a hard swallow, interrupting my spiraling thoughts. "If you are."

I nod and scoot further on the bed, crossing my legs to face her. With my wrists lying lightly on my knees, I send out branches of my magic—violet and emerald and fuchsia. I think of our last night in the Keep, when I'd intended to show her all the more . . . satisfying ways I can use it. When I'd planned to make her moan and writhe with pleasure.

As if reading my thoughts, the blaze in her eyes meets mine, and the air grows thick enough to slice like cold butter.

Patience, I remind myself again. I've lived for nearly three centuries and learned to cultivate it with some measure of skill and proficiency, but sometimes my emotions get the best of me. In that way, we're a lot alike. Ruled by the fire in our blood.

My magic wraps around her, twisting up her limbs, soothed by her touch. This is what it wants. This is what it craves. What *I* crave so fucking much. I spread my fist open and let it melt into her skin, where it strokes the sparking lines of her magic. It's different from mine. Less soft curves and tender caresses and more like the edges of cut crystal and the honed tip of a blade.

The tales of Heart's crimson lightning magic are the fodder of legends recited around campfires at night. When I saw her use it, I understood all the stories were true. It was awesome to behold, and I suspect it's only a fraction of what she's capable of.

Her magic is there. I feel it respond to my light.

As I coil through her limbs, she lets out a small gasp, her perfect pink lips opening. I *know* she has to feel this. She's practically vibrating.

Ignoring the desire to detour south through her abdomen and between her thighs, I direct my magic into the center of her chest, where that locked door sits. It's as tight as ever, like it's been welded over and nailed shut. I don't know what miracle allowed her to access it when she saved me from my father on the top of the Heart Castle, but that means she *can* get to it. It's just under the surface, waiting to be unleashed.

For several long minutes, neither of us speaks as our breaths grow heavier and the back of my neck flushes. Her cheeks turn pink, and she shifts on the bed like she can't find a comfortable position. This is driving me mad. It's not sex, but it feels almost like it. Waves of longing spread through my chest and down through my stomach until my cock stirs to life. I should stop this, but I'm helpless to resist. It's the closest she'll allow me right now, and it's evident from the sparkle in her eyes and the flush of her skin that she's having a similar reaction to my presence.

"Do you want me to stop?" I ask, cursing myself for uttering those words. I don't want to stop, but I also don't want to frighten her. I made that mistake once, and I've vowed never to do it again.

"No," she whispers, and the sound is so raw that my heart withers in my chest. "Keep going."

I don't understand what message she's sending by allowing me to continue, but I don't argue either. I keep digging away, prying at that locked space in her heart, but nothing I do makes any difference. She shakes her head, her shoulders sloping in defeat.

"It's no use."

I hate that I've failed her again. I wish I were stronger. I wish I could undo this. I wish I could go back in time and stop everything my father did.

"I'm sorry," I say, and I don't know exactly what I'm apologizing for, but I'm sorry for so many things. Some that are out of my control, but still, I want to be the one who fixes everything.

I slide my magic away from her heart, directing it through her limbs, where it twines with the echoes of her power. It feels like a dance, one of the most intimate sort.

Suddenly, it all coalesces into a wave that threatens to

drown me. It's too hard to pretend I don't feel this. Too hard to pretend I don't want her with every fiber of my fucking soul.

I yank on my threads, pulling them back into me abruptly, with such force that we both grunt. Then without another word, I scoot off the bed and stride for the door, desperate to escape.

"Nadir," she calls after me. "I'm sorry."

I nearly miss a step at the broken sound in her voice, but I continue walking.

I need air. I need to breathe.

I don't respond as I keep my gaze averted and leave the room.

Chapter Five

LOR

The Woodlands: Fourteen Years Ago

I run through the forest, my bare feet squelching in the mud. My tunic is streaked with dirt, the hem lost to the thorns of a rosebush an hour ago. Mother will be less than impressed. It's not often we venture into the city for new supplies or clothing. "Someone might see us," she always says with her hands clasped, her worried gaze pinned to the door. I don't know *why* no one should see us, but I've learned to accept this fact. Perhaps this is how all families live in the forest.

Tristan and Willow are off in the trees, concealed within the many paths and shadowed corners. It's Tristan's turn to find us today. Willow is the most skilled at hiding, but I'm taking a page from her book and being sneaky right now. I venture further than I normally do, splashing through a small stream that runs across my path. The icy water chills the tips of my toes, but my feet are accustomed to the elements, my soles toughened from the countless hours we spend exploring our isolated environment.

A rustle in the trees brings me to a stop as I listen intently. Is it my brother? He couldn't have found me already. Not even Tristan is that good.

Whoever loses today has to chop firewood for the week, and I hate doing it. I'm not strong enough to lift the axe, and Tristan loves to annoy me by pointing it out. Eventually, my father will take pity on me, all while grumbling at Tristan that this is actually *his* job.

But if I win, then Tristan has to grind flour for an entire month. The only task I dread more than chopping wood is pummeling wheat into a fine powder before sifting it for stones. It's mind-numbingly tedious, and I have better things to do with my time.

If Willow wins, Tristan and I technically have to handwash all the sheets, but she never actually follows through on making us do her chores.

A moment later, a squirrel skitters in my path, and I grin. Tristan hasn't found me yet. I plunge deeper into the trees, picking my way down a path barely worn into the earth. Far in the distance, I hear the screech that signals Willow's capture. I stifle a giggle and continue running, determined to evade my brother.

After shoving through a thick line of brush, I come to a

halt. A woman sits in a clearing, tending to a small fire with a charred stick. She looks up at my entrance and smiles, no hint of surprise in her serene expression.

"Hello there, little one. Who are you?"

I take a tentative step, instantly drawn towards her.

She's High Fae, with delicately pointed ears and glowing skin. I'm High Fae too, but no one else knows that. It's another thing Mother says we must hide from the world.

The woman is beautiful, with flowing silver hair and piercing blue eyes. I take another step, reeled in by her calm like she's a still lake on a hot summer day.

"I have some faerie cakes if you're hungry," she says softly, her smile hugging her eyes.

I nod as I take another step, bridging the distance. I'm not used to strangers, and her presence is a novelty I can't overlook. Besides our rare visits to The Woodlands' markets, my entire world consists of Tristan, Willow, Mother, and Father. I never get to meet anyone new.

She reaches into her bag and pulls out a package wrapped in white paper, the crinkle making my stomach rumble. Everything we eat is homemade, but sometimes, when we're in the city, we pass the bakeries and patisseries with their colorful towers of cookies and cakes and confections. We're never allowed to buy any, but I imagine what it would be like to swirl my tongue over their bright, sugary frosting as it coats the inside of my mouth.

The stranger unwraps the paper, producing a shiny white box trussed up with a wide gold ribbon. She eases the bow open and lifts the lid. By now, I'm standing directly over her as I anticipate its contents like a wolf sniffing out a burrow of orphaned bunnies. Six small cake squares are decorated with colorful icing and flowers dipped in sugar. They look like sculptures of art and are almost too pretty to eat.

"Go on," she says. "I don't mind sharing."

I hesitate for only a moment before picking one out and sinking my teeth through its moist layers. The flavors burst in my mouth like a rainbow unfurling. Lemon and vanilla and something else that can only be described as the taste of happiness. I chew slowly, closing my eyes and savoring every delicate note. The way it crumbles in my mouth and the way the sugar grinds against my teeth. While Mother's sweet buns are my favorite dessert, this is far and away the best thing I've ever tasted.

I devour it in three ravenous bites, and the woman holds up the box, offering me a second. This time I don't hesitate to select another, but I take my time with smaller nibbles as I attempt to parse out each flavor and sensation.

"You like it," she says with an indulgent smile.

"I love it," I say with my mouth full, a few crumbs spraying out. She laughs warmly and then closes the box, much to my disappointment, which I try not to let show. I watch her every movement as she wraps it up and then holds it out to me.

"You can have them."

My eyes widen. "Really?"

"Anyone who appreciates them this much should have them all," she says.

I look around the clearing. I'm not supposed to accept gifts from strangers. I shouldn't even be talking to her, but I can't help myself. She seems nice enough, and anyone giving me cake can't be all bad, right?

"What's your name?" she asks.

"Lor," I say without hesitating, and she smiles.

"Well, Lor, they'll go to waste if you don't take them. They were intended for my daughter, but I fear I'll have to make a detour on my return journey, and by the time I get home, these will have dried out. You'd be doing me a favor."

I find myself nodding, reaching to accept the gift. My fingers close around the slick surface, but the woman doesn't release the package. I frown at her, tugging on the box, but something has changed. Gone is her kind smile, darkness reflecting in the azure swirl of her eyes.

This was a mistake.

Finally, she frees the box from her grip. It rebounds from our opposing forces, crashing into my chest, where I nearly crush it.

"Oops. Careful," she says, her tone pitching into condescension. "You don't want to ruin them."

But she's smiling again, and it's warm and comforting. I must have imagined what just happened. I was up too late last night reading under my blanket with a lantern, and my mind is playing tricks on me.

"Thank you," I say and take a step back. "I'll leave you alone."

"No, don't leave yet," the woman says. "Won't you join me for a minute longer?"

She pats the spot on the log next to her and gives me another enchanting smile, but I'm sure I'm no longer imagining the vicious gleam reflecting in her eyes.

"No, I should really get back."

I take another step, searching the edges of the clearing, listening for the sounds of Tristan's approach. Where is he? Why hasn't he found me when I actually need him?

"I insist," says the woman. "I gave you those lovely treats. It's the least you can do."

"No," I say again, shaking my head, fear pricking up the back of my neck. "No, I have to go."

Then I turn on my heel and run, the box of cakes tumbling from my hands before I plunge into the trees.

But she's already pursuing me.

With her longer strides, she catches up easily, snagging the back of my tunic so hard I hear the stitches pop before she bands an arm around my waist.

"Not so fast, little one," she snarls in my ear. "I know who you are. *What* you are."

I kick and flail. I need to get away.

"You're coming with me," she says, her voice rough, devoid of her earlier kindness, as she turns and heads back towards her camp.

"Tris—!" I scream as a strong hand clamps over my mouth, muffling my terror.

"There will be none of that, little one."

I continue bucking and fighting, but she's so much stronger. I have to do something.

It all happens so quickly that I don't have time to think about it. I know it's forbidden, but I pull on my magic, feeling it spark under my skin. Lightning, bright and red, flashes from my hands, funneling into the spot where I'm gripping the woman's arm. She screams as she drops me to the ground, the plummet knocking the wind from my lungs before I roll away.

She clutches her forearm as she screams—the fabric of her coat singed and the skin beneath melting off the bone.

She snarls and stomps towards me, but I scramble back, throwing out my hand as another fork of lightning bursts from my fingertips, striking her in the chest. I'm screaming, too, tears running down my cheeks as I fling out my magic over and over, bolts of lightning sparking and cracking until it encases us both. She collapses to the ground, her body twitching as I siphon in more and more of my magic.

"Lor!" someone shouts, and I dimly register the sound of my name. "Lor! Stop it! She's dead!"

Finally, I force myself to let go. My fingertips hook inward as I seize on the last pulses of my power, tugging it in. When it's once again tethered under my skin, I find Tristan standing over me. The air crackles with remnants of lightning, hovering like errant wisps of smoke. We both stare at it and then at the body of the Fae. There's almost nothing left. She's just a black husk, barely recognizable as anything but a heap of scorched ruin.

"Oh gods," I sob, clutching my hand to my chest. I did that. I didn't just stop her, I *destroyed* her. "Tris. She grabbed me, and I didn't mean—"

I'm not sure what I'm trying to say.

I *did* mean to hurt her. She was going to hurt me, there was no doubt. But did I mean to do *this*?

"It's okay," Tristan says, understanding what I can't seem to say. "We should get out of here, though."

Tristan shoves his hands under my arms and lifts me up. The lingering crackles of lightning slowly dissipate into hazy red mist, like the atmosphere is burning. Tristan stares at it for a moment and then at me.

"Have you ever done anything like that before?" he asks.

I shake my head, wondering why he looks so worried.

"We should go," he says again. "Don't tell anyone about this, okay? Willow went back to the house, and it'll be our secret. We'll just worry Mother and Father. She's gone now, and no one ever needs to know."

"Okay," I say, understanding he's probably right, though I hate lying to my parents. With our hands linked, we head home, running as fast as our feet will take us.

Chapter Six

LOR

My eyes fly open, and I register the shape of a body hovering in the darkness. In one swift movement, my hand slips under my pillow, snagging my concealed dagger. I flip over, pinning the intruder to the mattress with the razor-sharp edge pressed to their throat.

It takes me a second to realize it's Nadir, highlighted in a sliver of moonlight, with his hands up over his head, his palms open in surrender.

My breath expels in a shaky rush, my entire body burning with adrenaline.

Nadir holds himself still, blinking up at me calmly despite the fact I'm threatening a vital artery.

That dream. That forest. That Fae who knew who I was. Somehow, I'd forgotten any of that happened, but it gallops towards me now with alarming clarity. Tristan and I should never have kept any of that quiet.

"What are you doing here?" I demand, waiting for my heartbeat to settle to a less stroke-inducing pace. "Why are you sneaking into my room?"

I don't know why I'm angry with Nadir other than he just scared the shit out of me. Ever since we escaped the Aurora King in Heart, I wake up at the slightest sound, certain that he's found us. I had a decade of practice inside Nostraza, always sleeping with one eye open.

"You were screaming," Nadir says, his words soft, still holding himself still. "I think you were having a nightmare."

My shoulders climb up to my ears, and I press the blade harder into his throat. It would be so easy to do it. Just the tiniest bit of pressure. A part of me knows he'd let me. It's so hard to look at him sometimes. To see the resemblance to his father. A constant reminder of everything I've lost. Of everything they both could still take.

"Lor," he says. "It's okay."

My gaze meets his. It swirls with violet light, and I remind myself that Nadir isn't his father. The tenderness in his eyes softens the pellet of rage I keep wedged in the center of my heart.

Finally, I relax, easing the blade from his throat.

"I could have killed you if I wanted," I say, not sure if that's entirely true. He could easily overpower me with his magic or good old-fashioned brute force before I ever got the chance.

"I know," he says without an ounce of condescension in his tone.

It's then I realize we're both practically naked.

I'm wearing only my bra and underwear, and Nadir's chest is bare but for the swirls of his colorful tattoos. I'm desperately hoping he has something over his bottom half. We both look down at each other and back up, and I shift, trying to determine if there's a layer of fabric between us. When a predictable awareness blooms between my thighs, I realize that is entirely the wrong move.

With my knees straddling his hips, it would be all too easy to give in to what my body craves. After what happened earlier today with his magic, the tension stretching between us hangs as heavy as an iron wall.

With the dagger still gripped in one fist, I plant my hands on either side of his head, leaning down as my breath tightens for an entirely different reason. I want him. I can't seem to stop wanting him. That night in Heart when he tried to claim me was an agonizing tease. I know I'm the one who pushed him away, but *need* squats in my chest, crushing my ribs, and the harder I try to push it away, the more it insists on being noticed. My magic hums softly in my veins as I lower myself down, slowly, so slowly.

Nadir's large, warm hands land lightly on the creases of my thighs, like he's afraid of making any sudden movements. His lips part, and I want to bite them. Suck on the bottom one until he's—

"Lor!" My door bangs open with a crash. *Shit.* I snap up to find Willow standing in the doorway. She takes in the scene, and her eyes widen before she covers them with a hand and fumbles for the doorknob.

"Oh. No. I'm sorry. I . . . heard you screaming." She keeps reaching behind her, trying to find the knob with her other hand clamped over her eyes.

"It's fine," I say, scrambling off Nadir and grabbing a robe to cover myself. I turn up the light, blinking furiously as I try to crush the swell of desire pulsing under my skin.

"It's not what you think."

I say the words firmly, hoping they sound a little bit true. It didn't start out the way she's thinking, but I wonder what might have happened if we hadn't been interrupted. I throw a look at Nadir, who is also scooting off the bed, relieved to note he's wearing underwear. However, it does nothing to conceal the effect of what we were just about to do, and he grabs a pillow to cover himself, tossing me a frown.

Willow lowers her hand and looks carefully between us.

"Is everything okay?"

"Yeah," I say, pulling my hair over a shoulder in an attempt to compose myself. "I was having a nightmare."

"Where the hell did you get a dagger from?" Nadir asks. "And why is it under your pillow?"

"Mael," I say, and Nadir shakes his head like he should have known. "He's been teaching me how to use it too."

Nadir's expression turns contrite. "I should have thought of that."

"Hmm," I say as I retrieve the knife from across the bed and return it to its hiding place.

"Is everything okay?" comes another voice. I turn around to find Tristan in the doorway, also half-dressed, his dark hair mussed from sleep. He looks at me and then at Nadir sitting on my bed, and his eyes darken. I am so not in the mood for this.

"Everything's fine," I say, running a hand down my face.

"Then why were you screaming?" Tristan asks.

"A nightmare." I bite my lip, considering how to approach this. "Tris, do you remember when we were kids, and there was that High Fae in the forest who tried to take me?"

I feel both Nadir and Willow physically react to my question.

"What?" Willow asks. "When?"

"I was about ten," I say. "The three of us were playing hide and seek, and she offered me a treat, and then she tried to steal me."

"How did I not know about this?" Willow demands.

I share a look with Tristan.

"We decided not to tell anyone."

"Why?" Nadir asks, already up, his entire body tight with tension. "Why did she try to take you?"

The tendons in his neck stand out, and I swear he's ready to hunt her down and tear a hole in her chest. Never mind that she's already dead. I sink onto the bed, pulling the collar of my robe tight.

"I used my magic on her," I say, and Willow's mouth falls open. "It was the only way to stop her. I called on my magic and just . . . obliterated her."

I recall the vivid details of my dream, thinking of the grotesque husk of her body lying in the grass. I'd blocked it out all those years ago, horrified by what I'd done, but I remember now. "Tristan and I agreed we didn't want to worry Mother and Father."

Willow nods with her mouth pressed in a thin line, but I catch the flicker of hurt in her eyes.

"I'd sort of forgotten about it in the passing years," I admit. "So many other things happened, and we never spoke about it, so it kind of sunk away."

"Until now," Nadir says.

I nod. "Until I just had a dream. And I think she must have known. She said something about knowing who I was. What I was. It makes sense that *someone* else knew."

"It would," Nadir says. "Someone beyond your parents and Cedar. How else would Atlas and my father have found out?"

"Atlas told me that he's friends with Cedar," I reply, and Nadir snorts.

"Maybe. But why would Cedar have kept that secret for almost three hundred years only to share it now? Cedar definitely isn't friends with my father and would never have given him information he could potentially use against him."

"We need to find out," Willow says.

"Why?" asks Tristan. "Is this the best use of our time? We need to get Lor to the Mirror."

"Don't you think this is important?" Willow asks. "Whoever knew told two powerful kings and clearly has an agenda. If the Mirror is the key to getting Lor her magic back, that person will emerge from the woodwork when she does. They had something to gain from all this, and we need to know what, for all our sakes and her safety."

I nod slowly. "But how do we even begin to uncover who it might be?"

"We'd need to go deeper," Nadir says. "Maybe find someone who was in Heart that day."

"What if we went to the settlements?" I ask, the idea stirring a wild longing in my chest.

Nadir shakes his head. "That's too much of a risk right now."

"But what Willow says makes sense. If I do get my magic back from the Mirror, then wouldn't it be better to already understand as much about the entire picture as possible before that happens? How long would it take?"

"We could be there and back in a couple of days."

"So what's a few more days while we figure out a plan?" I press my mouth together before whispering, "I need this. I want to see it."

I watch several thoughts cross his face. He's trying to keep me safe. He's trying to approach this from the most logical place, and I'm making that impossible with my request. But I couldn't see the settlements last time we went to Heart, and if things go poorly with Atlas and the Mirror, I might never get the chance.

"I'll send a message to Etienne. His last report said my father's soldiers have evacuated for the most part, but I'll ask him to do another sweep. We're not going anywhere near there unless I'm certain it's safe."

I blow out a breath. Nadir told me about his friend who watches over the settlements, sending reports. Thankfully, one of those missives stated that the king had stopped testing those women and let them go. It's the one positive side effect of my confrontation with the king. He had no further reason to search in Heart for the Primary—now he knows it's me.

"Thank you," I say.

"I'm not agreeing to anything yet," he says.

"They're coming too." I gesture to Tristan and Willow.

"Of course they are," he adds dryly.

He rolls his neck, attempting to loosen the tension I'm sure is partly due to me. Or maybe it's all due to me, but I'd like to think I'm not the sole source of his problems.

"Before we even consider this, we should try releasing your magic again. You are too vulnerable this way. While we wait for word from Etienne, we'll keep working on it."

I give him a sharp look, thinking of our encounter this afternoon. Like the last time he channeled his magic against mine, it had been one of the most intense experiences of my life. Did I like it? I certainly didn't hate it, but that dance feels like it's wobbling the rickety bridge I'm trying to keep between us.

"Not the way we've been," he says quickly. "Another way."

"All right," I say slowly, tipping my chin. "I'm willing to try anything." He nods before I add, "But then, I don't want any arguments about going to Heart if Etienne confirms it's safe."

His gaze flicks to me before he sighs.

Yup, I'm definitely one of the biggest sources of his problems.

"Fine. We'll take Mael too. The more the merrier, I guess."

CHAPTER SEVEN

After we gather a few more hours of sleep, Nadir takes me outside the city walls to work on my magic. Tristan tags along, too, since he has his own power to explore. While his Heart magic is a thin thread when compared to mine, he has other capabilities he's had to conceal for years. Something I know he's always despised.

Nadir performs some kind of spell on the horses, imparting them with speed. I remember when he took me through the Void on our way to the Keep. I knew that horse had been moving too fast to be natural.

With my disguise in place, we exit Aphelion through the western gate and venture into the dense forests surrounding the city.

Nadir rides in front, and after traveling for about an hour, he slows down, gesturing for me and Tristan to do the same. We're far from the walls of Aphelion now, and I pull off my hat, shaking my hair loose.

"What's that?" I ask as we pass what looks like a ruined stone building covered by overgrown vines and flowers. Nadir pulls up next to me.

"One of Zerra's old temples," he says.

"What happened to it?"

He shrugs. "A schism occurred many, many years ago known as the Burning. Her most ardent followers got out of hand, carrying out unspeakable acts in her name."

I look at him in horror. "What kinds of acts?"

"The legends say there was a conflict between the goddess and the Lord of the Underworld. That he tried to break free from his dominion where he's trapped. In her desire to suppress his growing power, she demanded unquestioned loyalty from everyone in Ouranos. But people were afraid, terrified of incurring the Lord's wrath, and so their support was... inconstant. To control them, her priestesses set about burning innocents in her name, claiming that anyone refusing to denounce him would pay with their lives.

"Eventually, people began to realize there was no actual evidence of the Lord's presence in their world, and they grew suspicious of the priestesses' claims. Thus, an uprising fought back, and her temples were ransacked, the priestesses shunned, and, in some more gruesome cases, struck down without mercy until they were all forced into hiding for a long time.

"Things were never quite the same again, and over time,

fewer and fewer followers find their way to Zerra with every passing year. She has no real power in Ouranos anymore."

Studying the crumbling ruin, I consider those words as we pass the temple. On one side is a carving of a woman, her face worn by time, but there's enough to make out the features of her mouth and an eye, along with a long dress that falls to her feet.

"Where did they come from?" I ask. "Zerra and the Lord?"

"That is a matter of debate amongst the scholars of Ouranos. They agree that Zerra created the High Fae and the Artefacts at the Beginning of Days, granting a select group of humans the magic of their lands and thus transforming them into what we are today."

"What about the low fae?"

"They were already here, living in peace in Ouranos's forests, lakes, and rivers. But as our cities spread, many were forced from their natural habitats and assimilated into society. There are still low fae dwelling in the most remote parts of the continent, probably hoping none of us ever notices them."

"Our parents didn't talk about her," I say, gesturing to Tristan, who watches our exchange. "But in Nostraza, her name was invoked regularly, and they prayed to her all the time," I say.

"Humans have, inexplicably, always had stronger ties to her," Nadir says. "I think since they possess no magic of their own, it allows them to feel closer to it. While the Fae, too, once openly worshipped her, their rituals and practices slowly died after the Burning. I think it became hard to believe in anyone or anything who could act so barbarically. In fact, many of the nobility and royal High Fae want nothing to do with Zerra's priestesses." He flicks his reins. "Temples like that used to be found everywhere in Ouranos—that's where her High Priestesses—her most devout and trusted servants—once lived."

"Is that the same type of High Priestess that was working with my grandparents?"

"Possibly," he says. "They also have magic, though their ability and capacity is a well-kept secret."

"Are there many High Priestesses left?"

"A few," he replies. "Scattered temples are left here and there, but they mostly keep to themselves, given their reputation."

I look over my shoulder at Tristan, noting the pinch of his brows. We both share similar frustrations that we know so little about our world. Everything we learned was filtered through a foggy lens, first by our parents and then by the years we spent behind the walls of Nostraza.

Finally, we arrive at a large clearing deep in the forest. High cliffs border the western edge, complete with a thundering waterfall that empties into a bright blue river winding along the far perimeter.

"This should be a good spot to conceal us," Nadir says before he hops down from his horse and ties it to a nearby tree. Tristan and I do the same before we proceed to the center of the clearing.

"I think we need to focus on what made your magic react when we were in Heart," Nadir says. "You felt threatened, so you released it. What you told me about your dream last night confirms the same."

Our gazes meet for an anxious moment before I look away. I wonder if he's thinking along the same lines. *I* wasn't the one being threatened at that moment. It was *Nadir* who the king had been tormenting when my magic broke loose.

I remember that utter rage coursing through me, so visceral it was like I'd been dipped in a boiling vat of anger thick enough to suffocate me. When I'd thought his life was in danger, I'd felt helpless and terrified, and I reacted. I wanted to protect him. Wanted to stop anyone from ever hurting him. It's a tangle of emotions I've found myself examining from every side ever since that night. No one has ever made me feel such an acute need to *protect*, and given my past, that's saying a lot.

"Right," I say, clearing my throat. "Makes sense."

Nadir turns his gaze to Tristan.

"You've never really explained what it is you're capable of."

Tristan chews the inside of his cheek before he steps away, putting a safe distance between us, and holds out a hand. He fires a blast of red lightning across the clearing, where it strikes the face of a cliff that explodes in a shower of gravel.

"I can do that," Tristan drawls, letting the words drift off.

Nadir picks up on Tristan's evasiveness immediately.

"And what else?"

My brother's jaw clenches, and he looks at me. I nod my head. There's no point in hiding this anymore. When Nadir and Amya asked about Tristan's magic in The Aurora, we'd claimed he wasn't capable of much.

But that was never the entire truth.

He turns to face the other direction and sends out another ribbon of magic, but this time it's green—it's similar to Nadir's light, though the essence differs. Richer and deeper and made of shadows instead of that bright and glowing Aurora power.

It forks out, wrapping around a copse of trees, twisting into a whirlwind of emerald as the trees start to stretch. Crackling sounds fill the air as their trunks expand, growing taller and broader, branches spreading and sprouting with thick, glossy leaves. After a moment, Tristan drops his hand, staring at his handiwork as though even he can't believe what he's done.

Nadir lets out a low whistle.

"You have Woodlands magic, too," he says, a touch of awe in his voice. "It makes sense, I suppose. Wolf would have been very powerful."

Nadir asks me, "You have none of this?"

"Not that I know of," I reply. "It seems I am all my grandmother."

He nibbles on his bottom lip as if contemplating a thousand possibilities and consequences of this knowledge.

"So when you both said Tristan didn't have much magic, you were lying."

"Well, I don't have much Heart magic. That part is true," my brother says.

Nadir lifts an eyebrow, but I know he understands why we kept this from him.

"And it *was* true," Tristan says, conflict in his eyes. "I didn't think I had much, but lately, it feels like it's . . . growing."

"Tris?" I ask. "Really?"

He nods. "I didn't want to say anything until I was sure, but sometimes at night, I wake up with red and green wrapping around me. During the day, it moves inside me, and I have to concentrate on holding it back. It keeps getting stronger."

"You said this might happen," I say to Nadir. "Do you remember? When you told me that after what my grandmother did, everyone in Ouranos lost their magic?"

"I remember," he says. "It was just a guess, though."

"Looks like you were right," I say.

"I usually am."

I roll my eyes at his smirk.

"I wonder if Willow is experiencing this too?" I ask, and Tristan shrugs.

"What else can you do with it?" Nadir asks my brother.

Tristan performs another demonstration, uprooting the same trees he just grew and tossing them aside like they're nothing but toothpicks.

"That could be very useful," Nadir says with a hint of admiration. Tristan almost smiles. He doesn't like Nadir, and I don't blame him for that, but they're so equally stubborn. I wonder if they can bridge this divide.

"Well, this got a lot more interesting," Nadir says, clapping his hands. "Lor. I think we need to put you on the defensive."

He turns around and points to a spot. "You'll stand there, and I'm going to use my magic against you."

I nod, seeing the validity of the idea. Maybe this could work.

"I'll help," Tristan says, cracking his knuckles, and Nadir snorts.

"Absolutely not."

Tristan glares at him. "Why not?"

"You haven't used your magic in over a decade and just said it's growing. You don't have the kind of control necessary for this exercise."

Tristan's jaw turns hard, his eyes flashing.

I repress a sigh. They're never going to get along at this rate.

"Nadir—" I say.

"No," he says, cutting me off. "If your brother values your life as much as I know he does, then he'll understand that we aren't playing around with your safety."

Nadir focuses his gaze on Tristan. "Right?"

Tristan pauses but then nods.

"Fine," he says before Nadir's face stretches into a grin.

"In fact, you can use this opportunity to practice, too. It's obvious you can become another weapon against whatever we might face. We're going to need every resource possible."

With that ominous remark, Nadir spins on his heel and jogs across the clearing.

I share a look with Tristan.

"You think this is a good idea?" he asks as I look back at Nadir, who is now a hundred feet away.

"I think it's worth a shot," I reply as Nadir stops and turns to face us.

"I don't trust him," Tristan says.

"I know you don't. I'm asking you to trust *me*."

I swallow the tightness in my throat. Do *I* trust Nadir? I've spent so much time pushing him away, determined not to believe him. Determined not to fall for the pretty words and pretty face of another High Fae royal. But my armor is forming a network of fissures liable to crack from the slightest pressure.

He's done nothing but protect me since we agreed to work together in The Aurora, despite our unconventional first encounters.

He makes me feel things I never expected to feel. Safe. Wanted. Beautiful. Like my flaws aren't a series of mistakes but rather the essential pieces that make me who I am.

And while he could be lying about all of it, I know he isn't. The truth is, somewhere in my determination not to trust him, I've grown to believe in him completely. I'm terrified, but of what exactly? Allowing myself to love freely and with abandon? Letting him have my heart to do anything with? What if I'm not enough?

"Ready?" Nadir shouts from across the distance, pulling me from my thoughts.

I nod, though I'm not sure what I'm supposed to be ready for.

Nadir raises his arms and sends two bolts of light streaming towards us—one at me and one at Tristan.

Tristan reacts instantly, a tendril of green light erupting from his fingers, slamming into Nadir's magic. I witness all of this from the corner of my eye as I focus on the streak of purple barreling down on me.

I grit my teeth, willing something to happen with my magic, but nothing comes. I duck at the last moment just as Nadir's light bends around me and harmlessly dissipates in the air.

"Fuck," I curse under my breath.

Nadir doesn't miss a beat, sending more streaks of magic

careening towards us. Tristan deflects as much as he can, focusing mostly on his forest magic, with flashes of shadowy green, leaping out of the way with each occasional miss. He's broken a sweat, his dark fringe of hair sticking to his temples, his breath coming in heavy gasps.

I'm amazed at his progress. It's obvious he's a natural at this. Clearly, that gift doesn't run in the family.

Nadir continues trying to provoke my magic into action, firing bolt after bolt towards me, wrapping around my torso, even going as far as singeing my clothing, but nothing I do makes a difference. My magic reacts to his in the same way it always does, fighting like a caged serpent trying to spring loose but ultimately failing to break out and act. I'm about as useful as a warning trapped inside an unbreakable bottle.

"Stop!" I finally yell, frustrated and angry that I can't seem to make myself function the way I need. "This isn't working."

Nadir drops his arms and jogs back towards us, stopping in front of me.

"It's no use," I say. "I know you won't really hurt me."

Those last words sit between us as Nadir's jaw tics. I know it's true. It's something I've understood for a while. That no matter what happens, he wouldn't ever willingly hurt me.

He doesn't argue, instead running a frustrated hand through his hair.

"He *would* hurt me, though," Tristan says, and Nadir's expression morphs from serious to gleeful.

"I'm not opposed to making you bleed a little," he says.

"I'd like to see you try," Tristan counters. "I had no trouble resisting you there."

Nadir barks out a derisive laugh.

"If you think that's all I could do, then you have much to learn about magic, little Faeling."

"Who are you calling Faeling?" Tristan demands.

"Stop," I say again, my hands rising between them. "That's enough from both of you."

I point to Nadir. "*You* are not using my brother as a battering ram. We need to think of something else. Something that actually makes it feel like my life is in danger."

We all fall silent for a moment, lost in our thoughts.

"No," Nadir says eventually. "Not your life, maybe. How about mine? It worked last time."

He moves back a few paces, his steps light and loose, and I can tell from the gleam in his eyes that he's planning something I won't like.

"What are you doing?" I demand as he tosses me a wicked smile and then turns and runs away.

"Nadir!" I call after him. "Get back here! I order you!"

He flips around, jogging backward and spreading his arms wide.

"I don't take orders from you, In—Lor!"

Then he turns around and continues running. I'm thankful he can't see my face at that moment. He was about to call me "Inmate" before he corrected himself.

He hasn't called me that since we left The Aurora. Not since that night. I used to hate that name, but something about him calling me *just* Lor sits like a cold stone in my stomach.

Like I'm not special to him anymore.

Like something has been lost between us, and I hate it.

And I hate that I hate it.

Fuck, I'm such a mess.

Nadir has stopped on the far side of the clearing and is now standing under a cliff where an overhang drenches him in shade. As he spins to face us, it suddenly occurs to me what he has planned.

"No!" I shout. "Are you insane?!"

Instantly, I start running, but even from this distance, I perceive his smug smile. He lifts a hand and shoots a blast of blue light into the protruding rock.

A loud crack brings me to a shuddering stop. He did it. He fucking did it. Frozen where I stand, I stare at the rock, watching pieces shear off, tumbling to where he waits below. He watches me. Testing me. Waiting for me to succeed.

I tell myself that he'll move before it collapses. He's only bluffing. He wouldn't really let that fall on him, just for my sake.

But a tiny voice screams in the back of my head. *What if he doesn't?* I've always known the Aurora Prince never does anything by halves. What if he's crushed under the weight of an entire cliff? Not even a High Fae would survive that.

"Nadir!" I scream, my voice cracking with fear.

"Use your magic, Lor!" he screams back. "I know you can do it!"

I *can* do this. He believed in me when we were in Heart, and I saved him then. He's the only one who's been able to rouse my magic since I locked it away, and I have to trust him now.

A boom draws my attention to the cliff. The rock shifts,

slowly crumbling as it succumbs to the pressure of gravity and its own weight. I don't have much time.

I search inside myself, prodding at that door keeping me blocked. Gritting my teeth, I pull at it, tearing at it like a crazed beast with a set of useless, dulled claws.

Another loud crack bounces through the clearing, echoing off the stones.

Nadir doesn't move. Doesn't even look up. He's staring at me. Willing me to do what I need to do.

It's then I understand that he won't move. He's going to force me to do this. Just like when he helped me release my magic inside the Heart Castle, he's never going to give up on me.

Another crack precedes the fall of a massive boulder. It plummets, landing just next to Nadir, barely missing him, tossing his hair around his shoulders. But still, he doesn't move. Doesn't even blink as he dares me to fail.

I can do this. I *must* do this.

And then everything happens at once.

Another loud pop bursts in my ears, and the cliff breaks away, rock tumbling as my hands fly out, and red lightning smashes into the stone, blasting it apart. I continue filtering lightning, pummeling the rock until the largest pieces crumble apart, becoming a harmless shower of gravel. Nadir covers his head as it drops, and my world stops moving until, a few seconds later, everything dims to silence.

Stumbling over my feet towards him, my head spins from the shortness of my breath, tears streaming down my cheeks.

When I reach him, he wraps me into his arms, but I batter his chest with my fists, screaming, crying, raging.

"How could you do that?! You scared the shit out of me! You could have died!" I sob as he holds me, saying nothing as I cling to the fabric of his shirt, balling it in my fists like I can stop him from ever leaving me.

Once I've suitably scolded him, I inhale a deep breath, waiting for my pulse to slow to normal. I push away, wiping my cheeks with the backs of my hands.

"Sorry," I say. "I didn't mean to yell at you. I just... You scared me."

He tips his head. "So you made clear."

Another moment passes between us. I can keep trying to pretend I don't care, but my cover has just been blown wide open.

"It worked, though," he says with a cocky tilt of his mouth. "Told you I'm always right."

Zerra, there will be no living with him after this.

"It did," I say, noticing Tristan on the other side of the clearing, practicing his forest magic on a group of trees, pointedly ignoring the two of us.

"He got all weird when you threw yourself at me," Nadir says, and I whip around to face him.

"I did not throw myself... Oh, shut up," I finish when I catch the smug look on his face.

I storm away, but he grabs my arm and pulls me towards him.

"Lor, stop this."

"Stop what?"

"You know what I'm talking about," he says. He moves closer, a bare sliver of space compressing between us.

I lick my lips and swallow the scratch in my suddenly dry throat. A quick check across the clearing shows Tristan is still ignoring us.

"I don't," I say, forcing the lie from my mouth. It tastes like ashes. "Please," I add, not entirely sure what I'm asking for. More space. More time. More distance to sort out the muddle of thoughts in my head.

Nadir's expression softens.

"What do you need, Lor?" Something about how he asks the question tightens the space behind my ribs. What *do* I need?

"A friend."

The words slip out. I hadn't really meant to say that, but as they land, I understand this feels right.

Nadir pauses only for a heartbeat before he nods. "I can do that."

Our gazes linger, and that feeling under my skin stirs, along with everything else that always reacts in his presence. I know he isn't *just* my friend. That's only one oversimplified layer of who we are to each other, but I'm not ready to explore the others yet.

It's hard to explain how much my previous experiences have twisted everything that has come after. My perspective. My relationships. My ability to trust.

Maybe it won't always be this way, but it was only a few months ago when I truly believed I'd die in Nostraza. When every day was a misery and surviving another sunrise became a reoccurring miracle. When I did unthinkable things to survive. Things that I want to forget but that will forever live in the stitched fabric of my soul.

I was a child when I was taken. I've lived so little. I'm not ready to plunge into whatever this will mean if Nadir and I continue on this path.

I want to get there. I think. But I need more time.

"Thank you," I finally say, and his jaw tenses before he lets go of my arm and steps away.

He turns towards Tristan, who's still pretending neither of us exists. Given his feelings about Nadir, I'm surprised he hasn't tried to interfere.

The prince and I watch Tristan use both forms of his magic, twisting them together as they spin through the air. He's obviously reveling in this ability to finally explore what he's capable of.

I smile at my brother as a tear slips from the corner of my eye. We haven't had much opportunity to talk about how we're all dealing with our respective releases from Nostraza, but I know it's affecting him in similar ways. None of us can escape that past.

"C'mon," Nadir says after a minute. "Let's try again. I know you can do this."

Over the next few hours, Nadir continues to force me to use my magic until it's starting to feel more natural. Almost. While I can drive it to the surface if I concentrate hard enough, it still isn't the extension of me that I remember from my childhood.

In those days, it was easy and natural. It's almost there, but it's blocked, trickling out instead of flowing freely, all because of that door I can't force open. I sense *more* pressing up against it, but this is all I can manage.

Still, it's better than nothing. And I have Nadir to thank for all of it.

Once we've all had enough, the sun is starting to set.

"We made excellent progress today," Nadir says, a hint of pride in his voice. "You did good, Lor."

"Amazing," my brother agrees.

"Thank you. Both of you," I say. Accessing my magic is still a struggle, but I don't feel quite as useless and helpless as I always have.

"Let's go home. I'm starving," Tristan says, heading for his horse.

Nadir is watching me, and I tip my head, giving him a small smile. I want to say thank you for this moment. For today. For giving me the space I need. For things I have no name for yet. I probably don't deserve his patience, but he's offering it nonetheless.

"Let's go," he says softly. "I'm proud of you."

It feels too hard to respond to that, so I just nod. And then we all hop back on our horses and head towards the walls of Aphelion.

CHAPTER EIGHT

Following a restless sleep, I head down to the kitchen the next morning. When Nadir, Tristan, and I arrived home last night, everyone had already gone to bed. So the three of us had a cold dinner of bread and cheese before we said our goodnights.

Laughter floats up the stairway, and I emerge to find Nerissa at the stove, tending to a frying pan, while Tristan leans against the counter with his arms crossed. He's smiling broadly as he says something that causes Nerissa to laugh again, her hand landing on his biceps in what I'm sure is a very deliberate attempt to touch him.

A knot of emotion forms in my throat as I watch them. This is what I want for my siblings. To find someone who allows them to feel again. To love and lose themselves with. This is what I was fighting for during the Trials.

Tristan catches sight of me and straightens up from his position.

"Morning," he says, looking down at his feet as he pulls up a stool around the large kitchen island and settles onto it. I'm sure he's blushing, but I decide not to embarrass him by commenting. I'm not sure why he's pretending he's not interested in Nerissa, but he has his own demons to contend with, and we're all dealing with it in our separate ways.

Nerissa peers over her shoulder and smiles.

"Morning, Lor. Breakfast is ready. Help yourself." Then she returns to the stove, humming to herself, but not before her gaze falls on my brother for the briefest moment.

I sit down next to Tristan, and one by one, Nadir, Willow, Mael, and Hylene also file in, helping themselves to pastries, waffles, and crispy strips of bacon. While Nerissa is more than content to cook for us, she absolutely refuses to clean up our mess, which is a fair boundary.

Mael's a bit of a slob, and I wouldn't want to clean up after this lot either.

A few minutes into our meal, Amya enters with a letter in her hand and a grim set to her lips.

"What is it?" Nadir asks.

"I just received a report from The Aurora," she says, scanning the page as though she's hoping the words will rearrange themselves. "The Savahell Mine collapsed two days ago, killing almost six hundred low fae, a group of prisoners from Nostraza, as well as every guard on duty."

We fall into silence at those words.

"The Savahell Mine?" Tristan asks, a raw edge to his voice.

As an able-bodied male, he was regularly assigned to work in the mines during our days in the prison while Willow and I were assigned to more domestic tasks. He'd come back covered in black dust, too tired to eat, often with lash marks torn into his back.

Willow reaches out and takes his hand, squeezing it.

"Yes. It's the largest jewel mine in The Aurora," Nadir replies, missing their exchange. "Dissent has been growing for months. The working conditions are vile, and even several members of the Aurora council disagree with its practices, but my father doesn't care. He just keeps pushing them to dig deeper and deeper."

That's when his gaze lands on where Willow is still gripping Tristan's hand so tightly her knuckles are turning white.

"Did you . . ." Nadir asks.

"I don't want to talk about it," Tristan says, cutting him off.

Nadir dips his chin in acknowledgment. "I'm sorry."

There's such anguish in that apology that my hands clench, my nails digging into my thighs.

Tristan nods and looks away, indicating he'd like to move on from the topic.

"Why does he keep digging?" Willow asks. "To what end? Don't you have enough riches and jewels?"

Nadir looks at my sister. "If only it were that simple."

"We have to stop this," Amya says, and she sounds so small.

"I know," replies Nadir. "I know."

He looks down at his plate and makes a show of returning to his breakfast, though I can see he's not really eating. The rest of us follow suit, chewing quietly in the kitchen's somber mood.

Nadir drops the piece of toast in his hand and stands up, planting his fists on the table's surface.

"We have a few things we need to take care of quickly. Gabriel can give us only a little time before he's forced to reveal our presence to Atlas. We need to accelerate our plans."

Everyone's eyes meet around the table. I can hear the strain in Nadir's words. The news from The Aurora has shaken him, but he's putting on his game face.

"Nadir," Amya says, but he holds up a hand.

"The plan hasn't changed. From the beginning, it's been our intention to get Lor's magic back so she can help bring Father down. That's the only thing that ends this. And to do that, we need to understand who's sharing the secrets of Heart around Ouranos and get Lor to the Mirror. Then we can focus on the rest."

Nadir glares at his sister, who dips her chin in agreement.

"But we still don't have a solid plan," Tristan says.

"What we need is someone who knows the layout well enough to draw us a map with alternate entrances and exits to the throne room and the building itself," Mael says.

"Gabriel," I say, but Nadir shakes his head.

"Only as a last resort. I worry we're already testing how far he can stretch this. If we ask him, we can never be sure when the line crosses into something he has no choice but to reveal to Atlas."

Nadir looks at Amya. "Any ideas?"

"Actually, yes," Amya says. "As luck would have it, I heard last night the future Sun Queen is looking for new lady's maids. Apparently, she fired her entire staff because they were all, and I quote, 'a bunch of ninny-headed fools without two brain cells to rub together.' She's holding interviews tomorrow. It might be the perfect opportunity to get us inside."

I almost smile at that, imagining Apricia tearing up a storm in the palace. It almost makes me feel sorry for Atlas.

"I'll do it," Willow says, and every eye swings to her. "Well, it can't be Lor. They'll recognize her. Nor can it be Amya."

"I could do it," Hylene says. "No one there knows me by sight."

"I have a feeling your skills are needed elsewhere," Willow says. "This is something I can do, and I want to help. I'm sure I can convince this Apricia I have at least three brain cells."

"It makes sense," Nadir says slowly, but Tristan and I trip over each other's objections.

"It's too dangerous," Tristan says.

"What if he figures it out?" I question, and Willow gives us both a sharp look.

"Oh, and everything you're doing is safe? Stop it. I can do this. I can stay beneath anyone's notice long enough to get a lay of the place."

"Servants usually know all the best routes to go in and out," Amya says. "It's a good plan."

"She looks too much like Lor," Mael says. "What if they make a connection?"

"I can dye my hair," Willow says, anticipating the comment. "I've always wondered what I'd look like as a blonde."

She flips her still-short locks and smiles at me. "I want to do this for you, Lor. For all of us. I don't have magic, and I'm no good in a fight, but this I can do."

"But, Willow—"

"No," she says, more firmly than I've ever heard her speak. "You and Tristan, you're always the brave and selfless ones. You're the one who protected me when those guards . . . You . . . They . . ."

She breaks off, her eyes filling with tears. I'm trying to understand what she's not saying. Does she think she owes me anything for our years in Nostraza?

"Just let me do this," she whispers.

An awkward silence hangs in the room, and I exchange a look with Tristan before I nod in agreement. Despite my reservations, this is a good idea. While we try to puzzle out who knows our secrets, we have to figure out how to get inside the palace. And we have to do it quickly, before Gabriel is forced to reveal our presence.

"Too bad we can't get Callias to deal with your hair," I say.

"Don't worry," Amya says. "I can take care of that."

"So that's decided," Nadir says, pushing past our uncomfortable confrontation. "Once Amya has altered your appearance, you'll present yourself at the Sun Palace and hope the future Sun Queen deems you intelligent enough for her highly exacting standards."

Willow holds up her hands with her fingers crossed. "One can only hope."

Chapter Nine

L ater that evening, I go in search of Willow, finding her in the back garden, seated at the long wooden table across from Tristan. They're sharing a bottle of something guaranteed to cause a regrettable hangover, their glasses sitting in front of them.

I haven't spent much time back here, but evidence of Nerissa's loving touches are everywhere, including the surrounding fence strung with small white lights, giving the entire space a warm glow.

"Hi," I say as I approach my brother and sister, sliding onto the bench beside Tristan. "Mind if I join you?"

Tristan nods and hands me his glass.

"Elven wine," he explains. "It's not bad if you aren't terribly attached to the lining of your stomach."

I peer at the dark green liquid and take a sip, tasting notes of mint and honey layered with the strong punch of alcohol.

Willow has been avoiding me since the discussion this morning, and even now, she refuses to make eye contact. It's clear she's spent the day with Amya, because her black hair has been lightened to a dark blonde streaked with copper. It's transformed her appearance so no one but the most astute observer would make the connection to me.

"Nice hair," I say. "You look good like that."

Willow scoffs and takes a sip of her drink, still avoiding my gaze.

"Willow, about what you said this morning—"

"I'm sorry," she says, her expression crumpling. "I shouldn't have said that to you."

"No, it's okay. But what did you mean by it? You understand that you owe me nothing for anything that happened in Nostraza? Right?"

She sighs and smacks her glass on the table. "How can you say that to me?"

I shake my head. "Willow, I don't understand where this is coming from all of a sudden."

"It's not all of a sudden," she says, raising her voice. "How do you think it felt knowing what those monsters were doing to you while I lay safe in my bed? Do you have any idea how much shame I feel that I let you take all of it? I'm supposed to be the big sister!"

"Willow." I reach for her hand across the table, but she snatches it away. "It's okay. That was all my choice."

"No! Don't do that. Don't try to baby me. I'm not made of glass."

I flinch at her words.

"Willow," Tristan says. "You're being a little hard on her."

"You're no better!" Willow yells at him. I've never heard her use her voice like this before. "Neither of you let me do anything."

"What did you want me to do?" I ask, my anger starting to crest at this string of unfair accusations. "Just let them have you?"

"Why not?" Willow asks. "Why did you think you had to do that?"

"I was trying to help you! I did it for you!"

"I didn't ask you to!"

My jaw drops. "Are you fucking kidding me right now?" I push up from the table. I don't know what to do with my hands or body, I just need to create some distance. "What good would that have done? Then we'd both be entirely fucked up, too scared to let anyone in! At least you don't have to close your eyes every fucking night and *remember*."

I'm furious now, my body trembling with rage and fear and the memories that threaten to crush me.

"No, I just have to remember the way you'd lie in your bed every night trying desperately not to cry, knowing that I was the cause of it. Knowing that I could have shared the burden with you!"

"Willow, you're not making any sense!"

She pushes herself up to stand.

"I can barely look at you," she says, tears streaming down

her cheeks. "It's my fault you're so *angry* all the time. That there's a prince in that house who looks at you like you're his entire world, and all you know how to do is push him away. It's my fault that my baby sister is *broken.*"

"Willow—"

"No!" She holds up her hands and steps back. "Don't come near me."

She heaves out a sob, covers her face, and then disappears into the house, slamming the door.

I stare after her for several long seconds before I turn to my brother.

"What was that?" I ask.

"I don't know."

"Should I go after her?"

Tristan rises from his seat, wrapping an arm across my shoulders. "Just give her a little space. I'll go and check on her." He picks up his glass from the table and presses it into my hand. "Drink this. I'll be right back."

Then he, too, disappears into the house, and I drop onto the bench, slamming the entire contents of my glass back before dropping my forehead to the table. I stay in that position for several long minutes, replaying our conversation over and over. I had no idea this was how she felt. She never hinted at any of these regrets.

I try to put myself in her shoes and realize I would feel exactly the same if our positions had been reversed, but I can't regret what I did. I meant what I said. At least only one of us has to live with those memories and that very specific brand of trauma.

I become aware of someone sitting down across from me before they drag the decanter of elven wine closer, filling up both glasses and pushing one of them next to my head.

"I know what it's like," comes a soft voice, and I look up to find Hylene. I'd been expecting Tristan. "To live with that darkness. To close your eyes at night and feel their rough hands. To hear the sounds of their breaths and remember the smell of their sweat as it turns your stomach."

I push myself up the rest of the way as I scrub a tear from my cheek.

"You do?"

She shrugs, one arm crossed over her body and the other holding her drink.

"My mother was a prostitute at a high-end brothel in the Crimson District. She fell pregnant with me when she was only sixteen. They allowed her to keep me with her until I could help with the chores, so I worked in the kitchens and did odd jobs until they deemed me old enough for more."

"More?" I ask, already dreading what she's going to say next.

"I was thirteen when I was forced to 'welcome' my first customer," she says, her eyes cold and distant. "I don't remember his name or his face, but I remember how he made me feel. Like I was small and worthless. Like I didn't matter and never would."

"I'm so sorry," I whisper.

She inhales a deep breath. "I found ways to survive. To block it out. I'm sure you understand."

I nod. I do.

"How did you get away?" I ask.

"When I was eighteen, I was invited as an escort to a party at a popular cabaret. The asshole I was with got blind drunk and dragged me out onto one of the balconies. He tried to fuck me, but he could barely get his pants undone, and I don't know what came over me that night. I'd just had enough. You know?"

I nod my head.

"I shoved him off me, and he flew into a rage because obviously he had a right to my cunt, and I owed him anything he wanted." She takes a long sip of her drink, and though she speaks with detachment, emotion simmers in her eyes. "He shoved me towards the balcony and was about to push me over when Nadir heard me screaming.

"He came out and pulled him off me, and then . . . someone went over the balcony that night, but it wasn't me."

My eyes are wide. "Nadir *killed* him?"

Hylene smirks. "Don't tell me you're surprised."

I bark out a laugh. "No. I guess I'm not."

In a weird sort of way, I'm kind of proud of him for that. Not kind of. Very. He might pretend he's all hardhearted, but I've seen what lies underneath.

"So what happened then?" I ask.

"Nadir checked that I was okay, and we got to talking. He asked if I wanted a job working for him. He needed someone to help with a few tasks, and I agreed immediately. I wanted out of the Crimson District so badly. He bought out the price of my indenture and set me up with a flat in the Violet District. And the rest, as they say, is history."

"Wow," I say. "How long ago was that?"

"Hmm, about fifty years or so."

"And have you two ever..." I move my fingers back and forth, and Hylene laughs.

"No. That's never what we've been to one another. Why? Would you have cared?"

"Of course not," I say far too quickly to be believable.

"Of course," she says, giving me a knowing look.

We both sip our drinks in silence for a few minutes, the distant sounds of the city and crickets floating on the breeze. A lightning bug buzzes through the air, and I watch as it twists and twirls, leaving a soft, glowing trail hovering against the dark.

"You really did that in Nostraza?" Hylene asks. "What your sister said?"

I nod.

"That was very brave of you."

I snort. "Tell that to my sister."

"She's not angry with you," Hylene says. "You must know that."

"I know. I'm not sure how to fix this now. What's done is done, and I've never blamed her for any of it, and I certainly don't think she owes me."

"You'll both figure it out. It's obvious how much you mean to each other. Just give her some time. We all deal with our ghosts in different ways."

"Thanks," I say, meaning it. "I really needed this. All of it."

The corner of her mouth ticks up, and her green eyes sparkle as she leans forward.

"You can repay me by telling me more about your friend with the wings."

My eyes widen.

"Who? Gabriel?"

Hylene lifts a delicate shoulder. "He had a certain long-suffering rage that was kind of hot."

I groan and grab my glass, tipping it towards her. "Then I'm going to need another drink for this conversation."

Chapter Ten

Gabriel

The Sun Palace

I stare down at Tyr, who lies in his bed, blinking at nothing, his gaze as distant as the stars. The arcturite cuffs around his wrists and neck pulse with an eerie blue glow that haunts me every time I close my eyes.

"I've been doing some reading," I say, looking up at Atlas, where he stands leaning against the wall with his arms crossed and one leg over the other. "They say prolonged exposure to arcturite can cause irreparable mental decay, making the wearer listless in some cases and manic in others."

I don't add what else I'm thinking. Tyr hasn't just experienced prolonged exposure, he's been wearing these fucking things for decades. I've always wondered what black market Atlas procured these from so many years ago. It's forbidden to mine or sell arcturite due to its unique capabilities against High Fae, and these must have cost a small ransom in some backdoor arrangement.

Atlas doesn't immediately reply to my comment as he stares at his brother, his mouth pressed into a line of obvious annoyance.

"So what do you want me to do?"

"He's getting worse," I say. "Take them off. Surely he can't pose any threat in this state?"

I watch while Atlas weighs my words as if testing them for poison before he shakes his head.

"No, I can't take that risk."

"But he can't give orders like this," I try.

For Atlas to control me and my brothers, he needs Tyr to say the words, but he can't do anything like this. It's partly why I can maneuver around the rules as much as I do. Tyr commanded that we obey his brother, but Atlas's own orders are thus delivered by proxy, giving them less weight. It's also part of why I wasn't forced to run to Atlas the moment I saw Lor.

What I told Nadir was also true—that Lor found me, not the other way around, and it's by existing inside these small deceptions that I'm able to find a pocket of air within the stranglehold of my chains. It's not much, but it's better than nothing.

"Instead of worrying about the cuffs, you need to get him to talk. He's no use to me when he's like this," Atlas says, his expression aloof. I tamp down my disgust. I don't know how Atlas can look at what's become of his brother and feel nothing about his role in causing this. "Without taking them off," he adds when he sees I'm about to speak, predicting my next words with more insight than I'd like.

"What if we let him out for a bit? Took him for a walk in the garden for some fresh air?"

It would be risky, and I'd have to find some way to conceal his identity, but Atlas cleared out every staff member employed during Tyr's rule, and he's hardly recognizable as the golden king he once was.

"Maybe," Atlas says. "I'll think about it."

I already know what that means—he has no intention of ever thinking about it. It's been this way for as long as I can remember. He'll tell me he'll "look into it" or "speak with his advisors" like a coward instead of just admitting he doesn't care.

Atlas looks outside and then pinches the bridge of his nose.

"Are we done? I need to go and meet with General Heulfryn. I've canceled it too many times and can't avoid it anymore."

"Sure," I say, glancing at Tyr one more time before I touch his brow, running my finger along the ridge of bone. He blinks, and I hope it's because he knows that I'm here and that I care. My thumb sweeps over his cheek, and he blinks again, my heart twisting in my chest.

I follow Atlas out of the room, locking the door and depositing the key into my pocket before we wind down the stairs. We make our way towards Atlas's study, where I know Apricia's father will be waiting, likely with his blades or fists prepared for a confrontation.

He's furious about the continued delays with the bonding ceremony, and I'm not sure how much longer Atlas can continue sidestepping the general's questions. Earlier, Atlas demanded to know if I had more news about Lor, and he seemed to swallow my carefully constructed lies.

I don't know why I want to give her time to accomplish whatever brought her back here, but something in my gut tells me I need to. Everything she revealed about her lineage was shocking but not completely a surprise. Obviously, there's more than what she revealed on the surface, given everything that happened and the fact Atlas wants to find her so much. I would never have guessed at the truth, though.

I find myself sympathizing with her. It seems like she's been thrust into something against her will, and I understand all too much how that feels.

"Stay with me," Atlas says. "I might need backup."

I nod and resist the urge to roll my eyes.

If Lor is the Primary of Heart, then she must have powerful magic, and given Atlas's obsession, the only logical conclusion is he wants to bond with her to access her strength. Though both Atlas and Tyr are able to channel the magic of Aphelion, their gifts aren't quite the same. Atlas has an unparalleled gift of illusion, but Tyr's most noticeable talent is the ability to use light as a weapon. Atlas has always been jealous of that, feeling what I can describe only as self-conscious that he has almost no offensive magic.

Lor's Heart magic—that legendary crimson lightning—would certainly give Atlas a different edge.

It could all work, and I suppose, when viewed at a distance, it's not a terrible plan, but I can't help but feel like this is all a house of cards about to topple at the slightest breeze. I don't know how he's managed to go so long without anyone uncovering his secret to begin with. Surely his clock is ticking towards ruin. All I can hope is he doesn't take me down with him.

I'm not well-versed enough in the relationship between rulers and their Artefacts, so I have no sense of how the Mirror figures into all of this. It chose Apricia, but for whom? Atlas or Tyr? Does it understand what Atlas has done?

What I do know is that Atlas avoids going anywhere near the Mirror, ordering the palace staff to keep it covered whenever it's not in use. Does anyone else see the way Atlas carefully keeps himself away from its line of sight? Or is it noticeable only to me? I have my theories about what's happening, but I have no evidence to support my suspicions.

Additionally, I can't comprehend how he thinks he'll ever convince Lor to bond with him after everything he did to her, but I already understand that he doesn't plan to *ask*. The Mirror rejected her, though, so unless he's convinced it to cooperate, I'm not sure how he's going to accomplish any of this.

What vital fact am I missing? I wish I could get into his head.

We enter Atlas's study to find General Cornelius Heulfryn pacing back and forth with his hands behind his back. He has Apricia's black hair and piercing blue eyes, his chin covered with a thick beard. He helped lead Aphelion's armies during both Sercen Wars, earning him his title and power. His position is mostly ceremonial after his retirement several years ago—an honor afforded to him for his service in the king's name. Apricia was always a natural choice for queen, given his legacy.

He stops at our entrance, straightening up.

"Finally," he says, in a way that suggests this conversation doesn't bode well for Atlas.

"General," Atlas says, smooth as silk. "It's such a pleasure to see you."

"Don't," Cornelius says, raising a finger. He's already shaking, he's so mad. "You have been avoiding me, and I am here to demand you set a date for the bonding ceremony. My daughter is beside herself with this constant dithering. What are you waiting for?"

Atlas tries to affect a calm demeanor, but I can tell he's holding back his frustration from the rigid set of his shoulders. I've known him long enough to read every cue others might miss.

"I'm waiting for the right time."

"Bullshit," says Cornelius. "You're hiding something. Why do all this?"

Cornelius stalks forward, coming to stand in front of Atlas. He nearly matches the king in size and is clearly not intimidated. It makes me admire him a little. "The council and I didn't make a fuss when you 'canceled' the previous Trials, but I will no longer stand for this. Those were the daughters of some of your most trusted friends and advisors, and even more were sacrificed in the name of a second Trial. How can you treat those lives so lightly? You're making a mockery of everything this kingdom and the Trials stand for."

"I do care," Atlas says, using his most velvet-smooth voice. "Of course I care. It wasn't my decision to end the last Trials. The Mirror made me do it. You know that."

Cornelius gives him a look that suggests Atlas is full of shit. If only he knew how right he was.

"Set a date. I've spoken with the district heads, and they're with me on this. They no longer care that their own daughters lost, but the longer you keep this up, the less support you'll have going forward. There's talk of selling property to the low fae."

Atlas's eyes narrow at that. "That is forbidden."

"And yet the tides are turning. There is less and less favor for these policies of yours, and the others have agreed that if you do not set a date, we will have to take more drastic measures."

The general stands straighter, clearly bracing himself for the impact of Atlas's anger.

My gaze volleys between them, mentally betting on who will win this. The heads of districts have the right to question the king's wishes when it seems he is acting against the interest of the kingdom, though I've never heard of it actually happening before. Cornelius is right, and Atlas's refusal to set the date is going to cause problems soon. It destabilizes us. Makes our traditions look pointless and like something to mock. No other realm holds such Trials, and most of them think it questionable to do so at all.

The Trials were the invention of Aphelion's first king after the Beginning of Days. The stories say that Zerra herself had bestowed upon each ruler both the Imperial magic of their realm and the Artefact that would help them rule. With that came the stipulation that each ruler must bond to another person of their choosing to tap into the full strength of their magic.

King Cyrus set out immediately to find a suitable companion but was overwhelmed with choice. Every noble in Aphelion wanted to put their daughter up for the role. Unable to make a decision, he came up with the idea of the Trials, and thus, a tradition was born that's carried on to this day.

Cyrus apparently also had a bit of an idealistic streak, leading him to include one Tribute from The Umbra to compete. While the official line is that the Final Tribute is meant as a message of hope, the true reason has become much less altruistic than that.

Atlas stares at Cornelius with his eyes flashing as his jaw clenches, but he has to see his hands are tied.

"Very well," Atlas finally says, his voice decidedly less smooth than before. "I'll set the date."

"When? I'm not leaving here until you pick one and it's announced."

Atlas rolls his shoulders, his gaze flicking to me briefly. But there's nothing I can do to help him, even if I wanted to. He's made this bed of schemes and deceptions, and now he can fucking lie in it. Die in it for all I care. I'm tired of saving his ungrateful ass from all his bad decisions.

"Two weeks," Atlas says, the words clipped. "Two weeks from today."

"That is too long," Cornelius counters. "You're just delaying again."

"We need time to make arrangements. We wouldn't want a ceremony that is anything less than the height of extravagance for our precious jewel of a queen, would we?"

Cornelius narrows his eyes, clearly trying to decide if Atlas has just insulted his shrew of a daughter. I'm pretty sure Atlas did, but I place no blame on him for that one.

Nevertheless, General Cornelius Heulfryn is a better man than I am because he simply dips his chin, his hands again clasping behind his back. "Excellent, Your Majesty. Shall I alert the royal notetakers so they can let everyone know?"

"That would be so helpful," Atlas says, the words barely containing their condescension. If Cornelius notices it, he pretends otherwise before bowing succinctly at Atlas and then at me.

"Excellent. It will be a wonderful event."

He says nothing else, his gaze flicking in my direction before he storms out of the room, slamming the door behind him.

As soon as he's gone, Atlas strides over to the bar in the corner and pours himself a generous glass of whisky. He tosses half of it back and runs his hands through his hair, tugging on it in frustration.

"Atlas," I say, wishing I understood anything.

Atlas whirls on me, his eyes bright with fury. "Gabriel, whose side are you on?"

I blink. "Sorry?"

He strides over with the glass in his hand and points it at me. "Your loyalty feels questionable lately. I sense something isn't right with you."

I shake my head. "I am always loyal to you, Atlas. You know that."

"But are you?"

"What is this about?"

Atlas snorts and takes another drink as if the answer should be obvious.

"You have two weeks to find her, Gabriel. Send out every spy you can get your hands on."

"Atlas, I—"

"Two weeks," he repeats. "If you don't find her, then I might have to make some replacements within my warders."

I bite the inside of my mouth, quelling the breathtaking desire to punch him in the face. After everything I've done for him, this is how he repays me? Losing warder status isn't like losing a job—it's the end of your entire existence. I am nothing without my king. Literally.

"Understood," I reply, and then before I say something I can't undo, I spin on my heel and leave the room.

I'm so angry right now that I can't think straight. I've gone through hell for Atlas, and he speaks to me like I'm no more significant than a worm curling over the toe of his golden boot. I've spent my entire life protecting him, even when I wasn't obligated to do so, and he's never once shown an ounce of gratitude. I stalk through the palace as servants and courtiers leap out of my way. Gods, I need a drink and a good fuck. I need to punch something. Hard.

It's too late to turn back when I realize I've walked right into the heart of the main hall, where dozens of people mill about.

"You there!" comes a sharp voice that drags me out of my internal spiral. "Come here!"

Apricia points at some poor young High Fae female, who shuffles forward with her eyes on her feet.

"Look at me," Apricia demands, and the girl looks up. Her blonde hair is clipped around her pointed ears, and her slight frame is clothed in a simple tunic. *Fuck.* The future Sun Queen fired half her attendants for being "a little too pretty" and is now on the hunt for a new set of victims. Why anyone would volunteer for this role is beyond me.

Before I'm dragged into another mess that is none of my business, I step back, slowly and cautiously, wary of making any sudden movements, lest I be noticed.

But my effort is wasted.

Both Apricia and the woman look over as Apricia's face darkens with a frown. From the pinch of her features, I can only surmise that no one has told her about the bonding yet. I debate being the one to do so but decide to let her stew in her irritation for a bit longer. I have so little to entertain me. Someone else can be the bearer of good news.

The woman she's speaking with is staring at me openly, her eyes dragging over my wings and down my frame. I frown at her, noting something familiar about her, but I can't put my finger on it.

"You," Apricia says, snapping her fingers under the woman's nose. "Pay attention. The first rule is don't gawk at the warders. Well, that's not the first rule. The first one is to pay attention to me at all times, but it *is* one of them."

She turns her gaze back to Apricia and nods before the

future Sun Queen starts rattling off an endless list of frivo-
lous duties her new attendant will be responsible for. Zerra,
I'd rather die.

I turn my attention back to the woman one more time,
wondering why she seems familiar, but it doesn't really matter. After that conversation with Atlas, I need something to
take the edge off. Something warm and wet and eager to distract me from this throbbing pain behind my eye.

Maybe I'll go find a guard or a courtier who doesn't mind
some teeth.

CHAPTER ELEVEN

NADIR

S tanding against the wall with my arms crossed, I watch Mael and Lor spar in the sheltered backyard of the house. He's teaching her how to use that dagger under her pillow, and she's a quick study.

It's obvious she's used to fighting, though I can tell from the lack of finesse and her brute force that it was with her fists and not a weapon. My jaw clenches at the thought. I know she spent her years in Nostraza defending herself against countless lowlifes. She told me. She hurled it in my face exactly the way I deserved. Sometimes I wonder if we'll ever be able to get past this rotten thing that sits between us like a decaying organ left to fester in the sun.

She had some training with Gabriel during the Trials, but

that was with a sword, and I'm assuming he didn't have much opportunity to finesse her skills. I wonder how hard he tried or if it was just another obligation he rushed through.

"Remember, a dagger is small, so you have to get close," Mael says. "It does no good to wave that thing around. I'm just going to walk up and snatch it from you."

"Try," she says with a challenge in her tone, and I can't help the smile that creeps to my face. Lor is fierce, but Mael is going to wipe the floor with her. There's a reason he rose through the ranks of the Aurora army as quickly as he did. He moves like shadows, and though he keeps his true power concealed, he has the ability to unleash hell when pushed to his limit.

That skill saved our lives in the prisoner camp where we first met, suffering side by side for months under a battalion led by Atlas, who did everything he could to humiliate and punish me. Aphelion captured us during a raid behind their lines, leashing me and anyone else they suspected of having magic with long, thin chains of arcturite. Mael stayed under the radar because they had no idea what he could do. I left Atlas alive that day, though I didn't have to, and he's always hated that he owes me anything.

Mael grins and then goes on the offensive as they duck and weave while Lor slices her blade. He's far too well trained to fall for any of her feints or tricks, and before long, he sweeps a leg behind her knees, sending her onto the pavers, where she lands on her back with an "oof."

"Fuck," she wheezes, and I tense, resisting every urge in my body to help her. I hate seeing her hurt in any way. Mael stands over her with his arms folded, wearing his signature irreverent smile, and she glares up at him with that ferocious expression that always makes my dick stir. I don't like it when she looks at anyone else that way, but then she might never look at anyone again.

When she asked me for friendship in the clearing, it nearly broke my fucking heart. Of course I want to be her friend, but I want so much more. I'm doing my best to understand. She needs time to come to terms with everything she's lived through.

Mael holds out his hand and pulls her up before they resume training.

"You just going to stand there?" Mael taunts me. "Afraid your girlfriend will realize I'm the better fighter?"

"I'm *not* his girlfriend," Lor growls, and those words explode inside my chest, making me wince. I push it away. Much like I've been doing with all my feelings lately. I don't know why it's bothering me so much. I'm used to this. Pretending I don't feel anything is how I've survived. But I do. Fuck, how I feel everything.

Mael rolls his eyes. "Sure you aren't."

Lor responds with a low snarl as they begin circling one another. I have a feeling Mael is about to pay for that comment.

The door to the courtyard bangs open, and to my surprise, Gabriel strides out. He stops and looks at the three of us as Mael and Lor pause in their fighting stances.

"What is it?" I ask, instantly on alert. "Does he know?"

Gabriel's anger is evident by the deep groove between his eyes and the lines cording his neck. His hair is wild, and his cheeks are pink. His shoulders are so tight I'm surprised they haven't snapped right off. "No," he grinds out. "He doesn't know yet."

My posture relaxes at that. "Then what is it?"

"You have two weeks. That's all the time I can give you."

"Why?" Lor asks. "What happened?"

"He set the date for the bonding with Apricia, but only because he was forced into it. He's ordered me to find you before then or else . . ."

He trails off, and he doesn't have to finish that sentence for all of us to understand what he's saying. It's Lor or him, and he's not choosing her.

Lor nods.

"Of course. Two weeks."

Her gaze flicks to me with alarm, and I try to maintain an outward show of calm for her sake, even if I'm roiling inside.

"Do you have a plan?" Gabriel asks. "Tell me you're working on something."

I nod. We don't have a very good one yet, but we'll come up with something.

"Good," Gabriel says.

"Thank you," Lor says. "For all of this."

Gabriel tips his chin towards her. "I'm going to go get drunk. And a blow job."

With that declaration, he spins on his heel without another word and leaves, slamming the door behind him.

"What was with him?" Mael asks.

I stare at the door and shake my head. "I don't know, but when I talked to him the other day, I sensed something was happening with Atlas."

"What?" Mael asks. "Trouble in paradise?"

As much as we joke about Atlas and his circle of winged babysitters, I've never gotten the sense that Gabriel is as loyal to Atlas as he appears.

I'll never forget Tyr's funeral. Gabriel had been a mess, barely holding himself together. He disappeared halfway through the ceremony, and no one else seemed to have noticed. When he hadn't resurfaced hours later, I went searching for him. Something about the look on his face told me he needed someone, even if it was me.

When I found him, he was sitting on one of the clifftops overlooking the city, surrounded by empty bottles of the strongest orc-brewed moonshine to be found between Aphelion and The Aurora. He stood at the very edge, swaying dangerously, too drunk to maintain his balance for long. Even with his wings, I strongly suspect that if I hadn't shown up, he would have fallen. Or maybe not fallen but jumped.

"It might seem that way," I say, answering Mael's question.

"So, what's the plan?" he asks as we all file back into the house and gather around the table.

The back door opens again, and Willow slips inside. Amya did a good job with her hair, turning her black tresses into dark blonde. It doesn't entirely disguise her, but combined with the short haircut, she looks a lot less like Lor.

We all overheard their argument last night about the things that transpired in Nostraza, and I can tell it's bothering Lor, but she's trying to put on a brave face. The accusations they flung at one another were enough to shame me yet again for allowing any of that to happen. No wonder Lor can't find it in herself to trust me.

"Willow," Lor says, her voice clipped. "How did it go?"

"I got the job," Willow replies triumphantly with a thumbs-up. "I start tomorrow."

I blow out a breath of relief. At least something's going right. Lor and Tristan may not want Willow to take on this risk, but after the way she stood up for herself, I'm positive she can handle it.

I smile at the determined look on Willow's face. She might be softer and quieter than Lor, but she's got a similar strength of spirit. It's no wonder Amya finds herself drawn to her. My sister has always been the sort to rescue every baby bird that's been shoved from its mother's nest.

"How was Apricia?" Lor asks, wrinkling her nose.

"Just as awful as you said."

Lor gives Willow a tight smile.

"But I can handle it. It won't be long, right?"

There's a pointedness in Willow's words, and Lor nods.

"Of course you can."

"I saw Gabriel," Willow adds. "He looked really pissed off."

"He didn't recognize you, did he?" Lor asks.

Willow shakes her head. "No, he barely looked at me. Apricia was too busy yelling at everyone."

"Did you see Halo or Marici?" Lor asks. Since we arrived, she's been wondering about seeing her friends in the Sun Palace.

"I didn't," Willow says, "but once I'm working there, I'm sure I will."

"I wish you could tell them I'm thinking about them."

Willow gives her sister a sad smile. "I'm sure they know."

"Okay, so Willow will get inside and find out more about the palace," Lor says, turning to face the rest of us. "What else can we do?"

"We should use the ceremony as a distraction," I say, just as Hylene enters the kitchen.

"Won't the bonding happen in the throne room?" Lor asks.

"Yes, but there will be days of pomp and pageantry. Plus, the castle will be full of people from the other realms for at least a week beforehand. This is an occasion everyone will be expected to attend. We might be able to blend in better amongst the crowd."

"But you're not getting an invitation unless Atlas had a change of heart about your banishment," Mael points out. "Do you think he'd still invite your father? Or Amya?"

"I doubt it," I say, my gaze sliding to Hylene. "You up for a task?"

She's leaning against the counter and smiles with her fist propped under her chin. "Always."

"You think you can get yourself invited? We'll need someone who has permission to be inside and who'll be privy to all the most exclusive parties. Then gather whatever intel you can."

Her smile stretches. "I'd be terrible at my job if I couldn't."

"What exactly is your job?" Mael asks and she glares at him. One of these days, she's going to rip off his balls, chop them into pieces, and feed them to a bear with a smile on her face. And he'll deserve it.

"It's to mingle with those of society who wouldn't touch a brute like you with a hundred-foot pole."

Lor laughs at that as Mael grins.

"Anyway," Hylene says, checking her bright red nails. "I'm sure there's some lonely minor noble looking for a piece of arm candy he can bring as his date. It'll be like shooting fish in a barrel."

"How will you get the attention of an Aphelion noble?" Lor asks, and Hylene winks.

"I have my ways."

"Okay, can we go to Heart then?" Lor asks, directing the question at me. "We can't do much else while we wait for these pieces to come together, right? I still think it's important we understand who was sharing our secrets before we speak to the Mirror."

I rub the arch of my eyebrow, feeling an ache build. I was hoping she'd let this go, but I understand why she can't.

"I'm just waiting for word from Etienne that my father's soldiers have left entirely." I pause. "He knows someone who was close to your grandmother and wants to speak with you."

I debated sharing this with her ever since receiving the message yesterday, but I know keeping it from her wouldn't be right. Also, it would do nothing to earn the trust I'm trying so desperately to win.

She sits up, now on alert.

"Who?"

"I'm not sure," I say. "He didn't want to put her name in writing, just in case."

"Okay, so when can he confirm it's safe?"

If Lor wasn't going to let this go before, then she certainly isn't now.

"Within the next day or two, I hope," I say. "We can't risk them getting wind of our presence."

Lor chews on her bottom lip, and I wish I could go over and take her in my arms and promise her that everything is going to be okay. I wish I knew *how* to make everything okay.

"What's wrong?" Willow asks her.

"Does it matter to you?" Lor asks, and Willow's expression collapses. Obviously, they haven't worked through their disagreement yet.

Lor scrubs her hands down her face.

"Nothing is wrong," she adds, but it's obvious that's a lie. "Sorry. I think I'm going to take a walk. I'll get us some of those meat pies we all like for dinner."

Then without another word, she grabs the hat and loose jacket she uses to conceal herself, heads out the back door, and leaves the rest of us staring after her.

Chapter Twelve

LOR

Without a backward glance, I storm out of the house, needing air and space to breathe. I shouldn't have snapped at Willow like that, but our argument weighs on my mind, and I'm not ready to forgive her yet. I'm angry she's blaming me for her feelings, as though everything I did wasn't for her. But that isn't really fair. I know that isn't what she meant, but I'm struggling to move past it.

We've always stuck together. Always been a unit. We never fight and have always supported each other because we were the only lifeline each of us had.

Now we've had our freedom for only a few weeks, and are we already drifting apart?

In addition to my drama with Willow, I also can't stop thinking about my dream from the other night.

The idea that someone is out there sharing my family's secrets for some nefarious reason sticks to the back of my throat. Who is it, and why do they hate us so much? Do they realize what they did to a group of children? Do they care? Or do they think we deserve everything?

The streets are busy at this time of day, and I pay little attention to the direction I'm walking. While I'd claimed I intended to go to Sonya's for the pies everyone loves, I first need to work off some of this building energy. I'll double back and pick some up on my return.

I'll also go and talk to Willow. She's been my best friend my entire life, and there's nothing we can't work through.

For now, I allow myself to get lost in the bustle and activity of Aphelion at the height of the afternoon. I've entered the Sixteenth District, home to entertainments of a carnal nature, evidenced by the dozens of bars, restaurants, and brothels all open for business and enjoying plenty of customers in the middle of the afternoon.

"Hey, gorgeous!" A male voice slices through my preoccupations, bringing me to a stop. He sits with a group of male High Fae, all nursing a round of drinks. The one who just cat-called me taps his thigh and winks. "Want some company?"

His friends start laughing, and I think of the dagger stashed in my boot. I don't know why I didn't start carrying one sooner. While Mael explained concealing a weapon without a proper grasp on how to use it is more dangerous than not having one at all, I'm not sure I believe that. I don't need any skill to stick a man in his gut or, better yet, slice off his dick. I curl my lip, my eyes narrowing as I stare back, unblinking, wondering where this idiot gets off thinking he has any right to speak to me this way.

Why does it always come back to this? Even when I'm dressed this way?

The conversation with Hylene last night loosened something tight living inside my chest. Knowing her past wasn't all that different from mine made me feel less alone. Though she spoke matter-of-factly about it, I recognized that same haunted look I know so well.

But she's also forged those experiences into a spine made of steel armor that I admire.

My scars will never be completely erased, but I hope they won't define the parameters of my present or my relationships forever. Willow claimed *she's* the reason I'm always so angry, but that couldn't be further from the truth.

The leering man is still laughing, but whatever he sees in my face causes his grin to slip. I don't move, glaring at him with the white-hot fury of my simmering rage, willing him to feel the shame of his behavior. Do I think he'll learn a lesson? I'm not holding my breath, but at least for today, maybe it's one less woman harassed by this prick.

Finally, he drops his gaze, muttering something to himself and then to his friends, who all cast wary, disgruntled glances in my direction, as though I'm the one to blame for ruining their fun. That's right. Be afraid. Or ashamed. Or something that makes you realize that every woman who passes you doesn't owe you her time.

When they've been sufficiently cowed to my liking, I turn away and scan the plaza. My nerves are still on edge. I wish I could tell what parts of that dream were real and what parts were simply conjured from the muddled haze of my memories. Did my subconscious fill in parts that didn't happen? Did she really claim to know who and what I was, or is my mind stretching over the blanks, trying to close the gaps?

There's a nicer-looking restaurant across the way where tables of women enjoy what look like tea cakes, along with sparkling wine. That seems a little more friendly.

As I make my way closer, I catch a snippet of conversation.

"A landslide in Tor," one female High Fae says. "Crushed half the city at the base of the castle."

"That's awful," says the second. "My Arthur says there are similar happenings in Alluvion. A hurricane wiped out half of the western coastline last week. Dead fish everywhere. Can you imagine?"

They both shake their heads as I frown. A second later, they catch me eavesdropping on their conversation.

"Sorry," I say, about to retreat in the direction I came, when a woman emerges from the building, and I nearly miss a step.

It's her.

It's been so many years, and my memories are hazy, but I'm *sure* it's the woman from my dream. I blink, reminding myself that can't be true.

I killed her.

I rendered her into a husk of charred skin and bones in the forest. I shake my head, willing the scene to change. It's just a coincidence. That woman is dead, and this one just bears a similar resemblance.

She says something to another group of High Fae females dining on the patio, and they air kiss each other's cheeks before she turns to leave.

She walks with a slight limp, though her posture is straight as her cane thunks against the stone pavers. She's the height of elegance in a long gown that seems a little fancy for this early in the day, but somehow she manages to pull it off. Her silver hair is swept away from her face and anchored at the crown, her long curls spilling down. It's impossible to gauge her age, even by Fae standards.

She stops and looks around the square, her lips pursing when her eyes fall on the group of Fae who harassed me, still loitering outside. Then she turns and continues her journey. Before I give too much thought to what I'm doing, I start to follow. This can't be the same Fae, and my imagination is working overtime, but I need to be sure.

I keep enough distance between us so she doesn't sense me on her trail, and we both weave through the crowds, dodging vendors and shoppers pressing through the throngs. She's clearly in no rush, stopping here and there to speak with this person or that or to survey a variety of wares as she passes. Everyone seems to know who she is, and she smiles at them all, moving in a regal way that suggests a life lived in relative comfort.

Finally, we approach the end of a street where a white stone building sits. It looks like a temple with its wide-angled roof and six round pillars gracing the facade. It reminds me of the ruin we passed in the forest, when Nadir told me about Zerra and her disciples.

Two stunning High Fae females stand at the top of the short set of stairs, wearing long white dresses that wrap around their bodies, very carefully displaying expanses of their luscious thighs, ample cleavage, and smooth stomachs. They smile and wave at passersby, who every so often stop and enter the building.

The woman I'm following heads up the stairs and into the building with a small bit of difficulty thanks to whatever is bothering her leg.

The gilded lettering inscribed on the front reads *Priestess of Payne*. I surmise this is some kind of religious-themed brothel, and from the look and regularity of the clientele, it's both very popular and catering to elites with a very specific type of kink.

I pause with one foot on the bottom step, wondering if I should follow the strange woman inside. This is ludicrous, and I can already hear Nadir and Tristan scolding me for not paying enough attention to my surroundings while stalking some rich High Fae through Aphelion.

Especially one who might have tried to steal me when I was a child.

But . . . I've never been one to let a bad idea get in the way of my actions.

"Come on in," one of the women beckons with a lilting voice, and I hesitate. But I need to see her up close. I'll never be able to relax if I don't. "There are many things to enjoy inside."

I nod and head up the stairs, hoping I won't regret this.

Inside isn't quite what I expected. I always pictured a

brothel to be dimly lit and draped in hues of red and black, but the religious-temple aesthetic continues inside with floors and walls of pale grey marble and windows cut into the ceiling, letting in thick beams of warm afternoon sunlight.

I think of the ruined temple we saw and wonder how Zerra feels about this place. Is the goddess a prude, or does she understand the power and influence of sex? Particularly when you're a woman who's been left with few other choices?

Another woman waits, this one even more scantily clad. Her priestess robe just barely covers her hips, the material sheer enough to hide almost nothing. She smiles with a set of perfect white teeth.

"The entrance fee is one hundred silvers," she says, and I vacillate again. I should let this go. I imagined it. That can't be the same woman. But I need to be sure.

I reach into the pouch at my hip and pull out the exorbitant sum. Thanks to Nadir and Amya, our mission is well funded. I don't really understand money other than as a concept. One unexpected side effect of living in Nostraza was never learning the idiosyncrasies of these mundane tasks everyone takes for granted.

While I initially felt weird about taking Nadir's money, he's assured me it's all part of his greater plan, and I'd be doing him a favor. Of course I don't really buy that, but it does make life easier when you don't have to worry about how to pay for anything.

"Did another woman come in here?" I ask, handing over the coins. "She had silver hair and was wearing a long blue dress?"

The female's eyebrows pinch together. "You mean Madame Payne?"

"Yes," I say, deciding that sounds right. The name outside had the unusual spelling of the word "pain," and I surmise this must be a clever play on a surname. Besides, she was clearly someone important. "Her."

"Yes, of course, she's here. She's probably in her office. I can send a messenger up if you tell me what your business is?"

Now I'm definitely unsure about this. What am I going to say?

I think I killed you fourteen years ago after you tried to kidnap me, but I just saw you in the street, and I want to be sure?

"Actually, it's okay. I'll just go in for now."

I'll get my bearings. Check things out and decide if there's anything to worry about. Maybe I'll return with Nadir, though the notion of him surrounded by these stunning, barely clothed Fae sits in my stomach like a rock.

Maybe Mael or Tristan then.

"Of course," she says. "Melianne will show you to a table."

She gestures to a High Fae with long red hair wearing another sheer white dress that hardly seems worth wearing at all. I nod as I follow her down a hall lined with intricate paintings of men and women engaged in various compromising positions. They're beautifully done, and it's hard not to admire the skill that went into creating them.

We emerge into a large, high-ceilinged room that looks like a conservatory with its tall windows, greenery, and colorful flowers perfuming the air. There's a sunken pool in the center where several nude men and women frolic in the water.

They're accompanied by what I assume are other patrons, most simply watching with drinks perched in their hands.

Plush benches tucked away in corners cradle couples, trios, and various groups who talk softly with gentle touches and suggestive looks.

Melianne leads me down a few steps to a velvet settee, gesturing for me to sit. Almost immediately, another woman approaches.

"Can I get you a drink?" she asks in a sweet voice that sounds like crystal bells. "Perhaps a glass of sparkling wine?"

"Sure," I say, "thank you."

She pulls out a card and lays it on the table. I can see it's a list of offerings. Spankings and whippings. Chains and canes and ropes. Degradation and praise, and some things I'm not even sure how to imagine. My thoughts can't help but wander to Nadir and the idea of exploring some of these activities with him. I'm still a little miffed I didn't get to see what he claimed he could do with his magic. But I really shouldn't be entertaining these thoughts.

The woman returns with my drink and sets it on the table with a smile before she walks away with her hips swaying. My gaze wanders around the room, and I try not to stare, but it's hard to ignore what's happening around me.

The longer I sit, the more foolish I feel. What was I thinking? I should go. This was stupid.

But that's when I spot her.

She's talking with someone across the room, and I'm instantly on my feet, making my way closer, her back facing me. I don't have a plan, but I stop just as she finishes her conversation and turns around. She startles when she sees me, a hand going to her chest.

"Oh! You surprised me," she says before her brow pinches together. "Can I help you?"

I blink because I was wrong. Now that she's standing in front of me, I can see that while she bears a striking resemblance to that woman from all those years ago, this woman is different. Her nose is longer, and her eyes are a different color. Gods, I'm so stupid.

"No," I say, shaking my head as her gaze travels up and down. "I'm sorry. I just thought..." I trail off. "Sorry to have bothered you."

Before she can stop me, I spin on my heel and leave.

CHAPTER THIRTEEN

KING HAWTHORNE

THE WOODLANDS: THE FIRST AGE OF OURANOS

The creak of branches dragged King Hawthorne's eyes upward to the snarled tangle that had grown so thick it nearly blotted out the light. Decay crunched under his heavy boots as he stalked through the forest with his sword angled over a broad shoulder. His nostrils flared in agitation. The taint on the wind was unmistakable and foretold of wicked things arriving on the breeze.

It had been another day and another endless list of reports about the forest behaving erratically. At first, it had been benign events, nothing to be overly alarmed about. A tree falling unexpectedly. The fruit from another suddenly dropping well ahead of the harvest. It was easy to dismiss them as mere anomalies of forest life. These trees weren't inanimate. They'd always had a sentience. They'd always had eyes. One had to expect they'd act out from time to time.

But things had shifted quickly, morphing from harmless to deadly. Missing children dragged from their beds at night by thorny vines. Holes unexpectedly opening in the middle of a worn path used safely a thousand times before, swallowing entire families up.

"Your Majesty," came a voice from behind, and he turned to find one of his soldiers approaching. "I found another one."

Suspended in the soldier's arms was a body. Hawthorne thought it might have been female, but it was hard to tell anymore. She'd been "infected," for lack of any better term to describe what was plaguing the forest. Her body had twisted like the trunk of an ancient tree, leaves and branches sprouting from her eyes and mouth and nose. The effect was grotesque, and he resisted the overwhelming urge to look away. These were his people, and they were dying at an alarming rate.

He had to be the one to look. Had to be the one to bear final witness to the life they'd given to this . . . monstrosity.

"Put her with the others," he said. "We'll bury them all, as is their due."

The soldier nodded and then walked away, disappearing into the trees.

The king waited, standing alone in the darkened forest. He had to figure out what was causing this. Rumors swarmed of similar events happening across the continent, though he wondered if any were as alarming as what transpired in The Woodlands.

With a grim press of his lips, he continued walking, heading to the Fort. A makeshift infirmary erected at its base treated those who could still be saved. His healers were having some success medicating the strange rot infecting the citizens of his kingdom, but no one wanted to admit the last part out loud. Any progress was only temporary; after a brief respite, the symptoms always returned.

He rubbed a hand against the back of his neck, feeling the weight of his people's lives press on his shoulders. Where could he go for help? There was no one to turn to and no one to ask. Perhaps he'd have to travel across the Lourwin Sea for aid. But the journey was long, and he feared what might happen in his absence.

The wind picked up, lifting his acorn-brown hair from his shoulders as his senses twitched with uneasiness. Lowering the sword still balanced over his shoulder, he spun around, but the pathway stood empty. He held still for a moment, listening for any foreign sound, but the forest was silent. Much too silent.

He shook his head, annoyed he was letting his nerves get the best of him before he turned and continued his journey.

When another rustle in the bushes drew his attention, it was already too late. Vines moving in a blur circled his limbs, squeezing his arms and legs and cinching his torso so tightly he couldn't breathe.

He tried to cry out, but another tendril constricted his throat, choking off his airway before he was dragged into the forest. The last thing he saw before everything went black was a canopy of dark green leaves closing over him like fingers.

Chapter Fourteen

LOR

Present Day

Two days later, we've finally received word that it's safe to return to Heart. I can't stop wondering about who knew my grandmother and whom I'm going to meet. I wait in the front foyer with Nadir, Mael, and Tristan, our bags packed with provisions.

One half of me is terrified about what we'll find in the settlements, while another yearns to see more of my home. My last visit to Heart was a brief taste of nothing—a dish uncovered, the scent curling on my tongue before it was snatched away with a slap.

Nadir's reluctance regarding this entire endeavor is worn

into the permanent furrow of his brow. But he's conceded my magic might be more accessible nearer to its source, and I've promised to practice once we arrive.

"Is everything okay with your sister?" he asks as we gather up the last of our supplies. Willow isn't here to see us off, but we sat down and talked things out last night.

I nod. "We're okay. We've just never argued like that before."

In the end, we both fell over each other trying to apologize. I told her I'd stop trying to shield her from every possible danger, and she had never felt worse for the things she said.

Because of her job at the palace, she had to remain behind, but I think she welcomed it. She isn't ready to see Heart yet. It's too painful and raw. Part of me understands.

"She's going to have to find a way to come to terms with it because nothing can change the past."

Nadir nods. "You had no good or easy choices in there."

"No, we didn't. And I will never regret anything I did to protect her."

"I know you don't," he says softly. "I just wish you hadn't ever had to make those decisions at all."

I've blamed him for so much of this. I've thrown my past in his face, and he's stared at it with wide, unflinching eyes. I admire him for it. He was wrong, and he knows it, and it takes a certain kind of man to admit his faults without passing the blame.

But if we're ever to be anything more than the friendship I asked for, *I* have to find a way to come to terms with this too.

"I know exactly what it's like to have a sister who thinks she knows what's best for you," he says with a wry smile.

"Are you referring to me or to Willow?" I ask, and he laughs. "I'm not answering that."

I snort and then sling my pack onto my shoulder.

Hylene is off, ingratiating herself with the local nobles, and Willow will be safe with Amya keeping an eye on her. Besides, we'll be gone for only a few days.

"Ready?" Nadir asks me, and I nod. "Then let's go."

Once we clear the outskirts of Aphelion, Nadir will fly me to Heart while Mael and Tristan follow on horseback, planning to arrive later this evening. Nadir magicked their horses to speed them through a journey that normally takes days.

Once we're out of the city, he scoops me into his arms, and I can't help how my entire body melts into his touch. Like this is where I'm meant to be, and this is the home where I will always return.

He looks down at me, and our gazes spark with a bright moment that leaves a hundred things left unsaid.

He's trying to give me some space, and I have to respect him for trying so hard. I no longer believe that he's trying to trick me or use me, at least not in the way I first thought, but I also refuse to get wrapped up in his territorial Fae bullshit.

I will not belong to him. I will never belong to anyone ever again.

We swoop over the treetops, his beautiful wings of colorful light beating against the wind, flying over the golden fields of Aphelion and the forests surrounding the place that should have been my home.

Eventually, we drop gently on the outskirts of Heart as Nadir sets me on my feet. From here, we'll walk to the settlements.

Our plan is to head for the largest, simply known as the "first," partly to blend in and, more importantly, because this is where we'll find the person who once knew my grandmother.

It breaks a part of me knowing the settlements were never fully named. They're just numbers filled with people waiting on the edge of what? It's hard not to worry about what they're expecting and how I might let them all down spectacularly.

"How's your mother?" I ask Nadir, partly to distract myself but also because I know he doesn't like to be away from her for long. I feel terrible for taking him from her on this possibly futile quest. I know he has a way of passing messages with her caregivers so he can keep tabs on her welfare.

"She's fine. The same," he says, the lines around his eyes tight. "She's taken care of and protected. My ice hounds are keeping her company."

"I'm sorry this is keeping you away from her."

He pins me with a fierce look. "Nothing would keep me away from this, Heart Queen. My mother doesn't even know I'm there."

He says the last part with such raw emotion that I reach out, grabbing his hand. He doesn't hesitate to thread his fingers through mine, a warm trickle leaking into my heart that feels far too good. "That's not true. She knows, and she appreciates it."

He lets out a huff that tells me he wishes that were true, but he's not holding his breath. I wish there were something I could do to ease her suffering. And his.

We continue walking in silence until the buildings of the first settlement come into view. They're only a few stories high, and even from here, their state of disrepair is obvious. The closer we get, the worse it looks. Everything is so fragile, like a strong gust of wind could blow it all away.

We join a line of people traveling from other settlements and other realms moving into the city. I've learned that Heart was once the center of healing and medicine in Ouranos, thanks to the magic that allowed the Fae to manipulate the body from within. I flex my hand, remembering when I was younger and could heal small cuts and wounds. It's another reason I need my magic back so desperately. What I wouldn't give to be able to help others in times of need.

Even if the actual magic of Heart is gone, a legacy of healing still subsists. People come from far and wide to purchase the potions and remedies made by what were once some of Heart's most gifted practitioners. I rub my chest as my magic bounces around inside me, hoping that what Nadir said about accessing it within the borders of Heart is true.

A few dilapidated inns line the main street, and we find one that looks marginally less run-down than the others. Of course there are only two rooms left for tonight, so we take one, leaving the other for Tristan and Mael.

We could wander around seeking another inn, but we're on a deadline and have things to accomplish. The room is comfortable enough, though the bed is much smaller than I would like. We both look at it and then at each other, the moment stretching into awkwardness. Maybe I can bunk with Tristan instead.

We should discuss that night in Heart, but I don't know what I'd say.

That I think about it constantly? That I regret what I said and did? But also that I know it was the right decision to make?

That despite what my mouth and the rational side of my brain say, I want to throw all my reservations away and just sink into this? Sink into him? While it's impossible to ignore my physical attraction, what I feel has become about so much more. I've spent the last twelve years pushing everyone away, save Willow and Tristan, and for the first time, I'm confronted with another person I want to add to the collection of jewels I store in my heart.

But...

There are just so many "buts."

I clear my throat and then drop my bag in a corner. We'll deal with the issue of the bed later. My fallback strategy when it comes to dealing with Nadir has become avoidance and a good dose of burying my head in the sand. It isn't a mature response, but I never claimed to be reasonable about anything.

"So, what now?"

"Let's go find Etienne," Nadir says, holding open the door. We head through the inn, passing through the common room, where about a dozen people dine on platters of food and drinks. There appears to be no distinction between humans, low fae, and High Fae, everyone mingling without artificial barriers.

When we step outside, I ask Nadir, "Do you know what it was like when Heart existed? How did my ancestors treat the low fae?"

"Not as poorly as Atlas or my father, if that's what you're asking," he says. "But they were mostly confined to positions of service, many of them inside the castle as far as I know."

I consider that, wondering again what kind of person my grandmother was. Was she a good Fae? Would she have been a kind and fair ruler? Was everything that happened a mistake or the result of greed? They say she craved power, but at what cost?

"And now? Here?" I ask as we continue walking.

"Necessity and time have done their work of eroding those class distinctions," Nadir says. "Ironically, these settlements are actually the most progressive on the continent in their own way."

"Can I give them their freedoms? When I'm . . . you know." I wave in the direction of the Heart Castle I know is in the distance, tempering my words lest anyone overhear.

Nadir's mouth lifts at the corner. "You can do whatever you want."

"Would I receive opposition from the other rulers?"

"Yes. You would. No one likes disrupting the status quo. But you'd have allies in Alluvion and The Woodlands."

"Would I?"

"Yes," he says, and I like the sound of that.

"I would fight the others about it."

"I know you would."

He gives me a meaningful look, and I press my lips together and nod. Good. Yes. That's what I want. I won't treat the low fae as slaves nor confine them to a corner of the city where I never have to interact with them. They'll be free to live their lives and follow their destinies just like everyone else. If it pisses anyone off, then so be it. We'll open our doors and welcome everyone, whatever it takes.

Nadir is watching me with a guarded expression.

"What?" I ask.

"Just wondering what you're thinking about," he says.

I give him a rueful smile that I'm sure he can't interpret. For once, I wasn't thinking about him, but I can't tell him that.

"Just picturing what it could all be like."

I can tell from the look on his face that he understands what I mean. His goals lie in a similar direction. I like that we have that in common.

We arrive at a rickety and nondescript building that squats on the street. Nadir opens the door and gestures me inside and up a flight of stairs. We proceed down a narrow hall, and he knocks on a door. There's a scuffle on the other side before it swings open.

A very tall High Fae male answers and peers at us wordlessly. He's dressed all in black, with straight dark hair that reaches his chin. His most notable feature is the patch covering his left eye.

After a second, he breaks into what feels like a reluctant half smile and embraces Nadir.

"Good to see you," he says warmly, and I assume this *must* be Etienne. A moment later, his gaze falls on me, his serious expression falling back in place.

"And this must be ..." He stops talking, peers out of the doorway, and ushers us inside.

Once the door is closed, he turns to us and studies me again, like he's trying to decide if I'm really here.

"Allow me to introduce you to Lor," Nadir says.

Etienne blinks with his good eye, and I note the edges

of a scar around the patch, immediately feeling an affinity towards him thanks to the similar scar on my own face. He's lean and muscled and absolutely fearsome, like an animal on the very edge of breaking loose.

"Hi," I say, giving him a little wave and feeling increasingly self-conscious about how he's staring at me. "Is everything okay?"

Then he does the last thing in the world I expect. He takes two steps forward until he's right before me and then drops to his knee. "Your Majesty," he says, his voice gruff and full of passion. "I am at your service."

I'm not sure how to react. I stare down at him and then at Nadir, who's watching both of us with wry amusement.

"Um, thank you?" I say, patting him awkwardly on the shoulder. "That's very . . . nice?"

Etienne looks up with reverence on his face. What is going on?

"Etienne is a citizen of Heart, Lor," Nadir finally explains. "He's been waiting for you for a long time."

Those words kick me in the stomach as I glance at Nadir and then back at Etienne.

"You didn't tell me that."

Nadir shrugs. "I wanted it to be a surprise." He winks, and I should be annoyed, but Etienne still sits on one knee, looking at me like I'm Zerra herself.

"He's waiting for you to tell him to get up," Nadir stage-whispers.

"What?" I flap my hands in his direction. "Oh my gods. Get up. Please get up."

Etienne drops his head again and then stands before bowing to me. "It has been an honor to serve you since we learned of your existence. When Nadir told me he'd found you, I knew our miracle had finally come."

I open my mouth, still not sure how to react. Nadir explained that those living here believed their queen would return, but being confronted by it twists my nerves into tangled knots. It's one thing to hear about it and think about it as a concept, but these are real-life people with thoughts and feelings who lost everything because of what my grandmother did. And I suspect they want me to fix all of it.

"Were you there?" I ask, whispering the words as though they might lash out and slice me open. "Did you know her?"

Why Nadir didn't tell me about Etienne's origins is a discussion we'll be having later.

He shakes his head. "I was there. I fought The Aurora's soldiers that night as they invaded the city. I saw and felt the blast from a distance and was tossed off my feet by the force. I think I must've flown at least a hundred feet." He gestures to his face. "That's how I got this."

Horror crumples in my chest at the knowledge my grandmother was responsible for his injury.

"I'm so sorry," I whisper, tears stinging my eyes, but he shakes his head.

"What's done is done. What matters is that you've returned, my queen."

I nod slowly, wishing that were true. *How* will I fix all of this? When my mother described the selective bits of our history, I couldn't have comprehended how vast the scope of all this was. She made it sound like we'd just show up one day and take over a castle and live happily ever after, but I realize now how naive that was.

Did she not understand? Maybe she hadn't wanted to scare us with the truth.

"Did you have magic that you lost?" I ask, but he shakes his head.

"I am not connected to the Imperial family in any way. My magic is not that of Heart, and it returned with the rest."

I recall when Nadir explained the different types of Fae power—common versus Imperial magic—and how the first could belong to anyone but the latter belonged to the land the Artefact was tied to. At least my family didn't take that from him.

"And no, I did not know the queen or her Primary. I was merely a common soldier in Heart's army," Etienne adds.

"Oh," I say.

"But don't worry," Etienne says quickly, as if sensing my disappointment. "As I explained in my last message, I know just the person for you to talk to. She can't wait to speak with you."

CHAPTER FIFTEEN

We follow Etienne out of his tiny flat and back into the streets of Heart. Evening has started to fall, the sky washing in pinks and reds. I look towards where I know the Heart Castle sits in the distance, empty and devoid of life, except for those roses growing all over its surface.

Nadir said he was sure they were evidence of my presence, and I hope that means this is the path I'm meant to be following. That as terrifying as it seems to try to make this right, perhaps I'll be able to find my way.

"Put up your hood," Nadir says as he does the same, darkening his face into obscurity.

Would anyone recognize me? Thankfully my physical traits—brown skin and dark hair and eyes—are common amongst the people of Heart, and all three of us blend in easily enough.

Nadir grips my hand as Etienne leads us through the bustling crowd. While things are rough on the surface, it's obvious people have built a life for themselves where friends and families meet over drinks, food, and conversation. Being amongst these strangers waiting for something that's potentially within my control causes my throat to knot with emotion.

Finally, we stop outside a shop where a pair of large windows face the street. Inside, we find an array of mismatched tables and chairs, along with the distinct aroma of brewing tea. A counter sits at the back, lined with rows and rows of silver canisters, all labeled with different flavors, from strawberry pear to something called ruby mint. I want to sample it all, but that's not what we're here for.

Etienne continues his determined stride as we pass through the shop to a door at the back that leads us into a narrow corridor. We continue up a flight of stairs, emerging into what looks like a workshop. Large tables are surrounded by stools where people scribble furiously on paper. Rows of weapons line one far wall, and against another is a shelf so stuffed with books that haphazard piles have begun to form at its base like teetering mountains.

At first, only one or two of the dozen or so Fae notice our entrance. A small gasp draws the attention of a few more before, suddenly, everyone in the room is staring at us. I exchange a look with Nadir, but he's got that usual half smirk on his face, clearly unfazed by all of this.

To my horror, everyone in the room slides off their stools and starts dropping to their knees one by one, their hands over their hearts and their heads bowing. There are murmurs of "Majesty" and "Queen," and I honestly want to melt into the floor. How am I supposed to handle this? What am I going to do if this becomes real?

Nadir squeezes my hand.

"It's okay," he says softly. "Consider this a warm-up."

"Are you used to this?" I ask, keeping my voice low.

"I grew up this way." I nod and then face the room.

"Hi," I say before remembering what Nadir said earlier, quickly adding, "Stand up. Please."

Everyone rises from their positions, staring at me like I'm a ghost who's risen from the ashes.

"You can all resume what you were doing," Etienne says, rescuing me from this increasing awkwardness. "Lor is here to see Rhiannon."

I shoot a look to Nadir. Who is Rhiannon?

Slowly, everyone turns away, pretending to resume their earlier tasks, but I can feel their surreptitious glances sneaking my way. I suppose I do need to get used to this. This isn't about *me*. This is about what I represent. The past and a future they've all been cradling in their expectant palms.

Etienne gives me a serious look and then gestures for me to follow. We wind past the tables and chairs to emerge in a sitting area at the far end. A large fireplace dominates the wall, with two armchairs angled towards it. In one sits a High Fae female with dark hair pulled up to the crown of her head.

She's wearing a long red gown, and though she appears as ageless as all High Fae, her presence speaks to something wise and ancient.

She's knitting, needles flying as she wraps the working strand around her finger, a basket of yarn lying at her feet. When we approach, she looks up, her dark eyes shifting as she takes me in. A rush of breath vacates her lungs in a sharp exhale. Everyone is silent as she puts her knitting aside and slowly stands.

"Is this her?" she asks, looking at Etienne and then back to me.

"This is Lor," he says, and Rhiannon closes her eyes slowly, her hand pressing to her chest as a stray tear slips down her cheek.

"I still can't believe it."

Then she surprises me by stretching her arms and enveloping me in a hug. It takes a moment to notice that she's shaking. As she looks up at me, I witness a thousand different emotions reflecting across her expression.

"You look just like her," she says softly, a delicate finger sweeping over my cheek and my eyebrow as if she's cataloging the pieces of my face to her memory.

"Who are you?" I ask, dying to know. This woman *knew* my grandmother, and from the look on her face, it was with love and fondness.

"I'm sorry. How rude," she says, stepping back and wiping her eyes. "Please have a seat." She gestures to the chair across from her. "Would you be a dear and get us something to drink?" she asks Etienne. He bends at the waist and scurries off. I raise an eyebrow, surprised this grizzled warrior is hopping to her request with such enthusiasm.

Nadir pulls up a chair beside me as Rhiannon briefly studies us both. She doesn't ask who Nadir is or why he's here, which must mean she knows something about what we've been up to.

"I knew your grandmother," she says. "We were cousins, and it took me a very long time to come to terms with her loss."

"Cousins? So we're related?"

She smiles softly. "Cousins many times removed, so distantly. But yes."

"How well did you know her?"

"Oh, very." She smiles. "I know all the things the history books either got wrong or completely missed."

"Will you tell me about her?" I ask, hardly daring to believe it. I'm having difficulty coming to terms with the fact I'm meeting family outside of my parents and siblings for the first time in my life.

"I'll tell you everything you want," she says. "But I would love to hear about your life, too. Where you've been and everything that's happened to bring you here today."

I nod slowly, checking with Nadir for confirmation. I don't know these people, and I'm trusting that he's looking out for my best interests. "It's okay. Everyone here is on your side. Etienne has been working with them for years."

I turn back to Rhiannon and allow myself to relax. It's hard to explain, but a peace settles over me that feels foreign but also as familiar as a warm blanket. Maybe it's being near

Heart. Maybe this is fate's way of reminding me that this is where I'm supposed to be.

"Okay," I say, and then I tell her almost everything as she listens patiently, asking me questions here and there, offering her sympathy and surprise. While we're talking, Etienne returns with a pot of tea and four mugs and pulls up another chair to join us. When I'm done speaking, Rhiannon lets out a charged breath.

"It seems history has repeated itself in many strange ways," she remarks, sipping on her glass.

"What do you mean by that?"

"They scrubbed this from the history books, but your grandmother was intended to bond with Atlas," she says, and I sit up in alarm, feeling Nadir do the same.

"What? When?" he asks.

Rhiannon looks at the fire and then back at me. "It was shortly before she met Wolf. Her mother, Queen Daedra, had allied with the Sun King, Kyros, and the intention was for Serce and Atlas to bond as a show of their allegiance. Then Aphelion would lend their armies to Heart to help take down the Aurora King." Her gaze flicks to Nadir, gauging his reaction, but he waves her off.

"Trust me, it's not a problem," he says, and Rhiannon smiles.

"But Serce found out they'd make her compete in the Trials even though his brother was the Primary. They gave her some preposterous reason, and she refused. Shortly after, she ran into Wolf, and the rest was . . . destiny." She waves a hand, and I sit back, stunned by this revelation.

My grandmother refused Atlas, yet there I was two

hundred and eighty-six years later, competing in those very Trials for the hand of the same royal Fae. What were the odds? Did this have anything to do with why Atlas wanted me there so badly?

"How did he suppress this information?" Nadir asks.

Rhiannon shrugs her delicate shoulders. "Only a few people ever knew, and most of them died at the end. I've always assumed that Atlas or Kyros bought everyone else's silence with either steel or gold. It was all a little pathetic," she says, and I snort.

Seems like Atlas hasn't changed much in all these years.

Nadir has a line between his brows, clearly running through a myriad of conflicting thoughts.

"Anyway, after she met Wolf, it was over for good. She fell in love instantly. There would be no changing her mind," Rhiannon says with a strong dose of nostalgia. "Serce was as stubborn as they come."

"Do you know what happened at the end?" I ask, and at that, her face darkens.

"I know some of it," she says. "After she left for The Woodlands, we exchanged letters frequently."

This knowledge perks me up. "More than what the books say?"

She nods. "More than that."

"What happened?" Nadir asks, sitting forward.

"They were working with a High Priestess to bond them. It had to be a different type of bonding since they were both Primaries. This priestess said that just like when a Primary takes a partner that is Fae or human, their power would increase, but with two Primaries, it would have an even stronger effect."

"Wow," I say, not sure what answer I was expecting.

"And then I'm not sure what happened," Rhiannon says. "When Serce returned to Heart with Wolf, I was away visiting friends in Alluvion, but we exchanged a few more letters. I know Serce was concerned her mother was reluctant to descend after she spurned the bonding with Atlas, but Serce was sure only she would be strong enough to beat Rion. She was probably right." She pauses and looks at me. "I've always wondered if something happened out of her control that day. Something she hadn't planned for, and that's what caused it. She would never have willingly destroyed her home or her people. She spent her entire life waiting for the moment she would rule."

"Who was the priestess?" Nadir asks. "Do you know?"

"Her name was Cloris," Rhiannon says. "Serce said she was kind of crazy."

"Do you know how Atlas could have found out about Lor?" Nadir asks, and she shakes her head.

"I wish I could tell you that."

Nadir takes on a thoughtful look as we all fall silent.

"What happened after everything broke apart?" I ask. "How did you end up here? How long have you been here?"

"I came back to see the destruction for myself and stayed to help, planning to remain only for a short while. But months became years, and before I knew it, this was my home. I've traveled here and there over the centuries, but something always draws me back, like I'm missing a piece of myself until I'm close to Heart again." She looks around the room. "We all feel it. It's why we're still here."

"Waiting," Lor says softly.

"Waiting." Rhiannon nods, but there's no admonishment in her tone, only a sense of near wonder.

"What was she like? My grandmother?"

Rhiannon smiles. "Oh, the stories I could tell you," she says with a wistful smile.

"Would you?"

"Of course. Why don't we send for some dinner, and I'll share everything I remember?"

Chapter Sixteen

Queen Amara

Queendom of Heart: The First Age of Ouranos

"A toast," Queen Amara said, raising her glass. "To gathering in the face of adversity and finding common ground."

She studied each skeptical face seated around the table, most of them well beyond her years and experience—a fact they brought up every chance they got. When her parents had passed suddenly, the crown had fallen to her. Not a single one of these nobles, most of them her father's former friends and advisors, felt she was ready.

Amara thought they were probably right, but she was doing her best to pretend otherwise. Occasionally, she succeeded.

Only two outcomes would make this lot happy: for her to step down or for her to marry one of these windbags and hand the reins to him. Amara would die before she did either of those things. Her father had tried to prepare her for this, and this was her birthright.

Reluctantly, they raised their glasses as she lifted hers higher, making a show of drinking heartily. It was the last of Heart's ruby wine stores, though no one around this table knew it yet. The vineyards on the outskirts of the queendom had been some of the first areas to succumb to the Sleepness.

Amara then took her seat and gestured for the food to arrive. The castle staff had been reduced to a skeleton crew as more and more succumbed to the mysterious illness every month.

"Tell us then," said one of her father's former advisors, a particularly uppity man with a pointy nose, beady eyes, and a chin as weak as milk. "What do you have in mind for the Sleepness? It's come to my attention that the last so-called witch you hired not only failed in her task but also fell to the plague herself?"

Amara pressed her lips together, hating that every word he said was true. She'd practically emptied the queendom's coffers to convince the witch to sail across the Lourwin Sea on a claim she understood the disease ailing Amara's queendom. It had started happening months ago. At first, it was a random incident here and there, but then it progressed at an increasingly alarming rate.

Amara had done her best to contain the news, hoping to stave off a mass panic, but she knew it was like a balloon filling with water, almost on the verge of popping. She'd done an adequate job spinning propaganda: the Sleepness mostly affected the lower classes, who lived side by side in less than hygienic conditions.

It meant no one around this table had paid as much attention to the Sleepness as they should have. If Amara had been gifted with anything in this life, it was a silver tongue that could sell ice to the Aurora King. But even her skills had their limits, and word was getting out about the poorer neighborhoods that had nearly been wiped out.

No one was dead, at least not that anyone could discern, though they might as well be for all the difference it made. Instead, they were simply falling asleep right where they were sitting or sometimes standing, in the middle of whatever they were doing, and just wouldn't wake up. Hence the apt, though slightly unoriginal name.

No matter what anyone did, the victims remained impassive, but their hearts beat, and their breath stirred, and Amara hoped that meant it was possible to revive them.

But the longer this went on, the worse things seemed.

"Yes," she replied to his question about the first spellcaster she'd hired, trying to quell her rising irritation. They loved putting her in her place. It had become a game to them. While they sat here attending to their ridiculous amusements and clinging to petty grudges, their home was falling apart, and none of them seemed to care. But soon the Sleepness would find them, and then they'd be forced to start acting. "That was unfortunate."

She didn't know what else to say. She'd gambled and lost. Anyone could have done the same thing. The advisor gave her a look, his eyebrows raising as though she were the greatest fool to have ever lived, and *he* would have known better. She resisted the urge to pick up her glass of wine and toss it in his face.

"I understand things didn't go quite as planned that time," she ventured carefully.

She had a specific reason for bringing them here today, and she'd need to govern her temper if she was to convince them of her increasingly desperate plans. "But I have a new lead. A sorcerer. They say he's the best and has broken curses from here and across the widest seas."

Before she even stopped speaking, a collective groan circled around the table.

"You can't really be serious," one of the advisors said. "Not another charlatan!"

Amara squeezed her napkin under the table so hard she felt the fibers giving way in her grip.

"I know I said this last time, but I have a good feeling about this one," she said, hating how needy and pleading she sounded. She had to make them see.

"I say let it take them all," someone said with a smug grin before he planted his elbow on the table and drained his glass. "Who needs them?" He belched, and she wrinkled her nose.

"If they're all gone, then who will bring your wine?" another noble countered, and Amara could have kissed him. Except he always smelled like onions, so it would be only a theoretical kiss.

"Right," Amara said. "So I need your help."

Her coffers were empty. They all knew it, though she had been careful to downplay the direness of her circumstances.

"Call it an investment," she said. "Once the Sleepness has been cured, you'll all be granted new land and titles befitting the glory you've brought on Heart with your generosity."

She held her breath as they all looked at one another, eyes meeting across the table. Several of them started talking at once, and her shoulders sagged as she fielded their questions and objections, willing herself not to cry. If her father were alive, he'd know what to do. But he'd died and left her alone with all this.

After what felt like a hundred years, the room again fell silent.

"I'm in," said the first noble, and Amara could barely believe her eyes as she witnessed several more heads nodding in agreement. She wanted to jump up and shout for joy, but she kept her composure, standing up and raising her glass as more and more acquiesced until everyone around the table grumbled their reluctant assent.

"To Heart and our glorious future!" she said with a huge grin.

That's when the man sitting at the end of the table dropped forward, his face landing in his soup. Everyone jumped, just as the man across from him also flopped over, his face crashing onto his plate.

Amara watched in horror, her mouth open in a soundless scream, as one by one, they all began to fall along each edge of the table like lemmings tumbling off the side of a cliff.

Her wine slipped from her fingers, exploding at her feet in a spray of glass and blood-red liquid.

And that's when she screamed.

CHAPTER SEVENTEEN

LOR

HEART SETTLEMENTS: PRESENT DAY

After dinner is brought up, I settle next to the fire with Rhiannon as she regales me with tales of her childhood with Serce. Stories of them causing mischief and Serce's bouts of independence and rebellion against her mother. I absorb it all like caked sand doused with drops of water. Or at least I'm trying to. My attention keeps diverting to Nadir, who's sitting in the middle of the room talking to a female High Fae that's shamelessly flirting with him.

What's worse is he seems to be flirting back. From the corner of my eye, I watch as she touches his arm and then *leaves* it there. Like she's claiming him, and how dare she? I definitely try not to notice how Nadir leans in and says something in a low voice that makes her laugh. He's not supposed to make her laugh.

He's the high-strung, broody Aurora Prince—he's not supposed to be making *anyone* laugh.

Rhiannon's soothing voice pierces the veil of my irate thoughts.

"Oh! And the time we stole an ancient faerie relic from the king's collection—it was said anyone who held it would gain the power to see the future. We got into so much trouble!" She's laughing, and I start laughing, though it sounds forced, and I feel terrible for ignoring her when she's giving me her time. I shift in my seat, attempting to turn my back to Nadir. It doesn't really work, but it's the thought that counts, right?

"Tell me about it," I say to Rhiannon, focusing back on her. Rhiannon continues talking as she works away at her knitting, her gaze periodically flicking up. It seems like this is cathartic for her, too, as she reminisces about the past with such fondness. As I continue listening, I try to picture my grandmother and Rhiannon, young and carefree, enjoying their lives.

The sky has grown dark outside, filling with stars, and it must be getting late. I wonder how Tristan and Mael are faring on their horses.

Once again, I'm distracted by Nadir, who's still chatting with the same woman, and am I imagining that she's moved even closer? He isn't deterring her advances, and I grind my teeth. I remind myself that I was the one who told him it was over between us. That I wanted friendship and nothing more. I have no right to be angry. And yet, I'm pissed.

I focus on Rhiannon, trying to block him out. He's not important. He's no one. My magic tugs under my skin, pointing in his direction, reminding me that I can try to keep telling myself that, but I'm fooling no one.

A few minutes later, I notice Nadir approaching. Rhiannon stops talking, and he tips his head her way. "Thank you so much, Rhiannon. I'm sure Lor appreciates all this very much."

I'm really not a fan of him speaking for me. I don't acknowledge it, because he doesn't know it yet, but I'm giving him the silent treatment right now.

"Lor, I'm going to take care of a few things. I'll return in an hour and walk you back to the inn. Okay?"

I don't answer him, annoyed in a way I don't have a right to be. *A few things* to take care of? What, like taking that woman somewhere private and fucking her against a wall? That image twists a sharp pain in my chest, and I bury it away, piling it with a heap of indigestion.

"Lor?"

"Sure," I say, conceding to single syllables purely out of necessity.

"Don't leave here without me," he says, giving me a look that suggests I'm going to be in for a world of trouble if I disobey his command.

"Fine."

He hesitates, and I widen my eyes as if to say *Are you done now?*

He nods and then turns on his heel, leaving the room. When he's gone, I let out the breath trapped in my chest. I look back at Rhiannon, who stares at the doorway where he just left with a half smile on her face before turning to me again.

"Where were we?" I ask. "Tell me more about my grandfather. What was he like?"

"Hmm," Rhiannon says. "I got to know him only for a short time during the summit, but he was both ferocious and exceedingly kind. He loved your grandmother fiercely."

I like the sound of that. Rhiannon's stories about my grandmother aren't exactly bad, but they don't always paint her in the most positive light. While I'm sure she wasn't evil, there's a definite theme of selfishness underpinning most of her actions. Maybe they were just young and foolish in the way of adolescents. They had the freedom to be children in ways I never did.

"You look a lot like him too," Rhiannon says. "Not your coloring—that's all Serce—but in your features, I see Wolf."

I like the sound of that too.

"Do you think he tried to stop her?" I ask.

"I'm not sure, but I never got that sense," Rhiannon says. "He would have done anything for her from the moment they met."

I consider that, wondering about how they fell in love so quickly.

"They certainly gave up a lot for one another," I say.

"Well, of course. They were mates," Rhiannon says as if that's perfectly clear.

" 'Mates,' " I repeat. "I've heard the term referenced once or twice before, but what does it actually mean?"

"Well, it's very rare," Rhiannon says, shifting in her seat, a sparkle dancing in her eyes. "In the thousands of years since the Beginning of Days, there have been only maybe a hundred true mate pairs to ever exist."

"Wow. What were the odds of finding each other, then?"

"Almost nothing," Rhiannon says. "She told me she knew the moment she met him. That there was this shift in the air around her, and she knew something had changed. Her magic started to respond to him, too."

My scalp prickles with heat, an alarm howling in the back of my head.

"What? How do you mean . . . respond?" I practically choke on the words as they wedge in my throat.

"She said it was like it was fighting to get out, sure it was fighting to get to *him*. If they were ever apart for too long, the feeling would get stronger, and once they'd both realized who they were to each other, it finally calmed down, like two opposing halves fitting together."

She knits her fingers together and smiles with a wistful look in her eyes.

My chest turns heavy, the air in my lungs moving like sludge as my magic tugs inside me, reminding me it's there. As if I could ever forget.

"Could that magical tug be a signal of anything else?" My voice has gone unnaturally high, and Rhiannon draws her eyebrows together, oblivious to my climbing panic.

"I'm not really sure. I've never heard of it happening otherwise. I've had plenty of time on my hands," she says with a dry smile. "I've done a lot of research on mate bonds purely out of curiosity. Sometimes I think it was their love that burned down the world, which in a way is almost romantic, I think?"

I give her a weak smile as thoughts roll through my head,

pinging against the inside of my scalp like razored arrows. When Gabriel had said Nadir's name that night at the Sun Queen Ball, I'd felt a shift too. An unmistakable bend in the course of my destiny.

Mates. Mates. Mates.

"Fuck," I whisper as it all calcifies into focus.

Nadir is my mate.

That's the only explanation for any of this.

For the way he's twisted me into knots from the moment I first saw him.

Does Nadir know about this?

What am I going to do?

"Lor?" Rhiannon is asking as I resurface from the quicksand of my inner spiral. "Are you okay?"

I look back at her and brush my hair from my forehead. "Yeah, I'm fine."

I am definitely *not* fine, but I'm not sure how to say these words out loud. First of all, what if I'm wrong? Maybe it's just a coincidence. Maybe it's something else. What if I give voice to this and look like a complete fool?

"Tell me more about mate bonds," I croak. "Please."

"They're very powerful," Rhiannon says. "Mate bonds can be the source and amplifier for magic. I'm not sure if Serce knew that part, but there are ways to use the magic of a mate bonding for various purposes." She keeps talking about the sacredness of the bond and how it's a mark from Zerra herself as I sit still in my chair, slipping down, down, down.

"Wait, what did you just say?" I ask, snagging on something she just said.

"When two Fae are mates, then they must bond," she says.

"What happens if they don't?" I ask, already dreading the answer.

"Then they'll both die. At first, it's a sort of slow and painful descent into agony and madness. And then they both just stop existing. No Evanescence. No nothing."

"I see," I say.

She falls silent, watching me as though she can sense the turbulence churning inside my head.

"Don't worry. It's rarely happened. The pull of one's true mate is hard to resist."

I contemplate those words before I frown.

"So fate just decides it for you, then? What if someone doesn't want to be mated to that person?"

Rhiannon gives me a patient smile and shakes her head.

"It's not like that. When Zerra bestows a mate bond, it's because those two people are wholly perfect for each other in every conceivable way. But it goes beyond the surface—it's far more meaningful and deep."

My frown deepens. "So what comes first, the chicken or the egg? Are they perfect because they're mates?"

"No, it's more cyclical. One begets the other. You'd still likely end up together, barring some drastic course of action altering your paths. It's about destiny and the purpose of those two lives. It's no different from any pair who choose the bond, but the mate bond has more powerful consequences."

"Doesn't sound like much of a choice if they die when they refuse."

She shrugs and tips her head. "Perhaps. But in the end, it is still your choice. Besides, there are also special advantages for mates."

"Such as?"

"One of the most notable is the ability to hear each other's thoughts. It can be very useful. It doesn't happen in every pairing, though."

"Why not?"

"I'm not sure. I've never discovered an answer to that. Serce never mentioned it, so I don't believe your grandparents were capable of it."

I run a hand down my face, on the verge of hyperventilating.

"Are you sure you're okay? You seem a little off," Rhiannon asks. "I have some tonics I can administer if you're unwell. I know this has all been a lot."

"Yes, I'm just tired," I say, the lie ringing hollow to my ears.

I *am* tired, but also, I've never been more awake in my entire fucking life.

Mates.

Nadir is my fucking mate.

"I've kept you long enough," I say. "I think Nadir should be back any minute."

"You don't have to leave," she says, and I get the sense that today, she needed me as much as I needed her.

"I'll be back tomorrow if that's okay? This has been a lot of information, and I think I just need some air. A moment to clear my head."

"Of course. I'd love it if you came back. I'll try to think of some more stories. I want to hear more about your siblings too. I know we've never met, but Serce and I were so close that you all feel like my own grandchildren. We're family."

"Thank you for all of this," I say. "Truly. You have no idea how much it means to me. And I'll bring Tristan—he should be here soon."

"Wonderful," she says with a soft smile, and I turn to leave, heading back the way I came.

The tea shop is closed for the evening, though many of the same Fae I saw upstairs linger at one of the tables, a pot of tea sitting between them. Instinctively, I search for the woman Nadir was flirting with, and when I see she isn't amongst them, my stomach twists.

Zerra. What am I going to do about any of this?

They all stop talking as I enter the room, and I can't help feeling like I'm a specimen on display.

"Hi," I say. I can sense they want to ask me a thousand questions, but after what I just learned, I need to be anywhere but confined to this stuffy room. "See you later."

I look down at my feet and then rush across the room, shoving open the door and taking a deep inhale of the cool night air. For several moments, I stand with my eyes closed and my face tipped up, trying to calm the thundering rush of my pulse. When I open them, I'm greeted with the breathtaking sights of a blanket of stars and a silver moon high in the sky.

I look around. The street is quieter than earlier, with just a few people nodding to me as they pass. Snow is gently starting to fall, dusting everything in a coating of icy sparkles. The temperature has dropped, and I rub my hands, peering down the street, both ready to call it a night but also anticipating the sight of Nadir.

What am I going to do when I see him? What do I say? We need to talk about this. Does he know? What does this mean? But what if I'm wrong? I can't stop the same unproductive thoughts from churning in pointless loops. This is not how I imagined this day would end.

I stamp my feet as the chill settles in my limbs, and now I'm getting annoyed. Where is he? I think of that small room and that tiny bed that we're supposed to share, and knots of desire and rage flare in my stomach.

Zerra. There's no way I'll ever be able to sleep next to him again and pretend it's innocent. My mate. I wonder if I'm having a panic attack as I struggle to breathe, my skin flushing and my temple throbbing.

Where the fuck is he?

He's with that woman. That's the only explanation. I check the watch in my pocket and then grimace. He isn't late. He still has fifteen minutes left.

I blow out a sigh and will myself to get my shit together. *Calm down, Lor.*

How am I going to look him in the eye ever again?

Pacing in front of the shop, I stew in my thoughts, when a sound catches my attention. Someone's crying—it sounds like a child. I notice a small boy standing at the corner with fat tears running down his face. He's sniffling loudly, his narrow chest heaving. I haven't spent much time around children, and it's hard to guess his age, but he looks small. And frightened.

I approach him cautiously, trying not to scare him. When I'm a few feet away, I crouch down on a knee.

"Are you okay?" I ask, and he looks over, hiccuping through his tears. He wipes his face with his hand, pulling out a string of snot. "I lost my mum," he says. "We were in the market, and I turned around, and she was gone."

I look around, hoping to find a harried woman already careening our way, but there's no one in sight. I can't just leave him like this.

"Okay, don't worry. I'll help you find her," I say.

The little boy frowns. "I'm not supposed to talk to strangers."

I nod. Smart kid. "Right. You're absolutely right. Can I just sit next to you until she returns then? Was the market close by?"

The boy's shoulders relax as I sink down on my heel.

"Not really," he says. "I was chasing a feather, and it was a long time, I think. When I looked up, everything was different."

Okay then. Well, still, he can't have gone that far.

"I want her," he whines, and I'm not really sure what to do.

"Are you sure you don't want to go look for her? My name is Lor. What's yours?"

"I'm Aris. It's spelled A-R-I-S," he says proudly, like he's just learned this and is eager to show off his new skill.

"Nice to meet you, Aris. And there, now we aren't strangers anymore."

I know that's not really how it works, but he's a kid, and maybe he'll go for it. I obviously don't mean him any harm, and just want to get him back to his mother.

He gives me a dubious look, and I offer up what I hope is my most *I'm not a threat* smile.

"Do you remember which direction you came from?" I ask. "We could just walk that way and see if we find your mom, okay?"

"Okay," he finally says. "I think it was this way."

He walks over, slips his hand into mine, and then tugs me down the road. I check the time, and I should make it back before Nadir returns. This kid needs me right now. I've never given much thought to the idea of motherhood, but I like the idea of a family someday.

Aris pulls me down a small street lined with doors that lead up to homes and other businesses. Then another one as we go deeper into the winding maze of dilapidated houses.

"Are you sure this is the right way?" I ask as we move further and further from the main thoroughfare. He nods his little chin.

"Yup, I remember this spot now."

"Okay," I say, looking around. I check my watch. It's now past time for Nadir to meet me at the tea shop. I wonder if he arrived on time or if he was too cock deep inside that woman to remember me. I shake my head. Gods, I can be so dramatic.

"Right up here," Aris says, tugging my hand again as we turn another corner. It's a dead end.

"I don't think this is it," I say, and that's when everything goes black.

I scream, but the sound is muffled against a swath of thick dark fabric. Surprise knocks me off balance, and I stumble, crashing into a wall before pain bursts at the back of my head, and then I remember nothing.

CHAPTER EIGHTEEN

NADIR

The sun has set and the snow falls in thick flakes as I head back towards the tea shop in time to meet Lor. A chill wind blasts through the seams of my clothing, but one of the gifts of my magic is a tolerance against the cold. The door chimes when I open it, and several heads look up as I enter. Though the shop is technically closed for the night, people file in and out at every hour of the day.

Etienne explained that Rhiannon is a sort of home base for so many of these displaced citizens—a mother hen providing an outlet for their despondency and lack of stability. A place to gather and rally and plan for their futures. I'm so grateful she was here and could provide Lor with some of the answers she needed.

I nod to the group, brushing past and heading up the stairs. The workshop is nearly empty except for Rhiannon, who sits at a table carefully chopping herbs as though her thoughts are a million miles away. She looks up as I enter and smiles.

"Hi," she says brightly. "What can I do for you?"

"I'm here to pick up Lor."

"Oh, she left about fifteen minutes ago. She was going to wait for you outside. You didn't see her?"

Instantly, sharp prickles crawl down the back of my neck, but I'm not going to panic. She's perfectly safe here. Etienne assured me she was safe. She probably got tired of waiting and wandered away, and we missed each other.

Before I realize what I'm doing, my feet are already thundering down the stairs, storming back onto the street. Most people have retired for the night, and the sidewalks are quiet.

As I scan the area, left to right, my throat swells. No sign of Lor. The door opens behind me, and then Rhiannon is there, her eyebrows furrowed.

"Maybe she went back to the inn," she says, repeating my earlier thoughts, and I nod. That has to be it. I try not to think about the fact that I just left Etienne there, and we should have passed one another in the street. Maybe she took a different route.

I'm going to kill her for not waiting and for scaring me nearly to death.

I don't bother saying goodbye to Rhiannon, because my feet are moving again, and I'm focused on only one thing. I attempt to maintain an even pace, but I don't know whom I'm trying to impress, so I break into a run, nearly bowling over the few stragglers navigating the street.

When I burst into the inn, I find Tristan and Mael have arrived. They're in the common room bickering like an old married couple as usual. Etienne sits with them, shuffling a deck of cards between his hands, trying to keep them busy. He says it helps calm his anxiety.

"Have you seen her? Did she come in here?"

They both stop talking. "No," Mael says. "You mean Lor?"

"Of course I mean Lor," I say, skirting past him and then pounding up the stairs. She's in our room. It's the only explanation I'll accept.

I fling open the door to find it empty, and now I'm plunging into full-blown panic.

"Where's my sister?" Tristan asks. "You lost her?"

I spin around, and I'm not proud of my actions, but I can't help myself as I grab him by the tunic and shove him against the wall.

"I didn't lose her," I hiss.

Tristan and I haven't gotten off on the best foot, and I'm trying to find some common ground for Lor's sake, but he can't stand me, and I can't really blame him. This isn't exactly helping matters.

"Then where is she?" he snaps, not intimidated by me at all, and why should he be? He lived in Nostraza too. He was surrounded by monsters his entire life. What's one more breathing down his neck?

"Etienne!" I'm shouting as I shove Tristan one more time and then barrel down the stairs. "Come!"

I pass through the common room with Etienne, Mael, and Tristan hot on my tail as I lead them to a quiet alley behind the inn.

"Tell me there are none of my father's men here," I say to Etienne, so very close to losing the tether on my self-control.

"There are no more of your father's men here." He sounds so certain that I want to believe him.

"Then where is she?"

Etienne swallows, and his eyes shift.

"Tell me! Tell me they don't have her."

"I don't know," Etienne says, his jaw clenching. "I suppose it's possible they were hiding."

"Fuck!" I roar. "How could you have gotten this wrong!"

His shoulders drop, and he runs a hand through his hair. "Nadir, I . . . was sure."

"Not sure enough! Where could they be?!"

He's pacing, and I give him a moment to gather his thoughts. Etienne is one of my closest friends—he was in the same prison camp with me and Mael all those years ago—but if he gets Lor killed, I can't be held responsible for what I do next.

"Etienne!" I say, losing my patience much quicker than I intend.

"I'm thinking!"

Mael and Tristan watch us warily, their arms folded as I try to hold back the white-hot lash of my temper. I need to hit something. Tear out my father's heart. Feel it cool in my hand as it slowly stops beating, his blood oozing between my fingers.

"I swear to Zerra—"

"You think I wanted this to happen?" Etienne yells, rounding on me. "She is my fucking queen!"

That's when I snap. I stride up to him, jamming my forearm against his throat and shoving him to the wall. "You have *no* idea what she is. She's your queen, but she is my m—"

I stop, practically biting through my tongue. Now is not the time for this. I catch the looks from Mael and Tristan. The first is studying me with surprised clarity and an expression suggesting he finally figured it all out, while the latter has the same confused look Lor has been giving me for weeks.

"Nadir," Mael finally says, muscling between us and pushing me off Etienne. "This is getting us nowhere. We're going to split up and look for her together." He lays a hand on my shoulder and squeezes. "We're going to find her, my friend. I promise you—we are going to find her if it's the last thing any of us do."

His dark eyes perforate the haze of my terror, reminding me he will go to the ends of the earth to make this true for me. I don't deserve him. I've never deserved him.

I nod slowly, doing my best to believe him.

"Etienne, think," he says. "Where might they hide her?"

"The warehouses or the river docks," he says. "There are plenty of abandoned buildings where they might have concealed themselves."

My jaw clenches so hard that my teeth are on the verge of collapse. How could he have been so careless? How could *I* have been so careless? I should have double-checked myself before letting her anywhere near this place.

"What if they've already removed her from the settlements?" Tristan asks.

"I'll signal the others to question the gate guards for anything suspicious," Etienne says. "But this late at night, the gates are closed, and they don't let anyone in or out. There's more than a good chance they're keeping her here until morning. Or until they can get a message out."

Our eyes meet, and no one says what we're all thinking. A message to the king. But which one? Some instinct tells me it's my father. This has his stink all over it.

"Okay, then do it," I say to Etienne. "Mael, you go with him and search the docks. Tristan, we'll head to the warehouses."

Everyone nods, and Etienne and Mael jog off while Tristan and I head in the opposite direction.

We haunt the shadows as we prowl past the buildings. It's probably best not to attract too much attention in the event more of my father's men are about. We need to get out of here and as far away as possible.

The deeper we wind through the narrow streets, the quieter it gets. It's clear this is an area best avoided at any time of day, but especially at night. Tristan and I look at one another and nod.

"Do you have a weapon?" I ask. Tristan pulls out a dagger from his belt. I'm not sure how skilled he is, but it will have to do. If he's anything like Lor, then he at least knows how to hold his own in a fight. "Be ready to use your magic."

Quietly, we stalk down the increasingly narrow streets, the towering buildings blocking our view beyond a few feet, casting long shadows where anything could be hiding and waiting. I try to focus over the panicked thoughts tumbling through my head. Listen for any hints or sounds of life or movement. I should be able to feel her if we're close enough. My magic responds when she's near, but we've always been in somewhat tight proximity when I've felt it.

Her name repeats on a loop in my head, over and over.

Lor. Where are you? Lor. Please be okay. Please be alive.

If anything happens to her, it will destroy me. Nothing will put the pieces back together if my father gets his hands on her. I'll be a shattered crystal statue, ground to nothing but razor-sharp dust.

Our heavy breaths mist in the cold night air as we wade through the darkness, which feels like a thick wool blanket closing around us. Why does it feel like these shadows are alive? I pray with every part of my soul that Mael and Etienne have already found her, but I also want to be the one who eviscerates anyone who dared touch her.

Zerra, how they will bleed rivers of red.

And fuck, I'm going to enjoy every second.

We round another corner, and that same unnatural darkness surrounds us. There's no doubt magic is at work here. It feels off, though, because I'm unaware of any power my father possesses to create shadows like this. I can barely see anything through it. I blink a few times, but it's no use.

Taking a calculated risk, I allow some of my magic to slip out, forming a glowing ball to light the way. But it's muted against the dark like a bright window dampened by a thin cloth. What is this? My only consolation is that it must mean we're close to her. Why else would someone use magic to conceal this area?

We turn another corner, and I blink again, wishing I could see better. It's like walking through layers of black gauze. Tristan stumbles next to me, and I instinctively reach out a hand to steady him, finding his arm.

"Thanks," he mumbles in the dark, but it's too loud in the stillness.

"She has to be close," I whisper, hoping it doesn't sound like a cannonball blasting through glass.

We round another corner, feeling blindly, using the walls to guide us, the darkness practically choking me. And that's when I feel it.

At first, it's faint, a weak thread of a voice I know like I know my own heart.

Nadir. Nadir. I'm here. I'm here. Find me, please.

Someone starts screaming. My name. Her muted echo bounces around in my skull, begging me to find her.

And then I start running.

Chapter Nineteen

LOR

U rgent voices churn somewhere between consciousness and the throbbing in the back of my head. Someone is arguing. A male voice followed by another. "We need to get a message out," one of them is saying.

"We can't until morning," the other replies.

"Do you think anyone saw us?"

"No."

"What did you do with the kid?"

"Gave him some coin to keep his yap shut. Told him I'll pull out his toenails one by one if he squeals."

They both snicker viciously as my mind meanders towards clarity, but I'm having trouble forming solid thoughts. The child and the darkened alley. That little shit tricked me. I have just enough presence of mind to lie still and continue pretending I'm passed out as I listen to them bicker. I shift, just barely, noting the prickle of scratchy rope binding my hands and feet.

I pray this is a random attack, and these two aren't working for the Aurora King. Etienne assured us that all his men were gone. Was he lying? Or was he just mistaken?

Their conversation continues as I resist the urge to open my eyes, sure that if they notice I'm awake, I'm destined for even more trouble.

"The king said we had to get a message out immediately," one of the voices implores with a nasally whine. My stomach buckles with terror.

The king.

But which Imperial Fae am I dealing with? What if it isn't Rion but Atlas? I have more than one king vying for my head, and how did I end up in this mess?

In comparison, life was so simple in Nostraza. All I had to worry about was filling my belly and staying away from the guards as much as possible. Simple. Straightforward.

Instinct tells me these are Rion's men, and I'm not sure which is the worse option. Ultimately, it doesn't matter all that much at this particular moment. The only thing that matters is getting as far away from here as I can. How long has it been since I was supposed to meet Nadir? Has he realized something happened? Would he come to find me?

That's when I remember what else happened before my abduction.

My *mate.*

Can that really be? Rhiannon claimed mates can sometimes

communicate with one another telepathically. We've never done so before, but I'm desperate enough to cling to this scrap of thin hope.

But maybe that's not true. I think of the dream I had back in the manor when Nadir was holding me captive. We both had the same fantasy about him coming into my room. Was that us communicating through . . . a mate bond?

My hip hurts from lying on the hard ground, and my head is pounding. My thoughts are still sluggish, like they're being dragged through congealed soup. Otherwise, I appear to be unhurt, at least for now.

Taking a chance, I open my eyes just enough to discern the blur of my surroundings. The room is mostly dark but for a flickering torch hanging off the wall where I can make out a door. The room's single window is covered with a thick curtain.

The men sit in chairs facing the door while passing a bottle of something back and forth. They're dressed in casual, nondescript clothes, not the uniforms of either king's soldiers.

I close my eyes as they continue talking. They've moved on from their argument, agreeing they'll have to wait until morning before they can do anything about me. Now they're discussing some woman, who's obviously rejected them, they both intend to fuck together. Pigs.

Shutting out the sounds of their voices, I start calling for Nadir using my mind. Maybe, if we really are mates, he can hear me.

Nadir. Nadir. I'm here. Find me.

Can he locate me based on a disembodied voice? How close

does he need to be? This is probably futile, but it's the only plan I have. Unless these idiots do me a favor and get drunk enough to drown in their own vomit, I have no clue how else I'll get out of here.

My magic stirs in my chest, and it feels easier than normal. Slightly less contained. Nadir's prediction that it might be more reachable while I'm close to the borders of Heart wasn't off base. But without the use of my hands, I can't even begin to guess how to control it.

Why am I so bad at this?

As I keep calling for Nadir, I try to access my magic, going into myself and focusing on that crackling red spark in my chest. It glows more brightly than it has in weeks.

Nadir. Nadir. I'm here. Find me.

I repeat the mantra every few seconds while I try to rally my power into something useful.

"Hey!" A gruff voice blasts through my thoughts. "She's talking."

Shit. My lips must have been moving without my noticing. I go still, but that is absolutely the wrong thing to do, because now they know I'm awake.

Shit. Shit. Shit.

Heavy boots stomp closer as my breath cuts off, vacating my lungs.

The steps halt, but I keep my eyes scrunched out of fear and some entirely displaced sense of self-preservation.

If I don't see them, they can't see me. Right?

Gods, I'm so fucked.

After a derisive snort, a sweaty finger touches my cheek,

and I flinch before my eyes fly open. I'm met with a sinister grin as one of the men leans over me. "How long have you been awake, darling?"

The words are soft, but there's a definite edge of gleeful malice in his tone like he can't wait to feast on the tender marrow of my bones. I see the shift of the second male out of the corner of my eye, and my stomach liquefies with pooling alarm.

"We can't do anything useful with you until morning," he says before he looks back at his companion. "What could we do to pass the time until then?" The meaning in his words is obvious, and why is the entire male gender so fucking predictable?

That's when I start thrashing, bucking against my restraints, but I'm like a fish tossed onto the beach, baking in the hot, dry sun. I can't do anything as I gasp for breath. The first man laughs.

"You're stuck, sweetheart. No point bothering."

Now I'm panicking. My entire body is seizing up with fear. Cold thorns claw over the back of my scalp.

No. No. No. This will not fucking happen again.

And that's when I feel it.

Not it. *Nadir.* He's close by. I'm sure of it. He's become like an extension of myself. His presence brushes against me, and I know he's here.

So I start screaming. I scream so loud my throat hurts and my ears ring, but I scream and scream, trying to get it out before these bastards silence me.

"Nadir! I'm here!" I scream and scream his name over and over.

It's then that several things happen at once.

The door blasts apart, ribbons of colorful light searing across my vision. Debris goes flying, and I do my best to duck my head as shards of wood and glass rain from above. Shrieks and shouts precede the ominous thud of bodies falling. I hear the crack of bone, followed by more screams through a haze of black fog. Flashes of Nadir's colorful magic and flares of velvety green.

A sharp pain at the back of my head blurs my vision, the edges smearing together like wet paint. Distantly, I register the sounds of fighting and the tang of blood filling my nose. It feels like forever and a minute before arms lift me up, cradling me against a warm body that smells like icy mountain winds and the crisp edges of frost.

We move swiftly, bouncing as Nadir flees with me to safety.

The pain in my head buzzes as I move in and out of consciousness, wishing my eyes would focus.

"This way!" comes a voice I recognize as Tristan's, and despite everything, my shoulders release.

"You found her," comes another voice. It sounds like Mael.

"We have to get out of here. Now," Nadir says, his words hard as steel. "If they got a message out, this place is going to be swarming with my father's men before morning."

"We'll go east." It sounds like Etienne. "Hide in The Woodlands until it's safe to travel."

Then we're moving once again. I moan, trying to wake up and make sense of anything.

"Hang on," Nadir says. "I'm getting you out of here. I'm so sorry, Lor."

I want to tell him it wasn't his fault and I shouldn't have followed that child, but I thought he needed me. I was only trying to help.

I open my eyes, the sky and the stars spinning above me as we continue running, gentle flakes of snow cooling my face.

And then everything shifts. One moment, we're in the middle of the city, and the next, we're in a forest where leaves and branches hang overhead, so thick they nearly block out the night sky. I blink, not sure what just happened. Did I pass out? How did we get here so quickly?

We finally stop, and Nadir lays me down on a soft patch of grass. I feel his hand on my cheek, his fingers gently probing my limbs and torso for signs of damage. He touches the back of my head, and I whimper as pain flashes across my skull.

"We need to get her to a healer," he says. "*Now*."

And, once again, my world goes black.

Chapter Twenty

Nadir

The Woodlands

I pace the length of the room, but this cottage is like the head of a pin, and there's nowhere for me to go as the walls close in. The healer, whose door I nearly split in two, sits at the side of the bed where Lor lies still with her eyes closed.

"It appears they gave her something. A sedative of sorts," Alder, the elf healer, says. "Does she have magic someone was trying to suppress?"

I stop, turning on him, a caustic warning curling up the base of my spine.

"No," I lie.

He offers me a skeptical look but doesn't push the matter

and turns back to Lor, continuing to dab her forehead with a cloth soaked in a potion of herbs he swears will help. I wish we could return to the settlements. Everyone knows the best healers live in Heart, even without their magic.

Elves are much smaller than High Fae, and Tristan and Mael sit at the tiny kitchen table, the furniture practically dwarfed by their frames.

Etienne wandered off somewhere after we arrived with his shoulders hunched and an even deeper scowl on his face than usual. I'm trying not to lash out at him for his nearly fatal mistake, but I'm finding it difficult to harness my temper. It was an accident, and he probably feels bad enough about it already, but I'm so angry I want to rip apart the sky.

Alder tends to Lor, mumbling something under his breath as he touches her here and there, once again examining the bump on her head. He's assured me it's a minor injury and it shouldn't cause any permanent damage.

"Can you wake her up?" I demand. "What's wrong with her?"

He looks up at me with dark green eyes, a tenderness I don't deserve crossing his expression. Then I feel a hand land on my shoulder.

"Come for a walk," Mael says. "He's doing everything he can."

I shake Mael off. "No. I'm not going anywhere."

"Okay, but then stop yelling at him."

I glare at my friend, but his patient smile doesn't falter. He holds up a glass of a dark green liquid clinking with balls of ice. "Have some Armata. It'll settle your nerves."

I take the glass and drain the entire thing in one gulp before I hand it back to him and roll my shoulders. "Nope. Didn't work."

I start pacing again, and Mael sighs as he returns to the table. Tristan is watching his sister intently, his pale face contrasting with the dark circles around his eyes. He was a huge asset tonight. His control over his magic, despite how little he's used it, is impressive. He helped me destroy those bastards without the slightest shred of mercy. In fact, I think he enjoyed it a little bit.

It makes me wonder if maybe we could be friends someday.

His gaze slides to me as though he can hear my thoughts, his expression shifting in a way I can't interpret before he looks back at Lor.

She groans softly, and I'm at her side in an instant, dropping to my knee and taking her hand.

"I think the poison is wearing off," Alder says. "It appears it was meant to incapacitate her for only a while. The effects should abate completely soon enough."

I drop my head against her shoulder, whispering a thank-you to Zerra.

"Give her a little longer," Alder says. "I'll brew some tea to help with the pain from that nasty bump when she wakes up."

Alder stands and claps me on the shoulder before he shuffles to the tiny kitchen. I remain in the same position next to Lor, gripping her hand between mine like she might dissolve through my fingers if I let go. I can't stand to think of how close I came to losing her. I remember her calling for me. I'll never forget her voice for as long as I live.

Sitting on the floor, I hold Lor's hand, watching her eyelids flutter and her forehead crease as though monsters are troubling her dreams. I wish I could reach out and take them from her. Take away all the pain she's suffered and make it mine.

Finally. Finally, she blinks awake, staring up at the ceiling. It's light out now, the sun having risen on what felt like the longest night of my life.

Her gaze moves to me, and an expression crosses her face that feels like she's cataloging me. Reading every cell and pore until she penetrates the very depths of my marrow. I get a peculiar sense of the world tipping on its side, but I have no idea why.

"What is it?" I ask, but she shakes her head and looks up at Tristan and Mael, who are now standing behind me.

"What happened? It was your father's men, wasn't it?"

Everyone's gaze flicks to Alder, who's standing at the stove stirring a pot and humming to himself. I place a finger to my lips, reminding her to be discreet. She reaches up and touches my cheek, her fingers gentle, and it's all I can do not to pick her up and kiss her until the sun burns out of the sky.

"You're covered in blood," she says. There's no condemnation in her statement, only distant observation.

"They had to die."

She blinks, her dark eyes simmering with rage while clearing with focus.

"Did they suffer?"

I raise an eyebrow and give her a crooked smile. "Very much."

She nods and presses her lips together. "Good."

"That's my girl," I say, and she gives me that same odd look again. Before I can ask her what the matter is, Alder thrusts a steaming mug into my vision.

"Here," he says. "Drink some of this."

I help Lor sit up, and she winces before she touches the back of her head. Rage, billowing clouds of icy vengeance, filters right to the tips of my fingers. What I did to those bastards wasn't enough. I hope they suffer from now until the end of eternity.

She accepts the mug and takes a tentative sip before wrinkling her nose.

"Tastes like death warmed over," Alder says. "But works like a charm."

He chuckles and then walks away as Lor forces down another gulp.

"Are you okay?" Tristan asks, sitting near her feet.

She nods on a hard swallow. "I will be. I thought they had me."

We all sit in silence for another few minutes while she continues to sip her tea. Color is returning to her cheeks, and the vise clamped around my chest finally eases—she survived this. Of course she did. She could survive anything.

"Do you think you can stand up?" I ask, preferring not to linger here any longer. Not only should we avoid staying in one place for too long, we should get back to Aphelion. Lor needs control over her magic now more than ever. My father will keep trying to get to her until it kills one of them. Of that I'm sure.

"I think so," she says, placing her now-empty mug on the

small table next to the bed. She pushes up to stand with Tristan's hand under her elbow.

"Whoa," she says, swaying on her feet. Before she can do anything, I've scooped her into my arms, and I'm rewarded with an angry glare.

"I don't need you to carry me."

"You nearly passed out just there."

"I'm fine. Besides, you're covered in blood."

She waves a hand over me, and I grin.

"The blood of your enemies, Lor. Ask me, and I'll slay anyone for you. Burn the world to ash if you desire." Though I mean the words to sound like a jest, they come out simmering with the fire of my truth.

She studies me again with that same puzzled expression as if she's finally fitting my various pieces together. The brightness in her eyes almost rips the air from my lungs, and I swear the corner of her mouth twitches as though she's trying not to smile.

Something happened between the moment I left her with Rhiannon and now. Something that feels like a tentative thread of . . . hope?

"Etienne's waiting outside," Mael says, rolling his eyes at my dramatics. "Let's go."

Despite her protests, I hang on to Lor, and she stops fighting me. I take that as a positive sign. Of what, I'm not sure yet.

Tristan and Mael head outside, but Mael comes to a stop so abruptly that I nearly crash right into his back.

"What are you—"

We're surrounded by a dozen High Fae guards, all wearing

the green-and-bronze uniform of the Woodlands army. Etienne has two spears pointed at his throat and his hands lifted in surrender, trying not to make any sudden movements.

In the center of this show sits an Imperial Fae male on top of a massive horse, his brown leather wings spread wide.

"Cedar," I say, trying to keep my tone unaffected and not like we're in a whole world of shit right now. Slowly, I lower Lor to the ground, keeping my arm around her waist. She's staring up at her great-uncle with the same unease we're all currently experiencing. "What brings you out here?"

Cedar smirks and then slides off his horse in one smooth movement, his feet kicking up a cloud of dust as his boots strike the earth.

"My dear prince. You didn't think you could waltz across my borders and I would remain ignorant of your royal presence? The forest has eyes and ears everywhere."

"We're just passing through," I say. "So, if you don't mind, we'll get out of your hair."

I attempt to pick up Lor again, when suddenly four more spears point towards us while more close around Mael and Tristan. I could attempt to use magic to get us out of this, but Cedar knows I won't. It would cause too much of a mess. Besides, I'm almost positive we'd never survive a chase through the forest with its king on our heels. This is his territory, which puts all of us at a distinct disadvantage.

"That's rude, Nadir. You enter uninvited, trample through my forest, make use of one of my healers, and then just leave without even saying hello? I'm wounded."

My jaw clenches.

"My apologies," I say. "I thought a king as important as you had better things to do than entertain a few wayward travelers. Surely The Woodlands doesn't trifle itself with such unimportant matters."

The comment is pointed, and he knows it, but he doesn't chew on my bait.

Instead, he grins. The egotistical son of a bitch.

"Of course, but I always have time for the prince of The Aurora. In fact, I think you should all come to the Fort and be my guests for a few days."

I feel Lor stiffen next to me, and my own sense of warning fires in alert. Is this an invitation or a detainment?

"That's very kind of you," I reply. "But we really do need to be going."

"What's the rush? Where do you need to go in such a hurry?"

He levels me with his bright green gaze, and I wonder just how much he knows.

"You haven't even introduced me to your companions." He scans over the group, nodding at Mael, whom he's already acquainted with, before his gaze falls on Lor and then flicks to Tristan.

This is very bad.

"This is . . ." I start, trying to think of a convincing lie.

"I know who they are, Nadir," Cedar says, his tone turning flat as he sweeps an assessing gaze over Lor and her brother. "You think I don't recognize my own flesh and blood?"

CHAPTER TWENTY-ONE

ZERRA THE SUN QUEEN

APHELION: THE FIRST AGE OF OURANOS

Queen Zerra lay on the divan, staring out the window. She had already stripped down to her golden underwear, but still her bronzed skin beaded with sweat. The window sat open, welcoming a tepid breeze off the water, but it wasn't enough to combat the oppressive stillness of this endless heat.

A servant stood over her, waving a giant leaf, and while the effort was commendable, all it really did was stir around the hot, soupy air. It was agony. She was wilting like flower petals packed in salt.

"Bring me some water," she ordered another servant, who

stood with her hands clasped. The girl scurried off, and Zerra wrinkled her nose. It had only been last week she'd finally conceded to allowing them to abandon their lovely gold livery in favor of looser cotton garments that made the heat more tolerable. She hated the way it made them appear unkempt and shabby, like broken-down furniture, unlike their crisp, starched uniforms.

But when they kept passing out from heat stroke, she'd conceded the sight of disheveled servants was better than having no one to fetch her a drink at all.

The girl returned with a crystal glass that clinked with ice. Zerra accepted it without a word and sipped before she pressed it to her forehead, seeking a moment of fleeting relief.

Around the room, more courtiers lay on their own divans with their eyes closed, all stripped down to practically nothing. This had been going on for two and a half months now. The endless heat. The lack of rain. Zerra had lost count of how many living in the districts had already died. She had people to worry about such matters, except they kept expecting her to do something about this. As if she had any control over the weather. She was a queen, not a god.

As she scanned the room, she caught the eye of Eamon, who regarded her with a raised brow, the suggestion in his expression clear.

Her eyes cantered down the length of his perfect body, admiring the cut of his chest and his stomach and the way a line of sweat lazily curved over his tight ridges like a cool stream winding through a mountain valley.

He used his chin to gesture towards the doorway, asking if

she wanted to move to a more private space. She gave the offer three seconds of serious consideration but decided she was just too fucking hot.

While she rarely balked at a stolen moment riding his cock, the idea of his hot body pressed against her hot body growing even hotter, almost made her faint. This was becoming unbearable.

She shook her head and mouthed the word "later" across the room. He tipped his chin and then laid his head back down, closing his eyes as his own leaf-waving servant arced her fan over him.

She enjoyed the view of his bronzed skin for several moments, contenting herself with daydreams of being fucked on her balcony, bent over the railing while he thrust into her from behind. It wasn't quite as satisfying as the real thing, but her imagination would have to suffice for now.

She laid her head back down and watched the ocean waves roll from the window, contemplating the idea of rousing herself for a swim. The water was one of the few places that offered a temporary sliver of escape from this torment.

Unfortunately, that also meant most of Aphelion had gathered on the coast. She frowned at the scene below, scanning the beach milling with hundreds of people dunking in the surf for hours on end. They were spending their entire days there and doing nothing else. Utterly lazy. Maybe she needed to enforce some curfews regarding the use of the water.

"The mist," she said, not addressing anyone in particular, but a moment later, the relief of a million tiny droplets sizzled over her flushed skin.

If this kept up, she'd need to cordon off a section of the beach for her private use, at the very least. She wasn't about to fight her way through the sweaty masses. Really, she should have done that years ago.

"Your Majesty," came a voice she knew, and her eyes drifted shut in irritation. "Your Majesty, I must speak with you."

Zerra sucked in a deep breath and then slowly rolled over with a clenched smile glued to her face. "What is it, Cyrus?"

"I've received word that we lost another hundred and thirty-two people last night. They can't tolerate this heat. We need to do something."

Zerra sighed. "Send them more ice," she said with a flick of her hand.

"Our production is lagging," he said. "There isn't enough to distribute to everyone."

He stared at her with his eyebrows drawn.

"And? What do you want me to do then?"

He blinked.

"Something. I want you to do . . . something."

The words were spoken softly, but Zerra flinched as though he'd pulled off a wet leather glove and slapped her cheek.

"There's nothing else I can do. We'll just have to wait this out."

Cyrus opened his mouth and then closed it before he tipped her a quick bow. She registered the disappointment on his face, but she wasn't sure what he expected of her.

"I'll direct people to the water then," he said, and she nodded.

"Yes. Do that."

He nodded and then turned to leave. She watched until he cleared the doorway, and then, with a heavy sigh, lay back down on her soft divan and closed her eyes.

She was listening to the sounds from the beach and the soft sighs of the courtiers when a cool breeze pulled her eyes open.

The scene around her had changed. She no longer lay on her divan but on a hard, foreign surface.

Above her curved an arched ceiling—at least it seemed like a ceiling, except that it looked like the sky. Most importantly, the air was cool. Blissfully, beautifully cool.

She sighed and brushed her arms and legs against the marble until someone cleared their throat, alerting her to the fact she wasn't alone.

Quickly, she shot up and looked behind her to find several figures she recognized.

Amara, the queen of Heart. Terra, the king of Tor. And though she'd never met him, she assumed the man with the long chestnut hair must be Hawthorne, the Woodlands King.

She pushed herself up as they watched her, and she became conscious of how little she was wearing.

"What is going on?" she asked as she tiptoed closer, taking a place next to Amara.

"We're not sure," she replied. "We're waiting. I think."

Zerra nodded, wrapping her arms around herself, and for the first time in months, she shivered.

Chapter Twenty-Two

LOR

The Woodlands: Present Day

King Cedar approaches me in two long strides as I process his words, exchanging nervous glances with Tristan. The king towers over me when he comes to a stop, long brown hair curling over his shoulders and the tips of his leathery brown wings stretching towards the sky.

He knows who we are? I remember him from the Sun Queen Ball. Had he known then?

"Did you think I wouldn't know when my kin returned home?" Cedar asks Nadir. "The question is, what are they doing with you, and why have you brought them here?"

Nadir rubs the back of his neck. Clearly, he hadn't antici-pated this development. "I didn't bring them here. Or at least I didn't bring them to you. We needed to hide."

I can tell it guts Nadir to admit that, but there really isn't any other reasonable explanation for our presence. "And as to why they're with me, that is really none of your business."

Nadir wraps a hand around my arm and pulls me towards him. "So, if you'd ask your goons to lower their weapons, we'll be on our way. We have no quarrel with you, Cedar. Don't start one."

Cedar raises a hand, and his soldiers press in closer, their weapons still pointed at us. "I'm sorry, but I can't let you do that." And then, before Nadir can protest, Cedar adds, "I mean you no harm. None of you. But I can't let you leave without some explanation and a moment to talk."

"How do you know who we are?" Tristan asks, attempting to approach only to find a pair of spears drop across his path. He stops short, glaring at the soldiers holding him back until Cedar waves a hand.

"Let him come."

As Tristan draws closer, Cedar watches him, his eyes scan-ning my brother from head to toe.

"I have wards set on my borders to trigger when anyone of Woodlands royal blood crosses the perimeter. I felt it the day you were taken, and I felt it a few hours ago."

Tristan and I exchange another glance, our expressions conveying the same shock at those words. He *knew*. He knew when we were taken. And he did nothing? I have so many questions that I can't figure out where to begin.

"Please," Cedar says. "I'd be happy to explain more, but I'd be remiss in my manners if we had such an important conversation standing out here in the middle of the forest. Come to the Fort and be my guests for a few days. I give you my word that you will be safe." He peers at Nadir. "And if your need to hide means no one can know of your presence within my borders, then consider your secrets safe with me."

"What about everyone else?" Nadir asks.

"My people are loyal, and the forest keeps secrets better than anyone."

I have no idea what that means, but the answer seems to satisfy Nadir, who nods.

"Only if Lor and Tristan agree," he says, yielding to us.

"Yes, I'd like to," I say, and Tristan also nods, though the expression on his face suggests he doesn't trust the Woodlands King at all.

Not only did we fail to learn anything about who's blabbing our secrets in Heart, we also need to get back to Aphelion, but I also need to hear what our great-uncle has to say. I've spent half my life wondering why this forest king sat on his ass when my parents were slaughtered.

"Wonderful," Cedar says, giving me and Tristan another lingering look. I'm not sure if it's the light, but I catch the silver of tears lining his eyes. "You both look so much like him."

There's a pause of silence, and then he turns on his heel and heads towards his horse before jumping into the saddle. The rest of his soldiers circle our group and herd us into the forest.

As we march along the worn earthen paths, I wonder how far we have to go. After the events of last night, I'm exhausted, and with the adrenaline of confronting the king and his soldiers wearing off, I'm swaying on my feet.

"Are you okay?" Nadir asks. "To walk? I can carry you if you want."

I look over at him, taking a moment to study his face.

When I awoke in the healer's cottage, when he was the first thing I saw, something shifted and flipped on its axis. Yet again.

I finally understood the way he's been growing up around me in a tangle of stems. That he's just like those roses blooming over the surface of the Heart Castle, despite the impossibility of their existence, filtering into the cracks and feeding on slivers of sunlight.

He sees into *my* darkness and stares at it with unflinching eyes.

I wasn't surprised to find him covered in the blood of those two men. This is who he is, and I will stare into his darkest corners, too, seeking his light.

"Thank you for coming to rescue me," I say, and his brow furrows.

He opens his mouth and then closes it before he says, "Why would you think I wouldn't?"

Why do I get the sense he had planned to say something else?

My mate.

Of course I knew he'd come.

And I . . . would have done the same. Without a moment's hesitation. With a fiery rage in my heart and a smile on my face. I would have made them suffer.

Everything Rhiannon said points towards him in blinking

red lights. It couldn't be more obvious if someone had tattooed it on his forehead.

How could I have ever thought these feelings for him were anything less than extraordinary? And it's then I realize that this whole time, I've been tending a patch of weeds while he's been growing me a garden.

Magic simmers under my skin, always stretching towards him, becoming stronger and stronger. Could it snap? Was this what she meant when she said it could kill us if we resisted?

I want to acknowledge this, but now is not the time. Not when we're surrounded by the soldiers of the Woodlands King.

This moment deserves to be honored. Given the space to breathe and flex, not hurried or rushed. His eyes meet mine, and they simmer with a universe of unspoken thoughts.

Do I worry about what he'll say or how he'll react? This might be one time in my life I'm absolutely sure of the outcome. He's made his feelings clear, and I no longer feel the need to crumble under their scorching weight.

"Are you sure you're all right to walk?" he asks. "You're a little pale."

My answering smile feels soft around the edges, like I'm being teased apart, the hardened pieces of me filtering out and then gently pressed back together into something new and whole. He's done this to me. Filed down the harsh cocoon I've worn for so long, giving me the chance to emerge reborn.

"Why do you keep looking at me like that?" he asks. I stare at him. At the arch of his brows and the line of his jaw. At the swell of muscle revealed by his open collar. He's so beautiful it makes my chest hurt.

"Like what?" I ask, blinking furiously, suddenly having trouble breathing. I accelerate my pace and focus my gaze ahead. I'm not ready for this conversation yet.

"Do you know how far it is?" I ask as he catches up to me, wanting to change the subject and really wishing we had a horse or something to ride. My head still feels woozy, and I should just let him carry me.

"I'm not exactly sure," he says, scanning the trees.

"It would seem 'family' is as loose a term as it's always been with the Woodlands King," I say. "Making your 'flesh and blood' walk behind you like a captive."

Nadir smirks. "Welcome home, I guess."

"Did I imagine how quickly we got here, though? I swear we were in the settlement, and then suddenly, we were here. Though it's entirely possible I passed out."

"No, you didn't. Etienne got us here." I give him a quizzical look. "It's his ability. He can shift people and himself from one place to another in the blink of an eye."

"Wow, that's pretty useful."

Nadir nods.

Etienne marches in the line ahead of him, his shoulders hunched and his eyes on his feet.

"He feels terrible," Nadir says, catching the direction of my stare. "I might have been a little . . . abrupt with him when you went missing."

"It was an accident, right?" I say before I look at him. "I know he's your friend, and I hate to ask this, but you're sure he's one hundred percent trustworthy?"

Nadir places a hand over his heart, his expression serious. "Absolutely. I would never ever have brought you to him otherwise."

I nod at that. "Okay. Then excuse me for a moment."

I rush forward, matching my steps to Etienne's long strides, until he finally looks up at me.

"Hi," I say. He doesn't reply, instead looking at his feet again as if trying to avoid tripping on an errant root. Or, more likely, avoiding me.

"I'm sorry," he mumbles after a moment, his gravelly voice even deeper than usual. "I fucked up royally."

"Mistakes happen," I reply. "I won't pretend that wasn't terrifying, but I don't blame you. I've been through much worse than that, and I got out alive. Okay?"

His dark gaze slides to me, and I see so much pain written in the depths of it. What is this man's story? "I don't deserve that. It was my job to make sure you were safe."

"And I appreciate that. More than you can possibly imagine. But that doesn't mean things always go the way we plan."

Etienne shakes his head and looks ahead as we continue our march through the forest.

"Nadir won't forgive me." He sounds so despondent that I almost want to wrap him in a hug. Something tells me he wouldn't appreciate the gesture.

"Well, you can ignore him," I say. "I'm the one in charge." I wink, and his expression softens, though I can tell he's still beating himself up about this.

"Really," I say. "I'm not blaming you for anything."

He grunts at that, and I guess that's the best I'm getting for now. I slow my pace to give him some space to process whatever he's going through.

Nadir catches up to me a second later. "Did that work?"

"Not at all," I say. "He thinks you're angry with him."

"Well, I am."

I give him a skeptical look, and he blows out a breath before running a hand through his hair. "We'll work it out. It's not the first time we've been pissed off at one another."

As we wind through the forest, something catches my eye.

"What is that?" I ask Nadir, pointing to a large black spot on the side of a tree, noticing more of them blooming in the branches.

"I suspect it's the same thing happening across Ouranos."

We look up, where many of the leaves carry the same taint. Even the air seems different. I take a deep breath, inhaling the clean forest scent of pine and soil, but it's mingled with a faint, cloying odor of decay. Our surrounding guards study the trees with grim scrutiny. They don't appear surprised, though, so this isn't new, only troubling.

"The mine collapse, those quakes we keep feeling, the depleting fish stocks, the other things we keep hearing about. There are too many events at once to be natural. Something similar happened when our magic disappeared, and I'm starting to wonder if it's all connected," Nadir says.

"Connected how?" I ask.

"I'm not sure yet. Maybe it's nothing."

I watch him for a moment, but it's clear from the concern on his face that he doesn't believe those words. I try to hold in my sigh. Not to be selfish, but the last thing we need is another wrench in our plans.

We continue walking, and I'm so tired now that my head spins. Just when I'm about to consider accepting Nadir's offer to carry me, I catch sight of the edge of the tree line. We emerge from the forest into a wide clearing where the biggest tree I've ever seen spreads into the sky. It's massive, practically a mountain. But then I note the windows and platforms suspended along its trunk and realize this enormous treehouse must be the Woodlands Fort.

I'm almost too tired to be impressed by the sight, and I start imagining a warm bath and a soft bed, hoping Cedar will allow us some time to rest before we "catch up."

"Welcome," Cedar says, having just dismounted from his horse. "You must be weary. We'll get you some rooms, and you can rest."

These are literally the best words I've ever heard in my life.

We enter the Fort through a set of tall gold doors into a grand hall with a curving ceiling braced with golden arches and a shiny green floor so smooth it looks like glass.

A female Fae, wearing brown leathers, approaches from down the hall, and at the sight of us, she breaks into a run. The queen of The Woodlands is as lovely as I remember from the Sun Queen Ball, with her long chestnut hair and bright green eyes along with a pair of those impressive wings. She leaps into Cedar's arms, and he spins her around as they smother each other in sloppy kisses. How long has he been away? If he came to find us this morning, it couldn't have been more than a few hours.

Watching them openly express their affection makes me seek out Nadir. When I find him, he's already looking at me, and our gazes hold for a tense beat before I look away.

"It's so nice to meet you finally!" says the queen. I remember her name is Elswyth. She takes my hands in hers and clasps them firmly. "I thought we'd never get the chance."

I frown at her words. They're all acting like they cared that we disappeared, and didn't leave us to rot at the hands of the Aurora King for half our lives.

"Okay," I say, not really sure how to respond, but she isn't deterred by my less-than-enthusiastic response. She's now hugging Tristan, her arms cinched around him so tightly that it's almost a little awkward. He's obviously as guarded as I am. We look at each other and shrug.

"We have rooms ready for you. And baths," Elswyth says, her gaze lingering on the blood coating both Tristan and Nadir. "Seems like you've been through something on your way here. Come with me."

She keeps up a string of chatter, describing the architecture of the Fort and explaining about the Winter Ball tomorrow, to which we're all invited. Great, another party. I think I already got my fill when we were in The Aurora.

Finally, she stops before a door and gestures me inside while the other four are taken to rooms along the same hall. My guest room is paneled with varying shades of polished wood, and the floor is made of planks of honey-colored beams covered with thick green rugs. I sigh out loud at the sight of a large wooden bed layered with emerald-green pillows and sheets.

"There's a warm bath for you if you'd like," Elswyth says. "I'll have some food sent up as well."

She stands with her hands clasped at her waist, giving me a bright smile. I move to the window that overlooks miles and miles of green forest sprawling in every direction.

"Great. Thank you."

"It's a miracle to have you here. I never thought we'd see you again," she says, repeating her earlier words, then dips her head. "I'll let you get settled."

Then she's gone. I take a turn about the room, checking the drawers and closet, finding a pair of thick green leggings and a tunic made of soft, stretchy fabric. I take them into the bathroom and then strip down to clean myself off. When I'm done, I find a platter of food on a low table near the window.

I nibble on the bread, but my exhaustion outweighs my hunger.

Instead, I climb under the sheets, savoring their cool crispness and sighing again before I drift into a dreamless sleep.

Chapter Twenty-Three

When I awake, the sun hangs low in the sky, and it seems I've slept away most of the day. Lying on my back, I stretch out, testing the aches and twinges of my encounter with the Aurora King's goons.

The hollow pit in my stomach rumbles, and I make my way towards the food left for me earlier. Someone has brought in a fresh platter of bread, cheese, and slices of cured meat. The jug of water is still filled with ice, suggesting someone was in here not long ago.

I try not to let that thought bother me. I was exhausted and slept like the dead. The healer had said the poison might linger in my system for a few days, making me more tired than usual.

As I'm nibbling on a wedge of soft white cheese, a quiet knock raps on the door.

"Come in," I say, and it swings open to reveal Elswyth.

She's changed from the leathers she was wearing earlier into a soft green gown the color of moss that sweeps to the floor. Her long hair hangs in thick ringlets so glossy and smooth, they might be made of marble.

"You're awake!" she says brightly. "How are you feeling?"

"I'm okay. Thank you."

"Wonderful. I'm not sure if you're hungry for a big meal, but I've arranged for a quiet dinner with me, the king, your brother, and of course, the prince and his companions. I hope you'll consider joining us?"

"Of course," I say.

Now that I've rested, I am ready for answers from Cedar.

"It's up to you, but I can loan you a dress to wear. Or if you're more comfortable like that, it's fine too. Tonight is casual, though you'll want something a little more festive for the ball tomorrow."

"I'm good like this right now."

She smiles. "Great, then let's go."

I find a pair of green slippers and slide them on before following Elswyth through the Fort.

"Where are the others?" I ask.

"They're already with Cedar."

She leads us through a clear glass doorway into an outdoor courtyard lined with flowers and greenery. A lit stone path winds us into a garden lined with hedges and hanging lanterns. In the middle is a round wooden table, and sure enough, Nadir and my brother are seated with the Woodlands King along with Mael and Etienne. Everyone stands as we enter.

Nadir pulls out the chair next to him, and I move to take it while Elswyth settles next to her bonded partner. The two of them kiss like no one else is in the room for a moment, and I wonder if these two are mates as well. Is this what it's like when you stop fighting it? My gaze slides to Nadir, who's watching the king and queen before his attention flicks to me, and my stomach freefalls.

Finally, Cedar pulls away from Elswyth and addresses me. I'm curiously impressed they aren't at all embarrassed by their unrestrained show of affection. What would that be like? I've spent so many years pretending not to feel anything someone could use against me.

"Lor, it's so nice to see you after so many years. You've grown so much since you were as high as my knee," he says.

"Did we meet when I was a child?"

He gives me a patient smile that feels incongruent with his rather blunt demeanor earlier in the forest.

"You probably don't remember. You were only a small girl the last time I came to visit your family in the woods."

"I don't remember," I say, looking at Tristan. The look on his face suggests he doesn't recall these visits either.

"Why did you come only when we were small?" Tristan asks, clearly thinking along the same lines.

Cedar presses his lips into a thin line. "Your parents asked me to stop."

I wasn't expecting that. "Why?"

"They worried it was dangerous and would draw too much attention to your location. I suppose they were probably right, though it pained me never to see you. My brother wouldn't have wanted it that way."

Is he telling the truth? I exchange another glance with Tristan.

"Where have you been all this time?" Elswyth asks. "When we felt you cross the border of The Woodlands, we came immediately to find out why." She pauses, her face paling as though the memory haunts her. "When we saw the destruction left behind, we feared the worst."

"You didn't know what happened?" I ask.

"No," Cedar says. "We tried for years to find out. Based on the state of the cottage, we had to assume someone had taken you, but there was no sign or trace of who. We thought you must all be dead."

"So you didn't tell him about us," I say, frustration and relief curdling in my stomach. If it wasn't Cedar, then *who* was it?

"I would never have told anyone. I swear it," he says solemnly, and despite everything, I believe him. "Tell who?"

Now I exchange a glance with Nadir, who nods his assent.

"The Aurora King," I say, my voice wooden. No matter how many years pass, those words will always catch in my throat like choking down the thorny stem of a rose.

Cedar lets out a whoosh of air, sitting back in his chair as he runs a hand over the top of his head, fitting the various pieces together.

"So he wanted to use you or keep you contained?"

I nod. "Very much."

"Which is it?"

"I'm not completely sure, but all signs point to using me for something."

The king and queen consider that for a moment, their expressions puzzled.

"Is that why you're in your human form?" Cedar looks me up and down.

"You know about that?" Tristan asks, and Cedar nods.

"Yes. Your mother showed me once to prove you were all safe without us checking in on you."

"It's partly why I am," I say, not interested in divulging the truth about my trapped magic until I'm sure we can trust them.

"But that was years ago. Where have you been all this time?" Elswyth asks, her voice soft with concern. "What happened to you?"

I hate this story. I hate having to relive it over and over, like pouring salt and lemon over an open scab. A well of tears burns my eyes. I used to be a master at holding them back and pretending they didn't exist.

Tristan rescues me from having to shoulder this burden and describes our years in Nostraza. As he speaks, I feel the pain and the heartache of those days knife into my chest like it happened only yesterday. I keep trying to shove it down. Pretend none of it existed, but I know that's impossible. Eventually, I must confront all the ugly truths I've been avoiding. Eventually, I must look in the mirror and decide if those years will finally break me or make me.

After Tristan finishes, we all fall silent.

"I'm so sorry," Cedar says. "I wish I had known."

"What would you have done?" Tristan asks with a thread of accusation in his voice.

"Everything I could," Cedar replies with conviction, and I want to believe that's true. He seems genuine, but I know how gifted Imperial Fae are at lying to suit their own ends.

"What about the rest of you? Where is your sister?" Elswyth asks. "There were three children, weren't there?"

"She's somewhere else right now," I say. "But she's fine. Or as fine as she can be, all things considered."

"That's good." The queen nods. "I can't help but feel like we met somewhere before now," Elswyth says to me next.

"The Sun Queen Ball. You look just like one of the Tributes."

Of course, I didn't just attend that ball. I became the center of attention when Atlas lost his shit on Nadir.

"And you . . ." Elswyth points to Nadir. "Atlas threw you out and banished you. That was quite a stir."

"I actually thought you'd banish me too," Nadir admits, and Cedar snorts.

"Atlas can throw all the temper tantrums he wants. That doesn't mean I'm going to indulge them."

"I thought you were friends," I say. "That's what he told me."

Cedar shrugs. "He overestimates what he means to me."

Why doesn't that surprise me to hear?

"I still don't understand what you were doing there," Elswyth says, studying us both.

"Right. Well, some more things happened," I say.

Nadir lays a hand over mine. "Some more things that the king and queen aren't going to force you to share, because, quite frankly, you owe them nothing."

I notice the way Cedar's jaw clenches before he dips his chin. He could argue that he protected us while we lived in The Woodlands. That he did keep our secrets, but I also see what Nadir is getting at.

"Very well," Cedar says. "Perhaps I can earn your trust in time."

He takes a sip of his wine, slowly and deliberately, like he's gathering his thoughts. He places it back on the table with a clink and then peers at me.

"None of this explains why you ended up in The Woodlands *now*, though."

It's Nadir's turn to jump in.

"My father still is after her. I won't get into the details of how Lor and her siblings got out, but as we've already discussed, my father wants to use her."

"For what, though?" Cedar asks. "He can't bond to her."

I notice Nadir's hand tighten on the armrest of his chair like those words make him angry.

"No, he cannot. We know he wants her magic, but we don't know why yet."

Cedar seems to consider that.

"Well, that would be a useful thing to find out."

Nadir arches an eyebrow loaded with sarcasm. "Hence the reason we were in the settlements and how we ended up here when his soldiers got wind of our presence. One that I'm again hoping I don't have to ask you to keep a secret."

Cedar's eyes dance with something that almost feels like amusement.

"With all due respect, Nadir, I cannot stand your father and have no interest in helping him achieve anything. Nothing he's planning would be good for anyone but himself."

At that, Nadir cracks into a grin. "Then we're on the same page."

The corner of Cedar's mouth quirks up.

"What about your parents?" Elswyth asks then. "Where are they?"

"They died when the king's men came for us."

"Oh, I'm so sorry," she says. "I just assumed they were with you."

"You didn't find their bodies?" Tristan asks, his tone sharp. "When you came to the cottage?"

"No. There was no one left when we arrived."

She says the words softly, as though they might hurt. And they do, scraping a fresh wound scored into the inside of my chest. I shudder to think what the king might have done with them.

Everyone at the table falls silent, the mood somber. No one has really touched their food.

Eventually, Cedar speaks, his expression grave. "I'm so very sorry for everything you've gone through, Lor and Tristan. If there's anything I can do to help you, then say the word. No matter what happens, you have an ally in The Woodlands. My brother loved your grandmother more than life itself, and he would've wanted to honor their union. I have no doubt our realms would have worked as one had they . . . survived."

He doesn't voice the subtext of what he's saying, but I understand his words for the declaration they are. If this comes to a war, then he will be on my side. I don't think he's lying. He seems like a man of his word, and while I don't understand much about the maneuverings of kings and queens yet, I understand there's a significance in drawing that line here among a group of witnesses.

"I appreciate that," I say, my throat tightening with the briny taste of the past.

"I know nothing will ever make up for everything you've lost, but we want to do whatever we can," Elswyth adds, nothing but genuine concern in her voice.

These two. Seeing how they are makes me wish that I could have known my grandfather more than anything.

"Thank you," Tristan says, voicing the words I'm having trouble articulating.

We move on from our grim history, finishing our suppers as we converse about lighter topics, namely the coming of winter and the ball to celebrate its advent tomorrow night. The more Elswyth talks about it, the more I find myself swept up in her enthusiasm.

"I know you need to get back," she says. "But please just stay for the party. It would be such an honor to have you there."

"Who will you say they are?" Nadir asks, gesturing to my brother and me.

"Distant family," Elswyth says. "It's not a lie. Is it?"

"No, I suppose not."

"But I think you should remain incognito," she tells Nadir. "Another relative, perhaps? Other than the nobles, few have reason to recognize who you are, and they can be swayed into silence. Our people are loyal."

My mouth stretches into a yawn. While I slept most of the day, I'm still feeling the effects of the previous night.

"And with that, I think you should all get some rest tonight," Elswyth says. "I promise you'll dance until the wee hours tomorrow!"

She lifts her glass, and we all do the same. As I stare across the table at the only other family we have left in the world, I feel lighter than I expected.

Maybe it's foolish, and maybe I'm putting too much stock into this interaction, desperate for the family we lost, but for the first time in a while, I feel a sense of hope burning in my chest.

CHAPTER TWENTY-FOUR

The Woodlands Fort buzzes with preparations for the Winter Ball. Despite my reservations, it's hard not to get swept up in the excitement. Shortly after lunch, Elswyth arrives with some clothing options for me to choose from.

"You're about the same size as me," she says, laying the outfits on the bed. "So something here should work."

She's brought two stunning green dresses, one accented with gold and the other with bronze, along with a pair of soft leather leggings that coordinate with an embroidered green leather vest worn with a fitted white shirt underneath.

"Why the pants?"

"Because it honors the hunt. Some prefer to wear a formal version of their hunting attire, though a dress is appropriate for the occasion too."

"I've never hunted anything," I say. Though Tristan and my father would catch game to feed us, I never had the chance to learn the skill myself.

Elswyth laughs. "That's hardly the point. It's tradition for everyone, whether they've ever shot an arrow or not. It's about the spirit of it."

Her eyes twinkle brightly.

"Well then, definitely the hunting clothes."

"Perfect. They'll look amazing on you."

She leaves me to dress, and I pull on the leggings, which slide like butter against my skin; the shirt; and the vest, which laces up the front with gold ribbons. She also leaves me a wide belt in a darker shade of green to wear around my hips and a pair of tall suede boots that come up to my knees. The ensemble is completed with an ornately jeweled dagger worn in a sheath around my thigh. I pull it out and test the razor-sharp edge.

I then curl my hair, tie it up at the back of my head, and finish off with some of the makeup the queen also left, including a sweep of green eyeshadow.

As I stare in the mirror, I consider the various threads of fate's hand leading me to this spot.

Maybe it was my mother's influence or the fact that it was lost, but I've always considered Heart to be my true home. The abandoned castle had always been her dream and her goal for us. Though she'd never lived there, *it* had lived in the essence of her thoughts.

But this place is a part of me too. My father and grandfather were both from The Woodlands. That blood flows in our veins, and Tristan bears its magic.

Could I forge the same alliance with The Woodlands intended by my grandparents?

I wonder who carries the title of their Primary and make a mental note to ask. Cedar and Elswyth have no heirs, so is it someone else?

A knock sounds at the door, and I walk over to find Tristan waiting on the other side. We haven't had a chance to discuss our conversation with the king and queen last night, but I'm sure he must be harboring many of the same questions.

"How are you?" he asks as I invite him in.

He looks so handsome in an outfit similar to mine, brown leggings and a green tunic with a brown leather vest, his dark hair hanging shaggy around his pointed ears. Like me, he's lost that gaunt edge of hunger, filling out into the man he was always meant to be.

"What did you think about everything they said last night?" he asks.

I sit across from where he's taken a seat, sliding my hands under my thighs. "I want to believe what they said about not knowing where we'd gone. They seemed genuinely remorseful."

Tristan nods. "I agree. They did, and I'd like to believe them too."

"But?"

"But we're right to always be on our guard. There's so much at stake here, and we don't really know who our allies are."

I nod at that, conceding he's right. I wish we lived in a world where we could trust the people around us. But maybe being of royal blood means that was never an option.

"What he said about supporting me," I say. "That felt like something one just doesn't say unless they really mean it."

"You're probably right. But still, we can't afford to go blindly into any of this."

"I know."

"Have you given any more thought to what Elswyth said about not finding our parents' bodies?" Tristan asks, peering at me through his thick, dark lashes. I can read everything on his face, but I can't let him wander down that perilous train of thought.

"Tris, no. If Mother were alive, I wouldn't be the Primary, right? They took them or buried them or did something else I can't even bear to think about," I say. "Don't do this to yourself. They're gone."

His jaw tics, and his gaze flicks to the window before it turns to me. I see the shine in his eyes, and I know how much he wants this. He remembers them better than either Willow or I do, but entertaining this hope will only lead to disappointment and even more heartbreak. I learned to live with their deaths once, and I don't think I can do it again.

"If they were alive, they would have come for us," I say with certainty. "Nothing would have stopped them."

"What if they couldn't?"

I shake my head. "They would have found a way."

Tristan's shoulders drop, and he lets out a whoosh of air. "I just thought..."

"I know. Trust me, I thought it too. But it's impossible."

I'm not as confident as I'm pretending to be, because I also want it to be true, but I won't let him do this to himself. We spent enough years conjuring up fantasies of vengeance and what our futures would be like with only Willow to keep us in check. Free from the walls of Nostraza, we have to focus on what's in front of us. We can't afford to lose ourselves inside daydreams that will only serve to distract us.

Tristan looks down at the floor and waits for a moment before sitting back up. He slaps his thighs and stands, trying to put on what I know is a brave face. "Then I guess we have a party to get to."

Still, his expression remains tight, the lines around his mouth and eyes tense, but he turns away before I can say anything else.

I get up to follow him, and we head through the Fort, directed by various palace servants. There are low fae everywhere I look, some working in positions of service, but many are also dressed for the party. I spy a pair of delicate-looking nymphs wearing green velvet dresses with golden antlers sprouting from their heads.

We enter a massive hall graced by a curved wooden ceiling that rises high over our heads with gold ribs running across its length. The walls and the floor are all made of various shades of wood inlaid with green enamel carved into leaves. Above us, hundreds of tiny golden lights zip about the room, and it takes me a moment to realize they're actually lightning bugs. They bounce around, racing past the guests before they zoom away. The sight is beyond captivating.

A long table bisecting the room is covered with food,

including a giant chocolate fountain and several ice sculptures shaved into various animal shapes—a deer, a bear, and an owl.

The wine flows and guests circulate around the food before they settle at rows of tables arranged along the walls.

We pass through the crowd, marveling at everything. When my gaze meets Tristan's, we both share a moment of disbelief. It's so hard to comprehend that a few months ago, we were both living deep in the bowels of a hellhole, and now we're here, surrounded by music and laughter.

I wonder how long this feeling of living on the edge of nothing will persist. When will this feel solid and not like an illusion about to be pulled out from under us?

The far end of the hall opens into a wide space where couples dance, spinning in circles to the strains of an entire orchestra outfitted in green and bronze. Beyond that is a long dais where the king and queen sit. Nadir, Etienne, and Mael are already at the front.

Nadir lounges next to Cedar, one leg casually slung over the other, chatting with the king. He looks up as I approach, his gaze sweeping over me in a way that makes my knees weak.

Suddenly, I want nothing more than to be alone with him as pressure expands in my chest. The words perch on my tongue, waiting to release and set off what I'm sure will be a chain reaction that marks a permanent alteration in the course of our lives.

My magic surges under my skin, battering me to the point of bruising. It refuses to stay away from him for much longer.

His head tilts, his expression probing, and I realize that I've been staring again. How long have I been standing here? By the skeptical look Tristan is giving me, it's been way too long not to be weird.

"You all right?" he asks, and I nod.

Sure. Not really.

Throwing my shoulders back, I approach the dais and bend at the waist in greeting to the king and queen. They stand and return my bow.

My gaze returns to Nadir, who's wearing his usual black, though it's obviously not the same blood-covered clothing he arrived in.

"How on earth did you manage to find the only black clothing in the entire kingdom?" I ask, and he smirks.

"I have so many secrets, Lor."

I roll my eyes as Cedar and Elswyth both embrace me warmly. It's so . . . cozy.

I really want to trust that these Imperial Fae have our best interests at heart. They're our family. They know our secrets and say they'll keep them. I'm going to need all the allies I can find. Even if this weren't about seizing my crown, I want a family. I want the comfort and safety of people who love us.

More importantly, I want that for Tristan and Willow.

A server approaches with a silver tray balanced on her hand and offers us all a drink. I pick up a small crystal glass filled with pale lilac liquid.

"The best Noma Violetta we have in our cellar," Cedar says, proudly gesturing to my cup. "It packs a punch, though."

I smile and take a sip that is both sweet and bitter and melts pleasantly through my limbs. I roll my shoulders, enjoying the sensation and deciding that I'm going to dance a lot tonight.

The current song comes to an end, the final notes echoing in the room as every eye turns to the front. Cedar and Elswyth stand with their hands clasped. They raise their free arms and then bow to the watching crowd.

"Welcome!" Cedar says, his deep voice booming through the hall. "As winter comes upon us again, let us all gather to celebrate the changing of the season. Our stores are full, and there is food to last us through the season. So please, drink up, have fun, and enjoy tonight!"

A chorus of cheers circulates through the crowd, and then Cedar and Elswyth sweep forward on smooth steps to the center of the dance floor. The music starts up again as they begin twirling before dozens more couples join them.

Over the next hour, I lose myself in the exuberance and the careless ease of people without too much on their minds. I've tried one of everything on the massive food table—it all tastes even better than it looks. Venison tartare with a raspberry reduction. Wild boar rosemary pâté. Forest mushroom toasts spread with goat cheese and honey.

I make another mental note to travel across Ouranos solely to taste the foods in every region. I wonder what delicacies they eat in the star queendom of Celestria. Moonbeam pie, perhaps?

Eventually, I find myself seated next to Elswyth as we watch the dancers swirling around the room.

"Are you having fun?" she asks.

"I am."

"I'm so glad you could stay for tonight."

I smile, my gaze circulating through the crowd, finding Nadir on the far side of the room. He's talking with Mael and a male Woodlands Fae.

I study him, appreciating every line of his shoulders and arms. The way his biceps swell against the black fabric. The narrow taper of his waist and the curve of his strong thighs. His face is my favorite, though. Those burning eyes that hide nothing from me. The way that eyebrow arches in a way that pisses me off but also makes me want to fall to my knees. That mouth capable of such biting wit and the filthy words that keep me awake and restless at night.

He's my challenge and my summit, and I am being tested in the deepest possible way.

The man whose father killed my parents is my fated mate, destined by Zerra. Who has apparently been made for me. That's no surprise, though. I think I knew that from the moment I threw my champagne at him.

I have only two choices before me now.

"Lor?"

I turn to the sound of my name, finding Elswyth watching me, a knowing smile on her face.

Gods. I was staring at him again.

"Yes?" I ask.

"I was wondering if you wanted more wine?"

I look down at my empty glass. Yes. I'll take the whole bottle.

"Sure." I get up to join her, refilling our glasses before we toast. We chat for a few more minutes before she excuses herself to tend to her queenly duties.

After she leaves, I consider going for another round at the food table just as my gaze tapers to a knife-sharp point.

Nadir is no longer with Mael. He's now talking to a gorgeous High Fae female with luscious curling brown hair wearing an outfit similar to mine. They're both leaning against the wall, standing far too close for my liking. Is he fucking flirting again?

I consider creating a distraction to break them apart. Maybe I'll light the tablecloth on fire or shove someone into the chocolate fountain. Cedar and Elswyth have been lovely, though, and don't deserve to have their party ruined because the Aurora Prince can't keep his dick in his pants.

Inexplicably, Nadir is also wearing a soft blue scarf over his shoulders, and I have no idea where *that* came from. The woman reaches out to touch his arm, her fingers wrapping around his firm biceps as she laughs, and that's when my vision turns crimson.

My fingers dig into my palms as I physically restrain myself from walking over and tearing off her arm.

He's not mine.

Fuck that. He *is* mine.

A few weeks ago, I said I didn't want to belong to anyone. I hated him and his father and everything they represented. But I know that isn't true anymore. The father, yes, but my feelings for the son are so much more layered than that.

But all I've done is push him away. Have I broken everything that might have come between us? Am I too late?

I wonder what that growling sound is and then realize it's me. I spin around to avoid facing them and take a deep breath that does nothing to settle the thrumming pulse of my current self-loathing.

An elf passes by, holding a basket over her arm filled with soft blue scarves like the one Nadir is wearing. She waves one about as an offering. A High Fae female with red hair and a long green dress snatches it from her and then drapes it over her shoulders with a giggle before she scurries off.

"What are those?" I ask the elf. She has pale green skin and soft pink hair to go with her large, pointed ears.

She smiles and pulls another one from her basket. "It's a Winter's Kiss scarf." There's a coy look on her face that suggests it's more than just a fashion accessory. I rub the fabric between my fingers. It's made of incredibly fine wool and might be the softest thing I've ever felt.

"What does it mean?"

She leans in closer with a sparkle in her eyes. "Eligible women take one and place it over the shoulders of someone they'd like a kiss from."

She grins and then winks.

Well, that sounds a little archaic and more than a little sexist, but given how many blue scarves I now notice draped over various shoulders, it's obviously a popular tradition.

When I catch sight of Nadir from the corner of my eye, wearing a fucking Winter's Kiss scarf, my rage twists into a pellet hard enough to crack a rib. Who gave that to him? I can only presume it's the woman who is *still* touching him.

Fine, two of us can play this game, and I have never ever backed down from a challenge.

"Can I have this?" I ask, and she nods.

"Of course. Enjoy." Then she gives me an airy wave and saunters off. I drape the scarf over my shoulders and search for a target. Someone devastatingly hot and sexy and really fucking tall. With good hair and a nice firm ass.

Nadir is still talking to the same woman, his gaze focused on her, and I grind my teeth so hard I swear the enamel begins to shear away.

I circle the large table, and thankfully, it doesn't take long before a very handsome and *very* tall High Fae male intercepts me.

"Hi there," he says, eyeing my scarf and then me. "I'm Declan. Who might you be?"

I flash him my most beaming smile, hoping I don't look like a lunatic. I can't say I have much experience flirting, but I've always managed well enough. Of course, most of the men I've tried to woo were confined to prison and didn't have too many options, but I try not to let that bother me.

He really is very nice to look at, with dark blond hair and bright green eyes that sparkle in the candlelight.

"I'm Lor," I say. "It's nice to meet you."

"I haven't seen you in the Fort before. Where did you come from?"

"Oh, I'm a very distant relation to the royal family. Just passing through, and Cedar insisted we stay for the night."

He grins and then leans down. "You're not secretly a princess, are you?"

My answering laugh is a little awkward, but I don't think he notices. I can tell he's teasing me, but he has no idea how close to the truth he is.

"Hmm, perhaps you'll find out if you're good."

His eyes glitter at that, his gaze again falling on the scarf for the briefest moment, and this is kind of fun. Maybe I'm not so bad at this.

Everything in me resists the urge to look at Nadir, but I can't help myself, and allow my gaze to wander for a fraction of a second before I pull it back. A swell of triumph sticks in my throat when I find him glaring at me, his eyes burning like the very fires of hell.

I immediately turn away and look up at Declan, stepping closer and placing a hand in the center of his chest. It's firm and sculpted, and I could do a lot worse.

"Would you like to dance?" I ask, and he nods.

"Absolutely."

He leads me to the dance floor and twirls me around. I don't really know what I'm doing, but he manages to make it feel like I'm keeping up. I try not to look at Nadir whenever we spin around the room. I attempt to shut Nadir out because I'm actually having fun.

After a few breathless reels, Declan leads me to the edge of the dance floor.

"Can I get you a drink?" he asks and then leads me to a table that puts me in direct line of sight with Nadir, who is now sitting on the other side of the room. His "friend" is leaning into him and laughing, and how long does he plan to talk to her? What could she possibly be saying that is so fucking interesting?

His gaze meets mine, and I know I'm winning. I'm just not sure what I've won yet. It's a wonder every single person in the room isn't suffocating under our seething animosity, which expands to fill every corner.

Declan returns with the promised glass of wine. He hands it to me before he pulls out a chair and sits. I cast another quick glance at Nadir and decide I'm raising the stakes so high they'll become a black dot disappearing into the sky.

I place my glass on the table and then slide onto Declan's lap before wrapping my scarf around the back of his neck and leaning in. He smells nice, like the forest and other green, earthy things. I feel bad. I shouldn't be using him like this. Maybe I should stop right now before I hurt his feelings.

Shit, I'm a terrible person. I've let myself get carried away.

Declan grins at me, and I'm about to call this whole thing off and apologize for my behavior. I'll blame the wine or something. It went to my head, and I'm not used to its potency. I'm from some backwater village, and I don't know how to behave in proper society. Hopefully, he won't become angry when he finds out he's getting nowhere with me tonight.

But that's when an ominous shadow looms over us like a fallen angel spreading his wings to block out the sun. Nadir's dark eyes flash with violet and emerald, his irises simmering with bottomless rage. Declan and I go completely still, and I can't decide if I'm afraid right now or if I'm feeling something else.

Something that is entirely inappropriate, making an ache bloom below my navel.

Should this be turning me on? Probably not.

Fuck, this is definitely turning me on.

"Get your hands off her," Nadir says with such bone-shivering menace that Declan sits back and slowly lifts both hands off me, holding them up in surrender. Nadir then leans over, whips off the scarf hanging around Declan's shoulders, and tosses it to the ground.

I'm too shocked to move. How dare he be angry? He's the one who's been flirting with everything that moves since we left Aphelion. The rational side of my brain has taken a long walk off a short cliff.

Before I can say or do anything else, Nadir bends down and picks me up, hauling me over his shoulder as he spins around and storms out of the room.

Chapter Twenty-Five

Nadir

My blood bakes under my skin as I storm through the Fort like a fucking hurricane. Lor kicks and flails where I have her caged against my shoulder.

"Put me down!" she screams, her fists pounding into my back. "Nadir!"

I laugh, but there is nothing warm about it. It's a steel knife digging into my sternum. Twisting, twisting deep. When I saw her sitting on the lap of that asshole, I lost it. I can't fucking *do* this anymore. We're going to have this out now if it kills both of us. I'm ready to flame out like a star across the sky, rendering me into nothing but smoking ash.

"I swear to you!" she threatens, but there's nothing left she can do.

She's ripped out my heart and stomped all over it until it's nothing but an anemic lump of desiccated flesh. I fling open the door to her room and walk to the bed, lifting her off my shoulder and dropping her with an unceremonious heave. She tries to scramble away, but I'm on her before she can sidle from my reach.

My body flattens hers to the mattress, and I grab her wrists, pinning them over her head. She's fighting me like a wildcat, and fuck, my dick is already hard.

My magic flares, an aura of color leaking out to surround me in soft light, bathing the planes of her face in a blue, green, violet glow.

"Nadir," she hisses, attempting to free her wrists, but she's helpless underneath me. "Get off me!"

"Not until you talk to me," I hiss back, pinning her with a glare. She shoots daggers with her violent gaze. She's so fucking beautiful like this. For the past few weeks, she's been so quiet, so subdued. Only a shadow of the woman I know she is. I want this fiery Lor, and I'll do anything it takes to get her back.

"Talk about what?"

"Who was that asshole you were with?"

Her grin turns wicked, her eyes morphing into diamonds that could slice through glass. "None of your business."

Oh no. I don't think so.

My weight settles against her as I feel *everything*. The softness of her breasts and her thighs and the way she has her legs wrapped around me. I want to fuck her so badly that the seams of my equilibrium are pulling apart, stretching to their very limits. I'm being dismantled piece by piece through the exquisite depth of my need.

"You're one to talk!" she screams, bucking at me again. "How many women can you flirt with in the space of two days, Prince of The Aurora?"

Flirting? What on earth is she talking about? Then it occurs to me. She thought a couple of harmless conversations was me *flirting*? She really doesn't get it.

But I'm not above using this to my advantage.

It's my turn to give her a wicked grin. "Jealous?"

"Absolutely not. How dare you rip me away from my . . . friend when you're out there rubbing yourself against anything that moves!" She screams so loudly her voice cracks, and the sound is the sweetest, most vindicating music to my ears. She *does* care.

"What difference does it make to you?" I snarl. "You've retreated into yourself and won't talk to me. But you keep looking at me like . . . like . . . Gods, I can't figure out what that look is!"

"Get. Off. Me." Her gaze burns with heat forged in the deepest fires of the Underworld. "I won't talk until you get off me."

"Fine," I say, loosening her wrists and then backing off. She sits up and then stands, smoothing down her tunic and her hair like she's a rabid dog about to meet the queen for tea.

"How dare you pick me up like I'm a sack of fruit and then toss me on the bed?" she shouts before she attempts to brush past me.

"You said you'd talk to me," I say, grabbing her.

In a flash, she has the dagger strapped around her leg

clutched in her hand. She points it at me, and I back up until I hit the bedpost, the sharp tip pressing into my throat.

"I lied," she hisses, pressing the dagger in more firmly, her breath heavy and her teeth bared. If she thinks *any* of this is deterring me, then she's about to be surprised. I literally couldn't be more turned on right now. "You have no right to tell me who I can talk to."

"I know," I say through clenched teeth.

"Do you?" she challenges. "Because you're acting like you do."

"Lor!" I grab her wrist and pin it against my chest, the dagger still clutched in her fist. "You're my fucking mate, and you are *mine*."

The words slip out and vibrate in the air, hanging between us. Forever said and never to be undone. I didn't mean to just blurt it out like that, but she's making me so crazy that I'm not thinking straight.

"I know that!" she yells as she wrenches her arm from my surprised hold and walks away. That's just about the last thing I expected her to say.

"You do?"

"Yes!" She presses a fist to her heart as though she can't draw enough air and then gives me a suspicious look, her gaze narrowed. "Wait. You knew?"

"Yes, of course I knew."

"How long have you known this?"

I shake my head. "I think I've always known, but I knew for sure after that night in the Heart Castle."

She approaches, placing her hand in the center of my chest.

My knees hit the back of a chair at the foot of the bed, and I collapse into it. She lands on top of me, straddling my hips, holding the edge of her blade under my chin.

"And you didn't tell me?" she hisses. With her cheeks flushed and her hair wild, I don't think I've ever seen anything more beautiful in my entire life. I'm trying to focus on her anger and her words, but I'm distracted by this *need* that throbs in my chest.

Not just physically, but the need for her to *see* me as I am, hands out, without armor, bleeding heart on the fucking table.

"You'd just told me you wanted me to never touch you again. What was I supposed to do?" I snap, grabbing her forearm as the blade digs deeper.

Her nostrils flare, and she breathes a long sigh before she pushes off me and walks towards the window, placing her hands on the ledge and dropping her head against it.

"When did *you* find out? Why didn't you say something?" I accuse, coming up behind her.

She whirls around.

"Rhiannon. She was talking about my grandparents and what she knew about mates, and then it all clicked! You're my mate! It was the only thing that made sense!"

"Okay! Why are you yelling about this?"

"I don't know!" She throws up her hands. "I don't know what to do with this!"

She's on the verge of tears, but I don't understand what they mean. Does she hate the idea of being mated to me so much? I know I'm the reminder of so many things she's lost, and I can never take away what my father did to her, but I am not him. I will do everything I can to protect her and prove that.

As she's about to turn away again, emotion tears from the center of my chest because I can't hold any of this in anymore. I *need* her to understand.

"Lor! When are you going to get it through your head that I am totally, completely fucking in love with you!"

She attempts to retreat, but I take another step until she's backed against the window. "You're all I think about. I've never felt like this about anyone, and I'd do anything for you. You've become my air and my blood and my only reason to exist. I love you, Lor. I love you so much it makes my heart feel ready to burst."

The rage in her eyes dims and turns into something else I'm not sure how to read. It's that same look she keeps giving me. Confusion and wariness and some third emotion that almost tastes like forever.

"You do?"

I place my hands on the window on either side of her. "Yes. Gods, Lor. How can you not see it?"

Tears pool in her eyes as she opens her mouth and then closes it. The tension in the air is so thick it feels like it might grow wings and fly out of the room. She stares up at me with her lips parted, and I read a million things in her eyes.

I see the hurt and the loss and the rage that she carries so close to her heart. But I also see the hope and the joy and bravery of her spirit. I see all the things she wants and how hard I'm going to try to give her every bit of it. What I see is almost too much, because even if she can't say the words, I'm sure at least part of her feels the same.

We're clashing hordes and falling stars. We've been existing on the ledges of two opposite cliffs, so close to touching, and either we grab hold now or plummet into nothing.

And then we're both moving.

Her mouth crashes into mine, and there is only heat and teeth and the frantic grab of our hands. This is bone breaking, lung crushing, and it consumes me.

I frame her face with my hands and kiss her like I'm drowning. Like I've forgotten how to breathe. My tongue plunges into her mouth, and she moans. The sound vibrates through every cell, ending at my already rock-hard cock.

We kiss as the room spins and the world melts away. There is nothing but this moment and her. Her. Lor. All she's done is fight me every step of the way, but I don't care. She's the summit of an unscalable peak. A distant, unreachable planet in the heavens.

I will fight back until the end if that's what it takes.

She tears at my shirt, fumbling with the buttons with her shaking hands. I pull them away and rip it open, the ping of buttons hitting the floor. She shoves the fabric over my shoulders, and then I press myself against her as her hands claw at my back, trying to get closer. I want her to mark me. Draw blood and leave scars staking her claim.

I don't even know what I'm doing as I fumble with the laces on her vest. I can't seem to make my hands work right. "Argh." I let out a sound of frustration and then reach for the dagger in her hand, finding it empty.

"Where is it?" I demand.

She grabs it from the window ledge where she left it and

holds it up. We both pause as our eyes meet. A moment ago, she wanted to slice me open, and now? Now her gaze simmers with that fire that drew me to her from the moment we met. It wouldn't have mattered whether she was my mate; I would have gone to the ends of the world for her even if we never exchanged a single word.

My hand closes around hers as I take the dagger, then slowly hook it under the first set of laces. The sharp edge slices clean through as she gasps. With my gaze on her, I move to the next as her chest moves up and down. I'm torturing myself, but part of me wants this moment to last forever.

We're on the edge of whatever comes next, and I want to remember her like this for the rest of my life.

We both watch the progress of my slow, deliberate movements as I slice through another set of ribbons.

"Nadir," she whispers, and the sound is so pained that my dick throbs. She wants this as much as I do.

"What, Lor?"

"You're fucking killing me right now," she says, and I smile.

"Good," I say before I finally slice through the last two ribbons, and we blow out twin gasps of strangled breath. My hand cups the side of her face as I press myself against her, and she looks up at me with that raw mixture of strength and vulnerability in her eyes. Then I kiss her as she melts against me. I take my time, luxuriating in the sensations consuming me, feeling every inch of her mouth and her tongue. Every whisper of her breath as I inhale her scent—that curious mingle of roses, rainstorms, and the crack of lightning that feels exactly like home.

But the moment stretches too thin, and we both snap, once again clawing at one another. I pick her up, folding her legs around my waist as I carry her back to the bed. I don't drop her any less gently than last time, but she doesn't seem to care. After dragging her closer by her ankle, I grab her shirt collar and rip it down the front.

"This time, I know you have more clothing with you," I snarl, referring to our night in the Heart Castle, and she nods before I capture her mouth with mine. Her hands fist into the strands of my hair, and she pulls me down hard enough to make my roots ache. I could lie here kissing her forever, but I'll also die if I don't get inside of her soon.

She palms my cock through my pants, and I nearly fold like I've been kicked in the chest. But I force myself to pull away. She looks up at me with that open gaze. The same one I saw that first time in Aphelion when I was already falling.

"What?" she asks.

"I just... I don't think I can do this again if you're not all in. It almost killed me last time, and I need to be honest with you because I've just told you how I feel and . . ." I break off, not sure how to finish. I've never been this vulnerable with anyone in my life, but with her, it feels right. It feels necessary. I can't hold anything back.

She sits up, smoothing down the sides of her hair like she intends to take this seriously.

"I freaked out that night. I've belonged to men trying to use me for half of my life, and hearing you say those words triggered every dark memory I've tried to suppress.

"When I realized Atlas had lied to me about so much, my

trust was broken. Not just in him but in everything. I'm trying to fix these pieces of myself with nothing but fraying threads."

I try to correct her. There's nothing to fix. That wasn't how I meant it, but she holds up a hand.

"I know that was never what you meant, Nadir. It just took me a while to come to understand that. I know you've never wanted to cage me. You've become not just my rock, but my soft landing too. All you've ever done is give me room to spread my wings."

She stares at me, and some feeble hope flutters in my chest. Is she saying what I think?

"I'm sorry," she whispers, sitting up on her knees and cupping my cheek with her hand. "I got scared that night, but I've regretted that moment so many times since it happened. I was worried that I—"

She looks away, but I direct her face back to me. "What?"

"That I ruined it. That this was over. When I saw you talking to that woman, I thought . . ."

"Lor," I growl, clamping a hand to her lower back and dragging her closer. "I told you that I didn't want anyone else. I meant it then, and I mean it now. Yesterday, when you thanked me for rescuing you, what I really wanted to say was that I would have torn apart the entire fucking world to find you, and how could you *ever* think that I wouldn't come for you?"

That's it. I'm laying it all out now. No more hiding my feelings. No more giving her room to run from hers. If she doesn't want this, then I'll find somewhere to sink into the dust forever until I pass out of memory.

But she's right there. I can feel it.

Her eyes fill with tears.

"I knew that," she whispers. "I think I knew that."

"Good," I say, and then we're kissing again. It's tender at first, but a storm has been brewing, and we cave to the pressure that threatens to suffocate us both. The kiss deepens, and then I can't seem to get her clothes off fast enough.

Now I know why she's always felt so familiar—she was destined for me from the very beginning.

I tug down her boots and then her leggings, and then I push her back so I can slide them off, trying not to tear every stitch, but really, who cares?

She's so beautiful and perfect, just like the first time I saw her. I can't believe she's mine. I hope she's mine this time. I'm sure this is what Zerra intended for us. How could anything else feel so right?

I stand up and pull her with me, just so I can take her all in. I'm torn between which I need more—my tongue or my cock inside her—but so help me, before we're done, I'm going to do both many times over. She tugs at the button on my pants and then slides her hand in, palming my cock, which feels like it's about to explode.

"Oh fuck," I moan as my head tips against hers. "You have no idea how much I want you, Lor."

"I want you, too," she says as she arches her head and sucks my neck, her hand tightening around me, pumping me with slow, firm strokes. My moan vibrates through every cell of my body, my orgasm already cresting, but I don't want to let go. I'm not even close to done with her yet.

She tugs at my waistband with her free hand, and I help her out, stepping back before I shove my pants down, stripping down to nothing. For several breaths, we just watch one another. I file every piece of her into my memory. The dusting of freckles on the swells of her breasts. The softness of her thighs. The mole on her left ribcage. The birthmark on her hip and the brand from Nostraza charred into her shoulder.

Her eyes drag over me, from my face and over my chest and down to my stomach, resting on my painfully erect cock.

She looks up slowly and then licks her lips, and I remember vividly what it was like to have her mouth wrapped around it. That was still the single hottest moment of my life. Tonight I have every intention of leaving that day in the dust.

But I'm trying hard not to take over. Though every primal instinct roaring through my veins wants to throw her down and claim her, I don't want to scare her again. I want her to feel like this is her choice and take exactly what she needs.

When she presses herself against me, my entire body shivers at the contact, every muscle tightening and melting at the same time. Her mouth hits the curve of my collarbone, her lips searing into my skin. Slowly, she trails them higher, up the column of my neck, stretching onto her toes, and I tip my head down until our mouths are an inch apart.

We hover there, breathing in each other's space, and this is the moment when I understand there will be no going back.

She's not just my mate. Not just the woman I've fallen in love with. She is every star in the sky and every wish I've ever wanted. This moment right now will define every single one that comes after it from now until eternity. I feel it in my bones. This isn't just true love. Lor has a destiny to fulfill, and I am sure that I am a part of it.

This is something so much bigger than either of us.

"Nadir," she whispers before she closes the distance, her mouth sealing against mine. She pushes me back until my legs hit the divan under the window. I collapse, taking her with me as she straddles my hips. With her hands gripping my shoulders, she slides her swollen, wet pussy against me, and I moan with the absolute exquisite ecstasy of every sensation.

Finally, I can't keep my hands off her anymore, and I grab her hips, grinding her down against me for more friction. My fingers dig into her soft skin as I cling to her for dear fucking life. More of my magic releases, twisting around my limbs. I see the faint crackle of red lightning dance at the edges of her body.

"Nadir," she gasps again.

"What do you want?" I ask. "Do whatever you need. Take me inside you. Use me. Fucking ride me, Lor. I'm here at your feet, ready to give you everything."

Her head snaps up, and I worry it's too much. Have I made the same mistake again? But she smiles, the corner of her mouth lifting in a way that makes me want to bite down on every inch of her.

She reaches between us and takes me in her hand, stroking me before she lifts herself up and then positions me at her entrance. I hold my breath as my entire body vibrates with want and need and everything I'm trying so hard to hold back.

Slowly, so slowly, she sinks down, gasping as her mouth forms a perfect "O."

"Gods, you're so fucking tight," I whimper.

My forehead falls against her as I groan. I can tell she needs a moment to adjust, so I give her that, holding back with all my strength instead of thrusting into her like I so desperately want.

"Look at me," I demand, and her gaze hits mine as her head comes up. She doesn't look away as she slowly takes me inch by glorious fucking inch. "Gods, you feel so good. You have no idea how many times I've thought about this."

Her mouth parts, and she leans in to kiss me, our tongues slicking together as she rolls her hips. Finally, she's fully seated, and our twin shudders practically ripple the surrounding air like it was also holding its breath.

"Lor," I growl.

"Hmm?"

"I need you to start moving, or I'm going to lose my mind."

She grins at me with a wicked light in her eyes.

"What's the magic word?" she asks, and I let out a low snarl that makes her laugh. That sound is like music, and I want to be the one who makes her laugh like that every single day.

"You haven't tortured me enough?" I ask, and her eyes spark.

"Not even close."

She leans in, rolls her hips, and then slowly fucks me while my fingers dig into her thighs. No, this isn't fucking. This is making love. I've never done this before. Not like this. It shakes something loose in my chest, and it's almost like I can breathe properly for the very first time.

Then she gently bites the lobe of my ear before she whispers,

"Take what *you* want, Nadir. I'm yours, but you are mine, too. I am not afraid, and I trust you. With everything. With my heart and my life. With everything that comes next." Then she pins me with a look that I feel straight to my toes. "I don't blame you for any of it."

My breath shudders out, the jagged edges smoothing away, the layers of myself peeling apart.

Until this moment, I didn't realize just how badly I needed to hear that.

My control snaps. I lift her up and toss her back on the bed because I need the freedom to fuck her until we both collapse. I fall to my knees and pull her towards me roughly, not giving her a chance to catch her breath before I bury my face between her legs.

"Oh!" she says, her hips lifting, but I pin them in place as I run the flat of my tongue against her pussy from back to front, savoring the taste of her on my tongue. Gods, how I've craved this. Her hand finds my head, her fingers pulling on my hair as I lap and nip at her until she's writhing under me.

"I'm...going...to..." she breathes out, but I pull back because I'm going to make her wait. She pouts as I stand up and then stretch over her, giving her a feral smile.

"Move back," I order, and she doesn't hesitate to scoot to the middle of the bed. I'm pretty sure that's the first time she's ever just listened to me without arguing. I watch her for a moment, my gaze lingering between her legs, reveling in the sight of how wet she is for me.

Then I crawl towards her, kissing my way up the length of her body as she moans, her breasts arching into me. I'm so close to the edge. I've wanted this for so long, and it's almost too much.

"Nadir, please," she says, and it's my turn to torture her.

"Please what, Inmate?"

She pierces me with her gaze, her expression vulnerable. "You haven't called me that since we left The Aurora."

I hate the way she's looking at me like I hurt her. "I thought you wanted me to stop, and you didn't like it."

She bites her lip. "Maybe it grew on me."

"And after everything that happened, it didn't feel right anymore."

"And now?"

"And now I think we're different."

She smiles. That answer seems to please her.

"Wait? In . . . *mate*. Was that some kind of clue?"

I grin at that and chuckle. "Not at first, but it did turn out to be a happy coincidence."

She shakes her head and pretends to look angry.

"How can I make it up to you?" I ask, leaning down and kissing her navel before I circle my tongue in the space below it.

"Oh," she gasps. "By not making me wait any longer."

I crawl over her, peppering her with more kisses. On her thigh and her hip. Up her ribs before I pull a nipple in my mouth and then bite down hard enough to make her cry out.

"You kept pushing me away, Lor. Now it's your turn to suffer."

She gives me that fierce look that always makes my cock ache, but who the fuck am I kidding? I possess no willpower to carry out that threat.

I lift up her leg and then position myself at her entrance, and this time there's nothing gentle about it. I'm inside her within a moment, and we both gasp.

"Tell me if it's too rough," I order, but she shakes her head.

"It's not," she says, clawing at my back. "Don't stop."

"Then eyes on me, Heart Queen. Because I'm going to fucking *ruin* you."

Slowly, I pull out, savoring how hot and tight she is, the way she fits me so perfectly. And then I thrust back in with force. This is it. This is my claiming. My mate and my heart. I will love her from now until the day that I become dust. All I can feel is her. All I can think of is her.

We both moan as I push in again, inch by inch, until I'm fully inside. I'm standing on the edge of a precipice, and I'm about to jump, and it's both terrifying and exhilarating at the same time. The wind in my face and that tumbling feeling in my stomach. I want to hold on forever, but it's too late. I've already fallen.

I keep thrusting, and she keeps trying to pull me closer like she can wrap me into her soul. I press my mouth to hers as my hips churn, and I can feel her getting close as she clenches around me. My magic filters out, twisting around us as her faint, barely there traces of red lightning rise to the surface, our individual powers melding. Soft curves and hard edges, fitting together like two pieces that were always meant to be one.

"That's my girl," I whisper. "Fall apart for me."

She cries out, and then her back arches as she comes, squeezing me so tightly that I follow a moment later, my orgasm tearing through me with a force that nearly splits me wide. My mind whites out, everything spreading apart. I keep riding her, wanting to prolong this feeling forever. She moves with me, and we kiss again, panting into each other's mouths.

"I love you, Lor," I say as our magic hovers around us like curls of smoke. "I love you. From now until the Evanescence takes us, I will love you. Even then, I'll follow you to the ends of time."

She looks at me, not saying anything.

"And if you never feel the same, then I—"

She silences me by pressing her finger to my mouth and shaking her head.

"No, stop that. I love you too," she says, and my heart nearly explodes out of my chest. "I love you too. I'm sorry it took me so long to see it."

Chapter Twenty-Six

LOR

I stare up at Nadir, the warmth of my declaration spreading through my limbs. The look on his face makes my heart melt out of my pores. I know it's true. I love him.

I want to say it happened in a blinding flash, like some great awakening, because I fought so hard against it. But it didn't. It was there all along, happening with each touch and look and word, stacking and forming themselves together until I had no choice but to acknowledge what was there.

"Zerra, you really made me work for that," he says, but he's grinning from ear to ear, and I can't help but laugh as he leans down and gives me a deep kiss that fills the dark space behind my heart with liquid drops of sunshine.

"I've known it for a while," I say. "Though I've been too scared to admit it. It's been so hard to get past everything you once represented to me, but I know that's not who you are. And I understand you were never trying to claim me in a way I didn't want."

He revealed his hand, and now it's my turn to lay it out, but this no longer feels like I'm stumbling through silver fog, trying to reach for safety. Along with my growing but complicated feelings, I've come to trust him with everything. My heart. My soul. And now my future.

His face softens, and he rolls off me, tucking me into his side. "I understand that. I'm sorry for everything he did. For every moment of hurt he caused you."

I shake my head and touch his face. "I don't want this to come between us anymore. I should never have been so hard on you. None of it was your fault. I was just so angry."

His eyes darken, and he pulls me tighter. "What if he'd killed you, and I never got the chance to meet you? If Atlas hadn't stolen you, who knows what would have happened? Maybe I should be thanking him."

I smile at the echo of the same thought I've had before. "I'd probably still be there, wasting away."

Nadir shakes his head. "No. I don't actually think so. Fate meant for all of this to happen. I'm sure of it. It felt like destiny the first time I laid eyes on you in Aphelion. I just knew something had changed."

"I did, too," I say. "When Gabriel told me your name and that it was your ring I had to 'borrow' for the challenge, there was this moment when everything just...shifted."

He smiles and tucks a lock of hair behind my ear before he bends his head and nuzzles my neck.

"So, what does this mate thing actually mean?" I ask, and he blows out a breath.

"Honestly, I'm not entirely sure. I know it means we're connected, of course, but I'm not sure what else it means. Like for the long term."

"It means it's you and me," I say, touching his chest, and he clasps my hand against it.

"Yeah. It does. You aren't going to freak out about that, are you?" He smirks as he tips his head.

I slap him playfully on the arm. "Okay, I deserved that."

He laughs warmly, and I just stare at him, wondering how we got here.

"Why are you looking at me like that now?" he asks. "What did I do?"

"Nothing. I've just never seen you like this."

"Like what?"

I shrug and then consider my response for a second. "Happy?"

But that has the opposite effect I intend, because the smile drops off his face, replaced by that fierce expression that gives rise to some violent part of my soul. I love that look and the way it feels like I am the sum of his every desire.

I don't know how, but somehow, he draws me in even tighter.

"Lor. I've spent my life on the edge of happiness. I've had happy moments, and I have happy memories, but everything was tainted by my father and the pain he caused my mother. By everything that happened in the war and everything that's happened since. But I can say with the most undeniable certainty that the moment when you said you loved me was the first time I've ever known what it's like to be free."

He stops talking, his intense gaze burning through the layers of my very soul.

"Oh," I whisper, because that's a lot, and I feel the same way, but it sounds trite to echo his words. I need words of my own, but everything feels inadequate, and they won't come over the knot swelling in my throat.

"Fuck," I blurt out, like the articulate troll I am. "You are really, really good at this."

His grin returns, and then he rolls back on top of me. "I'm glad you think so, because I plan to tell you the same thing every day of our lives, Lor."

I hold his face between my hands. "This is it then. You and me?"

"If you'll have me."

"Rhiannon said that we have to bond, or eventually we'll waste away and die."

"I'm ready whenever you are," he says.

"She said there was something special we'd need to do because we're both Primaries."

"Then we'll do whatever we need." He brushes my cheek with his thumb. "Don't worry, Lor. Nothing is going to come between us anymore."

"We probably need my magic back first."

He dips his chin. "I saw it. Just now. It was coming to the surface. Did that change anything?"

I shake my head. "I felt it, but it's still locked in there."

His eyes darken with a wicked spark. "Then maybe lots and *lots* of sex is the answer."

I laugh. "Do you suppose that, too, is what fate has in store for us?"

But he's not really listening anymore, because his mouth is against my throat, sucking the skin.

"Oh, are we done talking?"

"Keep talking," he breathes. "I'm listening. I'll just..."

He slides a hand between us, a finger pressing against my clit, and my hips arch.

"...be right here."

"Mmm," I moan as his finger slides into where I'm already wet. Or still wet? It doesn't matter. All I know is my body craves him with a ferocity that would destroy worlds.

"Wait," I say, and he pulls up. "That night in The Aurora when your father figured out who I was. You promised me something very specific, and yet you've failed to demonstrate what toe-curling things *your* magic can supposedly do." The smile on his face is growing as I speak. I tip my head and raise an eyebrow. "Or was that all talk, oh Prince of The Aurora?"

He lets out a growl and sits back on his knees. He's absolutely beautiful. All warm brown skin and taut muscle painted with the colorful images of his magic, his hair wild and loose. His generous cock sits erect and waiting, and I stare at it and then at him, licking my lips, remembering the last time I had it in my mouth, when I wouldn't let him touch me.

He lets out a low rumble as if he's reading my mind.

"Don't lose that thought," he orders, and I laugh. "But first, I'm going to show how much that wasn't talk."

I lift up onto my elbows and pin him with a challenging look. "Put your money where your magic is, Your Highness."

The title slips out, feeling so right this time. I remember when I swore to him I'd die before I called him that. He must remember, too, because something curls in his expression, his entire demeanor arching into the shape of a ravenous predator who's been denied his quarry for far too long.

A moment later, multihued ribbons of glowing light peel off him and circle in the air, twisting around my arms and my legs in mesmerizing spirals of color.

When he tied me up in his bedroom, they had felt like nothing against my skin. When he'd used them to go inside me to unlock my magic, they'd been only gentle touches, no more forceful than a spring breeze. But they're entirely different right now. They feel just like his hands—warm and soft and insistent.

I lie back, luxuriating in the sensation like a cat who's found a sunbeam. Inexplicably, the space overhead begins to fill with lightning bugs, just like those I spied in the ballroom. They filter in through an open window and circle around us, bouncing happily.

"Where did they come from?" I ask as Nadir watches them with a crooked smile. "I think they like your magic."

We both watch as the lightning bugs zig and zag, waltzing with his ribbons of color.

"You are so beautiful," he says, pulling my attention to him. "I could sit here all day and stare at you."

"Fine, but could you get on with it while you stare? I'm dying here."

His eyes go dark at that. "Was that an order?"

"So what if it was?"

He waves a hand, and more magic spirals out, wrapping around my torso and my waist before thin tendrils cuff each of my wrists, binding them together. My magic slips through my limbs, swirling and twisting, but I don't know if this is what it needs to truly break free.

Nadir raises my hands over my head and then secures them to the bed so I'm helplessly restrained under him.

"You're going to pay for that."

I tug on the restraints, pretending to be put out but definitely intrigued by what comes next.

His magic continues swirling around me, and his gaze is acute as a ribbon of magic glides down the center of my body, dragging like a fingertip. The violet light is warm as it travels lower, spreading heat through my limbs and my stomach before it passes my navel and then pauses at the very apex of my thighs, so close yet so far from where I want to be touched. *Need* to be touched.

"Still think I'm all talk?" he asks with an evil smile.

"I'm not sure. You really haven't done anything yet," I say, completely breathless, as the magic tightens in a way that rolls through my entire body. I gasp as he lets out a dark chuckle, and then slowly, that teasing ribbon slides down further between my legs and into the heat of my wet aching center.

I moan as Nadir spreads my legs wider and sinks down on his elbows so his face is poised close enough that I can feel his warm breath along with the tantalizing touch of his magic.

I want to reach for him, but I'm still trapped, and that helpless feeling shreds the threadbare control I'm keeping on my nerves.

He continues touching me—or rather his magic does, dancing along my clit—and then there's an electric spark, and I cry out as my whole body attempts to fold in on itself.

"Still all talk?" he asks again, and this time I shake my head as he sends out another spark, lighting me up like a bloody chandelier.

"Oh gods, no," I say, not sure what I'm saying no to. Every sensation is so extreme I can barely stand it, but I also don't want him to stop. Magic touches me everywhere, tiny shocks peppering my breasts and nipples and stomach, and there, right there, his magic slips inside me, finding my hollow place slick with need. It feels almost like his fingers, only slightly different. Smoother and less dense but just as present. My entire body is writhing, and I tug on my restraints because I can barely handle all these conflicting tingles.

"Nadir," I gasp and moan over and over as my hips move and buck. He sends out another spark, and that's when I snap, my orgasm tearing through me with such force that I scream. Wow, that has never happened before.

Then he's on me, his mouth crashing into mine as the magic around us shifts, and he releases my hands right before he flips me onto my stomach and then presses his chest against my back. I feel the wide head of his cock at my entrance, and I lift my hips and push my butt back.

"Please," I beg.

"What do you say?" he asks with a dark laugh, and I know what he wants.

"It wasn't all talk. It was definitely not just talk," I whimper as he hitches his arm around my waist and thrusts into me.

"Fuck," he moans. "Lor, I'm never ever going to get enough of you. This is the most fucking perfect feeling."

And then he's moving, pounding into me as I grip the bedsheets while he drops long, wet kisses on my shoulders and my back and my neck. The bed creaks under the force of his thrusts, and his magic returns, circling around my limbs and then sliding under me until it finds my clit, sending out more of those little sparks until I come apart again with a rough moan.

Nadir picks up his pace, his movements turning frantic. He lets out a low grunt, and then I feel the shudder that ripples over him as he spills into me, and we collapse into a warm heap of tangled limbs.

After we're done, we lie there for several minutes, holding each other.

"You okay, Lightning Bug?" he asks, and I nod.

"Definitely," I answer with a smile that he returns, one that brightens up every shadowed corner of his face. He tucks me close, his big body wrapping around mine as his hand traces gentle circles on my skin.

"Lightning Bug?" I query.

He shrugs. "Seemed like it was time for a new name, and this felt...appropriate." He holds up my hand, lacing his fingers with mine. "Heart Queen with the wicked red lightning."

I look up, watching the tiny creatures who continue to hover around us like our own personal sky filled with a galaxy of golden stars.

"I love it," I say, a crest of emotion swelling in my chest.

In this moment, everything feels right.

We bask in the lazy perfection of our afterglow, my eyelids growing heavy. I want to sleep, but I also don't want to miss one solitary second of this chance to be next to him. We might not get much time. If I ever unlock my Fae form, we should have centuries, but nothing right now is certain.

As I continue to fight the pull of sleep, a vivid memory comes hurtling towards me.

The conversation I had with the Torch in the Aurora Keep throne room when I asked it about Nadir.

The prince wants something from you, but it is not your power.

I think about my grandparents.

Two Primaries who tried to bond and tore apart the world.

But . . . that way lies only heartbreak, Your Majesty.

That way lies only ruin.

Chapter Twenty-Seven

King Herric

The Aurora: First Age of Ouranos

King Herric stood under the dark sky, peering up. They hadn't seen the northern lights in months. The stars sparkled with their usual brightness, but without the lights, they were like a flower without its petals. Mournful and lonely and an aberration of nature.

The wind blew off the snow-capped mountains, tossing his hair and his cloak. He closed his eyes and inhaled the crisp air, hoping it would do something to cool the uneasy simmer in his blood.

He shivered against the bite as it nipped at his nose and fingertips, but he refused to pull up his hood to shield himself.

He craved the discomfort as a reminder of what they might lose if this continued. He was a king, and it was his duty to ensure the power and position of his legacy.

"Your Majesty," came a voice, stirring him from his reverie. "They're ready for you."

Herric peered up at the sky again, hoping someone would answer his calls. Maybe tonight they'd receive the miracle he'd pleaded for over and over. Where had the lights gone? Why wouldn't they come back? What had happened to cause this?

Finally, he turned to face the cave entrance, squaring his shoulders, maintaining a confident set to his posture. His people were relying on him, and he would fix this. Somehow.

He nodded and marched towards the line of his waiting inner council. They shuffled out of his way as his boots crunched over the snow, his fur-lined, leather-clad legs protected from the chill.

He'd been avoiding this, but it had been weeks, and the emerging reports had become increasingly alarming. This was a problem he couldn't afford to ignore any longer.

"Follow me, Your Majesty," their guide said as he turned around and led them further into the mountain.

Herric picked his way over the small pebbles and rocks that littered the path, pressing one hand against the wall to maintain his balance. The temperature dropped the further they went, winding deeper and deeper into the mine.

On a normal day, he would have heard the sounds of activity. The clink and echo of metal hitting stone as the workers chipped at the bedrock, digging up the emeralds, rubies, and diamonds that grew here in abundance.

Or had grown, until the northern lights disappeared. He was sure these phenomena had to be connected.

When it had first happened, it was curious. Sometimes the lights were invisible, but that was normal—if it was cloudy or the conditions weren't right. But those days were usually sporadic and occasional. When three nights passed without the barest hint of color in the sky, Herric started worrying. When another week passed, he truly wondered if something was wrong.

But that had been minor. After all, while the lights were beautiful, their absence didn't pose a threat to his kingdom. Or so he thought.

It was a week later when word surfaced from the mines. Something that had the potential to ruin everything.

A line of torches lit the way, casting their surroundings into shadow. Herric took another step, his hand landing on a small cluster of faded stones that crumbled beneath his fingers. He stopped and studied the remnants in his palm before closing his fist, feeling each grain give way under the gentle pressure.

They were jewels. Or rather, they had been jewels once. Now their color had leached out, leaving behind not even stone but this frail mass of decay that dissolved at the merest touch.

"It's what we told you about," his guide said, apology and maybe a hint of admonishment in his tone.

"Is it like this everywhere?" he asked, already knowing the answer.

The guide swallowed and linked his hands behind his back.

"Not yet..." He paused, as if debating what to say next. "But it's moving quickly."

Herric nodded. "Show me."

The guide nodded and turned on his heel, leading Herric and his retinue deeper into the mountain. Finally, he caught the distant strains of axes against stone. As reports of the disappearing jewels flooded in, he'd ordered them to dig deeper and further. Surely everything hadn't been affected.

Eventually, Herric and the others entered a massive cavern, the ceiling arcing high over their heads. In the center sat a crystal-clear pool, the bottom of which had once been lined with thousands of sparkling jewels.

It was forbidden to mine from the water—plenty of gems were available elsewhere, and the pool's beauty was far too precious to ever consider destroying.

But what once had been a glowing circle of light, reflecting with a million facets, now sat dull and dark. The crystal-clear water allowed them all to see straight down to the monochrome bottom.

The only reasonable explanation was that the jewels' presence was a direct function of the northern lights. But they were gone, and Herric had no idea how to bring any of it back. They would have to keep digging. They couldn't give up.

"They're still digging deeper," his guide said as if reading Herric's thoughts. "Trying to mine what they can, but the rot... It travels faster than they can move."

"You have every able hand working?" he asked, and the guide nodded.

"Of course, Your Majesty, but the progression is rapid. And appears to be traveling faster with each passing day."

Herric stared at the pool.

Without the mines, his kingdom was in peril. They lived at the base of the mountains, where the climate was too cold for them to grow much, the ground rocky, and the soil thin. Their precious jewels were coveted by all the realms, offering his people the opportunity to trade for anything they desired and needed. It put them in a position of great security and power.

"I want to see," Herric said. "The areas where there are still stones. I want to see them."

There was a desperate edge to his voice, but he had to confirm it with his own eyes. It would be the only thing that would quell this twisting vise in his chest.

The guide tipped his chin, conflict in his expression, before he said, "Of course. This way. There is something else I'd like to show you."

The guide turned on his heel, leaving Herric to wonder what else could go wrong.

They descended further, moving deeper and deeper as Herric shook off the feeling he was being buried alive. It was incomprehensible to think about the weight of stone perched over their heads.

"This," said the guide, coming to a stop inside a small cavern where several miners were busy chipping away. They all looked over at Herric and his party, their heads dipping in deference. The guide then waved the torch towards the wall, and the light caught a vein of dark sparkling rock.

"What is it?" Herric asked, moving in for a closer look. It glittered with presence, weighty and dense, like solid smoke curling and shifting in a gust of air.

"We're not sure," the guide said. "But we just started noticing it recently. It seems the deeper we go, the thicker it becomes."

"We should get a sample," Herric said, running his fingers along the vein, a foreign twist tugging in his chest. "Test its properties."

"Of course. I'll have some sent up to the castle."

Herric studied the unfamiliar material for a moment longer before turning back to their guide.

"What of the jewels?" he asked.

The guide was turning to lead them down to another tunnel when Herric heard it.

A rumble from deep in the mountain.

"What's that?" someone else asked, alarm already in his tone. The floor vibrated beneath their feet as another rumble shook the entire cavern.

Debris sheared off the ceiling, first as pebbles but then in larger chunks as their surroundings shook and shook.

"Run! Everyone out!" their guide screamed. "It's coming down."

Herric spun around to witness the fleeing backs of his advisors scrambling over the fallen rocks as they all made their way back up the route they'd taken. He brought up the rear, willing them to move faster as the ground trembled so hard he lost his footing.

His knees struck rock, and he peered over his shoulder

as black mist belched from the recesses of the mountain. It fogged over him, filling his mouth and nose.

He tried to scream, but the clouds choked off his air, and then the ground gave way beneath him as he began to fall, his limbs circling wildly as he tumbled end over end and then landed with a painful thud onto a hard surface.

For several long seconds, he lay with his cheek pressed to cold marble before he realized he was somewhere else. This was no longer The Aurora and it certainly wasn't the inside of a mountain.

Voices in the distance pulled him to his knees as he surveyed his new surroundings. He appeared to be in some kind of hall, the walls and floors covered in marble, while a row of arched windows lining each side filtered in bright sunlight.

His head spinning slightly, he staggered to his feet and peered out, but all he saw were white clouds pressed against the glass. The same voices drew his attention, and he moved towards them, entering a large round chamber where six people stood facing one another.

He recognized most of them. King Nerus of Alluvion, with his pale bluish skin and indigo hair, and Queen Astraia of Celestria, with her silvery-white locks and those big black eyes.

King Terra of Tor was speaking, his deep voice rumbling like stones tumbling down a landslide.

"We had just returned from the fall hunt," he said, "when we found everyone frozen in place, turned to stone."

As Herric circled the perimeter, the rulers stopped, eyeing him as he moved into the remaining empty space around the circle.

"Continue," Herric said.

"We made our way up the switchback to the castle, and every level was the same," Terra said, rolling his neck. "Finally, we came upon a rock troll." He stopped, his grey eyes blinking rapidly. "I didn't even know they were real. But it was there like some nightmare from a storybook, and it had turned everyone to stone. I tried to confront it, but it faced me, and then everything went grey, and here I was."

Queen Astraia spoke next. "It was a meteor," she said, her musical voice devoid of emotion. "We did everything we could. My star wielders tried everything, but its trajectory was set. We all stood in the main square and watched it come." She swallowed hard, her throat bobbing. "I . . . What happened to them?"

Her question finished on a whisper that shivered around the room.

The Alluvion King spoke of the sea dragon terrorizing the shores of his kingdom. How he'd sailed out with a group of his most trusted soldiers until, one by one, they'd all been lost to the deeps. The Sleepness in Heart, the plagued forests of The Woodlands, and a heat wave in Aphelion.

When Herric's turn came, he spoke of the lights and his jewels. Of the black fog that had consumed him in the cave collapse.

When he finished speaking, everyone stared around the circle. Each of them had encountered such tragedy. Such loss, but why?

And where were they now?

A flicker in the center of the circle drew everyone's attention.

It wobbled in and out until a figure stood in the middle. Herric squinted, trying to sort through its blur. It wouldn't stand still. First, it appeared like a woman with dark skin and black hair, then like a man with a snowy complexion and blond waves. They continued to shift, appearing as a dozen different people.

"Welcome," they said, the strains of many voices, high and low, soft and harsh, all mixing together.

"What is this?" King Terra demanded. "Who are you?"

The figure continued to flicker, and that same multitudinous voice spoke.

"You are at the end of the First Age of Ouranos," they answered as they swept out their arms. "But when one door closes, another one opens. And the Second Age is about to begin."

Chapter Twenty-Eight

LOR

PRESENT DAY

N adir and I eventually cave to sleep, and I awake to the warmth of sunlight filtering into the room. We didn't get around to closing the curtains last night, and I cover my eyes from the assault of brightness, shifting under the blanket, snuggling deeper into our cozy cocoon. It's so comfortable with his arm wrapped around me, his mouth gently parted with soft, sleepy breaths.

My eyes take in the regal lines of his face as the ominous words I recalled in the haze of near unconsciousness spin into the front of my thoughts.

Heartbreak and ruin.

Another recollection jogs my memory. Something that Rhiannon said.

Sometimes I think it was their love that burned down the world, which in a way is almost romantic, I think?

While it seems farfetched, I can't help but see these pieces arrange themselves in the jumble of my mind's scope. What if *that's* what caused the breaking?

The Mirror alluded to it, too, when I stood before it.

This *can never happen again.*

I hadn't understood what those words meant at the time, but I wonder if I do now.

I shake my head, attempting to dislodge the stones piling up in my thoughts. Whatever happens, we're going to find a way around or through anything fate can throw in our path. If there's some catch to sealing our bond, then we'll find someone who can help us. I don't care what I must do to make that happen.

My singular goal for so long was to exact my revenge on the Aurora King, but my desires and wants have broadened, spreading like water over cracked, parched earth, nourishing the dead ground under my feet. I want more than just the cold hard need to make him pay for everything. Despite the rage that fueled me for years, I want more than that, and I think I'm slowly learning to accept that I deserve it.

When you've been treated like nothing for most of your life, it's easy to forget that you're *something.*

I continue studying Nadir's face, tracing the lines of his nose and his cheeks. I once said he isn't attractive in the traditional sense—he's far too extraordinary for that. But he's so achingly beautiful that I could lie here all day memorizing every fascinating detail.

The plan is to return to Aphelion today, but we're no closer to figuring out how Atlas or Rion knew about my origins. This ever-present unknown congeals in my stomach, burning like acid. I feel vulnerable and exposed and wary of everyone. Whom can I really trust?

My gaze falls on Nadir, and in spite of everything, I smile to myself, because, in him, I finally trust.

"How long do you plan to stare at me, Lightning Bug?" Nadir says with his eyes still closed, making me jump. "I understand how devastatingly good-looking I am, but this is getting a little awkward."

I shove his shoulder, and his eyes snap open before he grins.

"How long have you been awake?" I demand as he pulls me closer while I attempt to shove him away.

"Long enough to know that you were swooning over me."

"I was not," I say, but it's so obvious I'm lying that I can't even pretend to be serious.

He nuzzles into my neck, his hand sliding down my back to where he finds my ass and squeezes it firmly. "You can't fool me. I know how much you want me, even when you were working so damn hard to pretend otherwise."

I snort, but he's already kissing me as he rolls me over, pinning me to the mattress.

"Are you sore?" he asks, his hand sliding down my stomach and across my hip, his touches like tender kisses.

"A little," I admit.

"Hmm," he says, his fingers dipping into the space between my thighs. "And yet, you're dripping for me."

"I can be both things. They aren't mutually exclusive occurrences," I say, and he grins as he gently massages my clit. He leans down and sucks on my neck, carefully and lovingly bringing me to the edge until I shatter underneath him again. I wonder if you can go blind from orgasming this often?

When he's finished, he rolls away and then scoops me up, carrying me to the bathroom, where we spend another solid hour in the shower "cleaning up."

Once we finally emerge from the haze of steam and a heady rainbow of orgasms, I find a note under the door inviting us for breakfast with Cedar and Elswyth before we depart.

Nadir comes up behind me, wrapping his arms around me and kissing my shoulder. "I was hoping we could stay in this room, just the two of us, until the end of time," he says, reading the note. "But I suppose we have shit to get accomplished."

I look over my shoulder and arch an eyebrow. "And here I thought vengeance was the foundation of your personality and not just a side hobby you'd abandon at the first opportunity for a roll in the sheets."

He lets out a low growl and spins me around, backing me towards the bed, and tipping me over as he lands on top. "My need for vengeance is fully intact. Never doubt that."

Then he peppers me with kisses as his fingers find all of my ticklish spots, and I dissolve into a fit of giggles.

This feels really . . . nice.

When he's done torturing me, he pulls up and catches something in my expression.

"What is it?" he asks.

"Nothing. I just . . . I like this." My hand settles against his cheek, my thumb pressing his bottom lip, as his mouth crooks up at the corner. He nips my finger with his teeth, and I snatch it away with a laugh.

"This is everything," he says.

Finally, we manage to dress and head to the dining room with our fingers laced together. We've walked like this before. We spent most of our time in the Keep holding hands, but its significance has shifted. This isn't for show anymore, and now that we've declared ourselves to each other, it means something else. It's such a small, innocuous action, but it strikes me as momentous.

We round the corner to find Tristan, Mael, and Etienne already seated with the Woodlands King and Queen.

"Finally," Mael says. "I thought we were going to have to send out a search party for you. What happened last n—"

His eyes drop to our clasped hands and then flick back up as a beaming grin crosses his face. He slaps the table with enough force to rattle the glasses and cutlery.

"You finally fucked," he declares, and I feel my face turn beet red. Especially when Tristan sits up, glowering at Mael and then at me and Nadir like he's not sure what he's supposed to do but knows he definitely wants to do something about this.

"Good gods, Mael," I say, covering my eyes. "Can you ever behave like a normal person?"

He smiles and shrugs. "For me, this is normal."

"That would be the problem," Nadir says as he leads me

into the room and then pulls out a chair next to Mael for me. As I sit, I nail him with a withering glare, but he couldn't care less, grinning at me and then at his friend.

"Maybe now you won't be so fucking moody all the time," Mael says, and Nadir smiles.

"You can certainly hope."

Cedar and Elswyth are now watching all of us with bemused looks on their faces.

"I'm sorry," I say, not entirely sure what I'm apologizing for, but this is the height of embarrassment. "He's not fully house-broken yet."

"I suppose," Elswyth says, tipping her head with a coy tilt to her mouth, "congratulations are in order?"

My face scorches as Nadir's hand lands on my thigh and squeezes it.

"Thank you," he replies as I drop my face into my hands in mortification. Did he just accept a congratulations . . . for sex?

Nadir chuckles softly, leaning against me before he drops a kiss on my shoulder. I look up, planning to tell him to stop, but he's staring at me with such adorable reverence that I don't have the heart.

"Can we talk about something else, please?" I ask instead.

"You have a mark on your neck," Tristan says, zeroing in on me, his eyes narrowing. "Like someone was sucking on you."

I slap my hand over my skin, sure the tips of my ears are about to incinerate. Oh gods, we should have just stayed in my room. Mael snorts out a laugh, and even Etienne cracks a rare smile.

"Tris!" I hiss. "Stop it." My eyes dart around the table, and

I sit up straight, trying to pretend I have some control over what's happening right now. "A gentleman wouldn't draw attention to it."

He rolls his eyes. "Then don't let random dickheads suck on your neck, little sister."

He raises a hand and bumps his fist with Mael's as they both laugh.

"Seriously, though," Tristan says, turning to Nadir, the smile dropping from his face. "Hurt her, and I'll kill you. Just... absolutely destroy you, Aurora Prince."

Nadir raises an eyebrow, and I expect him to say something cocky and irreverent, but instead, he dips his chin. "I wouldn't expect anything less. You have my word that I will never, ever do anything to hurt her. I love her more than you can possibly understand."

Their gazes meet, and some kind of testosterone-induced understanding passes between them. It would be nice if they got along better, though I'm not really caring for this overt display of male aggression.

"If you two are done acting like I'm a piece of furniture to be discussed, can we *please* talk about something else?"

I turn to Cedar, who's studying me curiously.

"You two," he says, his finger flicking between us. "The Aurora Prince and the Primary of Heart?"

Gods. Is this the only topic of conversation we can come up with this morning? Surely we have more important things to discuss?

"We're..." I say, not sure how to continue that thought, when I'm temporarily rescued by a low rumble that shakes the table and the ground beneath us. We all reach out to steady our glasses as we wait for the quake to subside.

"Has that been happening a lot?" Nadir asks, and Cedar answers with a grim nod.

"More and more."

"The trees," I ask. "We saw them on our way in. How long have they been that way?"

"A few months," the king replies.

"And you have no idea what's causing this?" Nadir asks.

"None at all," Cedar says. "Do you?"

"No," Nadir replies. "At first, I'd hoped it was just the natural ebb and flow of the environment . . ."

He trails off, and it's becoming obvious it's more than that.

"Anyway," Nadir says, picking up the thread of our previous conversation. "We're mates."

Etienne drops his fork with a clatter on his plate before it bounces off and then lands on the floor with another clatter.

Elswyth leans forward, her eyes wide. "Is it true?"

I shrug, suddenly feeling incredibly self-conscious.

"Mates?" Tristan asks. "What does that mean?"

"It means she's stuck with me," Nadir says, his usual expression reserved for Tristan back in place. "Which I guess means you are, too."

"I don't know what that means." My brother is understandably confused.

"It's a thing that happens sometimes," I say, waving a hand.

"Not sometimes," Cedar says. "It's incredibly rare. Your grandparents . . ."

"I know," I say. "Someone told me that they were. You knew?"

He nods. "Wolf told me before they left for Heart when they..."

"Blew everything up," I say.

"This is remarkable," Elswyth says. "So all this time, you were right under each other's noses." She clasps her hands together. "How romantic."

I exchange a look with Nadir. I wish we had more time to talk about this and explore its many layers.

"I'm very glad you came here," Cedar says. "It seems that destiny has something very big in store for both of you and fate meant for our paths to cross after all these years. I meant what I said about offering my allegiance, Lor. I've always felt that the loss of Heart was a detriment to Ouranos. Your queendom's healing magic was an invaluable asset, and we will never be as safe without it."

"Thank you," I say. "You don't know how much that means to me."

"I'm sorry for everything," Cedar says. "I should have tried harder to find you. The guilt has sat with me ever since that day."

I shake my head. "None of it was your fault," I say, meaning it. He had no obligation to protect us, and I've spent enough time blaming myself. There is no one responsible for anything that happened other than Rion himself.

After all the years of yearning, we have a sort of family again. I wonder at the sincerity in Cedar's heart, but I want to give him the benefit of the doubt. I've spent so long mistrusting everyone that I also want to break down those walls for my own sake. This anger I've clutched in my heart will consume me if I don't find some way to release it.

"Still. I should have tried," Cedar says as he looks at Tristan, perhaps seeking his absolution. My brother is less inclined to trust or forgive right now, and I don't blame him. He needs more time, and he's entitled to as much as he wants.

"Thank you for welcoming us," Tristan says, leaving the rest unspoken, but it's clear from Cedar's expression that he understands there are bridges yet to mend.

"It was truly the least we could do," Elswyth says, laying a hand on the king's arm. "You have a home here any time you need it."

"Thank you," I add.

"I never thought I'd see the day The Woodlands would be working with The Aurora," Cedar says to Nadir, leaning forward. "This is quite a turn of history."

"Well, I'm not officially The Aurora yet," Nadir replies, and Cedar nods.

"I've never liked your father. Just so you know."

My eyes widen as I look between them, but Nadir grins. "You are far from the only one, Your Majesty."

Cedar belts out a warm laugh before he turns to me. "Before you leave, is there anything else I can do? Just say the word."

"Actually," I reply, because there is something.

Nadir and I discussed it this morning in our sex-drunk daydream and agreed this made sense in our quest for answers. "I wonder if you'd let me see the Woodlands Staff?"

CHAPTER TWENTY-NINE

"The Staff?" Cedar asks.

Nadir and I exchange a look. Does Cedar's generosity extend to his most precious relic? Does he trust me enough to let me near it?

"I want to hold it," I say, biting the inside of my lip. Should I reveal the truth about how they talk to me? Nadir is still confused about this phenomenon, and I wonder if this is another secret I must keep.

Cedar looks me up and down, saying nothing for a moment, before nodding.

"Very well."

My shoulders drop in relief when he doesn't seem intent on forcing out the reasons for my request.

"Come with me."

We all rise from the table and slowly proceed through the Fort until we come to a large archway twisted from greenery and decorated with flowers. After we pass underneath, we wind through more verdant pathways until we come to a clearing. A dome fabricated from vines and leaves arches over our heads, filtering in sunlight on a crisp breeze.

Ahead of us sit two wooden thrones bound in more vines and flowers.

My breath catches at the sight.

This also could have been my home.

This is our other half.

I take a moment to study our surroundings. The air smells sweet and fresh—flowers mixing with pine—and the grass is so green and lush that it looks like velvet. My brother stops next to me, and I reach out, his hand finding mine before we squeeze each other's fingers.

"I've wondered," Cedar says, approaching on my other side. "Do either of you have the blood of your grandfather in your veins? Can you channel the magic of The Woodlands?"

Tristan and I exchange a look. This is his truth to share.

"I do," Tristan says, the words rushing out of him like he's been clinging to them with his life. Every eye in the room falls on him.

"Do you?" Cedar asks, rubbing his chin with a shrewd, narrow-eyed look that lingers on my brother before he finally addresses me.

"And you?"

I shake my head. "Only Tristan has it."

"When you're ready, I'd love to discuss it," he says to

Tristan. "Perhaps help you learn how to use it and control it. I suspect you haven't had much opportunity to do so."

Tristan nods as several vivid emotions cross his face. "I would like that," he says. "Very much."

"I'm glad to hear. My brother would have wanted that . . . as do I."

Cedar smiles and gestures to the Woodlands thrones, where the Staff sits propped at an angle on the left seat.

About the same height I am, it resembles a sturdy tree branch, knotted and slightly bent. Its design is simple when compared to the Mirror's, or the Crown's, or even the Torch's, but it's been polished to a glassy shine, and there's a quiet beauty in its simplicity.

"What do you plan to do?" Cedar asks as we both approach.

"Do you mind if I pick it up?" I don't know the proper etiquette for handling these precious Artefacts. I can only assume one doesn't just walk in and grab one without permission from its ruler.

"No. Please go ahead," Cedar says, with his dark eyebrows drawn. He's obviously not sure what's happening, but I appreciate his willingness to place his trust in me. "But can I ask why?"

My lips roll together before I decide to answer. "They talk to me."

"I don't understand."

"The Mirror. The Torch. They both spoke to me and told me things, and I'm hoping the Staff will do the same."

"Why?"

"I wish I knew."

Cedar's mouth parts and he dips his chin. "Very well. I hope it offers you something useful."

Then I look back at Nadir, who stands off to my left, his hands stuffed in his pockets, wearing that fierce determination he carries like a shield.

You can do this.

I blink. Did he just . . . ?

Did you just speak to me?

This time his forehead folds into confusion.

Did you just speak to me, *Lightning Bug?*

The mate bond. A smile creeps to my face as one teases the corner of his mouth. Why does that make me so happy?

We'll talk about this later.

He nods, and I turn back and reach for the Staff, picking it up and clutching it with both hands. The wood is warm and as smooth as it appears, the surface burnished with swollen knots and veins. Up close, I'm able to appreciate its gilded beauty, the grain of the wood, noting how it shimmers in the light.

With a deep breath, I close my eyes and then try to search for its presence.

"Hello?" I ask in my head. *"Can you hear me?"*

I wait, pleading for a response. When none comes, I ask again, worried it won't answer. What if the Staff refuses to talk to me?

"Hello?" I try again, squeezing the wood so tightly my hands ache.

Is that who I think it is?

The voice pops into my head and relief collapses my lungs.

Again, just like with the Torch, I'm somewhere else, no longer in the Woodlands throne room, but in a place that seems lost between the earth and the sky. This time I'm surrounded by leaves creeping in every direction. It feels both like they're right next to me, brushing my skin, and also like they're miles away. The sensation throws me off-kilter, but I spread my feet, clinging to my balance.

"Hello!" I call again.

Heart Queen, the Staff replies. *You've finally come to see me and brought the Primary, I see.*

"You know about me too?"

Indeed. So close and yet so far for all those years. When I felt you leave the borders of The Woodlands, I thought you had been lost. But I felt him across the miles and hoped you would return someday.

"I'm here," I say. *"Can you help me?"*

With what?

"Anything. Everything. I have so many questions. Do you know how to unlock my magic?"

I am not the keeper of Heart magic. You'll need the Crown for that.

"That's not working. I've tried."

Perhaps the ark then.

"The what?"

The Staff pauses. *The arks are objects of immense power, but many were taken.*

"Where do I find them? What are they? Taken by who?"

She who was there knows.

"There? You mean . . ."

I mean when the Heart Queen tried to take too much.

I swallow hard. *"Who was there?"*

One of Zerra's blessed sat at the feet of my lost king.

"What do you mean?"

I can show you. If you like.

"Yes." The word escapes in a whispered breath with a pulse of anticipation.

Show me. Can I see what really happened that day? A bend in the air around me tells me that what I witness next is about to change everything, yet again.

A moment later, the scene melts away, and I'm standing inside a castle with white marble covering the floor and walls.

A group huddles together in a corner, and a baby cries, and then I see it all. My grandfather Wolf holds a child in his arms while my grandmother watches from the settee where she lies. She's covered in sweat and surrounded by a group of women cleaning up the blood between her legs. She's clearly just given birth to a child.

To my *mother*.

I almost choke on my grief, a strangled sob threatening to drown me. I can't tear my eyes away as I take in her round face and her soft limbs. My mother.

No one marks my presence, and it becomes obvious I'm not really here. I'm watching this scene only as it happened.

Another woman, with dark hair and wearing the Heart Crown, speaks in hushed tones with Wolf. Daedra. My great-grandmother.

She moves to the door and speaks with someone beyond it before a pair of guards enters the room. A noise diverts my attention to another figure lying on the floor.

A woman balled up with her arms wrapped around her knees rocks back and forth, babbling to herself. She looks like she's been through hell. There's something vaguely familiar about her, but I can't put my finger on it. This must be the High Priestess.

My attention redirects once again as the scene flashes in and out of my vision. Wolf is now transferring the baby to his guards as my great-grandmother looks on. Tears streak his face, and my heart cracks apart at the depth of his loss. It breaks for my mother, who never had the chance to know her parents at all. And for all of us who would never get the chance to know one another.

The guards prepare to leave, but my great-grandmother stops them and unhooks the chain around her neck. A red jewel glints from it, and my breath hooks into my throat. I know that jewel. I spent half my life protecting it. That's how my mother got it. Why did my great-grandmother give a piece of it away? What was the purpose of that?

After the guards leave with my mother, a blast rocks the room, and a ball of light hovers outside like a star drawing too close. The unmistakable colorful ribbons of light tell me it is Aurora magic. Rion is here.

The scene warps as my grandmother levers herself up from the sofa. She's surprisingly nimble for a woman who just gave birth. She snatches the Crown from her mother's head and places it on hers, the steely glint in her eyes veering from lucid to manic.

I don't need to hear every word to understand that my grandmother stole that crown.

She tried to take the magic of Heart.

My blood turns to ice as I bear witness to this unspeakable crime. One that was scrubbed from history because no one *knew*.

And now, I've been granted this glimpse that has become my curse to bear.

My grandmother grabs the High Priestess by her collar, dragging her to the center of the room as the woman babbles incoherently. My grandmother stares down at her with such naked loathing that something twists in my chest. It's clear she's balancing on the edge, ready to tip, and nothing will stand in her way.

She rips a book from the woman's pocket and then flips to a marked page. Wolf joins her as she begins to recite a series of lines, and it's then I truly comprehend what else I'm witnessing.

This was the moment. This was the end.

I back away, but there's nowhere for me to go. I remind myself I'm not really here. Nothing can hurt me, at least not physically, but what will this do to my heart and mind? I force myself to look. This is my lot to bear. My burden to shoulder. I am her heir, no matter the mistakes she made, and it's my job to fix them.

My grandmother continues speaking as her magic sparks around them both, the entire room glowing and flashing like we've been trapped inside a star. What is she doing? What is she saying? I can't make out the words.

Red and green magic—her lightning and his dense green ribbons—flashes through the room, the edges trimmed with the faintest line of black smoke, like smoldering ruins. The air crackles as the hairs on my arms lift.

I take another step back as a high-pitched whine pierces the atmosphere. It drills into my ears, and I cover them as I watch the moment my grandmother realizes she fucked this all up. It's there in the frantic widening of her eyes, the certainty of their deaths written with indelible ink, before suddenly, everything blasts apart in an explosion of blinding light.

I'm not really here, but I practically feel the heat of the air as it tugs against my hair and clothes. I shield myself with my arms, but there's nothing to protect myself against. It all passes me by like mist.

The blast seems to go on forever until, finally, silence descends. Everything is gone. I'm surrounded by nothing but a black ring where my grandparents were standing. In the distance, I see the night sky overhead, the stars twinkling from above. Even the magic of The Aurora is gone.

My heart pounds in my chest, and there are tears running down my face. She did this. She stole the Crown, killed the Primary, and brought this destruction on them all. I'll never forget the look in her eyes while she teetered on the edge of reason. Like she didn't care whom she hurt as long as she got what she wanted.

I want to leave this place. I don't want *this* to be where I came from. My legacy is a stain, blotting out everything. I take another step back, feeling behind me and wondering how I'll get out of here. I can't seem to make my voice work.

The Staff. I'd almost forgotten that was how I got here at all.

"Hello!" I yell, wondering why it's still forcing me to witness this. It's over. Everything is gone.

But then, a movement catches my eye, and I go completely still as a pile of rubble shifts before I hear a cough.

Someone is alive.

I'm not sure if this is worse than thinking everyone was dead. How did *anyone* survive this?

After another moment, the debris shifts again, and a head emerges from the wreckage. It's the babbling woman. The High Priestess. At least, I think it is. She's so covered in soot it's hard to tell, but her silver hair shines through the layer of grime.

She no longer seems devoid of her wits. No, she struggles to her feet and surveys the damage with a wicked but entirely coherent smile. Her eyes have lost that rolling wildness and are now as clear as crystal.

She shakes her head and rubs her hands down her face as she dislodges some of the dust. Then she takes a careful step, her knee clearly bothering her, but she presses on. Slowly, so slowly, she makes her way across the room as I watch her, unable to believe my eyes.

Someone survived.

Someone who knew there was a child.

That's when she stops and turns her head, looking directly at the spot where I'm standing. I hold my breath as I go perfectly still. She can't see me, but the way she looks right into my eyes sends a chill over the back of my scalp.

And that's when I recognize her.

She's the High Fae female I killed when I was a child. I'm sure of it. I'd stake my entire life on it.

She stares at me as her face stretches into a smile. Then she looks up at the sky and pauses for several long seconds before she hobbles away.

A moment later, I'm once again standing in the throne room inside the Woodlands Fort with the Staff clutched in my sweating hands.

I gasp as my lungs fill with air like I've just emerged from the bottom of an ocean trench.

"Lor," Nadir growls, his hand coming to my lower back. "Are you okay? You're pale."

"I'm not sure," I whisper.

"What happened?"

I shake my head as Cedar approaches to take the Staff carefully from my hands and places it back on his throne.

"Lor?" Nadir asks, his jaw set. He looks like he wants to go and punch someone, and he's just waiting to hear who the unlucky victim will be.

"I was there. It showed me that day in Heart. I saw my grandparents and our mother." I look at Tristan, wishing I could somehow share the images in my head. Some of them. Not all of them. How will Tristan react when he knows what she did?

"Someone survived," I say, focusing on the most important thing first. "A woman. She had silver hair."

"Cloris Payne," Cedar says. "She was the priestess they were working with."

"I think she might have tricked them. Or things didn't go the way anyone planned."

FATE OF THE SUN KING   293

I don't have the courage to voice what I saw in my grand-mother's eyes. Her malice and greed and the way she *took* her mother's crown.

"She got up and walked away." I swallow. "But that's not all. She's the same woman I killed when I was a child. She's who knew. She's how your father and Atlas must have known."

"Who?" Cedar asks, because I hadn't shared this with him the other night. After I fill him in, everyone comes to the same conclusion.

"But if we're assuming Atlas ended the first Trials because he found out about you two years ago, then someone else told him, because *you* killed her fourteen years ago," Nadir says.

I shake my head. "I didn't. She isn't really dead."

"What are you talking about?" he asks.

"I saw her in Aphelion. Or at least I thought I did."

I describe the day I saw her in the city and how I followed before believing it wasn't really her. But it was. Did she know it was me?

"I think she used some kind of glamour to fool me. I'm sure it was her. Her name was on the fucking building."

"We need to see her immediately," Nadir says. "If she knows who you are and is working with Atlas, then she might have told him she saw you."

"No. She had days to do that, and Atlas didn't come for me. It's likely she had no idea it was me. I was a child the last time she saw me."

"So we need to know what she knows."

"I think so."

I take in the shell-shocked expressions of my companions,

knowing how much more surprised they'd be if I revealed the rest.

Nadir holds out a hand for Cedar. "Thank you for everything. But it seems we really need to go. Can we continue to count on your discretion?"

"Of course," Cedar says. "Let me know if you need anything at all." He says the words to me and to Tristan, and we both nod.

"Please come back and see us when you can. And we'd love to see your sister, too," Elswyth adds.

"Of course," I say. If any of us ever get that chance.

We finally prepare to leave. We're riding back to Aphelion together on horses provided by Cedar.

Just as we're about to depart, I remember something else the Staff said. It had remarked that I'd brought the Primary with me and that the Staff had felt *him* across the miles. At first, I assumed it had been talking about Nadir as the Primary, but now I realize it couldn't have been. The Woodlands Staff has no connection to The Aurora.

"Can I ask?" I say to Cedar. "Who is the Woodlands Primary?"

He presses his mouth together. "Unfortunately, the Staff hasn't seen fit to share that with me."

"You mean you don't always know?"

He shakes his head, and I sense Nadir react, ever on the alert.

"Not always. Sometimes the current rulers know from the moment the Primary is born. Sometimes it's revealed later, but almost always before the king or queen descends." Cedar tips his head. "Why do you ask?"

I shake mine in response. "Just curious. Until a few weeks ago, I'd never heard of one, and now that I am one ..." I trail off. None of it is a lie, but it isn't the complete truth.

"Of course," Cedar says. "That's only natural."

"Thank you again."

I turn to leave with the others as Tristan catches my eyes. He's got a perplexed look on his face, and he's rubbing his chest.

He feels the Staff.

Just like I felt the Crown in Heart.

I may not have any Woodlands magic. *I* might be all Heart, but Tristan has always straddled the line, and now ... I'm sure that he's The Woodlands' next Primary.

CHAPTER THIRTY

CLORIS PAYNE

APHELION: TWO YEARS AGO

Cloris entered the city on a tide of bodies, no one marking her entrance. She gripped a long wooden staff in one thin hand as she hobbled along the golden paved street, squinting at the opulence of her surroundings. The bones in her knee had never set right, and that old injury caused by the Heart Queen always flared when storms were brewing. What she wouldn't give to go back in time and rip out that brat's throat. What an absolute fool she had been.

But Cloris was the one who'd had the last laugh, wasn't she?

While Serce and her mate had dissolved into nothing but memories and ash, tainted by their mistakes, Cloris had

Zerra's divine protection to thank for her narrow escape. The arcturite cuffs had dragged her into near madness, but Cloris had never lost her faith in her god, and in turn, she was rewarded with life beyond the worst disaster since the Beginning of Days. Zerra *had* refused to heal her knee as punishment for her missteps, but it was better than the alternative.

After that, Cloris had been forced to go into hiding for years. There were those who knew she'd been present at the end when Serce had botched that cursed bonding. Some knew Cloris had been working with the queen, and she refused to be held accountable for that wretched woman's actions. None of that had been her fault. Cloris was still furious that bitch had locked her in a cage like she was nothing but a slobbering animal. If she weren't already dead, Cloris would have made it her life's purpose to ensure Serce suffered painfully until she took her final breaths. Now Cloris would settle for her offspring instead.

A little over two decades ago, Cloris finally emerged from the shadows of her seclusion. The dust had settled enough so she could move out into the open once again. Memories were short, and the history books all asserted she was dead. It was a reasonable assumption. No bodies had been left to identify after the chaos.

Some small alterations to her appearance—the color of her eyes and the shape of her chin and nose—and a change of name completed her transformation. It was the perfect cover. She couldn't return to her sisters at Zerra's temple yet— another thing she'd never forgive Serce for—but she would forge new plans. When she was finished, they would welcome her into their fold with open arms. She would finally realize Zerra's purpose when the goddess had given life to the priestesses so many years ago.

The ark of Heart. It had been her goal when she'd tried to steal the girl and once again found herself rescued from death by the divine hand of Zerra's mercy.

She tried again when she'd approached Rion twelve years ago. Of course, none of *that* had gone as planned. The rulers of Ouranos were too absorbed in themselves to see the bigger picture. They were too myopic to appreciate the scale of what they could accomplish if only they'd open their eyes and *see*.

Looking up at the towering Sun Palace, she hitched up the hem of her skirt, rolling her lips together.

First Serce. Then that little brat. Then Rion. She hoped a fourth time would be the charm.

Slowly, she wove her way through the crowd, arriving at the gated entrance. Two guards in golden armor flanked the archway to the Sun Palace, their postures stiff and their gazes watching everything.

As she approached, she sensed their judgment. The curl of their lips and the shifting of their eyes. She knew how she appeared. Feeble. Broken. Not quite whole. Thanks to those cuffs, something had cracked in her mind, and though she'd spent so many years trying to heal, there would always be something not quite . . . right.

She shuffled towards the guards and stopped before dragging her eyes up. They watched her with bored looks, and she resisted the urge to slap the disdain off their faces.

"I'm here to see the king," she said, standing as straight as she could and trying to project a confidence she hadn't felt in a very long time.

One of the guards snorted as he exchanged an amused glance with the other guard.

"I don't think so," he said. "Move along. You don't belong here."

He made a shooing motion with his hands, and her jaw clenched in anger.

Instead, she shuffled closer and lifted a hand to her collar. She'd used this only once in the centuries after the destruction, when she'd gone to see the Aurora King after emerging from the forest on the same misguided errand.

The guard's thick eyebrows drew together as she pulled on the fabric of her dress, exposing the mark of a High Priestess tattooed into the curve of her collarbone.

Referred to as Zerra's mark in the common tongue but known as the Empyreal Seal to all of Zerra's true disciples. The mark would grant an automatic audience with any ruler in Ouranos when presented. Or at least that had been the case once upon a time.

She knew it stood out in stark contrast to her paleness. A midnight mark against a snowy canvas that had seen little sunlight in over two hundred years. The seven Artefacts formed a circle, each rendered in precise miniature detail.

The guard's eyes narrowed as he took in the marking, leaning closer to get a better look.

"I come on behalf of the goddess," Cloris said. "Here to demand an audience with the king." It wasn't entirely the truth. After the last time Zerra had rescued Cloris, she'd stopped speaking to her as further punishment for her failures. But she was trying to earn her way back into Zerra's grace, and sometimes one had to massage the truth in support of a nobler cause.

The guard peered at the mark as he rubbed his chin, clearly lacking enough brain cells to assess the situation.

"I think we better let her in," the other one said, obviously the more superstitious of the two.

"We can't just let her in." The first one again. "The king will have our heads. It's the middle of the Trials."

The second guard's gaze shifted to Cloris. "She's with the goddess." Then his gaze flicked upward before it landed on Cloris again. "We should let her in."

The first guard hesitated again. "I'm not sure."

"Do you want to incur her wrath?"

"What about the king?" the first one said, and Cloris was ready to crack their heads together. But she reined in her temper and smiled pleasantly enough while these two tried to remember that one plus one added up to two.

"I'd be far more worried about angering the goddess than the king. You know, eternal damnation and all that. I heard the Lord of the Underworld burns off your skin, and you just have to walk around like that. All bleeding and muscly, screaming in agony."

"Hmm," the first one said, clearly skeptical about the other's claims. "I suppose."

He eyed Cloris up and down one more time, but she sensed victory at hand.

"Fine. Come with me," he said. "But don't touch anything."

She nodded and dipped her head as the guard turned and gestured for her to follow. They wound through several resplendent corridors, passing rooms full of merry High Fae cavorting and drinking. She caught sight of a group of young women, all in gold dresses, huddling together at the end of a salon watching an acrobat twist through a golden suspended ring. She recalled what the guard had just said about the Trials and realized she had arrived in Aphelion just in time.

Another sign from Zerra that she was on the right track.

"Wait here," the guard said to her as they came to a stop outside a set of massive golden doors. The guard went to confer with yet another pair of guards as they cast looks at her and then argued with each other. This was getting so very tiresome. There was a time when a High Priestess of Zerra would have been welcomed with open arms and bestowed with every luxury the kingdom could afford. Not treated like a common criminal here to abscond with the silverware stuffed down her shirt.

"Need I remind you that the mark of Zerra is to be respected and that it begs an immediate audience with any ruler in Ouranos? Surely you haven't forgotten what the *goddess* does to those who disobey?"

They might fear the Lord's wrath, but his would be a damp flickering match compared to what Zerra could invoke when tested.

One of the guards standing outside the king's chamber finally nodded and disappeared inside. Well, at least this was progress.

They all waited in silence for several long minutes, the tension stretching into gossamer.

Finally, the guard returned.

"You may come." The guard gestured her towards him. He ushered her into a study lined with pale yellow tiles and golden shelves filled with knickknacks and other curios. A large arched window at the end looked over onto the bright blue sea of Aphelion.

"Have a seat," the guard said. "His Majesty will be here in a moment."

She did as he asked, dropping into the shiny leather couch tufted with golden buttons, and waited.

And waited.

She lost track of the hours, but the sun started sinking over the horizon, and her stomach rumbled with hunger. How long was this king going to make her sit here? Perhaps this had all been a mistake. She lifted a hand to her forehead, feeling the twinges of a headache cresting at her temples. They'd plagued her ever since that fateful day in Heart, their intensity so fierce that sometimes her vision went blank. None of the usual remedies worked, and all she could do was lie in her bed for days with the curtains drawn, waiting for them to pass.

This was an insult. This was ridiculous. When she was about to get up and demand to see the king, the door finally swung open, and there he was.

He shot a beaming smile in her direction.

"Thank you for your patience," said the Sun King. "It's been a day."

He strode into the room and walked over to the bar cart in the corner. "Can I get you a drink?"

"No," she said, her tone clipped. "I'm fine."

He poured himself a good measure of whisky and then walked over and sunk down in the seat across from her. Crossing one leg over the other, he took a sip. He was all casual grace and easy elegance with that coppery hair and bronzed skin, like he didn't have a care in the world. Like he hadn't made her sit here for half the day waiting for him.

"Now, to what do I owe the pleasure of this visit?" he asked. "I didn't catch your name?"

"It's Mathilde," she said, using the fake name she'd adopted years ago. It had been the name of a childhood friend who'd succumbed to the Withering when they'd been girls.

"Mathilde," Atlas said. "What can I do for you? I can't say that I've ever had the pleasure of meeting one of Zerra's emissaries before. Imagine my surprise when I was told you had come to speak with me."

Cloris sat forward, twisting her hands in her lap. She needed to approach this carefully.

"I have come to you on a matter of some importance." He waited, studying her with those piercing aqua eyes as he sipped his drink. "There is a girl who lives inside Nostraza. One who may be of some interest to you."

His eyebrow raised at that. "Why should I care about a girl inside Nostraza?"

"She is no ordinary girl, you see. She is . . . the granddaughter of Queen Serce."

Atlas paused with his glass nearly at his lips, narrowing his gaze. "You interrupt my day to bring me lies? Is this behavior becoming of Zerra's disciples?"

She had expected this. It had been the same with Rion.

Though just like with the Aurora King, she could tell she had piqued his interest.

"It's not a lie," she said. "I would never come to you without being absolutely sure it is the truth."

"How do you come by this information?"

A fair question, and one she'd have to answer truthfully, at least in part.

"I knew Cloris Payne," she said. "She was my sister. I knew she'd gotten involved with the future Heart Queen, and I cautioned her against it. But she was resolute. I was worried she was getting in over her head, so I traveled to Heart to check in on her. But I was too late. I was nearby when it all happened, and I saw them leave the castle before the breaking."

"Who did you see leaving?" Atlas asked, sitting forward and uncrossing his legs, his attention entirely focused on her now.

"The child."

Atlas blinked, several things shifting in his expression.

"The child perished with Serce and Wolf."

"She did not," Cloris replied. "Serce delivered her just before the end. King Wolf's soldiers secreted the baby from the castle and back to The Woodlands. It was *their* child. I followed them to the Fort, where the baby was passed to Prince Cedar for protection and his guardianship. She was sent into the forest to live out her days undercover, never to reveal who she was."

Atlas furrowed his brows, clasping the glass in his hand.

"This doesn't seem possible. How do I know you're not lying about all of this?"

"I am not lying. What reason would I have to make this up?"

Atlas smirked. "What reason indeed? Why are you coming to me with this information?"

This was where she knew he'd balk. "Because I need you to get Serce's granddaughter out of Nostraza."

Atlas snorted a laugh. "And how do you propose I do that? Walk up to Rion and ask for him to release the supposed heir of Heart into my care? Do you have any idea what would happen if this girl were to be discovered?"

Cloris nodded. "Of course I know. That's why I'm here." She said it softly and witnessed the deviation in the king's expression. It was at that moment that she knew he believed her.

"But no, you cannot go to the Aurora King and ask for her. He will not let her go."

"Does he know who she is?"

Another fair question. "Yes."

"Then why is she locked up? Why hasn't he brought her out? Made use of her in some way? Or better yet, killed her?"

"Because he broke her," Cloris said.

Oh yes, Rion had made a grave misjudgment in his treatment of the girl. She'd locked away her magic, and he'd tried and tried to pry it out. Cloris had stood by, watching her scream and writhe and cry. Watched her fight against him until he had no choice but to give up.

But rather than admit it, Rion had declared she was useless, and there was no point in bothering with her. If there was magic, then it was gone. But Cloris was sure the girl had merely been bent but not broken.

What she did know was the girl would forever be useless

to her if she remained inside Nostraza. She'd tried again and again to make Rion try something else with her, but he refused, saying it was no use. He was afraid. He must have known what it meant that she'd withstood him.

Cloris had pleaded with him not to kill her, and he reluctantly agreed once she reminded him that if the girl died, the magic of Heart would transfer to someone else, and they might have no idea who. At least with her safely inside Nostraza, he could keep an eye on her and keep her contained.

It had been years, but Cloris knew the girl still lived. And now what she needed was to get her hands on her and undo the damage Rion had caused. It might be the only way to find the lost ark of Heart.

"What do you mean he broke her?" Atlas asked.

"I mean he tortured her until her magic . . . died."

"There is no magic left in Heart," he declared, but there was an edge to the words, as though he already realized they couldn't be true. She'd never heard much about the Sun King's intelligence, but he was astute enough to keep up with her at least.

"There is," she whispered. "There is magic left if you know where to look."

He blinked again, a wall dropping behind his eyes. She understood this was a lot to take in. Rion had reacted similarly.

"I still don't understand what this has to do with me," Atlas said, though she could tell he was eager to know just *what* it might have to do with him.

"You are not yet bonded," Cloris said, and Atlas nodded

slowly. "Do you really want to tether yourself to one of these simpering girls?"

"A bonding with the Heart Queen?"

Clarity flickered across his gaze like he'd wiped a fogged-over mirror with his sleeve and could finally see a glorious future shining in the distance.

"I know your truth," Cloris said. "What *did* you do with your brother?"

She tipped her head and blinked at him, allowing him to fill in the uncomfortable pieces himself. Thanks to her connection with Zerra, Cloris had always known Atlas wasn't the Primary. Until now, she hadn't concerned herself with how exactly he'd claimed the title of king, but now she would use that knowledge to her advantage.

"My brother died of the Withering," Atlas said. "Everyone knows that."

The Withering was a rare affliction that affected only High Fae. It happened when their magic began to turn on them, essentially eating them from the inside. No one knew what caused it or why only certain Fae were afflicted, and there was no known cure. Sometimes Fae could live for decades with the Withering as it slowly chewed away at their bodies, while other times it came on suddenly, and a once-healthy High Fae would find themselves dead within a few weeks.

The story was that the former Sun King, Tyr, had been one of those who'd succumbed quickly.

Cloris pressed her lips into a thin line, resisting the urge to fill the prickly silence between them. Let him be the one to hang himself.

"I'm in the middle of the Trials as we speak," Atlas said, as though he wasn't quite ready to accept what she was offering, poking her story with holes. "It's too late."

"Is it? Has the fourth test been completed?"

Again, she said nothing as she let him work through this process on his own. No, it was not too late.

"Let's say I believe you. How would I bond to the Heart Queen? How would that work?" He sharpened his gaze and added, "What do you ask for in return for all of this?"

This was where Cloris had to play her cards carefully. She'd let too much slip to Rion in a moment of weakness. Her thoughts became so muddled sometimes, and he spoke so harshly to her that her tongue had loosened against her will. She'd revealed things she had never meant to. It wasn't a mistake she'd make again.

"She is the key to finding something I've lost," Cloris said. "Or rather, the sisterhood lost many years ago. Once I have her then I can use her to find this item, which will then allow her to bond to you."

There. She hoped that sounded reasonable enough.

"What kind of object?" he asked.

"One of great power. One that can bend the will of the Artefacts. Once I have it, I will help you get everything you desire, and then I will return the object to where it belongs, with my goddess."

It was partly the truth. She knew the arks could channel the magic of the Artefacts, though she wasn't privy to the true extent of their power. She was almost certain she couldn't actually force a bonding with the heir of Heart, but she just needed Atlas to believe she could long enough to get her hands on the girl. Once she had the ark, she'd do away with her and hopefully end Serce's miserable line forever.

"And what if I refuse?" Atlas asked.

She hadn't quite worked that part out yet. Go to another ruler? Could she risk yet another one of them knowing? Alluvion would be the only remaining kingdom that made sense, but Cyan already had his hands full.

Atlas was far more malleable towards this proposal. A pretty young face and a promise of power—that would sway him. Cloris hoped the girl was pretty enough, though she worried what the years in Nostraza might have done to her.

"How long have you been waiting, Your Majesty? To bond with someone who holds real power? When Queen Serce . . . declined you, was that not . . . troubling?"

His gaze flashed at those pointed words, the subject clearly still a sore spot all these years later.

"How do you know about that?" he snarled.

"Does it matter?" she asked, watching him with an unwavering expression.

But there it was. The moment she knew she had him.

This would be his chance to redo history. To take back what he'd lost.

"Do we have an agreement?" she asked.

He nodded, his eyes far away, as though he was turning over a thousand thoughts in his head.

"I'll have to make some arrangements." He'd long abandoned

his drink and was sitting with his elbows on his knees, a thumb running across his bottom lip. "It might take time to get her out without alerting Rion."

"Of course," Cloris said. "It will need a deft hand to maneuver it, but I'm sure someone with your skills and resources can accomplish the task."

"You'll stay in the city then," Atlas said. "As my guest, of course."

"It would be an honor," she said, concealing her triumphant smile with a deferential bow of her head. "I look forward to working with you."

Atlas stood up then, rubbing his palms on his thighs. "I must get back."

"Thank you for hearing me out."

"I'll make arrangements for you to stay in the city. It will be comfortable."

"Thank you again," Cloris said, once more dipping her head. When she lifted it, the Sun King was already gone.

CHAPTER THIRTY-ONE

LOR

ON THE ROAD TO APHELION: PRESENT DAY

We make our way back to Aphelion. I haven't said anything to Tristan about what I've learned, because I'm
not sure how to break this to him. The Woodlands Primary.
Will he be happy? Scared? As overwhelmed as I am?

Somehow, we'd always imagined it would be me on a
throne with Tristan and Willow at my side—that was the
story our mother painted for us. But maybe we should have
anticipated our paths would eventually diverge.

"What's wrong?" Nadir asks after we stop for a rest.

Mael and Tristan have gone off to explore, arguing with one
another about what kinds of fish inhabit the nearby stream,

while Nadir and I remain by the fire. Etienne has returned to the settlements to ensure everything is stable after the king's men evaded their previous surveillance. After another sweep to ensure they've truly evacuated this time, he will meet us back in Aphelion to help with the next phase of our plan, whatever that is.

"Nothing," I say.

He takes my hands in one of his and gives me a serious look.

"You can't hide from me anymore."

"I learned something else from the Staff," I say, biting the corner of my lip. "About Tristan."

Nadir's gaze turns shrewd. "You should talk to him first."

"Thank you," I say, grateful he understands the need to speak to my brother alone. It wouldn't be fair to Tristan.

"Is that all?" he asks.

"There's something else about my grandmother," I admit.

"What about her?"

"She did it on purpose, Nadir. Her mother. The priestess. They all warned her it wouldn't work. That she was destined for ruin. She tried to take the magic of Heart, and she did it. She stole the Crown off her mother's head and tried to take it. None of it was an accident. Or at least not in the way people assume."

Nadir is quiet for a moment, and I listen to the crackle of the fire and the stirring of the leaves in the breeze.

"What bothers you the most about knowing that?"

The question forces me to consider several options. What *is* bothering me?

"I suppose it's knowing that she was selfish and didn't care what happened to anyone else in her desire for power. When Rhiannon told me about her, none of her stories painted my grandmother in the most flattering light. I thought maybe she was just young and foolish, but after seeing what really happened, now I'm not so confident about that."

"But you understand none of that is a reflection on you and the person you are?"

Zerra, how does he always see straight through me?

"Isn't it, though? They already curse her name throughout Ouranos, and they don't even know the whole truth. What do you think everyone will believe of me if they learn this too?"

Nadir leans down and presses a soft kiss to the space below my ear. "They're going to judge you for the queen you are. Not the one that died centuries ago."

My answer is a wary look.

"Right. Because I'm sure you've never been judged against the evidence of your father's actions."

"That's different," he says, his jaw clenching. "My father is still alive and very much indulging in said 'actions,' but your grandmother lived many years ago. They can judge me because I am his son and have been under his thumb for my entire life."

His eyes darken with some unvoiced trauma, and I decide not to push him on what he's saying, knowing there are things he hasn't shared with me yet. Perhaps in time he will. Still, I'm not sure how it's actually different, and I am positive no one will overlook what my grandmother did. Everyone wants a scapegoat for the wrongs done to them, and if it can't be her, then it will be the one who wears her crown.

I lean my head against his shoulder and let out a sigh. His arm wraps around me, his hand running up and down my arm.

"Nadir?"

"Yes, Lightning Bug?"

I peer up at him, and he cocks a smile.

"What?" he asks.

"That's going to take some getting used to. You calling me that. Us like this."

There's a brief flash of uncertainty in his expression, and I sit up, taking his face in my hands.

"I don't mean that in a bad way. Just that we've been one thing since the day we met, and now we're something else. And it's just like that. There was no transition. From enemies to mates."

The last word echoes in the silent clearing. A promise and an oath.

"You were never my enemy, Lor. I never saw you that way, even when I was tearing my hair out in the manor house because you were driving me insane."

I snort out a laugh. "You had just *kidnapped* me."

"*Rescued* you," he counters.

"You were *my* enemy," I whisper. "I was so... angry. I needed somewhere to direct all that rage, and you made the most sense."

"I know." His smug smile says it all, though, and I'm so grateful he's not holding my behavior against me. "But I knew in my heart of hearts that you and I were meant to be. I just had to be patient."

I bark out a laugh. "Patient. You stole me from the middle of a party and threw me over your shoulder because I looked at another man. And you broke another one's wrist because he was nice to me."

He spreads his hands. "Look, I did the best I could."

"Thank you for giving me the space I needed these last few weeks. It was killing me. I wanted you, but I didn't want to want you."

He snorts a dry laugh. "You have no idea how close to madness I came, Lor."

"I aim to always keep you on your toes, Aurora Prince."

He touches my cheek, the tips of his fingers both rough and soft in the most delicious and perfect way.

"I know you do," he whispers as his thumb presses into my bottom lip.

"It was unfair to ever blame you for any of it. Thank you for putting up with me."

"Lor, I—" I lean in and kiss him, silencing whatever contradiction he wants to voice.

"No. You're not going to blame yourself. Your father. Atlas. My grandparents. They are the ones to blame. The only thing I ask now is you give me whatever strength you can to help me work through my . . . issues."

He tips his head with a soft smile. "You mean like the anger and the reckless impulsiveness?"

I know he's only teasing, but it's not far from the truth. "That would be a start."

"Listen to me, Heart Queen," he continues. "I love those things about you. They're what make you, you. So yes, I'm here to help you face whatever demons you need to slay, but don't ever lose that fire. You might be my mate, but I would have fallen in love with you anyway because you are impossible to ignore."

"Okay," I whisper as those words touch something deep in my chest. I've never had someone see and understand me so clearly. Yes, I've had Tristan and Willow, but they could only be so much. The love of a sibling is different from that of a partner—especially one destined to stand by your side.

"I'm here for you, too," I say, looking up at him. "If you need."

He cracks a wry smile, and I get the sense he's holding something back. I don't let that bother me, though. Anything he's holding close has nothing to do with me—he just needs the same space I've needed. With everything I know about his mother and what he's told me about his father, I know I'm not the only one with monsters prowling through their memories.

So, about this?

His voice enters my head.

What about it?

I'm thinking about all the filthy things I can now say to you when we aren't alone.

I roll my eyes.

That's hardly a respectful use of this talent.

His smile widens, and the way he looks at me feels like a gift wrapped in shiny paper and curled ribbon.

"Rhiannon said sometimes mates can hear each other's thoughts," I say out loud now. "I assumed we had to bond first, but I guess not."

"I realize I heard you in Heart that night those men took you."

"I called to you," I say. "Maybe we just had to acknowledge the mate bond to make it work."

He takes my hand and kisses the back. "I love you," he says.

Ruin. Heartbreak.

The Torch's words stalk through the chambers of my mind.

"Nadir, there's something else we need to talk about regarding the bond. I think two things happened that day with my grandparents."

"What?" he asks.

"My grandmother tried to take the magic of Heart, but I think something went wrong with the sealing of the bond. That's what they needed Cloris for. But she couldn't help them at the end, and my grandmother tried to do it herself. That's what caused at least some of the damage."

He watches me with a serious expression.

"If we want to bond, then we have to find a way to do so that doesn't blow up half of Ouranos again."

He rubs his hands down his face. "Fuck, nothing is ever easy with us, is it?"

"At least we're never bored."

"We'll figure it out, Lor," he says, wrapping his hand around the side of my neck. "Whatever we have to do."

I nod. He's right.

That is not our destiny. I won't let it be.

We look at each other, and my heart squeezes.

The sun is starting to set, the air growing cooler as his eyes turn hungry.

He leans down and sucks gently on the curve of my neck.

"I want you," he says, his voice rough. "Here. Now. Spread out on the floor, where I feast to my heart's content. I want to fuck you somewhere we can be alone, where no one can hear us for weeks, so I can make you scream my name until your voice gives out."

His hand slides from my knee and up my thigh, sending shivers over my skin, even through the leather of my riding pants. I wonder if there will ever come a day when I stop craving him like air.

"Say the word, Aurora Prince," I gasp as his hand slides between my legs, the heel of his hand pressing on the seam of my pants with just the right amount of pressure.

"Somewhere on a mountaintop perhaps," he says. "Or deep in a forgotten forest where no one will find us."

A moan slips from my mouth as he grinds his hand against me. I grab onto his arm, and my head tips back as he places a row of kisses along my jaw.

First, we have to get into the Sun Palace. First, we have to get past Atlas and avoid Nadir's father, who is out there somewhere hunting for us. If we survive any of this, maybe we'll have the chance to live out this fantasy.

"I'm going to do everything in my power to make sure we get that," he says, once again reading my thoughts. His hand continues to press into me, and my back arches as my eyes flutter closed.

"What the fuck are you two doing?" comes a voice that makes Nadir go still. My brain takes a moment to catch up, and I want to protest this unwelcome interruption. "Is this what we have to put up with now? The two of you behaving like horny rabbits whenever I turn my back?"

Nadir snarls as he retrieves his hand from between my legs, and Mael offers us a smarmy grin, his eyes dancing with joy.

"What's going on?" comes my brother's voice next, as he looks from me to Nadir while my face warms. It's one thing for Mael to show up, but it's quite another for my brother to catch us in the impending throes of lust.

"We walked in on something," Mael says in a singsong voice, and Tristan's face darkens as he takes the two of us in.

Tristan is dripping in water, his hair and his clothing completely soaked.

"Why are you wet?" I ask, eager to change the subject.

Mael barks out a laugh and slings a limp fish off his shoulder.

"We found a log in the river, perfect for rolling. We made a bet, and he lost." Mael grins at Tristan, who throws him another glower.

"Well, glad to see you're getting along?" I ask, as Tristan leans down to dig into his pack and pulls out a tunic.

"The bastard cheated," Tristan says, yanking off his wet top and exchanging it for the dry one.

"I did not cheat," Mael says, pressing a hand to his chest. "I really did think I saw a bear."

Then Mael looks at me and winks.

"It was a squirrel."

Mael waves a hand. "Squirrel. Bear. I get them mixed up sometimes. I'm more of a city guy."

Nadir and I exchange a glance as they continue to argue, trying to suppress our smiles.

Mael sets to preparing the fish, and before long, he hands us all a tender piece.

"Did you learn to cook in the army too?" I ask as I accept the food, remembering what Nadir told me that night in the Heart Castle.

Mael snorts. "No. I wasn't born with a silver spoon in my mouth. I had to learn to cook at an early age. I was the oldest of eleven brothers and sisters, and we all had to pull our weight."

It's hard to imagine Mael outside his role as Nadir's captain, but obviously, he had a life before that too.

"Where are they now?" I ask as he sits down across from us.

"In The Aurora. After the war, Nadir made me his captain, and I moved my mother from the tiny house where we grew up and helped all my siblings get settled in homes of their own. I don't want for much living in the Keep, and my compensation is . . . generous."

He and Nadir exchange a look, and it's obvious they're sharing a message. I'm not sure what Mael means by "generous," but I have a sense I understand.

"It's a good thing I've never had a head for numbers," Nadir says. "I'm sure you drink more whisky from my stash than I pay you in a year."

Mael snorts and smiles. "At least twice as much."

"Well, maybe one of you can teach me someday," I say. "I never really had the chance to learn how."

"Right," Tristan says. "Because she was tossed in prison as a—"

"Tris," I say, interrupting him. "Don't. That isn't necessary."

I understand. While I've forgiven Nadir for everything, Tristan has no reason to do the same.

"What?" Tristan asks. "Is this about protecting him?" He gestures to Nadir.

"No, it's about protecting me."

"Lor, I don't get to dictate who you . . . choose to spend your time with. You've always made that clear, but—"

"No, you don't. That's always been true. But I also understand why you aren't ready to trust him. It took me a long time too."

"Not really that long," Tristan says, and I nod.

"You're right. It must seem fast, but we've spent a lot of time together, and I need you to accept that he's a part of my life now, even if you're not ready to make him a part of yours."

"Lor," Nadir interrupts. "It's okay."

"No, it isn't. Tristan, please. You and Willow are two of the most important people in my life. You know that. But it's not just the three of us against the world anymore."

It's been only a few months since I was nothing but a prisoner who never knew if she'd see the next day. And now I've competed for a crown, I'm being hunted by two rabid kings, and I've met the man I'm supposed to spend the rest of my life with. Everything has changed.

When Willow and I argued a few days ago, I was the one worried about how she might already be slipping away from me, but now that our lives have expanded in ways none of us ever imagined, I understand all of this was inevitable. It had been naive for any of us to think that if we ever got out of

Nostraza, we wouldn't have to contend with a million outside influences vying for our attention.

Tristan's eyes flicker from me to Nadir and back. "Why, because he's your *mate*?"

Mael chuckles, and Tristan tosses him a dark look. Mael raises his hands in supplication.

"Sorry. I'm not laughing at you."

"Then who are you laughing at?" Tristan demands.

"Him." Mael cocks his head towards Nadir, who raises an eyebrow in response. "You've been such a fucking mess since she showed up. It's a relief to know there was a reason, and it wasn't only down to your sparkling personality."

Nadir opens his mouth as if to argue and then snaps it shut before he gives me a small smile. "I might have been a little in my head the past few weeks."

"So you're destined or something?" Tristan asks. I explain everything I've been feeling and what Rhiannon told me about the bond. When I'm finished, Tristan is quiet.

"Remember our grandparents were mates too," I say, and that makes something flicker in his expression. "Rhiannon said they loved each other very much."

Tristan rubs a hand down his face. "So that means you're stuck with him. With the son of the king that killed our family and locked us up for half our lives."

I nod. "The very same one," I say softly. "I hope that in time you can learn to accept him. I know why it's hard to trust him, but believe me when I say Nadir has had only my best interests at heart." I pause, thinking of how he stole me from Aphelion so he could interrogate me and told me he would have disposed of me had I turned out to be no one of importance. "Mostly," I add.

I understand why he did those things, and they had nothing to do with me. Not really.

"It means you're stuck with him, too, Tris. Because any future I have beyond what we're trying to achieve is one that includes both of you in it."

Tristan lets out a deep sigh and peers at Nadir as if looking at him properly for the very first time.

Nadir grins and leans forward, holding out a hand. "Welcome to the family, Brother."

Tristan's glare is hard as stone, and Nadir winks.

"Okay, too soon for that. We'll work on it."

Chapter Thirty-Two

Gabriel

The Sun Palace

I already hate today. Lately, I sort of hate every day, if I'm being honest. Ever since Atlas set a date for the bonding with Apricia, I can't get a moment of fucking peace. She's everywhere. Screeching at anyone within firing distance, and no matter how hard I try to hide, she manages to sniff me out like a bloodhound...or maybe a rat or some equally unpleasant pest with an unnaturally gifted nose and a penchant for bestowing misery.

It seems she's decided that because the warders exist to do Atlas's bidding, we're also there for hers. Fuck that. Even if I didn't want to toss her into shark-infested waters, the very last thing on my to-do list would be picking up flower arrangements and holding up the train of the ridiculous dress she ordered.

I almost burst out laughing when she came into Atlas's study wearing it. It's about as wide as a house, and it has so many crystals and gold beads, I was shocked she didn't tip right over. Even Atlas had a hard time holding in his grimace, though he made a good show of pretending he thought she looked beautiful.

Atlas has changed a lot in the past few weeks. He's lost weight, and there are bags under his eyes. I know he isn't sleeping because I haven't found Lor yet. With one week until the bonding, he's pressuring me with increased urgency every day. I really hope Lor is figuring out how to get inside the palace so I don't have to continue lying. Not because I care about being truthful with Atlas, but because the strain of keeping this secret—the aches and pains plaguing my joints and my limbs—means I can't hold out much longer.

Today I find myself inexplicably standing inside Apricia's entertaining salon, having been summoned by a shrill screech echoing through the halls. Was she this insufferable during the Trials, or has the power of her position made her worse?

She's currently outlining the seating arrangements for dinner after the ceremony, though I have absolutely no idea why. Does she think I'm going to remember any of this? Or that I care which spoiled noble sits next to another? As she turns to face the window, still talking, I pinch the bridge of my nose. In just a few more days, all those said nobles will start entering the palace, not only from the twenty-four districts but also from the rest of Ouranos.

Apricia whips around, and I look up, feeling like a school-boy caught with his hand down the front of his pants. Which is ridiculous. Zerra, how does she do that? Part of me is considering giving up Lor to Atlas solely so Apricia doesn't actually become my queen. But even I'm not that much of a bastard. I think. At this point, the chances are fifty-fifty.

"Are you paying attention to me?" she demands, and it's literally all I can do not to roll my eyes far enough to see the inside of my skull. My forehead cramps from struggling to keep them in place.

"Of course," I say, tipping my head. But she's not technically my queen yet, and I'm not required to add "Your Majesty" to that, a detail that she must notice, because she narrows her eyes.

"Then who did I say should sit next to Lady Boliver?"

Fuck me. I scratch my chin, wondering if I should try to answer this or simply walk away. I do not care if Apricia is angry, unless it means she'll follow me down the hallway waving her broomstick until my eardrums burst and leak out of my ears.

"Lord Ferdinand?" I say, because I decide answering incorrectly will be more fun and lord knows I need all the comic relief I can get right now.

Her eyes narrow into knife-sharp points dedicated to slicing through my vital organs.

"I said Lord Summers," she hisses. "If you ruin this ceremony..."

"Perhaps..." I say, interrupting her, which makes her cheeks turn pink and her neck flush in a decidedly unattractive way. She looks like a lobster that tried its mother's lipstick with unflattering results. "... I'm not the best person for this discussion? I've never had a good head for names."

"You are the captain," she says. "It's your job to know these people better than anyone."

"I assure you that of the many illustrious and honorable duties I am burdened with, that is not one of them," I say, and I'm not sure how she turns redder, but somehow, she does. "I couldn't tell you the difference between Lord Summers and Lord Spring Flowers if my life depended on it. Surely this is your arena."

She stares at me, considering my words, and I wonder if this might work. If I might manage to convince her to afflict some other hapless fool with this painful task. She blinks and nods her head, and my shoulders sag with relief.

"You're right."

"Perfect. Then I'll leave you to it," I say, and turn on my heel, attempting to escape like my boots have been doused in oil and lit on fire.

"In that case, I'll put you in charge of the deliveries," she says, her voice pitching up at the end, and I freeze. "There will be dozens and *dozens* of them over the next week. Flowers. Fabrics. Food. Wine. Someone will need to figure out where it all goes."

Slowly, I turn around, exhaling a paper-thin breath.

"Apricia—" I cut myself off at her glare, which suggests she'd gladly scoop out my spleen and serve it as an appetizer drizzled with butter. "*Your Majesty.* I am already quite busy with the king's security. Surely someone else can do that."

My teeth are grinding so hard I'm going to wear them down to blunted nubs. My gaze darts to a Fae female who stands off to the side, her hands clasped and her lips folded together as though she's trying to restrain a laugh. I think I remember her from her interview a week ago, and I feel rather sorry for her that she got the job.

Who is she laughing at? Me? Apricia? She looks up, and our gazes meet before she quickly looks away and covers her mouth, her narrow shoulders shaking. I decide that, yes, she's laughing at Apricia and is sympathizing with me, because only a masochist would ever take Apricia's side.

The snapping of fingers draws my attention back to the golden menace currently making my life hell.

"No, it makes perfect sense. You're already in charge of who's coming and going, managing all the extra deliveries is only logical. See that it's done."

She spins around and starts firing orders at her maids. I wonder if that means I'm dismissed. I want to protest that I really don't have time for this, but I'd be a fool not to seize my chance to escape. I'll discuss it with Atlas. Until now, I've resisted going to him with his future queen's demands, but I'm truly at my wit's end.

Ducking out of the room, I breathe a sigh of relief. Somehow Apricia's voice manages to follow me through the palace until I'm far, far away from her wing. Even then, I can hear her nattering like it's been tattooed on my brain.

After a while, I double back and head down a dark hallway, making my way to the entrance of Tyr's tower. When I arrive, I check again, but the coast is clear, the hall as silent as always.

I pull out my keys and unlock the door. I don't have anything for him today—this is a spontaneous visit. I just feel the need to say hello.

I close the door behind me and then wind my way up the stairs. Tyr sits by an open window when I enter. His eyes are closed as he allows the soft breeze and warm sun to land on his face. I can't remember the last time I saw him do this. I'm not sure if he knows I'm here, but he remains still, so I take the opportunity to study him for a moment.

I recall those years that feel like a lifetime ago when Atlas locked him up.

Atlas and Tyr's father, Kyros, chose to descend after the Second Sercen War, making room for Tyr to take over. Aphelion suffered many catastrophic blows during the battle that Kyros took personally. He wasn't the same after the dust settled, and I think he was content to let his son take over while he descended with their mother into the Evanescence to put the pieces of himself back together.

Despite those failings, he was a good king and wherever he is, I hope he's at peace.

Tyr named ten new warders as part of his ascension, including me. I'd trained for it for years, knowing this was my only future. I had no name and no family, only the memories of my childhood to haunt my waking dreams.

My father had been an abusive piece of shit and a mean drunk whose favorite pastime was pummeling and then raping my mother. He'd lock my twin brother and me in the larder when he was angry so he could hit her in peace without—as he so eloquently put it—"our sniveling making his dick soft."

After he'd knock her out, he'd start in on the two of us. We tried to shield one another, but it was no use. We were so small, and he was a cruel, broken man.

One day, he lost control. He went too far and killed my mother and brother. I fought against him, cracking a chair over his head. I still don't know how I managed it. It knocked him out, and I finally saw my chance to escape. I hated leaving my mother and brother, but there was nothing left I could do for them.

I lost myself in the woods, where I wandered for weeks, alone, hurt, and hungry, until King Kyros and a hunting party stumbled upon me when I tried to ambush them with a stick. I had little idea of how to forage for sustenance myself. I'd found some berries and mushrooms and other smaller items, but I was too scared to eat most of it, never knowing which bits were poisonous.

I lied and told them I was all alone. It was mostly true. I didn't know if my father still lived, but for all intents and purposes, my family was gone, and I was utterly solitary in this world.

When I was ordained as one of Tyr's warders, it was both the end and the beginning of my life. While I was now a servant with no autonomy of my own, I also would never want for any comforts in this life again.

Atlas ruled at Tyr's side for many years, but I could sense he was always on edge and couldn't quite settle in his role, constantly wanting to do more. He hated that he didn't have the same destructive powers as his brother, having to content himself with his more docile illusions. He'd also never gotten over the way he'd been rejected by the Heart Princess all those years ago, even if there was almost no one left alive to remember it.

Never underestimate the enduring fragility of a man who suffers from a lack of confidence.

He started to undermine Tyr every chance he got, trying to strip away the king's confidence instead, telling him that all of Aphelion's problems were a direct result of Tyr's failings. I tried to open Tyr's eyes to the games Atlas was playing, but Atlas has always been a master of manipulation, weaving his illusions to support his truths. Sometimes I wonder who truly held the real power.

I was with Atlas the day Tyr walked in to find the two of us, clearly stricken about something. He stared at Atlas with the most haunted look in his eyes before he paced the room, running his hands through his hair and muttering to himself.

Atlas had demanded to know what the problem was, and after a lot of coaxing, Tyr admitted the Mirror had spoken to him.

It had just revealed the Primary of Aphelion. And it wasn't Atlas.

I'll never forget that moment. It was as though our entire lives had just been knocked off course, our fates all careening towards disaster. Though it was just a feeling then, I had no idea just how much everything would change.

Atlas lost his shit, tearing up the study—smashing windows and objects, ripping books and pictures from the walls—until finally Tyr and I subdued him. Several of the other warders arrived to help, but only I had been privy to the truth Tyr had revealed.

After that, Atlas calmed down, though I could tell it was a thin veneer layered over the restlessness that had dogged him since the war.

Then one day, Atlas declared Tyr was being taken by the Withering. That he was too weak to see or talk to anyone, save me and the other warders.

To this day, I don't know what Atlas did to him, but I've always suspected poison, drugging Tyr until he was too weak to do anything about it. I don't know what lies he whispered in his brother's ear, but somehow, he managed to convince him to give the order to the warders—that Atlas would be taking over and that no one was ever to speak of Tyr's existence in the tower.

But Atlas couldn't kill Tyr, because the magic of Aphelion would transfer to the true Primary, and he would risk losing it forever.

A body was procured for the funeral, and Atlas worked his magic to make it look so much like Tyr that it almost fooled even me. Then he sequestered his brother into this tower and cuffed him with the arcturite, where he's been ever since.

Eventually, Tyr recovered from whatever Atlas had done to him, but his life was over.

The secret we've all had to keep is the worst thing I've ever had to do.

"How are you doing?" I say to Tyr as I sit down in the second chair that faces the window. Atlas rarely comes to see him, and the other warders aren't comfortable with being in his presence. Not because of anything Tyr has done but because he's a reminder of their forced betrayal. The prickly truth of what we're all complicit in, though none of us has much choice.

In the months after Atlas locked him away, I convinced Tyr to move against his brother's wishes only once. Tyr ordered the warders to gather Aphelion's council inside their usual meeting chamber so we could expose Atlas's lies. We knew they'd never believe it without the proof of seeing Tyr alive in the flesh.

But Atlas's paranoia extended further than I imagined, and he'd already placed spies in every district head's household. With twenty-four districts and only ten warders, word got to Atlas before we could execute all the parts of our plan.

When the council arrived, Atlas was ready to greet them. He convinced everyone he'd summoned them to discuss building a monument to each ruler in the center of their district, and thanks to his flattery and their delicate egos, no one questioned that the facts didn't quite add up.

After they left, I'd never seen Atlas so furious. He railed at Tyr and then he turned his rage on me and my brothers. He had each of us tortured before Tyr's eyes, saving the worst for me.

I don't know if Atlas was jealous of the relationship between me and Tyr and resented our closeness, but whatever it was, he finally found a way to use it against both of us.

My mind has done its best to block out those days.

The pain. The blood. The burns. The screams.

The scars on my chest, back, arms, and legs will never truly let me forget.

After that, Tyr refused to move against Atlas's wishes ever

again. And so, we dance this vicious dance, twirling in circles, neither one of us knowing how to break out of its ever tightening noose.

"The palace is in shambles thanks to the future queen," I say, and I swear I catch the slightest hint of Tyr's smile.

I desperately want to know how this will all go down if Atlas gets his hands on Lor.

She's a Primary, which means anyone she bonds with will receive the benefit of her magic when she ascends. After I learned of her origins, it all made much more sense. That's what Atlas was after. He resents the fact he doesn't have a Primary's magic. But will it work if he uses the Mirror?

Does Lor have the Artefact of Heart? The Crown was lost as far as I'm aware, but I'm assuming Lor and Nadir haven't been entirely truthful with me.

"She's a right pain in my ass," I add, and Tyr slowly turns his head, his blue eyes simmering with so many things that we haven't said in so many years. There was a time when I thought Tyr and I—

I shake my head, refusing to torment myself with things that might have been.

It doesn't matter. That future died a long time ago.

Maybe it never even started, and I've been kidding myself all along. Tyr was the king, and anyone he bonded with had to be chosen through the Trials. I was probably never really an option, at least not officially.

But now I'll never know.

I settle back and listen to the sound of the waves crashing on the shore as we enjoy the solitude together. This is one of the few times in my week when I finally feel at peace. When I can escape the tumult of my churning thoughts.

After being tethered to this family since I was a small child, there are days when I think I would have been better off abandoned to the forest where Kyros found me.

After he got over the initial shock of my entrance, he scooped me up and brought me back to his hunting lodge in the forest. I thought I'd died and gone to heaven, and that was when I met Atlas and Tyr, both of them only a few years older than me. We spent weeks together running around, learning how to catch small game, and getting into the kinds of mischief small children are known for. It might have been the happiest time of my life. I'd escaped a nightmare and woken up in a dream. I thought about my mother and brother all the time, but I wanted so badly to forget.

It wasn't until they brought me back to Aphelion that I learned I was being conscripted into service. I was too young to know any better, but I joined a group of young High Fae who were all being trained as the Sun King's future warders. It was a grueling process—only a few ever developed the skills demanded of them—and openings in the king's inner circle were rare.

The warders were also a creation of King Cyrus—the same king who'd orchestrated the Trials. Much like his misplaced optimism regarding the Final Tribute, he used the warder corps as an opportunity to elevate those who'd come into this life with nothing more than a name. In theory, it sounds nice. In practice, it's more complicated.

Atlas, Tyr, and I were already friends, and the others

resented my closeness with them. I was determined to prove that I belonged there, so I trained until I collapsed each day. That dedication won me a spot as the youngest warder the Sun Palace had ever seen, though I know there were those who claimed I'd only been given that honor because of my relationship with the princes.

Nevertheless, I underwent the painful process of growing my wings. It's an unusual and rare bit of magic that I couldn't explain if you held a crossbow to my chest, but an enchanted object was used to perform the ceremony.

I'll never forget the agony that ripped across my body when my new appendages tore through my skin like a butterfly cracking out of its cocoon. It took months of training my muscles so the weight didn't cause my back to ache and many more to use them for flight. Despite the pain, I'd considered it an honor and a stroke of luck that Kyros found me in the trees that day.

Little did I know it would all become more like a curse.

My thoughts wander back to the present and to Tyr, who is now watching me.

His brows furrow as though he's wondering what I'm thinking about. I wish he would speak. I sometimes wonder if he's forgotten how.

He used to be such a different person. Bold and loud, sometimes to his detriment, but he's only a shell of the man I knew. The man I thought I might fall in love with once upon a time. And it's not that I don't love him like this, but it's the kind of love bred by the need to protect. It's not the love either of us wanted.

"I was thinking about how we met," I say, answering his unspoken question. "The look on your father's face when I jumped out with that stick." I laugh at the memory, and Tyr's mouth tips up into the smallest of smiles.

"I was no more cultured than a bridge troll," I add, hoping to elicit another, but he sighs and then turns away, looking out the window.

"Is there anything you need?" I ask. "Anything I can bring you?" I hate how helpless I feel whenever I'm around him. It's enough to dread coming here, but if I stopped too, then Tyr would truly have no one left, and I can't do that.

He shakes his head, still not looking at me. And I take that as my cue that he's done for the day.

"I'll bring you some new books," I say, looking over the shelves of stories I know he's heard a hundred times. "What if we did those exercises? I'll come back tomorrow."

I try to get him to move as often as I can. I'm worried about him wasting away to nothing confined to this small space. Sometimes he humors me and does what I ask, but I can tell his heart is never really in it. I need him to fight harder. I need him to fight against this becoming his only fate. With Atlas spiraling and playing games, I'm more sure than ever that Tyr is vulnerable.

"Tyr," I say, crouching down as I grip his forearm. "I need you to be strong. I don't know what's going on, but I think that whatever Atlas is doing has the potential to go very wrong for him. I need you to be ready."

He turns and looks down at me, and I swear that for the first time in decades, I see something flicker in his gaze that looks like more than just resigned defeat. I squeeze his arm, and he looks down to where I'm holding him before he looks up. He tips his chin ever so slightly, though I'm not entirely sure what it means.

"Please," I say again. "I'm ... I don't know yet, but I can't keep doing this, and you can't either."

He nods again and swallows, and I stand to leave, a burning weight burrowing through my chest.

After I close the door, I wind down the stairs, lost in my thoughts. I forget my usual protocol and open the door without listening to check if anyone is walking by. There's the sound of someone stumbling and an "Oh!" as I emerge. A High Fae female is currently bending over, picking up a pile of towels. She appears to be trying very hard to avoid my gaze.

I watch her, wondering if she was leaning against the door. Was she listening?

"What are you doing?" I ask, and she looks up. I recognize her as the same lady's maid I saw with Apricia earlier. The same one I saw at the intake interviews. There's still something familiar about her I can't place my finger on.

"Sorry, I was just passing, and I tripped," she says, scooping up the towels into an armful, not bothering to fold them back up. "Sorry to have disturbed you."

And then she ducks her head and scurries away.

Chapter Thirty-Three

Zerra the Sun Queen

The Evanescence

Zerra listened as every ruler in Ouranos recounted the horrors that had befallen their people. She heard the pain in their voices. The passion in their words. The ends they all went to trying to save their homes.

Still feeling self-conscious in nothing but her scant golden underwear, Zerra stood with her arms wrapped around her waist as she took her turn around the circle, describing the heat. The lack of rain. The thirst. The sluggish ennui that plagued Aphelion.

"What did you do?" Queen Amara of Heart asked. "How did you try to stop it and ease their suffering?"

The question was innocent enough, but it picked at a sore spot. Zerra recalled Cyrus's face, the last one she'd seen before she'd found herself here, when he'd begged her to do something. The way she'd dismissed him with a wave of her hand, more concerned about fucking Eamon and clearing off the beach for her own private use.

"I ... encouraged them to use the water," she said, tucking a loose strand of golden hair behind her ear in a nervous gesture. Shame burned her cheeks as she stammered.

"And?" Astraia, the Star Queen, asked. "What else?"

"I gave them ice. Well ... until we ran out."

Zerra wasn't sure if she imagined the judgment on their faces, but why were they questioning her when they hadn't interrogated anyone else?

When Zerra had nothing else to add, they moved on to King Herric of The Aurora.

He'd been the last to arrive, and after they listened to him describe the withering of his jewel mines, their attention was pulled to a glowing flicker in the center of the circle.

A figure appeared, and Zerra attempted to make out its features, but it shifted. Transforming from a woman with silver hair and lined skin to a young man with a shaved head and a sprinkle of stubble on his cheeks. "Welcome," the figure said with a hundred voices, all blending together like an untuned melody. Zerra blinked, trying to bring them into focus, but the effort made her dizzy, and she rubbed her eyes with the back of a hand.

"What is this?" King Terra demanded. "Who are you?"

The figure continued to change from being to being and

then spoke in that same disorienting voice. "You are at the end of the First Age of Ouranos," they said. "But when one door closes, another opens. The Second Age is about to begin."

They all stared at one another across the circle.

"What does that mean?" Amara asked.

The figure turned to the Heart Queen, and as Zerra watched, she noticed it wasn't an infinite number of people but the same handful of faces flipping over and over. She squinted, trying to count them. Twelve of them. Maybe. It was hard to be sure.

"We are the Empyrium," they said. "You may consider us your gods. We are caretakers of this land and countless others since their first inception more years ago than you can comprehend. And while you were of little importance in the majestic cosmos of the universe, it seems your time for governance has arrived."

"What are you talking about?" King Nerus of Alluvion demanded. "What do you mean we're of little importance?"

The Empyrium turned to face him next.

"When your people first arrived, this was a fledgling land, devoid of magic, save for the first seedlings churning deep in the soil. Over time, it gave rise to the Fae."

Magic, Zerra thought. She knew there was magic in Ouranos. Fae lived deep in the forests and mountains, where they made flowers bloom and birds sing. Magical creatures with wings, colorful skin, and glowing eyes. Weary travelers spoke of being rescued when they'd lost their way, and farmers recounted miraculous tales of their crops recovering from droughts. Some claimed they were nothing but stories and the ravings of lunatics, but Zerra had always believed they were real.

"But the magic continues to grow, and the Fae do not possess the strength to contain it any longer. The plagues and the illnesses besieging your homes are a result of this burgeoning power. It must now be harnessed, controlled, and channeled," the Empyrium said. "And so we've brought you here."

They waved their hand, and seven objects appeared, hovering around them in a circle. A golden mirror. A silver crown with a red stone. A black torch. A wooden staff. A shimmering rock. A pearlescent coral. And a white diadem inset with moonstones.

"These seven Artefacts are tied to the magic of your homelands. From this day on, each of you will be bound to them and, in turn, to the magic itself."

The Empyrium waved their hand again, and the objects floated closer, each one choosing a benefactor, until the mirror hovered over Zerra's head.

"With magic comes your ascension to High Fae, which includes gifts that elevate you above your mortal status. Long life. Increased physical strength. Sharper senses."

Zerra watched the faces around the circle, wary but hopeful. This proposition sounded very promising, but there had to be a catch.

"What do they do?" Amara asked, her gaze studying the silver crown spinning slowly above her.

"With these objects, you will gain a unique ability known as Imperial magic." The Empyrium went on to describe each ruler's magic in turn. Zerra, as the queen of Aphelion, would be granted the power of light to use both as a weapon and in the manipulation of illusions. She was having difficulty containing her disbelief.

"When you come to the ends of your lives," the Empyrium continued, "you will then live on forever in the fabric of your Artefacts and hold the enviable task of selecting the most worthy ruler to follow in your stead. Never again will someone gain the leadership of a people through birthright alone."

Though the Empyrium hadn't acknowledged her specifically, Zerra could have sworn they meant her with those pointed words. She'd inherited the title of queen by default, not because she'd deserved it.

"However, one of you will remain here."

The wary hope circling around the room morphed into something sharper.

"One of you will be stationed to watch over Ouranos. You will act in our stead as the caretaker of the Artefacts, functioning as an additional layer to ensure the stability of the continent."

"Stay here?" Amara asked. "For how long?"

"For as long as Ouranos exists."

Amara's lips pressed together, her dark eyes filled with mistrust.

The Empyrium tipped their head. "It is a lot to ask, we understand."

"Can we visit our homes?" Terra asked.

"You cannot. You will remain here, in the Evanescence."

Zerra watched Terra's face pale as he took a small step back. She knew he was married to a husband he loved very much.

"Can we bring our loved ones here?" he asked.

"You can, but they will not be meant for this plane."

"What does that mean?" Amara asked.

"It means that while their physical bodies may be with you, their spirits and their minds will slowly wither away until they are but empty shells of the person you knew."

"But our people need us," Astraia said.

"Our families need us," King Nerus of Alluvion added.

The Empyrium nodded but said nothing as everyone looked at each other from across the circle. Zerra drew into herself, trying to make herself appear small. It wasn't that she had anyone important on the surface waiting for her, but this sounded like a big job.

Silence stretched across the room until, finally, someone broke it.

"I'll do it," Herric said, his chin up. "I accept this task."

The Empyrium swung around to face him, their hands clasped in front of them. They stared at the Aurora King wordlessly for several long seconds.

Zerra watched Herric watch them. The king's eyes gleamed with promise and cunning. He'd always been wildly ambitious, and this was a task of the highest honor.

Not just a king.

Not just High Fae with magic.

But a god.

"No," the Empyrium said. "You are needed at home."

"But you just said—"

They lifted their hand and cut him off. "Our decision is made. It is not you."

"This is preposterous! No one else wants to do it. I'm the best choice!" His voice rose, bouncing off the room's hard corners, echoing with his frustration. He continued shouting as Zerra stared at the Empyrium. Though their body faced the Aurora King, Zerra noticed a face peering directly at her, as if emerging from the back of their head. A woman with kind eyes and soft blonde waves tumbling down either side of her face.

She smiled at Zerra and dipped her chin.

Zerra had the strangest sense this god was sending her a message, and the hairs on her arms stood at attention.

"Enough!" the Empyrium said, slicing off Herric's tirade. The command vibrated through the room with such force it shook the very walls. "We seek another."

Herric glowered at the Empyrium, his expression bruised with malice. He clamped his mouth shut, and at that moment two things occurred to Zerra.

One—this would not be the last of this from Herric.

Two—the Empyrium were expecting her to stand up.

The woman she'd seen a moment ago flickered into view again, her form solidifying for several seconds as she nodded, her image holding steady.

Zerra had never been a good queen. She knew that. She wasn't too blind or foolish to understand that while her queendom had suffered, she had chosen to do nothing.

When she'd listened to the stories from the others—about how broken they'd been, about how relentlessly they'd searched for solutions—she'd felt the gripping shame of her idleness.

She had never deserved to be Aphelion's queen, and standing amongst the noble rulers of Ouranos, that had never been more obvious.

Zerra had never sought greatness for herself. She'd never sought out glory or recognition, but a part of her at least wanted to be remembered for *something*.

And so Zerra lifted her head, dropping her arms as she threw her shoulders back.

Finally, she would do something noble. Something that might make up for this life of selfishness.

"I'll do it," she said, and every eye turned to her.

The Empyrium smiled, and for the first time in her life, Zerra felt the glowing shine of worthiness spill across her skin.

"And who shall you appoint in your stead?" they asked.

"Cyrus," she replied immediately. He deserved it. He had tried everything, and she had resisted him at every turn. "My advisor."

"It will be done."

"This is a mistake!" Herric said, taking up his cause once again, his entire body trembling with rage. "I am a better king! I can rule over these people! You don't want her!"

He shouted and screamed, his eyes wild, but the Empyrium and Zerra had made up their minds.

The Empyrium ignored Herric's ranting, lifting a hand before the six other rulers disappeared, leaving Zerra standing alone in the echoing silence of her new and eternal surroundings.

Chapter Thirty-Four

LOR

APHELION: PRESENT DAY

After leaving our horses on the outskirts, our return to Aphelion goes unnoticed thanks to a cresting wave of people flowing into the city. It seems the Sun King plans to host quite an affair for his bonding, but why? Is he hoping these preparations will result in my capture? Or worse, what if his plans have changed and he has something far more sinister in store for me?

A cart speeds by, nearly trampling a group of traveling minstrels as it barrels past.

"What's the fucking rush?" Nadir growls, the corner of his lip curling up.

I peer over my shoulder at Tristan and Mael, who follow close behind. We plan to return to the Priestess of Payne tomorrow, hoping to corner Cloris, but tonight I need to talk to my brother about what I've learned regarding his destiny. When I look back, Nadir is watching me, and I'm sure he's plotting ways to leave me behind, as if that will keep me safe.

I taper my gaze, hoping I'm accurately conveying the message that I'll carve out his heart and eat it raw if he so much as thinks of trying to stop me.

But he just gives me a smug smile, making me glare harder.

I love you.

His words filter into my head, making my breath catch and my cheeks flush. This is all going to take some getting used to.

After a moment, I reply with *I love you too.*

His smile struggles to remain casual, and I sense the turbulence of his swirling emotions.

My gaze tears away as we maneuver through the congested city. Nadir gestures for us to follow, and we all turn down a street, hoping to circumvent the chaos. We end up on the northern perimeter of The Umbra, where signs and posters, all depicting Atlas's face, are plastered everywhere.

I approach one and study it. The word "tyrant" is written in big, bold letters at the top, under which his image is rendered, along with a list of the low fae's grievances. Many of the posters have been defaced—some are more humorous, like a thin mustache or a pig's snout or horns sprouting from his head, while others are more sinister, with slashes scribbled across the parchment along with violent red splashes I assume are meant to portray his blood.

The four of us exchange a glance. I'm wary of our presence in the middle of all of this. While the bonding is a useful distraction to access the Mirror, we didn't account for this potential snag in our plans. I wish there was more we could do to help the low fae without drawing attention to ourselves.

"Come on," Nadir says, turning into a plaza. "We shouldn't linger out here."

We cross quickly, sensing the growing agitation of our surroundings. It isn't the same as the crowds arriving for the bonding; this has the echo of wildness and danger.

"What do you think is going on?" Mael asks, clearly noticing it too.

"I don't know," Nadir replies. "Keep moving. I don't like this."

We follow him across the square, but a moment later, I'm thrown off my feet to the sound of an explosion.

A shriek tears from my throat as I crash into the ground, my hands scraping against the cobbles. Through the ringing in my ears, I hear a cacophony of screams and shouts. The sounds of people yelling and wailing. The rumble of stone and mortar cracking.

After several deep breaths, I attempt to stir my limbs into action. Slowly, I roll over, my joints protesting in pain. Sitting up, I'm stunned by the sight that surrounds me.

An entire section of the city has been blown away, leaving a black spot of scorched rubble. Thankfully, we were at the edge of the blast and appear to have escaped the worst of it.

Frantically, I search for Nadir and my brother. When I spot Nadir, I scramble to him on my hands and knees.

"Nadir!" I call. He's lying on his side, and I tip him onto his back, struggling to heft his large body. He groans as I place my ear to his chest, a sob cracking out of me when I hear his heart beating. His eyes peel open slowly, and he blinks up at the sky once and then twice.

"Are you okay?" I ask, leaning over as I press a kiss to his lips.

He nods. "Yeah, I think so. What was that?"

"Someone must have set off a bomb or something."

Nadir groans, and I notice the trickle of blood near his temple.

"You're hurt," I say, digging a cloth out of my pocket and dabbing the wound at his hairline gently. He winces.

"Ow," he groans.

"Don't tell me the big bad Fae warrior has a boo-boo," I joke, trying to stem a flow of tears. He grabs my wrist, yanking me towards him. I yelp as he pulls me on top of him and crushes me into a tight hug, his hand cupping the back of my head.

"You're okay?" he breathes into my hair, and I nod against him.

"I'm fine."

"Thank fuck."

"Nadir!"

We both glance over to see Mael, and the sight makes my blood harden into blocks of ice.

"Tristan!" I'm up in an instant, running towards Mael, who's carrying my unconscious brother in his arms. Tristan's tunic and neck are covered in blood, his face darkened by soot.

"He won't wake up," Mael tells me as Nadir approaches from behind.

"Tris!" I sob.

"Come on," Nadir says. "This place is going to be swarming

with Atlas's soldiers at any moment. Let's get him back to the house. It's not far."

Mael is already moving, and I follow behind as we wind our way through the wreckage. People and bodies lie everywhere, some hurt and some only shocked, but so many are dead. Who did this?

I peer over my shoulder at the smoldering ruins, noticing a group of rebels have circled a destroyed building with Erevan, their leader, at the front, his fist raised to the sky, shouting words I can't make out. Whatever he's saying is rousing up the low fae, and I notice that whatever caused the blast very carefully avoided destroying The Umbra, forcing the worst of the damage into the adjacent Twelfth District.

It's clear this was a message to Atlas. He can't keep ignoring them much longer.

I share a look with Nadir before we all dash through the streets, finally arriving at the back gate of our safehouse.

"What happened?" Nerissa asks as we enter. As usual, she's in her garden, her implements abandoned in the dirt. "I heard an explosion."

Her eyes alight on Tristan's prone form in Mael's arms, and her pallor turns to ash.

"Get him inside. Now."

We all enter the kitchen, where Mael gently deposits Tristan on the long table as Nerissa scurries about, gathering bandages and supplies.

"What's wrong with him?" I ask as Mael rips open the front of Tristan's tunic. There's a gash across his chest that makes bile climb up my throat.

"Oh gods," I whisper.

Nerissa returns with an armful of first aid supplies. "We need a healer. I can't fix this."

Tristan's skin is pale and clammy. I pick up his wrist, feeling for a heartbeat. It pulses faintly, nothing more than a whisper.

"There isn't time," Mael says. "I've been on enough battlefields to know what a fatal wound looks like. Besides, they're going to be busy with the injured in that blast."

A choked sob escapes my mouth as I cling to Tristan's cold, limp hand.

No. Not my brother. Not after everything we've been through. He can't leave me.

A gentle hand cups the back of my neck, and I look up to find Nadir, his eyes focused on me.

"Lor," he says softly. "You told me once that your magic allowed you the ability to heal people."

Before the words are out of his mouth, I'm already shaking my head.

"I can't," I say. "It's not..."

"You can," he says. "You can do this. It's there. It's inside you. I need you to believe it. He's going to die if you don't help him."

I stare at my brother. His black hair sticks to his forehead. The dark circles under his eyes contrast with the ashen sallowness of his skin. My handsome brother, who has lived through more than any young man should ever have to. One who was saddled with the care of his two little sisters and did everything in his power to protect them.

With my lips pressed together, I nod. If there's anyone in the world I can do this for, it's Tristan. I owe him everything, including my life. I would never have made it this far without him.

Approaching him, I lay my hands on his chest.

"What's going on?" Nerissa asks, but Nadir shakes his head.

"Trust us. Trust Lor."

I focus on that locked door inside my chest. It's not as firmly shut as it was a few weeks ago, but it still resists like it's being forced on rusted hinges. Bit by bit, Nadir has helped me inch it open. He stands across from me, and our gazes meet.

"He was a child, too," I say. "He had to protect us, but he had no one to protect him." Tears run down my cheeks, flowing freely as they spill down my chin, mingling with my brother's blood.

"I know that," Nadir says. "But I promise you he doesn't regret a single thing he did to protect either of you."

I nod with a knot caught in my throat, and then I force myself to concentrate. It's been so long, but I remember the cuts and scrapes we'd sustain exploring the forest in our youth. When my mother stopped us from using our magic, it was a piece of myself I'd lost. I've spent so much of my life wondering if I would have been able to save my parents if the Aurora King hadn't taken us away.

The magic inside my chest crackles like static sparks, and I force it out, bit by bit. My brother is going to die if I don't do something, so I do everything I can. I will *not* let him die.

"What's going on?" I hear my sister's voice distantly. "Tris!"

She screams, the broken sound nearly shattering me into a pile of splinters on the floor.

"Stay back," comes Nadir's soft voice. "She's healing him."

I keep my gaze focused on my brother's face, but I feel Willow standing across from me too.

"Willow," I whisper as magic filters slowly out of me. "We can't lose him."

"We won't, Lor. You can do this. I know you can do this."

I draw it out of me bit by bit, small threads at a time. When I was practicing with Nadir earlier, it was an unrestrained torrent, but I can't rely on brute force this time. This task requires more precision and more finesse. Lightning sparks in my veins, but I pull it back because it isn't what I need right now.

I go deeper, closing my eyes, rooting around in the pieces of myself I know once existed, buried for so long. I find the softer ribbon of my magic. It's not like Nadir's, but there's a sinuous quality different from my lightning magic. It's dense, like thick satin ribbons instead of his airy light.

It's the healing magic I remember. I let it twirl out down through my arms and then to my fingertips, slowly, so slowly easing it into Tristan. My body trembles with the effort of holding it back, but this is what I must do. I remember this part. If I allow too much out, it transforms into the more destructive form of my magic. Gradually, I feed it into my brother's chest.

I forgot how hard this is.

A pair of warm arms circles my waist, and I recognize my sister's scent. The magic resists at the same time it tries to break free. It's like holding two pieces of string pulling in opposite directions by the very ends of my fingernails.

"It's working, Lor," Willow says, her body pressed to mine. "Don't stop."

I tremble as more and more magic bleeds from my fingertips, and I finally tear my gaze away from Tristan's face and study the wound on his chest. It is working. The jagged edges of his shredded skin start to pull together like interlocking teeth. I'm crying. I don't know if I've ever cried this hard. The day my parents died was the worst of my life, but I know it will pale in comparison if I lose Tristan now. I'd never be the same.

"You're doing it," Willow says. The room falls silent as everyone witnesses the red haze of magic that slides around Tristan until, a few minutes later, the wound is completely gone. When I'm sure every mark has been erased, I gasp and pull my hands away, stumbling back as the world tilts at an angle. A pair of strong arms catches me before I fall.

Nadir pulls me close, his hand cupping the back of my head as he whispers softly into my ear. "I knew you could do it."

"Is he okay?" I ask. Nerissa and Amya are standing over my brother now.

"He's breathing," Nerissa says. I catch the firm set of her mouth. She's trying to be brave, and it's obvious that my brother has come to mean something to her. "And his heartbeat is stronger."

I let out a breath of relief, clinging to Nadir as I sob against his chest.

"Let's move him somewhere more comfortable," Mael says to Nadir, and he pulls away to help carry Tristan up the stairs. They maneuver him into his bed, and Amya and Nerissa deal with the rags of his ruined tunic.

I bring over a basin of water with a cloth and sit on the edge of the bed to wipe the blood and soot from his face as he sleeps. His color is already returning, and I can't believe I actually saved him. The magic in my heart stirs, still with that muted energy, but it's there, and I get the strangest sense that it's proud of me.

I *need* to free myself from this cage. I could help so many with this.

"Do you think he'll be okay?" I say to no one in particular. I just need someone to reassure me that my brother is going to be fine.

"Yes. Thanks to you, he will," Willow says softly as she comes to sit next to me, and my gaze flicks to Nadir. I hope he can see the gratitude in my expression for his help. For the way he believed in me again.

He approaches and rubs a hand down the back of my head. "I'm going to go find out what happened out there," he says. "And maybe the rest of you can get some food for all of us?"

Everyone around the room nods before they disperse, and Nadir plants a kiss on top of my head. I'm so grateful he's here to take charge when I feel like I'm crumbling to pieces.

Willow arches an eyebrow at the intimate gesture.

"Well done, Lightning Bug," he whispers before he leaves the room, and my sister pins me with an inquisitive look.

"I think you have some explaining to do," she says.

I wrinkle my nose. "You could say that."

CHAPTER THIRTY-FIVE

While we wait for Tristan to recover, I fill Willow in on everything that happened, first in the settlements and then at the Woodlands Fort, including the somewhat momentous update about Nadir. My sister has always been the more forgiving type, and when I explain what it means to be mates, she couldn't be more thrilled for me.

"Lor," she says, her big brown eyes filling with tears. "I see the way he looks at you. I know it must have been so hard to learn how to trust him, but I think I'm a pretty good judge of character, and that man would walk through fire for you. I don't think you could be in better hands."

I smile at Willow, recalling her words during our argument. That she was the reason I kept pushing him away. Some might mistake her kindness for weakness or naivety, but it isn't. I've spent so much of my life angry and mistrusting everyone around me, and I think the way Willow sees the good in everyone, despite everything she's been through, is the greatest strength a person can possess.

"You're not angry because I'm essentially sleeping with the enemy?"

"Essentially? You're telling me you two haven't had sex yet?"

"Willow!" I exclaim. "What a thing to ask!"

She scoffs. "What? I'm supposed to pretend that the two of you don't practically make the walls melt when you're together?"

I make a wry face. "Fair enough. I just wasn't expecting that question from you."

She sits up straight and smooths back a piece of her hair. "Why not? Just because I'm less experienced doesn't mean I can't be a sexual being too."

"Oh really?" I ask, affecting a coy tone. "And who are you being sexual with, my dear sister?"

Willow's cheeks turn pink instantly, and I burst out laughing.

"Shut up," she says, and that only makes me laugh harder.

"Sorry," I say through my giggles. "Tell me. I want to hear. Perhaps a certain Aurora Princess?"

Her cheeks grow even pinker, and she ducks her head like she wants to whisper something in my ear.

"Maybe," she says softly, and I grin at that. Despite everything, I like Amya. I really think she is the nice one, and I'm confident her intentions lie in the right place.

"Care to elaborate?" I say, and Willow's smile turns soft, her eyes alight with a sparkle that transforms her whole face into a version of her I've never seen before. I like it. I *love* it.

"We're taking things slowly, but we've kissed."

I grin even wider and then wrap her in a hug.

"I'm happy for you, but be careful, okay?"

She opens her mouth to protest, but I interrupt her. "I'm not saying that because I don't think you can't handle it, but we've all been through a lot. I'd say the same thing to anyone in our circumstances."

Willow nods and pats my hand. "Okay. Thank you. I am being careful."

"You always are," I say, earning me a smile.

"Tristan isn't happy about it," I say then. "Me and Nadir, I mean."

"He's just as stubborn as you are. He'll get over it," Willow says.

"That might be the meanest thing you've ever said to me," comes Tristan's groggy voice.

"Tris!" we both exclaim.

He slowly peels open his eyes, his mouth stretching into a lazy grin.

"How long have you been awake?" Willow demands, and he rolls his eyes.

"Unfortunately, long enough to hear that both of my sisters are fucking the offspring of the man who killed our parents."

"Amya and I aren't fucking!" Willow exclaims, and then Tristan and I exchange a look as we both start laughing. I don't think I've ever heard Willow curse before.

"Look at you," I say. "A few weeks out of prison, and *now* you become a cursing, kissing, *sexual being*."

A pillow whacks me in the face, and I fall off my chair, laughing so hard I'm clutching my stomach. I look up to find Willow with her feather-filled assault weapon gripped in her hand and a grin on her face.

"Did you just hit me?" I gasp, still laughing.

Willow looks at the pillow and then at me with a satisfied smile. "I did. That felt good."

"Oh gods," Tristan says. "What have you done, Lor? She's going to turn into you."

"Shut up," I say as I drag myself back up onto the chair, but I'm laughing so hard that I keep missing the seat. "It's rude to pretend you're asleep while people are talking, by the way."

Tristan shrugs and then winces. Willow drops the pillow and is instantly at his side.

"Are you okay?" she asks. "Do you need some water?" She picks up the glass on the nightstand and helps him sit up.

"I'm okay. Just sore and tired." He takes a sip of water. "What happened?"

We fill him in on the bombing in the square and how it knocked him out. Mael and Nadir have been out trying to gather information, and I'm trying not to worry about how many hours they've been gone.

"You healed me?" Tristan says. "A wound that severe? You haven't done anything like that in years."

"I don't think I've ever done anything like that," I say. "But I couldn't let you die, Tris."

He nods, a shine appearing in his eyes. "Thank you," he says.

"I couldn't have done it without Nadir's help." I say the words pointedly, hoping they'll make some kind of impression on my brother. His expression darkens.

"I'm trying, Lor. You can't expect me to just trust him after everything that happened."

I dip my chin. "I know. I'm only asking you to try."

"I will. I am. I promise."

I blow out a breath. "Thank you."

"It's not like Tristan can claim innocence, though, can he?" Willow says, batting her eyes. "Why don't we talk about Nerissa?"

Tristan's brow furrows as though in confusion, and it's my and Willow's turn to laugh at our brother's expense. I think I like this sassy version of my sister.

"Are you seriously pretending you haven't been making googly eyes at her since the day we got here?" I ask, and Tristan frowns harder.

"I don't know what you're talking about," he says. "Maybe she's kind of . . . pretty."

Willow rolls her eyes, and Tristan shrugs with a sheepish grin. "Hey, if you two are allowed to explore things, then so can I."

"Fine," I say. "Fair enough."

We all fall into silence, enjoying this comfort of being together, but I already know I'm going to have to pull us back to the teetering edge.

"There's something else I need to tell you," I say to him. "I wanted to talk to you as soon as we got back, but then all this happened."

"What is it?" Willow asks, a line of concern furrowing between her eyes.

I don't think Tristan will mind if I share this with Willow too, and I can't keep this information to myself any longer.

"You remember how I told you I held the Woodlands Staff?" I ask her, and she nods. I take her hand, and then I look at Tristan. "It . . . hinted at something about you."

"What?" he asks and tries to sit up but winces. I lay a hand on his shoulder.

"Don't move. You're probably better off lying down for this anyway."

"You're worrying me," Willow says, biting the corner of her lip.

"It's not *bad*. At least, I don't think it is."

"Lor, just spit it out," Tristan demands.

"Okay, so I think it told me you're the Woodlands Primary." The words fall out in a rush, and I wince before rearranging my face into a strained smile as Tristan's expression blanks.

"What?" he asks.

"I mean, it didn't say that explicitly, but it commented about how I'd brought the Primary with me and that it felt *you* when we were gone. Not us. *You*."

"That's why you asked Cedar who it is?"

"Yes. It all makes sense, doesn't it? You have Woodlands magic that neither of us does, and our grandfather was their king. And you felt the Staff, didn't you?"

He rubs his chest, clearly recalling that enigmatic tug.

"But I have Heart magic, too," Tristan says.

"Maybe some of it 'leaked' into you. From what I've read, our grandmother was really powerful."

"What am I supposed to do with this information?" he asks, a thread of panic bleeding into his voice.

I open my mouth and then rub a hand down his arm, hoping to offer some comfort. "Nothing right now. I think. But eventually, Cedar will find out."

"But this was supposed to be you," he whispers. "Not me. I was fine with that. I was comfortable with that."

"I know," I say. "You don't have to do anything right now. Get used to the idea. When you're ready, you can go back to see him and discuss it."

"Do you think he'll be happy about this?" Tristan asks. "What if he hates the idea?"

"I don't think he gets any say in the matter."

He blows out a long breath. "Great." He shares a look between me and Willow. "Will you come with me?"

"Of course," Willow says, grabbing his hand and squeezing it.

"Tris, absolutely," I say. "Whatever you need."

"Did you tell Nadir?" Tristan asks, his tone sharp.

"No. I wanted to talk to you first."

His shoulders relax. "Thank you for that." He presses his mouth together, conflict struggling in his gaze. "You can tell him. If he's really what you say, then you need to be open with him about stuff."

"Thanks, Tris."

It's not quite acceptance, but it definitely feels like progress.

A knock comes at the door, interrupting our conversation.

"Come in," I call, and the door swings open to reveal Nadir with Mael on his heels.

"Hi," I say, the tight band in my chest loosening. I get up and wrap my arms around Nadir, pressing my cheek to his chest. "You're back."

Miss me, Lightning Bug? he asks through our bond, with his lips against the crown of my head.

Yes.

He tightens his arms.

Me too.

I look up. "What did you find out?"

Amya and Nerissa arrive next with two trays covered in food and drink. They set them down on the table in the corner, and we all fill our plates, taking seats on the floor and various chairs around the room.

"We can go downstairs," Tristan says as he shifts with another wince.

"You're staying in bed until you're fully recovered," Nerissa says, her tone offering zero room for argument as she fusses with his pillows. She hands him a plate and Willow and I exchange looks, trying to contain our smiles.

"It's not good," Nadir says, everyone's attention swinging to him. "It seems the low fae are getting more proactive the longer Atlas ignores them. Today's attack was intended to force an audience. All of their requests to meet with him have been declined thus far."

"So what does that mean?" Amya asks. "What are their bigger plans?"

"We couldn't figure that out," Mael says. "Not without revealing ourselves to Erevan, and I don't think that would be wise. He may not be a friend of Atlas's, but who knows what kind of leverage knowledge of Lor's whereabouts could offer?"

"You don't really think he'd turn her in?" Willow asks.

Nadir shakes his head. "I don't think so, but it's not a chance I'm willing to take unless we get desperate. We're still operating under the idea that the fewer people who know about this, the better."

We all fall into silence for a few moments.

"Do we have any other news?" Nadir asks then, looking at Willow. "Have you had any luck in the palace?"

Willow nods. "I'm not sure if it's anything, but I followed Gabriel."

"You what?" I ask, but she holds up a hand.

"He went into this strange dark part of the castle. At first, I swear I couldn't see the hallway—my eyes just passed over it, but then he turned and walked down it."

"*Why* were you following him?" I demand.

"I didn't mean to. I was carrying towels, and I saw him, and he looked so serious. Then he disappeared into that weird hall, so I followed."

Nadir bites the inside of his cheek. "An illusion. Atlas must be hiding something there."

Willow nods. "He had a set of keys in his hand, and he unlocked a door and then disappeared for a while. He was gone for about half an hour, and then he came back out."

Willow rubs the tip of her nose. "I pretended to get in his

way. He knocked over my towels, and he was shocked to see me. He told me I shouldn't be there."

"Willow," Tristan says from his position on the bed. "I can't believe you did that. What if he'd recognized you?"

She shakes her head. "I don't think he did. Besides, isn't that why I'm working there? To gather information? I am capable of doing things, you know."

Willow pins Tristan with a look, and I'm staying out of it because I'm not having this fight with her again.

"Sorry," Tristan says. "But you need to be careful."

"I am," Willow says.

"You were supposed to be getting a map of the palace," Mael points out, his mouth half-full.

"And I've done that," Willow says, standing up and retrieving a bag from the corner where she dropped it earlier. She pulls out a rolled-up piece of paper. "I'm not completely finished yet, but you'll see I've got a rough outline."

She unrolls the map in front of her, spreading it out on the floor as we clamber around it. She points to where she's marked out the throne room and the king's and queen's quarters.

"This is good," Nadir says, dragging the paper closer. "Do you know where this leads?" He points to the door at the back of the throne room.

"I thought Lor could use this as an exit. There's a spiral staircase that descends to the lowest levels of the palace," Willow says. "If you look here, I've mapped out a route through these tunnels should she need it."

"This is amazing," Amya says with admiration in her tone. "Maybe you have a future as an artist or a mapmaker."

Willow gives Amya a soft smile. "Maybe."

We eat in silence for a few minutes, everyone baking in their thoughts.

"So, what is Gabriel, or more likely Atlas, hiding?" I ask eventually. "And do you think it has anything to do with all of this?" I wave my hand around in a circle to encompass the Trials and my liberation from Nostraza and everything that's happened between.

Nadir shakes his head.

"I'm not sure, but it might be important to know, just in case."

"I'll see what else I can find," Willow says, and Tristan and I are about to protest when she raises a hand and silences us both. "I'm going to find out," she says firmly enough that I stop pushing. We both snap our mouths shut. Old habits die hard, but I'm trying to do better.

"Good," Nadir says. "The more information we have, the better."

"So, what's the plan now?" Mael asks.

"We go to see Cloris," Nadir says. "You and me."

"And me," I say, and I know he's about to list off all the reasons I should stay behind. "I'm coming. Don't even bother."

"But if she tells Atlas . . ."

"She would have already done so. If she recognized me, then she already knows I'm here. I need to confront her myself."

Nadir gives me a defiant look, and I return it.

"Fine," he says. "We'll go tomorrow afternoon."

"Good," I say, folding my arms with a glare.

"Good."

CHAPTER THIRTY-SIX

NADIR

SIXTEENTH DISTRICT

The following afternoon, Lor, Mael, and I stand outside the Priestess of Payne. Though I wish Lor had let me take care of this, there was no dissuading her. Not that I really thought I could. She can handle herself. I know that. But the idea of Atlas getting his hands on her makes me seize with breathless fear. If I understood what he wanted from her . . . Well, maybe we'll find that out today.

"Why haven't I been here yet?" Mael asks, scanning the ornate facade in between exchanging smiles with a hand-some High Fae male wearing nothing but the scantest bit of fabric covering the bulge at his hips. Which, even from a distance, is very impressive.

Lor is scrutinizing him, too, with a hint of mild curiosity, and I resist the urge to pick her up, carry her over my shoulder, and remind her that I'm the only man who will ever touch her again. Her gaze meets mine, and she narrows her eyes as she hears my possessive thoughts.

I grin because she can pretend all she wants. She knows she's mine now, territorial Fae bullshit and all.

She looks away, admiring the woman flanking the other side of the door. She's beautiful, wearing a sheer white dress that leaves nothing to the imagination, and I'm not surprised to find that none of these "offerings" holds the slightest bit of allure anymore. My only interest is my mate.

She takes my hand. It feels so small in mine, and I can tell she's nervous about what we'll encounter. I squeeze her fingers and her shoulders straighten, setting off another wave of primal desire.

That's right. I will be her rock and her strength whenever she needs me.

"Come in," the male Fae says to us with a crook of his finger and a bright white smile. "Pleasure and pain await in the house of the priestess."

"Don't mind if I do," Mael replies, clapping and then rubbing his hands together. It'll be a religious miracle if we get him out of here before the sun rises tomorrow or even the day after.

Mael bounds up the steps like an eager puppy, and Lor and I follow with our hands still clasped. We're greeted by another beautiful High Fae female inside, dressed in clothing meant to mimic the religious wear of Zerra's blessed but with some very notable and scandalous alterations.

"For three?" she asks before her gaze falls on Lor. "You came back with friends this time."

Lor nods, and I flex my jaw.

I can't believe you followed Cloris into this place all on your own.

Her gaze wings to me.

Save the lecture, Aurora Prince. You don't own me, and I can do whatever I want.

I arch an eyebrow.

Fine. Maybe it wasn't the best decision, but what's done is done.

No problem. I'll find a way to punish you later.

If it's possible, her gaze darkens even further, and I'm surprised my hair doesn't light on fire.

Don't worry. We'll both enjoy it. This place is giving me all kinds of ideas.

The glare drops off her face as pink creeps over her cheeks.

I love throwing you off, Lightning Bug.

"Stop it," she hisses, and the hostess peers over her shoulder with a curious look before leading us through an archway into a large atrium decorated to look like a temple. I wonder how the goddess feels about her name being used this way. Something tells me she wouldn't mind. The stories of her early days, when she brought drink and food and fucking aplenty to her first followers, are the stuff of legends.

"Can I get you a drink?" the hostess asks as she gestures us to a booth.

"We'll have a bottle of your best wine," Mael says, and she tips her head before placing a card in the middle of the table.

"I'll bring that right out. In the meantime, this is our menu. We cater to singles, couples, or groups, depending on what you'd prefer."

At that, Mael grins at me. "What do you say, Nadir? How about the three of us get naked?"

A low snarl rips from my throat at the idea of anyone touching Lor, even if he is my best friend.

Mael just laughs, and Lor rolls her eyes.

"Thank you," Lor says. "We're not actually here for that. We're wondering if we can have a word with the mistress of this fine establishment, Madame Payne?"

The woman blinks, evidently surprised by the request. Then she tips her head.

"I can certainly find out if she's willing to see you, though my mistress doesn't entertain visitors often. Who may I ask is inquiring?"

Lor exchanges a wary glance with me as she nibbles her lip. We discussed this beforehand and agreed she'd likely have to reveal who she is. I don't like it, but I have to reason that if Cloris Payne planned to do something to Lor, then she's already had ample opportunity. At least Lor didn't come here alone this time, so I can protect her.

"Tell her..." Lor pauses, and I know it's carving out a piece of herself to say this when she was expected to smother the truth for so long. "That Wolf's granddaughter is here to see her."

I study the server's face, searching for any signs of recognition. Any clue that those words might mean something. We agreed to use Lor's grandfather's name instead of Serce's, given its far more common usage across Ouranos. While it's a Woodlands name through and through, it isn't unique enough to arouse suspicion.

"She'll know what it means," Lor adds, and the waitress nods. "I assure you."

"Of course. I will let her know. And I'll get your wine."

"Thank you," Lor says as the woman drops into a quick curtsy and then walks away, exposing everything her sheer dress fails to conceal from behind.

"You think that will work?" Lor asks, leaning against me. I love how she fits like this under my arm, where she has always belonged. "Do you think she suspected anything?"

"I don't," I say. I'm not entirely confident about that, but I see no reason to worry Lor. We've revealed at least some of our hand, and now we'll wait to see where the chips fall.

After a few minutes, the woman returns with a tray holding the bottle we ordered, along with three glasses. She deposits them on the table and then addresses Lor.

"Mistress Payne said she is willing to see you, but she has some business she must attend to first. She invites you to enjoy the club's entertainment on the house, and someone will retrieve you when she's ready."

Lor opens her mouth, obviously ready to protest. I squeeze her hand, and she closes it. I suspect this is a power play to make us squirm, but we can wait. It won't do us much good to make a fuss.

"Okay," Lor says. "Thank you. We'll wait then."

"You can remain here or move over to the performance area if you like. There will be a very exciting demonstration happening soon."

The woman gestures to a small round stage at the far end of the room surrounded by silk-covered divans, where other High Fae are already gathering.

"Thank you," I say. "We might do that."

"Of course. Please let me know if you need anything else."

With another quick curtsy, she walks away.

"You don't think Cloris is busy running to Atlas right now, do you?" Lor asks, nervously twisting an end of her hair.

"I don't think so," I say. "Remember, if she recognized you then she already knew you were in Aphelion. You're the one who keeps reminding me of that."

"But what if she didn't know it was me, and now we've just told her I'm here? Are we sitting ducks?"

"Lor, it's going to be fine," I say, taking her hand. "I'm not going to let anything happen to you."

She gives me a wry smile. "Where do you get this confidence from?"

I wink. "I come by it honestly."

She snorts out a skeptical laugh just as a High Fae male approaches our table. "Would anyone here care for something?"

He's nearly naked, save for the tiny shorts barely covering the swell of his massive cock, revealing stacked bronzed muscle over every inch of his body. Mael grins, and I'm pretty sure we've just lost him for the day. My friend has always had a thing for blonds.

"Perhaps," Mael replies, stretching his arms along the back of the couch. "What are you offering?"

The male crooks a smile. "Anything you want." He leans down, planting one hand on the back of the booth, his nose inches from Mael's. "But I happen to be extremely gifted with my mouth."

Mael lets out a low grunt. "I like the sound of that." His gaze flicks to me.

"If you don't need me for a short while . . ."

"Go," I say, knowing this was likely to happen. "Just don't be too long."

"You know me, lightning quick," he replies as he's already sliding out of the booth. The male takes his hand and drags him away without another word while Mael waves half-heartedly back at us over his shoulder.

Lor is laughing. "How long do you really think he'll be?"

"Oh, he's never coming back," I say, and she giggles. "Should we go down to watch the show?"

"Sure," she says. "You know, the first time I came here, I thought about what it would be like to visit with you."

I stand and pick up the wine and two glasses in one hand while I hold out my other for Lor. She takes it before we start walking towards the stage.

"And what did you think it would be like?" I ask.

"I didn't like it. I didn't want you looking at anyone else like that."

My answering grin is feral. "I love it when you're posses-sive." I reel her closer, wrapping my arm around her waist and whispering in her ear. "You can complain about my primitive

Fae nature, but deep down, you're exactly the same." She gives me an annoyed look that never fails to stir something inside of me. "And you never have to worry about me looking at anyone else like that ever again. There is only you."

We arrive at the seating area, and I place the wine on a small side table before I sit down and draw her onto my lap.

"I know," she whispers as she wraps her arms around my neck. "There's only you too."

Those words. The way she feels against me. The way she smells. My eyes close, and I exhale a drawn-out breath. I've waited for this for so long. I don't just feel for *her*, I feel *everything* when I'm with her. Every bit of joy and sorrow. Every laugh and tear I've ever shed. I think of all the things I want us to experience together, and I pray we'll get that chance.

"Where did you go?" she asks, stirring me from my thoughts.

"Just thinking about the future," I say, and she gives me a sad smile.

"Pour us some wine." I hand her a glass just as the lights dim above and the crowd mutes to an excited hush.

Lor twists so she's facing the stage, and I love that she stays on my lap, not that I'd let her move if she tried.

A moment later, two High Fae, a male and female, walk onto the stage. They've dispensed with any pretense of clothing and are already nude and stripped of pretty much every bit of hair on their bodies. They're both specimens of magnificent perfection, obviously chosen for this purpose to excite and inspire every savage feeling and emotion.

The man brings out a long silken cord and then proceeds to wrap it around the woman's body in a series of complex knots and twists, highlighting her breasts and ass. A hook descends from the ceiling, and he hoists her up, attaching her to it before he hikes up her knees, wrapping more cords around them so she's spread open like a dragonfly snared in a spider's web. Slowly, she starts to spin.

"What do you think?" I ask, sliding my hand up Lor's back and whispering in her ear. I don't miss how she shivers at my touch, and my gods, that is the greatest feeling I could have ever imagined. I can't believe this incredible woman is mine.

"It's interesting," she says, leaning to whisper in my ear. She cocks her head, studying the performers as if trying to determine if this excites or scares her.

"Maybe we should take them up on the offer of that room," I say, and she tips a smile. We have important things to do, but I just want to touch and be with her. I want time to explore this momentous thing we're becoming without distractions.

I tamp down the fear that we may never get that. That my father and Atlas are after her. That everyone seems to want something from Lor, and I live with the terror that I *won't* be able to protect her.

"Maybe," she whispers, and I'm about to say fuck it. Who cares about responsibilities right now? But then, a figure stands over us.

It's the same hostess who delivered our message to Cloris.

"Madame Payne is ready to see you now," she says. "Please follow me."

Chapter Thirty-Seven

LOR

At the sound of the hostess's voice, I look up, trying to organize my thoughts. It's grown warm in here, and I wave my hand at my face, trying to cool my flushed cheeks.

"Thank you," I finally say, sliding off Nadir's lap and standing up. He takes my hand before the woman beckons us to follow her through the club. We exit the solarium, head down another marble-lined corridor, and then up a spiraling gold staircase.

At the top is another hallway, this one lit by flickering sconces and lined with thick dark carpets, the walls covered in rich paneled wood. At the end stands a set of double doors. Our guide knocks softly twice before she swings it open. As we pass, she dips into a small curtsy.

"Madame Payne will be with you in a moment," she informs us before sealing the door behind her.

We enter a sitting room decorated with more rich dark hues and velvet-covered furniture. The whole aesthetic almost reminds me of the Keep.

Neither of us is able to relax as we wait in nervous dread. I perch stiffly on the edge of the sofa in the middle of the room while Nadir paces back and forth behind me.

After a minute, a door on the far side swings open, and I blink. There she is.

Silver hair pulled up into a high knot and bright blue eyes, her skin smooth with a quality that belies her age. She wears an expensive-looking dress of luxurious purple silk and pauses in the doorway, lifting her chin as we all scrutinize one another, sizing each other up like opponents facing off across a battle-field littered with dead bodies.

When her eyes fall on me, her nostrils flare delicately. Her expression reveals nothing, but I get the sense she's holding in a torrent of repressed emotions.

She grips an ornately carved cane in her hand, and after another moment of silence, she takes a step, her knee hampering her movements. I remember how she'd limped away in the Woodlands Staff's vision and assume this must be an injury from that day that never fully healed.

How much does she resent what my grandmother did? Has all of this been about revenge?

Cloris slowly proceeds across the floor as Nadir and I watch her. The clip and clop of her shoes echo hollowly against the room's corners.

Then she stops in front of me and lets out a long breath.

"I never thought I'd see you again," she says. "You've grown up so much."

Her voice holds no sense of the nostalgia usually accompanying that statement. It's cold and assessing, as though she's evaluating my mettle, trying to decide how much of a threat I pose.

"Well, it's been over a decade," I say, stating the obvious, to which she tips her chin.

"Indeed."

I'm waiting for her to tell me I look like one of my grandparents or another sentiment that speaks of the past, but she says nothing, staring at me for so long that I'm starting to get uncomfortable.

Nadir has stopped pacing on the far side of the sofa, and we exchange a wary glance.

Keep our relationship a secret. The less she knows about either of us, the better.

Nadir's voice enters my head, and I resist the urge to nod, worried that will give us away. He's right. Nothing good can come of Cloris knowing who we are to one another.

"I would not have thought to find you two together," Cloris says to Nadir at long last.

He doesn't react, though I note the slight hardening of his jaw. "Why is that?"

Cloris tips her head, a dry smile crossing her lips as if to say *Let's not play games here.*

Finally, she settles onto one of the chairs, resting her hands on the head of her cane and peering at me.

"What can I do for you, Lor?"

I don't like this woman. Everything about her makes my skin crawl.

"Are you the one telling everyone who I am?"

Nadir sits down next to me but keeps his distance.

"I hardly think two people count as everyone," she sneers.

"Why?" I ask, trying to sound detached and not like an angry rush of blood is making me dizzy. Like I'm in control of my emotions. But all I feel is an acrimonious sense of betrayal from someone I don't even know. "Why would you do that to us?"

Cloris lets out a derisive laugh.

"My dear, it had nothing to do with you."

"You ruined our lives," I say, and there's no mistaking the threat of tears in my voice. I can't let her see me cry. "You took everything. Why?"

Cloris sits back and regards me with cool detachment. She really doesn't care, but I need to know. I don't seek contrition from her, nor do I expect it. What's done is done. What I need are fucking answers.

"It's curious," Cloris says. "How events can transpire. How schemes you set into motion can fail, and yet, somehow fate serves to orchestrate a favorable outcome you don't foresee until one day the Primary of Heart, herself, comes knocking on your door."

I chew the inside of my cheek, baffled and afraid and waiting for her to continue.

"I told them, yes," she says. "Did I do it because I loathed your bitch of a grandmother? If I were to examine my motivations, that might have been part of it, but anything her family suffered was collateral damage. It just happened to make the outcome all that much more satisfying."

Her lips stretch into a thin, brittle smile. She's enjoying this.

"Please," I say, noticing Nadir shift as though he wants to reach out to me. I keep my gaze focused on Cloris, determined not to allow her any information she can use as leverage. Of course, it's suspicious that I'd show up here with the Aurora Prince, but she doesn't need to know the full extent of it.

"Your grandmother came to me," Cloris says, "because she needed me to perform the bonding between her and Wolf. She had discovered that joining two Primaries requires additional precautions compared with a regular bonding."

My nails dig into my palms as I try to keep my breaths even, knowing another hurdle has just been thrown into our path. My earlier hunch was right.

"I knew how to do it," Cloris continues. "She promised me something I sought in exchange, but I did not trust her."

She pauses and picks a piece of lint off her skirt. "So, I went behind her back and told the Aurora King of her plans to double-cross him. You see, the two of them were conspiring to take your great-grandmother's crown from Heart, and then Serce claimed she would help Rion conquer all of the realms and hand Ouranos over, save her queendom and The Woodlands."

My breath catches on that revelation. I recall the conversation with Nadir in The Aurora when he reminded me that everything Rion claimed about past events was up against the word of a dead queen. I'm not surprised to hear he massaged the truth to make himself look better.

"Why go to my father?" Nadir asks.

"Because I didn't like her, and I didn't trust her. I wanted to keep my options open," she replies. "And Serce had no intention of honoring her agreement and planned to use the bonding with Wolf to overpower Rion and take everything for herself. I gave the Aurora King everything I knew, and my instincts proved correct because she imprisoned me the moment I assured her I understood how to perform the ritual."

Cloris pauses; her expression is almost dispassionate, but stifled rage flickers in the depths of her eyes.

"So I pretended to descend into madness to the point she no longer believed me capable of performing the task. Her short-sightedness and her impatience proved to be her downfall. She attempted to perform the ritual herself..."

Cloris stops as if for dramatic effect.

"And you all know how that turned out."

The room falls silent as my chest twists. I have so many questions that I'm not sure where to begin. My grandmother didn't just try to take the magic of Heart, she tried to conquer all of Ouranos. She was a monster. A tyrant. A power-hungry murderer.

"Why do that? Surely you knew letting her do it herself might kill everyone, including you?" Nadir asks, and I shoot him a grateful look because I'm not sure I can speak.

Cloris scoffs. "I am one of Zerra's blessed. The people of this ungrateful continent may have forgotten. They may have let her temples fall into disrepair. They may use her name only in vain, but Zerra lives, and she protects those who serve in her name."

Cloris's eyes glaze over with something that feels like it's hovering just on the fine edge of sanity. Her words stirred from ancient grudges and possibly a less-than-firm grasp on reality.

"I see," Nadir finally says, and she tapers her gaze as if reading the insincerity in his words. It's hard to argue with her statement entirely. I saw the blast. Saw the destruction it caused, and she had gotten up and walked out of there almost no worse for wear. Divine intervention might be the only reasonable explanation.

Cloris gives us both a patronizing smile. "Oh, I know what you think of me. These are just the ramblings of a crazy woman, but soon enough, all of you will see that you are wrong. That Zerra lives and grows weary of being ignored."

Though her words are confident, I sense something hesitant buried within them.

"But?" I ask, hoping my instincts are correct. "Something is not right? What did you want from my grandmother?"

Cloris sniffs, looking down her nose at me.

"The goddess is weakening. Her power fades. Do you think all these stories of the trembling earth, plagued forests, and droughts are mere coincidences? You think there isn't some bigger purpose at hand?"

Nadir shifts next to me, no doubt thinking about the mine collapse that killed all those low fae. I think about the blackened forests of The Woodlands. The talk in Aphelion of low fish counts and the constant rumbles we've felt beneath our feet. Though it was impossible to say why, I felt these events had to be connected. To hear it confirmed sends a prickle of alarm down my neck.

"That's because of Zerra?" I ask carefully.

"It's not because of her," Cloris snaps. "It's because of all of you. You use your magic with impunity, draining the land and the goddess. It was never meant to be this way."

"How was it meant to be?" I ask.

Cloris pauses, and I can see her weighing how much she wants to reveal to us.

"You asked what I wanted from your grandmother," she says, and I nod, perching on the edge of my seat. "Your family had a powerful object called an ark. In exchange for my help, I asked that she relinquish it to me."

"What is it?" I ask.

An ark. It's then I remember the Staff mentioned an ark too, but another memory is sticking in the back of my head.

"It's an object used to channel and amplify magic."

"Did my grandmother know what it was?"

"At the time, I didn't believe so."

"So you were trying to manipulate her?" I accuse.

Cloris presses her lips together, her eyes dimming.

"Your grandmother was the manipulator, Lor. Don't act like I was the only one who was wrong here."

"So why did you tell Atlas and the Aurora King about me?" I ask. "What was the purpose?"

"Because I still seek the ark, and your magic is tied to it."

She says the words swiftly, like she doesn't really want me to hear them.

"What does that mean?" Nadir asks. "Be specific. None of these evasive answers. What *are* they?"

"Each Artefact has a corresponding ark," Cloris says, though I can tell it guts her to admit that to us. "And their magic is bound together."

"So you want to use me to find it," I say, my voice devoid of emotion. All I am is a pawn in everyone's fucking schemes.

"Would the ark have saved Serce and Wolf?" Nadir asks, already one step ahead of me. "Was that what they needed to complete their bond?"

Cloris laughs, surprising me with the sound.

"Oh, Aurora Prince. I will not be revealing all of my secrets today."

Again, I exchange a look with him. Was that a yes or a no?

"Why are you telling us any of this?" Nadir asks. "None of this explains why you revealed Lor to Atlas and my father."

Cloris taps her bottom lip.

"Well, *that* is all a very good story," she says. "Shall I tell it?"

"If you want my help, then you will tell me everything," I say.

Next to her is a small table with a decanter of bourbon and a crystal tumbler. She pours herself a measure and takes a long sip. She doesn't offer us any as she refills her glass, acting like we're not even here. I wonder just how much she was pretending to go crazy to fool my grandmother or if it was a short walk off that cliff.

"I searched the castle after the explosion. Sorted through the rubble for days, keeping myself hidden from those who came to search for survivors, but the ark was nowhere to be found. I suspected Serce had known all along what it was. She had double-crossed me in ways I didn't even realize. Or maybe something else happened. I couldn't be sure.

"At any rate, I continued searching. Not just in and around Heart—because I had no true way of knowing if it had ever been there—but all over the continent, lying low. I had to stay hidden. No one could know that I had survived. They cursed me nearly as much as they did her for a long time, and it suited my purpose to let everyone think I was dead."

"Why did you want it?" I ask. "For what purpose?"

"For Zerra," she said. "I was tasked with finding it centuries ago and have been hunting for it most of my life."

"Why? What does *she* need it for?"

"I will tell you anything that pertains directly to you," she says. "However, my relationship with my goddess is private."

The hard glare she gives me suggests she will not waver on this point.

"So then what?" I ask, brushing past it for now, resolving to come back to this later.

"Eventually, I realized I'd need someone with the magic of Heart to find it. And while the magic was ostensibly gone for the whole of Serce's mistakes, I knew someone else had survived that night and that someone *else* had carefully safeguarded the magic from being taken from the Primary."

"What do you mean?" I ask. "Safeguarded it?"

Cloris pierces me with a penetrating stare. "Do you have it?

The piece of the Heart Crown that Daedra bestowed on your mother?"

Again, I try not to react.

"I don't know what you're talking about."

Cloris studies me, and I'm almost positive she doesn't believe my lie.

"Daedra saw her daughter for who she was that night and understood that Serce had gone over the edge. I watched the Heart Queen send a piece of the Crown with the next Primary."

"Why?" Nadir asks, sitting forward.

"I suspect it was a way to escape punishment when Serce tried to steal the magic of Heart. The gift of the Primary would pass over her and on to the next. Only no one could have predicted what would happen instead."

"The explosion. That was the punishment?" he says.

"No," Cloris says. "That was the bonding she tried to orchestrate herself—there was too much power between them to seal it without precautions. The punishment was when everyone lost their magic for fifty years."

My vision swims at that revelation. I remember the story Nadir told me. That everyone hated my grandmother because they all lost their magic. *None* of it had been an accident.

His mouth opens and then closes, a grim set forming to his mouth. "How did Daedra know to give away a piece of the Crown?"

I'm glad he's the one asking questions, because my mind can't stop tilting.

Cloris shrugs her bony shoulders. "I can only assume the Crown must have revealed it to her at some point. Perhaps it

388   NISHA J. TULI

was as desperate as she was. Whatever the case, I found the child. And lo and behold, not only was she still alive, she was in possession of the magic her grandmother had saved.

"And had *three* children."

She levels another look my way.

"I wasn't expecting to find such strength in someone so young. While my initial goal was your mother the day I encountered you in the forest, I wondered if perhaps she wasn't the Primary after all. The magic had skipped to you instead. I had intended to use you as leverage against your mother, but you should not have been able to do that to me. It was then I knew *you* were the reason the Crown had seen fit to protect your family from Serce's greed."

I grind my teeth, wishing I *had* killed her that day. I can't believe I ever felt bad about it.

"When you managed to best me, I knew I had to find another way. I returned to the most ambitious king in Ouranos, told him what I knew, and waited for him to root you out."

She sits back and allows those words to settle. She doesn't need to tell me what came next. Twelve long years behind those bars. I've lived those days over and over so many times.

"But you were a tricky thing," Cloris says with a wrinkle of her nose. "Rion was skeptical of my claims. Suspicious of me despite the way I'd handed Serce's betrayal to him on a platter. And you refused to let him see your magic. You nearly convinced him you weren't who I promised you were."

She purses her lips as though all of that was my fault. I want to stand up and slap her.

"My, how you *screamed*," she says in a nearly musical voice, and I'm on my feet in a flash. Nadir's arms wrap around me as I swing with my fist, barely missing her face. She leans back only a fraction as she clings to that thin, horrid smile.

"You were there," I spit. "You saw what he did?"

She waves her hand as if it's of no importance, and I lunge again, but Nadir holds tight.

"Lor," he whispers softly. I know he's angry too. I can feel him shaking, but he's also right that clobbering her will get us nowhere.

Let her keep talking.

Cloris narrows her gaze, her eyes flicking between us, and I hope I imagine the knowing spark that flashes in her eyes.

"When you refused to reveal yourself, I convinced him to let you live," she continues as though nothing has happened. "So he threw you into that prison for safekeeping, but he was done with me."

Drawing a deep breath, I attempt to settle my temper as I gather my thoughts. I don't need to hear Nadir to know he's doing everything he can to stop himself from tearing apart this entire room.

"And then what?" I ask after a moment. "Why Atlas next?"

"Because I still needed someone to get you out of there. Someone with proper motivation. When I showed up, he was about to bond to someone else."

"You're the reason he canceled the first Trials," I say, and she nods.

"Indeed. When I told him about you, he immediately called them off and started working on a plan to get you out of Nostraza."

"He wanted to bond with Lor?" Nadir asks. "Can he actually do that? Wouldn't he have the same issues that Wolf and Serce did?"

"Technically," Cloris says after a brief pause, but there's something false in it. "But I didn't tell him any of that."

I drop onto the sofa, cradling my face in my hands, stunned at everything I've just heard. I've wondered for so long what series of events brought me to that throne room in Aphelion, but I never imagined any of this.

"Did you know it was me the other day?" I ask. "Did you recognize me?"

"I did," she says.

"So why didn't you go to Atlas then?" Nadir asks.

"Why are you so sure I didn't?"

Nadir levels her with a look, and she rolls her eyes.

"Because he failed, didn't he? The Mirror rejected her as I suspected it would, and now I have no use for him. I just needed her out of Nostraza. He's fulfilled his purpose, and now what I need is Lor."

She looks at me, and I snort in derision before she leans forward.

"Did the Mirror reveal anything to you?"

I arch an eyebrow. "You've got to be kidding me."

Cloris pinches her mouth together and sits back.

"Have you recovered your magic?" she asks carefully, as if she knows she's crossing a line.

"Yes," I say with a pointed glare. "And it's incredibly strong."

She doesn't need to know how much I'm still struggling with it, but let her think I'm dangerous.

"And before you ask, I have no idea where the ark is."

But her question about the Mirror knocks something loose, a fragment rattling as it hits the floor.

A gift for you.

What if it's not my magic at all, but something else that was lost?

"Hmm," Cloris replies. "I figured you'd say that, and I am inclined to believe you."

"So what do you want then?" Nadir asks, gritting. His teeth "You're doing an awful lot of sharing right now."

Cloris smiles. "There is nothing I've told you that can harm me in any way. Your father was a fool not to believe me, but now he knows the truth, and I don't give a whit about what happens to Atlas."

"Then *what*?" Nadir asks again.

"I want to make a bargain," Cloris says. "You find me the ark, and I won't reveal your location to either king currently hunting for your pretty little neck."

I scoff. "I've already proven once that I can kill you. I'll just end you now and be done with it." I point a thumb at Nadir. "And I have backup. This time, I'll make sure you're dead for good."

Her nostrils flare and her mouth pinches together before her expression smooths over.

"You think you're both so clever, don't you? That you can fool me?"

"What are you talking about?" I ask, and she looks down, picking at the fabric of her skirt and rearranging it around her ankles before she addresses me again.

"You think a High Priestess can't detect a mate bond when

she's in the presence of one? I was the first to know your grandmother was pregnant, too. I might not have the flash and destruction you possess, but I still hold power in my own ways."

An evil light shines in her eyes.

She doesn't need to voice the threat or the offer now dangling at the end of a dead olive branch: I help her, and she helps us overcome whatever obstacles we need to seal the bond.

My gaze bounces to Nadir, and I'm sure I can guess what he's thinking.

Cloris rolls her eyes. "You two couldn't possibly be more obvious."

A low growl gathers in my throat.

She laughs, once again reveling in the power of the upper hand.

"Do we have a bargain?"

"I'll think about it."

"You do that. It would be such a shame to see another love like yours go"—she springs her fingers apart—"poof."

Once I get my magic back, maybe I can use it to force the answer out of her.

And then fry her to a crisp.

Nadir and I stand and head for the door.

"You still bear his mark, I see."

"What?" I spin around.

She's standing now, and she flicks her pointer finger in my direction. "On your face."

My scar. I touch my cheek, cold dread slithering down my

neck. I've always borne this scar proudly, because it reminded me of what I would do to protect the people I love most.

"I got this from the prison guards. I was protecting my sister."

A wicked glee crosses her expression.

"The mind is a funny thing," she muses. "The way it can twist a truth and bury a memory we'd rather forget, turning it into something that feels a little more manageable. A little more . . . noble, perhaps?"

Her meaning becomes clear a moment later. This is a mark from Rion. From what he did to me. His magic made this mark, and I've been wearing it around like a fucking brand to match the one on my shoulder. A reminder that no matter how far I run, I still belong to him.

Suddenly, I feel like I've been dipped in toxic sludge as heat spreads over my chest and back. I stare at her, my heart sinking down through my ribs and tumbling to my feet.

"I'll await your answer, Lor," she says, and then slams the door in my face.

Chapter Thirty-Eight

My limbs tremble as I stare at the door. My fingers completely numb and my lungs filled with cement.

"Lor?" I hear Nadir say, but he sounds too far away over the ringing in my ears and the black spots snowballing in my vision. White flashes burst in the corners of my eyes, and I stumble as vertigo tips me on my axis.

"I ... can't ..." I clutch my heart as it ricochets against my ribs, but I'm breathing against a brick wall, the air solid as granite. Cold sweat drips down my back as my face burns like smoldering embers.

"Lor!" I feel his strong arms around me, catching me before I sink to the floor like an anchor fighting the tide, and then I break.

"It...was...him..." I wail as my body shakes and I claw at my face. "I want it gone! I want it gone! Take it away!"

My voice resonates against cold marble with the hollowness of a tomb.

"Take it away!" I scream so loud my voice cracks. "It wasn't for them! It was him! Take it away!"

"Lor. It's okay. We'll get rid of it." Nadir's soothing voice is the gentle calm at the eye of my storm. "We'll find someone who can take care of it." He folds me into his arms, holding me tight, pressing my face to his chest. I'm shaking. I can't stop shaking.

I fist the fabric of his tunic, clinging to him like I'm toppling down a landslide. I cry and cry, allowing myself to shed the tears I buried for twelve fucking years. He holds me, gently rubbing my head and my back as we rock in the sea of my wretchedness.

Slowly, my heartbeat settles, no longer threatening to rip out of my chest. I pull away with my hair sticking to my cheek, and Nadir sweeps it away with a gentle fingertip. A large dark spot of my tears stains the front of his tunic.

I wipe my nose with the back of my sleeve as I sniffle.

"Sorry."

"It's okay," he says, tucking my hair behind my ear. "We'll find someone to take care of it immediately."

"Callias offered," I say, my voice scraped raw and thin. "He said he could fix it during the Trials, but I wouldn't let him because I'm a fucking idiot. I thought I was being...I don't know—brave? Or strong? Trying to prove to those guards they couldn't hurt me. But they were probably all laughing at me."

"Lor, you are all of those things," he says softly. "You *are* so brave and so strong. I meant what I said when I told you it was noble. It isn't your fault that he did this, and your reasons for keeping it are yours. Don't let him take that from you. It doesn't change who you are or how fiercely you love your brother and sister."

"Can we find a way to get a message to Callias?" I ask.

I'm falling and I need him to catch me. I have no doubt he'll be waiting with open arms.

Nadir's answer is a skeptical look. Sending a message to the palace isn't the most prudent idea, but I need someone whom I trust with this. Whatever he sees in my face causes his expression to soften.

"Of course. We'll figure something out. Okay?" He captures my chin between his finger and thumb.

I nod, pressing my lips together to stem another swell of tears balling up my throat.

"It's okay if you need to cry," he says so tenderly that a sob cracks from the center of my soul. I can't believe this is the same man who tied me to the foot of his bed not that long ago. For some morbid reason, the reminder causes my sob to turn into a laugh.

"What?" he asks, clearly bewildered by my sudden mood swing.

"I was just thinking about the time you made me sleep on your floor."

"Lor, I—"

I shake my head, snorting out another laugh as I fall apart.

"It's okay. I'm not mad. Pissing each other off. It was our thing. Remember when Mael called it foreplay?"

The corner of his mouth tips up. "I barely slept that night. All I could feel was you."

"That makes two of us," I say, wiping my face and nose again. "Gods, I must be a mess."

He shakes his head. "You're the most beautiful thing I've ever seen."

"I'm sure you say that to all your mates." He smiles again.

"We should get out of here." He glances at the closed door of Cloris's sitting room, and it's only now I remember where we are.

"Do you think she heard all that?"

"No," he says, expression deadpan.

"Liar." He gives me a wry smile before his jaw hardens and his eyes dim down to black inky pools.

"Lor. I need you to understand that someday I'm going to make a choice when it comes to my father. One that might show you I'm not a good person, and I hope that you'll be able to forgive me for it."

"I understand," I say. "There will be nothing to forgive. There's nothing you can do that will ever make me question you."

Then he kisses me deeply before he pulls away and touches his forehead to mine.

"Let's go," Nadir says, helping me stand and tugging me back the way we came.

"Where do you think Mael got to?" I ask.

"Not sure, but he can find his way home."

We spill out into the bright street, blinking against the sunlight.

"We need to get your magic back—the full force of it. I can't stand the idea of you being vulnerable around my father again."

"Did you know any of that?" I ask as we walk. "About the arks?"

Nadir shakes his head. "I've never heard of such a thing, but we need to know what they actually do. I don't believe a single word she just told us."

"No, me neither." I stop walking, forcing Nadir to do the same. "Do you think it's possible the Mirror has it? What if that's the gift and it was never my magic? The Staff hinted it might help unlock mine. Cloris said the ark is an amplifier too."

"I'd considered that. We have to get inside the palace soon. There is absolutely no way we can let her get her hands on it."

"What about the other thing?" I ask. "Sealing our bond?"

"If she knows how to do it, then someone else must know too."

"What if we can't find anyone else?"

As the crowd surges around us, he pulls me in close with a hand cupped around the side of my neck.

"If we have to give her the ark, then that's what we'll do."

"But what if—"

He reels me in and kisses me fiercely. "No. I told you once that I don't let anything get in the way of what I want, and I meant that. There is nothing I want more than you."

I blink at him and nod.

"We're going to figure this out," he says with all his usual bravado, and I believe him. One way or another, we will.

We start walking again with our hands clasped, both lost in our thoughts. The silence between us is comfortable, despite the way I just reacted. I realize I don't have to be anything around him other than myself. He has accepted me, warts and all.

We duck into the alley leading to the house's back gate and enter to find everyone gathered in the sitting room.

Willow's map is spread out on the table, and I can see she's filled in more details since yesterday.

At our entrance, everyone sits up, watching us expectantly. A moment later, the back door bangs open, and Mael appears in the doorway, flushed and smiling like the cat that caught the canary.

"Enjoyed yourself?" Nadir asks, and Mael smirks as he drops onto the sofa with a satisfied sigh.

"Immensely."

"Were you crying?" Willow asks. "What happened?"

"Did you talk to her?" Tristan asks, and I nod.

"We did." I opt not to share the details that sent me into a spiral. I'll explain the true source of my scar to my brother and sister later.

I do share what Cloris told us about the arks as everyone listens intently.

"Anyway, we're now wondering if this is what the Mirror wants to give me," I say.

"How do we find out more?" Amya asks. "I don't understand how we've never heard of this."

"I get the sense it's the kind of information reserved only for the ascended," Nadir says.

"I have a friend who works in the archives," Nerissa says. "I could ask her if there's anything written about it?"

"That would be amazing," I reply. "Thank you."

She dips her chin, clearly happy to be useful.

"What about you?" Nadir asks Hylene next. "Any luck on your end?"

She tosses a red curl over her shoulder. "Of course. I'll be attending the festivities with one Lord Cedric Heulfryn."

Nadir nods. "Well done."

"Wait," I say. "Heulfryn. As in Apricia's family?"

Hylene's eyes sparkle. "Her brother, in fact."

I bark out a laugh, not sure why that's so amusing.

"Impressive," Mael says. "I guess you are useful around here."

Hylene narrows her gaze, and I'm sure that one day, Mael will find himself with a dagger pressed to his throat. Or maybe his cock, depending on Hylene's mood.

"That's good," Nadir says. "You'll be invited to the palace to stay for a few days."

"I'll get my bags packed. I'm expected soon. So we need to get moving on whatever plan you're hatching."

"She's right," Willow says. "I won't be able to come back here either. Apricia has made it clear we're to remain by her side in the days leading up to the ceremony."

Nadir pinches the bridge of his nose, and I feel his mounting frustration.

"Have you had any luck getting your hands on a schedule of the events?" he asks her.

She grins and pulls out a piece of paper. "Yup. This is everything."

Nadir grabs it, and I read over his shoulder.

"What's the presentation?" I ask, noting its place on the timetable the day before the bonding.

"It's when Atlas and Apricia will greet the citizens of Aphelion one by one. It's kind of like the second-tier invite for those who aren't important enough to garner an invite to the real ceremony," Amya says.

"Anyone can attend?" I ask.

"In theory, yes."

She presses her lips together and doesn't voice her other thought. The low fae are definitely not invited.

"They're already setting up a huge tent outside the gates," Willow says. "That's where it will happen."

"So the throne room will be empty?" I ask.

Nadir nods as he rubs his chin. "It'll be a partial distraction. It might be what we need."

"How do we get in without being seen, though?" I ask.

"There's a side entrance," Willow says, pointing to her sketch. "This is where the deliveries are coming in. What if you entered there?"

"It's an idea," Nadir says as Mael proceeds to grill Willow on who guards the entrance, what kinds of questions they ask, and how closely they scrutinize the carts and vendors coming in and out. Willow answers as best she can, but we're still working with a lot of holes and guesses.

As we talk, I grow more and more nervous. Can I do this? Can we possibly get in and out of there undetected?

"Lor, I think you need to practice your magic some more," Nadir says to me. "You're getting better with it, but I would rest easier if you had a bit more control."

I nod. "Sure. Me too."

"Perfect. We'll go back to the clearing tomorrow. Nerissa, if you could see what you can find as soon as possible, so we know what we're dealing with? I'm not entirely happy with the plan yet, but we're getting closer."

We all murmur our assent.

Zerra help us all.

Chapter Thirty-Nine

CLORIS PAYNE

Aphelion: A Few Months Ago

Cloris waited in Atlas's study, once again a casualty of his inconsiderate timekeeping. She'd been summoned here in the middle of the night and dragged out with barely a chance to change out of her nightclothes. Three of those winged abominations—the king's warders—had stormed into the Priestess of Payne, barged into her private chambers, and demanded she come with them.

She didn't bother protesting. Resisting would be futile, and nothing would stop them from fulfilling the king's wish.

Now she paced the length of his study, peering out the window and marching back to the middle of the room until she repeated the circuit. How long would he make her wait this time? Her glance skidded over the bookshelves to her left, when she came to a jarring stop.

Hidden in the shadows was a small glass case where an object sat nestled into a stand, propping it upright. She listened for the sounds of anyone approaching before she tiptoed towards the shelf, worried the slightest noise would cause it to dissolve into a puff of smoke.

Her fingers reached for the case, finding it locked. It couldn't be what she thought. With another check at the door, she used a small flare of magic to get a better look.

The ball of light in her hand illuminated the figure of the woman carved into an almost rectangular-shaped object, the top part wider to accommodate her shoulders before tapering to her feet.

Her goddess.

Made of dark material infused with silver sparkles, it shimmered softly in the glare of Cloris's light. Cradled in Zerra's hand was a mirror—a direct copy of the Artefact sitting in the Sun Palace throne room.

Cloris blinked, unable to believe her eyes.

This was Aphelion's ark. What was it doing here after all this time?

Many years ago, Zerra had sent Cloris and two of her sisters, Rosa and Adrienne, in search of the three remaining arks. Zerra held the rest in her possession but hadn't been able to secure them all.

Rosa had been assigned to Alluvion. Adrienne to Aphelion. And Cloris was to find the ark of Heart. Adrienne had died a few years back—she didn't understand why Zerra hadn't saved her too—and she hadn't heard from Rosa in years. But as far as Cloris knew, neither had ever succeeded. A fact that was confirmed as she looked upon Aphelion's ark now.

Cloris didn't understand what the goddess wanted with the arks, but it had never been her place to ask too many questions.

She'd set out on her quest, coming up against dead ends over and over. That was until she'd gotten wind of an heirloom named the Ark of the Coeur residing in the queen's collection—the name slipped from the lips of a drunk noble during a soiree where she'd posed as a courtesan.

Though the name was a bit ridiculous, she was sure it had to be the object she sought. That after many lifetimes of hiding, the ark had resurfaced. She had spent years orchestrating a way to get close to the royal family when she happened upon Serce. Of course, none of that had worked the way she planned, setting everything back to zero, yet again.

Despite the fact Zerra no longer spoke to her, Cloris had never given up her quest, hoping that one day, she'd find her way back to her goddess's side.

Voices drew her attention then, and Cloris jumped just as the door banged open. She snatched her hand away, dousing her magic, tucking it behind her back as if that would make her look any less guilty. She arranged her face into a mask of calm innocence, but she needn't have bothered.

The Sun King was furious—his hair and eyes wild—and he saw nothing as he slammed the door behind him so hard it nearly shook the entire room off its foundations.

"The Mirror fucking rejected her," he hissed, and Cloris froze before she swallowed down a nervous knot of tension. She had anticipated this. Why would the Mirror ever select the Heart Queen for its own?

"I see," she said. "That is unfortunate."

"Unfortunate?" Atlas spat, approaching her with his shoulders hunched. "Unfortunate?! I ended the last Trials for this. I had those girls killed because you told me to bond with Lor! And now the Mirror rejected her and chose someone else!"

Cloris rolled her neck and clasped her hands at her stomach.

"I cannot control what the Mirror chooses to do. It seems this isn't her destiny."

"Her destiny? What about my destiny?! You promised me—"

"*Nothing* has changed," she said, raising her voice. "Once I have my hands on the object I seek, you can use it to reverse the Mirror's decision."

"You lied to me!" Atlas roared, taking another step towards her as he grabbed her throat and shoved her against the bookcase, the shelves digging painfully into her back. "What game are you playing, witch? Tell me the truth."

Cloris opened her mouth as Atlas squeezed while a small pit of fear quivered in her stomach. "I wasn't," she choked out. "Please."

She clawed at his arm, but in his fury, she was no match for him. He squeezed harder as he trembled with his teeth bared.

"Please," she gasped. "I ... swear ... to ... you ..."

"I'm not listening to any more of your lies," he hissed.

"No ... just ... please ... this ... isn't."

Atlas eased his grip just enough so Cloris could breathe. She inhaled a shallow breath.

"Talk," Atlas said. "And if you try to fuck with me, I'll crush your windpipe and never give you another thought."

"You can still use her," Cloris said. Her voice was raw, and she was sure bruises were already forming on her skin.

"How can I do that when the Mirror chose someone else?"

Slowly, she straightened up. "I told you what I need is powerful."

He glared at her. "And?"

"And if you release the girl to me, I can find the object, and we can reverse what the Mirror has done."

"You said she'd bond to me!" he said.

"Yes, but I can't do that without what I seek. I thought I made that clear," she said, trying to keep her patience. Was he really this dim? "You'll also be able to finally do away with your brother, once and for all."

Again, Cloris was lying, but she would say anything to convince Atlas to believe her. She'd deal with the fallout of these deceptions later. The Sun King wasn't just dim, he was also gullible because she saw the way his eyes lit up at her words.

"For real?" he asked, and she almost felt bad for seeding this tender blossom of hope.

"You will be the king."

It was a noncommittal answer that confirmed nothing either way, but he seized on it.

Atlas crowded her space, bringing his face so close to hers, she could feel the drops of spittle as he hissed, "If you do anything I deem suspicious, I will not hesitate to kill you. Is that understood?"

"Yes," she said as she nodded, trying to hold back the tears of rage and frustration building in her eyes. All she wanted was to serve her goddess. Was that too much to ask? "Yes."

Finally, he eased off, his lip curling in a snarl as he paced away, running a hand through his hair and muttering to himself.

Cloris could practically feel the ark's presence behind her on the shelf and wondered if Atlas understood what he had in his possession. It sat amongst what appeared to be other objects of great value, safely locked in a case she suspected could be opened only with Imperial magic. But the ark wasn't valuable; it was beyond value. The second most powerful object in this kingdom.

"Can I ask?" she ventured. "That's a lovely piece you have there." She gestured to the ark, testing Atlas's face for any signs of recognition.

"Yes? And?"

"Where did it come from?"

He shrugged. "How should I know? It's used to transform the warders."

Atlas spun on his heel, still dragging his hand through his hair. She wondered if he'd meant to let that bit of information slip. He really was quite distraught.

"Oh," she said. "Is that all? Does it have a name?"

Atlas gave her a look like she was a lunatic. "Why should it have a name?"

"No reason. I thought I saw one like it in the market the other day."

His face deepened into an ever skeptical scowl.

"Why the fuck are we talking about this?"

Cloris smiled. Atlas was not the Primary nor the true king. He had no idea.

"You're right," she said. "About the girl. If you'll release her into my care, we can proceed."

"Where will you take her?"

"That is yet to be determined."

"How can I trust you'll return to do what you've promised?"

Cloris pressed a hand to her chest as though she were offended by the question.

"Your Majesty, I am a messenger of Zerra. I would never lie."

Atlas narrowed his eyes. "You'll take an escort of my guards with you. My captain will see that you're watched." He paused.

"And protected," he added as an afterthought.

Cloris shuddered at being in the presence of those creatures, but she dipped her head. It made sense, and Atlas was actually doing her a favor. When Lor's magic released, she might be hard to control. Cloris would need someone to contain her. Once she had her hands on the ark, she would simply disappear, leaving the girl with Atlas's guards.

She'd also have to find a way to return and get her hands on Aphelion's ark, but one problem at a time.

"Very well," Cloris said, bowing at the waist, ever the obedient servant.

Atlas clenched his jaw. "Fine. But if I find out you're lying to me again..."

"Understood," Cloris said. "Just bring her to me."

They turned their heads at a knock.

"Come in," Atlas called.

The door swung open, and two of the king's warders entered.

"Your Majesty," one of them said. "The Final Tribute has escaped the palace."

CHAPTER FORTY

LOR

PRESENT DAY

The following day, Nadir and I ride for the clearing where we practiced with Tristan last week. As we pass the same ruined temple, I stop to study it with new perspective, thinking of the task Zerra assigned to Cloris. Though she changed the subject, Cloris seemed to suggest Zerra needed the ark to save herself. But from what, exactly?

The stillness in the clearing is a direct contrast to the chaos building inside Aphelion. Between clashes with the low fae and the mounting spectacle of the bonding, the city walls have become a noose, cinching a little tighter every day.

Despite the calendar showing it's winter, the temperature has been creeping up all week, and sweat is already beading on my forehead, a line running down my temple. I wear a light sleeveless top, the fabric clinging to my flushed skin.

We dismount from our horses and walk to the middle of the clearing.

"Do I need to put myself in mortal peril today?" Nadir asks, eyeing the pile of rubble we were responsible for creating last time.

"No," I say. "I have to learn to do this without that being the reason."

He approaches me and circles my waist. "I never properly thanked you for saving me from my father that day in Heart," he says, his voice rough. "Without you protecting me, he would have won."

I blow out a shaky breath. "It was strange, but at that moment, all I saw was white-hot rage, and I didn't understand yet why it affected me that way. I would have done anything to protect you. I wanted to make him suffer for that moment and for everything he's ever done to you." My words pitch lower until I'm practically growling them, and Nadir smiles.

"I love it when you're possessive, Heart Queen. It makes me so fucking hard."

To prove his point, he grabs my ass and yanks me closer, where I feel the proof of his claim.

"Well, get used to it," I whisper as he kisses the curve of my throat. "If anyone dares lay a hand on you, I will make them bleed. I once broke a woman's arm for stealing my soap. Imagine what I'd do if someone hurt my mate."

"Zerra, I will never get enough of you," he murmurs into my skin, and I believe him because I feel the same.

"Maybe we don't need to practice. How about a skinny dip under the waterfall?" I tease, and he groans.

"Yes, we do." Then he pulls up. "Maybe if you're a good girl and do as I say, I'll reward you."

Then he winks, spins, and walks away as I roll my eyes at his back.

"I heard that!" he calls.

"I didn't say anything!"

"Let's go, Lightning Bug," he says, turning around with a smirk. "Show me what you can do."

My hands ball into fists, and I squint at him, focusing on the churning in my veins. That door that's still locked but has taken on a less dense and solid quality. I'm tearing it down, bit by bit, but can I do it in time for it to matter?

As I concentrate, a trickle of magic sparks through my limbs while Nadir continues backing up, putting more distance between us. When he seems satisfied, he sends out ribbons of light towards me but not in aggression. They wind gently around me as my magic responds to him with bottomless want.

A shiver ripples over my body as my lightning emerges. Only this time, there's no uncontrolled torrent. This time it surfaces slowly, twisting up my arms in jagged lines following the curve of Nadir's magic as they twin together like dancers waltzing over glass. I exhale in surprise, mesmerized by how this feels like an extension of me. I remember this sensation from so long ago.

I look over at Nadir, and even from across the clearing, I can see his pride. He pulls his magic back, leaving only mine, and I continue to marvel at it. It's so remarkable, this gift. I truly thought it was gone forever. It's still not all *quite* there. It's muted, and that door is still closed, but it's leaking out, and I'm sure it's getting stronger.

When I healed Tristan, it crested so close to the surface and to breaking free.

Two abilities live inside me: one to destroy and one to create. Something tells me I will call on both many times before all of this is over.

Nadir sends another burst of magic hurtling my way. I lift my arm and block it, and our magic meets, crashing together and spreading apart in a halo of red and green and blue and purple suspended in the air. I can't help but think it represents the two of us, contradictory and at odds but also yielding to each other to create something that makes my bones ache and my blood simmer.

He does it again, and I go on the offensive, countering with more control than I've had in years.

He stops and stares at me, breathing heavily, waiting for me to do my worst. So I take the lead, spearing lightning bolts from every direction as he fends them off. I'm not worried about hurting him. It's obvious he still has far more control and power, so I keep going, giving him the full brunt of my strength.

I've always wanted to be the sort of woman who makes monsters kneel. Who brings down empires. Who holds the world in her hand. And for the first time in my life, it feels like it's within my reach.

Finally, I stop, pulling everything back as the magic dissipates around me. Sweat runs down my temples, but I'm not done just yet. I fling out my hands, aiming for a spot high on a cliff. My shot clashes with the rock, falling just short of my intended target. I try again and again, shooting blasts around me as my aim slowly improves.

Nadir circles behind me, pointing at this spot or that spot as I aim over and over. My control is returning, though I never pushed my magic this way as a child. We didn't have the freedom, worried about exposure, and my mother was too nervous to allow us to try anything more.

Finally, I stop. My body shakes with exertion, and sweat coats my back, plastering my tunic to my torso. The sun sits high, beating down on us with unrelenting heat.

Arms circle me from behind.

"You are fucking incredible," Nadir says into my hair. "Beautiful. Fearless. Absolutely amazing."

Suddenly, I have the overwhelming urge to cry. A sob builds in my throat, and I spin around, throwing my arms around his neck as I let go, weeping against his shoulder. He holds me, squeezing me tight, every once in a while kissing my neck or my cheek or my temple.

They feel like messages. Reminders that he's here, a poem or a love letter written in the ashes.

I'm crying for everything. For everything we lost. For my parents. For my brother and sister. For everything I want to give them. For Nadir and his mother and Amya. For Mael and even for Gabriel. For everything I want to give Nadir too. I've been so entirely helpless for so very long, and finally, this one thing is almost within my control.

Eventually, my sobs taper off and I pull back. Nadir tucks a strand of hair behind my ear. "Are you okay?" he asks, and I nod.

"I am. Zerra, all I do is cry lately." He crooks up the corner of his mouth. "Thank you for allowing me to let go."

He touches my cheek, peering at me with a look in his eyes that makes my heart twist.

"I want to be your safe place, Lor. No matter what happens, I will always be there for you."

I nod, tears threatening again at the earnestness of his words.

"Me too," I say. "I want to be that for you too. You've given me something I never thought I would have."

Nadir gives me a troubled look.

"What is it?" I ask.

"You don't know all of my darkest secrets," he says. "Sometimes I'm afraid if you do, you'll change your mind about me."

I shake my head. "I could never do that."

He hesitates.

"You don't have to tell me now," I say. "When you're ready. But I hope that someday I can earn your trust."

His hold on me tightens. "I trust you. With everything. It's myself I don't trust."

I let out a sigh, understanding what he's trying to say. I still have demons to share from my time in Nostraza that I'm not ready to give voice to yet. Not because of him but because of me.

"Okay," I say. "I understand."

He kisses me then, his lips brushing mine softly. Our mouths work together with gentle nips and touches. It's tender but also deep.

When we pull away, a haze of lust clouds his eyes.

"It's scorching out here. I think it's time for that swim you mentioned."

A mischievous smile creeps to his face as he drags me towards the stream where the waterfall topples from above.

"Oh, did I earn my reward?" I ask, and he grins as his hand slides over my ass and squeezes it.

"And then some."

I burst out laughing, pulling my tunic over my head while kicking off my boots.

I watch as he strips down, already salivating at the idea of touching him. Before long, we're both naked, the sun warming our bare skin. I dip a toe into the water and then screech because it's colder than I expect.

A moment later, Nadir scoops me up and plunges us into the stream. I cling to his neck, screaming as he laughs. I playfully batter his shoulders as he walks towards the falls and then floats us across the pool where they deposit.

He wraps my legs around his waist as we kiss, his fingers digging into my hips. I feel him kicking as we move across. He releases his mouth from mine for a brief moment, sending out an arc of magic that splits the tumbling water, creating a space for us to pass underneath.

"Where are we going?" I ask, tipping my head back to welcome a gentle spray of cool water.

"Aren't you curious about what's on the other side?"

NISHA J. TULI

He's sucking on my neck, rubbing me against his hips, where the friction is already starting to drive me wild.

"You don't seem to be paying much attention to our surroundings," I joke, but it comes out breathless as his hand works its way between us to find my clit.

"You caught me," he says. "I was just hoping there was somewhere private I could do this."

He backs me up against a rock and then lifts me up to sit on the edge.

It feels incredible to be out of the beating sun, the tickle of water soothing our skin. I lean back on my hands, the mist painting my face, breasts, and stomach as Nadir's hands slide down to my ankles.

He pushes them up so my heels perch on the edge of the rock, with my legs spread wide. He looks up at me with a dark glint in his eyes before he lifts my ankle and kisses the inside, slowly placing more kisses higher and higher—the inside of my knee and then my thigh.

My body shakes in response, my legs quivering and my flesh dimpling.

"Nadir," I whisper as he places a kiss in the tender spot at the crease of my thigh on one side and then the other.

"Hmm?" he asks, taking his time, slowly exploring me with his lips and his tongue, touching me every place except where I desperately need him.

"Is there something you want, Lightning Bug?"

I glare at him, and he gives a wicked laugh before he lowers his head once again, making me tremble as he takes his time exploring me.

Finally, the tip of his tongue touches my clit, and I moan, dropping my head back.

"Gods, I love it when you make that sound," he rumbles before he uses the flat of his tongue, lapping me up from top to bottom. My back arches, and I gasp as he hooks his hands around my thighs, his tongue driving into me as he groans. "You taste so fucking good."

He buries his face against me as the rough stubble on his chin provides a point of friction that makes my hips start to writhe.

"Nadir—" I gasp as he nibbles my clit, causing my stomach to pull tight as I feel my release building.

Then he pulls away.

"Back up," he orders, and I do as he says, making room for him to join me on the ledge. He levers himself up and then pulls me to stand before hooking his hands under my thighs and lifting me.

We kiss, my hands tangling in his hair while his fingers dig into my flesh.

Slowly, he maneuvers us towards a wall, distancing me a few inches from the surface that's been worn smooth by nature's gentle hand.

"Hang on," he says, gesturing to the rock where protruding sections offer handholds.

"I love you," he says. "My heart. My mate. I fucking love you."

"I know," I whisper. "I love you too. So much."

Slowly, he lowers me, positioning himself at my entrance. My eyes flutter at the sensation of the wide head pressing into me. We both watch where he enters as I slide down inch by inch, moaning at how he fills me up, touching every nerve in the most exquisite way.

"That's my girl," he growls. "You take my cock so fucking good."

Once he's fully seated, he pauses as we both catch our breath, my chest tight from every emotion crowding in the back of my throat.

"Nadir," I gasp as he pulls out and then slides back in with agonizing slowness. I'd expected him to take me fast and hard right now, but this is exactly what I need. After everything that's happened in the past week, I need a moment to hide here under this waterfall, clinging to the person I fought against but who has somehow become the softest spot for me to fall.

I will always have my brother and sister, who will always mean everything to me, but how I feel about Nadir feels divine. If Zerra does indeed hold dominion over the fate of mated pairings, then this does feel like something ordained. I was wrong when I told Rhiannon the mate bond didn't feel like much of a choice.

This feels like a choice I've made. That no matter what happens between now and forever, this was inevitable. Like morning sunlight spilling through a window. Like the tide giving way to the ocean's pull. Like blood beading on a fingertip at the prick of a thorn.

He is my choice. And he would have been my choice over and over until the end of the world.

"Lor," he says, his voice thick with ragged breath as he

pulls out again and slides back in. With one hand protecting my back, he uses the other to gently touch my clit as he churns his hips, slowly fucking me long and deep.

My legs tremble, and my fingers ache from gripping the stone above my head as he spears into me like I'm an angel served up as an offering. A moment later, he braces his hands on my hips and then thrusts into me hard, being careful not to let my back collide with the wall.

"More," I gasp as he does it again, and my head tips back. "Harder."

And then he snaps. We become a blur of motion as he pumps his hips, thrusting into me with force. With one hand braced on the wall behind us, and the other pressed to the small of my back, he pounds into me as he peppers open-mouthed kisses down my throat and my shoulder.

Our moans fill the space, backdropped by the rushing of the waterfall. Our magic surfaces, spinning around us, filling the cavern with Nadir's light and the pale, inconstant flickers of my lightning. I feel them twist, melding together, finally allowed to play.

Here we are free. Here no one can see or hear us. Here I can forget for a moment about everything that's working against us and everything we're trying to accomplish.

I hold so many warring pieces of my soul and my heart cupped in my hands. There are so many paths for us to travel. Threads splitting apart to form a future that's yet to clarify into something I recognize. I just know that Nadir is a part of it.

We have only one goal now, and I don't know how close it

will take me to the object of my desires. The reclamation of my home and revenge on the Aurora King. Because no matter what happens. No matter how broken I am. No matter how hard I fail, Rion is still the focus of every bloody fantasy I conjured every night I lived in Nostraza.

For what he did to my parents. To my siblings. For what he's done to Nadir—and I get the sense I've only just scratched at the surface of the torment the king has inflicted on his only son.

As Nadir continues his deep thrusts, he captures my mouth with his. We kiss like these are our last moments and every time, every single time he does this, it feels like I'm falling all over again.

I feel his cock twitch as it thickens, and then he comes with a shuddering groan that ricochets over his entire body.

He continues pumping in and out of me, slowing down before one of his hands finds my clit. He circles it with a rough finger, and then I blow apart, too, my back arching into him, my hands gripping the stone as I cry out. My legs clamp around him as my orgasm rolls in heavy waves, filtering through my fingers and toes until it feels like I've been wrung out and turned upside down.

When I finally stop shuddering, he gathers me into his arms. I loop mine around his neck as he leans me against the wall, and we just stand there, feeling the spray of the water and the cool air that coasts over our fevered skin, holding each other. Silently promising one another that in the layers of uncertain darkness, we are each other's light.

Chapter Forty-One

Gabriel

"That was a really fucking stupid thing to do," I say to Erevan before I groan, my head dropping back on the settee where I'm currently being serviced by a blonde with the most perfect tits I've ever seen. She's sucking on me like I'm a fucking lollipop, offering the only form of stress relief that seems to make any difference lately.

Erevan sits a few feet down from me, a dark-haired beauty kneeling between his legs, supplying him with similar entertainment. As Atlas and Tyr's cousin, Erevan has known me almost as long as they have. We all grew up together as boys, finding ourselves in the sort of trouble typical of royal children without much parental oversight. Of course, I wasn't an heir or part of their family, but my proximity to the princes offered me certain advantages.

As we grew older, our paths diverged. Tyr was training to be a king, with Atlas as his possible second. I was destined for the warder corps, and Erevan was sent to study in Alluvion to learn history and politics with the hopes of leading Aphelion's council someday. I think his mother hoped he'd find some nice young woman to bond with, but something happened during his time on the western coast. He dropped out of school and returned to Aphelion, where he renounced any claim he had to the royal line and moved to The Umbra. We lost touch for many years, until he resurfaced with a list of demands on behalf of the low fae.

By then, Atlas was king, and he dismissed Erevan with cold words, declaring that if Erevan ever darkened his door with requests of a similar nature again, he'd see to it that he was tossed out of Aphelion, but not before suffering for his insubordination first.

But Erevan wasn't to be deterred. Instead, he returned to The Umbra, where he began to rally support amongst the low fae. At first, he was met with resistance—the low fae had been cowed thoroughly into submission and were reluctant to fight back, afraid of what further punishments Atlas might force upon them.

But Erevan has a way of making people believe in him, and not in the same duplicitous way as Atlas. Even as kids, we all felt the pull to be around him. There was something that made you want to earn his pride, but he never abused that power.

Anything he desired was a path he truly thought would be in your best interest. I believe that if the Mirror hadn't chosen Tyr when Kyros descended, Erevan would have made the best choice of king for Aphelion. I've wondered countless times if Erevan would have fallen for Atlas's tricks and if we'd all be stranded in the positions we are now.

"We needed to send a message," Erevan says, picking up on my earlier admonishment about blowing up the Twelfth District days earlier. Hundreds died in the blast, which destroyed a chunk of the city. I've had guards working around the clock, patrolling the border of The Umbra, worried the city will devolve into a full-out war. With the extra visitors here for the bonding, our forces are stretched as thin as paper and rips are forming everywhere. "Atlas can't keep ignoring us."

The woman between my legs sucks hard, directing my attention away. I can't quite form a response yet, so I let her continue, feeling myself grow thicker with each enthusiastic hollowing out of her cheeks. My hips move of their own accord, thrusting up and sliding down the back of her throat, causing tears to run down her cheeks.

She grips my thighs as I fist my hand into her hair, taking over as I fuck her mouth, letting all the frustrations of the past few months melt out of me for a fleeting moment of relief. After another minute, there's a tingling at the base of my spine before I spill into her as she swallows every drop like the pro she is.

When she's done, she slides off me with a pop before she stands up, giving me an eyeful of her lithe, toned body. "Anything else?" she asks with a tip of her head, and I wave her off.

"Just another drink." She picks up my glass and walks away as I study her round ass in appreciation. Erevan is tucking himself back into his pants, having also just finished.

"Atlas is furious," I say, picking up the conversation now that I can think again.

"You think I give a shit?" Erevan asks, accepting a drink from the woman who was just blowing him a moment ago. My girl returns with a tray for me as well.

"What was the point of that? You killed some of your own, Erevan."

Erevan's mouth tightens.

"I know. That was an accident."

I run a hand down my face with a long sigh.

"You need to be more careful. If you keep doing shit like this, you'll lose the little support you already have from the council. Some of them lost property in that explosion."

Erevan casts a sharp glance at me. "*Property*. You think I care about a few ruined buildings when the low fae have nothing?"

"You're absolutely right," I say. "But that's not how they think. You need to speak their language. Appeal to what moves them. And unfortunately, that's money. Talk to them. Convince them that changing the laws would benefit their businesses and fill their coffers."

Erevan takes a long drink, his gaze focused away from me. "We've been over this before. I refuse to be a sellout. I want them to do this because it's the right thing to do."

"Erevan," I say.

"No." He turns to me with a sharp look. "If their benedictions extend to only what's profitable and not what's *right*, then how long will it be before we're in this position again? They have to do this for the proper reasons, or it means nothing."

I blow out another long sigh. "I know you're right..."

I trail off. He *is* right, but he's also too idealistic for his own good. The bastard won't even use his magic in solidarity with Aphelion's low fae. I admire his principles, but he'll have to learn to fight dirtier if he has any hope of victory.

"What I need is a way to shame Atlas," Erevan says. "Something that destroys his credibility so thoroughly they'll be calling for his head."

My gaze slides to Erevan, who is rubbing his bottom lip with the tip of his finger.

"What are you thinking?" I ask, and he shakes his head.

"I don't know. I'm wondering if we can use the bonding ceremonies in some way."

I sit up in alarm.

"Don't. If you pull another stunt like that, you're going to ruin everything you've been working for. You'll lose all the support you have from Aphelion."

"We're not," he snaps at me. "But we need to get everyone's attention. Not just here in Aphelion but across Ouranos. Other than The Aurora, no one treats the low fae this poorly. Surely another of the rulers can be rallied to our cause."

"I think you're a dreamer," I reply.

Erevan lets out a derisive snort. "Perhaps."

He takes another long sip of his drink.

"Remember when we were children and Atlas locked all three of us in that shed and left us there for hours?" he asks with a crook of his mouth.

I snicker and shake my head.

"Then he pretended he saved us to make himself look like a hero?" Erevan adds.

"How could I forget? Remember you were so scared you pissed yourself?"

"That was *water*. I spilled *water*. How many times do I have to say it?" Erevan exclaims, and we both start laughing at the well-worn joke.

"Gods, he's always been such a fucking prick," Erevan says after a moment of silence. "Why did we ever let him get away with that shit?"

"He was a royal heir," I say. "And he was very good at getting his way."

When I say that the four of us played as friends, I truly mean that there was a hierarchy within our tiny group, and I was always at the bottom, with Erevan coming in a close second.

"What do you think would have happened if Kyros hadn't found you in the woods that day?" Erevan muses. It's a question I've asked myself a thousand times.

"I would have died out there," I say, knowing it's true. Part of me is sure I would have tried to return to my father to make him suffer for what he did to my family. But he probably would have killed me in the process, and I'm not sure if I would have had the courage anyway. In the end, this was the better fate.

Now that I'm no longer a frightened child, I've considered

returning to see if he's still there, toiling in his hollow, miserable life.

Erevan doesn't respond to that, and I stare at my now empty glass.

"So, what are you going to do?" I ask. "How are you going to . . . embarrass him?"

"I'm not sure. I'll think of something. Surely that bastard has some skeletons I've yet to uncover."

He looks over at me, and I wish I could tell him everything I know. Would it be the thing he needs? If Aphelion were to learn that Tyr is alive, nothing would save Atlas's neck. But I can't. The words stick to my tongue. It's one thing to skirt around Atlas's rules and utter a few half-truths sprinkled here and there, but it's quite another to spill out his secrets like poison injected directly into a vein.

"If you know of anything?" Erevan suggests.

"Fuck off," I bite. "You know I can't."

My anger coalesces into swollen clouds, threatening to drown me as Erevan gives me a grim, pitying look.

"Yeah, I know. I'm sorry. I'll think of something."

After my talk with Erevan, I head back to the Sun Palace, doing my best to go unnoticed by the dozens of courtiers filtering in from every part of the continent. But no matter how much I avoid eye contact, keeping my head down, there's no hiding these fucking wings on my back. I stand out like a flashing red light over an inky pond.

Though I look straight ahead, I feel every curious eye peeling me apart. Thankfully, I know this palace like I know the back of my hand, and before long, I'm able to maneuver my way into a quieter area of the building.

Breathing a sigh of relief, I sag against the wall, running a hand through my hair.

"Gabriel."

Callias, the palace stylist, storms in my direction, flanked by two of the Tributes. I remember them as the ones that Lor became friendly with, Halo and Marici.

"We've been looking for you," Callias says, and I suppress a groan. Why the fuck can't everyone just leave me alone?

"Where is Lor?" the one on Callias's left asks. Halo, with her dark curly hair and deep complexion and her lips currently pulled into a frown.

"What?" I ask.

Callias's guilty smile is sheepish.

"I might have let it slip that I'd seen her," he says, and I sigh loudly.

"You're really shit at keeping secrets," I say.

"I know," he agrees.

"We want to see her," the other Tribute, Marici, says. "We've been worried sick about her."

"Is she okay?" Halo asks. "Where is she?"

I hold up my hands, this barrage of questions making my head pound.

"I can't tell you that," I say, and Halo plants her hands on her hips, her eyebrows drawing together. "I promised."

That softens her expression.

"We just want to know she's all right," Halo says. "Does she need our help?"

I shake my head. "I don't know."

The looks on their faces are brimming with concern, and some soft, pathetic place buried deep in the center of my heart wavers. I'm such an idiot.

"Look, I'll try to get a message to her," I find myself saying, already regretting this. "If she's okay with you knowing her whereabouts, then I'll let you know. Until then, do not bother me with this again."

Halo opens her mouth as if to protest, but I cut her off.

"It's the best I can do," I say. "I swore I'd keep her location a secret."

"Right," Halo says. "I can respect that. Tell her we just want to see her and hope that she's safe."

I roll my neck and massage the bridge of my nose. "Sure. Of course."

Then, before they can demand anything else, I spin on my heel and walk away, hopefully to lose myself where no one will fucking talk to me ever again.

CHAPTER FORTY-TWO

KING HERRIC

THE AURORA: THE SECOND AGE

"**K**eep going," Herric ordered as he paced back and forth, casting out a tendril of Aurora magic, watching the colors swirl against the dark sky.

It had been years since he'd been granted this gift by the Empyrium, and it was still difficult for him to control. While the Torch did its best to help, it was just an enchanted object, and most of the heavy lifting fell to him. It was a similar tale across Ouranos—the magic was strong and unpredictable, and though fewer tragedies plagued the land, complete control was still elusive. No one knew if it would get better with time or if they could expect this as their permanent state of being.

For months now, Herric had assigned his workers to dig up the wreckage of the mine collapse that had preceded the moment he'd been taken to the Evanescence. He wanted to recover that strange black stone they'd encountered.

It had come to him in a dream one night. The memory of what he'd felt down there before they'd been forced to flee. Magic. He hadn't recognized it right away, but now that he'd been gifted with his own, he recalled the way it had pulsed around him. Now that he was familiar with its essence and flavor, he was sure he'd experienced its presence buried deep in that mountain.

"A message, Your Majesty," came a voice, and Herric stopped pacing. One of his guards handed him a letter written on golden paper, which meant he already knew from where it came.

He slid his finger under the gold seal, popping it open. An invitation from Zerra to dine with her next week. He smiled.

He had never gotten over the fact the Empyrium had declined to give him dominion over the continent, tossing him out and selecting that useless airhead as the god to rule over them. He could never let that choice lie.

As far as he could discern, Zerra was doing nothing in her palace in the sky. Though she couldn't touch the surface, she could summon people to her, and Herric had acquiesced to her invitations. She wanted to smooth things over, and he pretended to go along with it, but only to learn where her weaknesses might lie.

When he'd first arrived in the Evanescence, he'd found what could be described only as a scene of debauchery, fueled by wine and food and sex. She had the world in the palm of her hand, and she chose to squander her power for the sake of parties and luxury. It was an affront.

She clearly hadn't troubled herself with the notion that anyone she brought up from the surface would, after a time, become an empty shell of nothing. A body without a soul or spark. Herric had been careful to limit the length of his visits in the Evanescence, keeping a watchful eye on himself for any signs he might suffer a similar fate.

He had always been adept at understanding what people wanted to hear, and he'd used that to convince Zerra to let down her guard. She was a vain thing. A few well-placed compliments and the suggestion that he was attracted to her were enough to have her also inviting him to her bed.

He'd obliged, performing the carnal duties with enough enthusiasm to make it seem believable. He didn't feel anything for her, but she was a beautiful woman, and he couldn't complain about the physical release.

His goal was to find a way to usurp her position. She wasn't particularly bright, and he hoped fooling her into revealing her secrets wouldn't prove too much of a challenge.

"Thank you," Herric said. "Please send a message back stating that I would be happy to visit."

"Very well," said his guard with a bow before he stalked off. At that moment, a resounding crash drew Herric's attention towards the tunnel where they'd been digging.

"We've broken through!" came the cry that had Herric making haste towards the worksite. Someone was already heading up to retrieve him, and they stopped at the sight of their king and bowed.

"This way, Your Majesty."

Herric wound down into the bowels of the mountain, arriving inside a large cavern. The walls were made of dark, glittering stone, like someone had trapped the night sky underground.

He felt it again. That humming that vibrated in his bones and suggested evidence of magic. He would take his time and thoroughly test the substance. With the unpredictability of Ouranos's magic, he didn't dare try anything here in the bowels of the mountain, lest he risk another collapse.

"Well done," he said to the workers, who watched him with their tools gripped at their sides.

"How would you like us to proceed, Your Majesty?" asked one of the site leaders.

"Bring some to the surface," Herric said. "We're going to find out what it can do."

Chapter Forty-Three

LOR

Present Day

"**P**ut that book down. We're going out," Nadir says from the doorway of the living room.

I'm seated on the floor with Nerissa, a mountain of books spread around us. We have just two more days until the presentation ceremony, and our plans are still in flux. While we hammer out the details of our somewhat nebulous ideas for infiltrating the Sun Palace, we're scouring through texts for mentions of the arks, hoping to learn something about them.

"Where?" I ask.

"I can't tell you."

"You expect me to just walk out of here with you without

any sort of explanation?" I ask, closing the book in my lap. "Have you met me?"

He smirks. "Sure, and that's why I know you're already dying of curiosity." He stops and smiles. "I promise it'll be worth it."

I roll my eyes. "Fine. But there better be food involved. Chocolate and cheese and decadent things stuffed with other things."

He chuckles and then holds out a hand, drawing me up.

"Enough talking. Let's *go*. We're going to be late."

"Late for what?"

"Lor," he growls.

It's true that I am curious, so I relent as he drags me out of the back gate and through the streets of Aphelion. We arrive at the docks, where a small ferry waits, bobbing in the ocean as the setting sun transforms the waves into watercolor hues of orange and pink.

"This way," Nadir says, tugging me onto the small boat decorated with tiny white lights. After we both take a seat on the small bench at the back, Nadir wraps an arm around my shoulders. The captain pushes us from the dock before the ferry putters through the water.

"Tell me where we're going," I demand again, but he just gives me a smug smile and refuses to answer. I cross my arms and sit back, pretending to pout as he leans in and kisses the spot behind my ear.

"Patience, Lightning Bug. Enjoy the ride."

I try to contain my smile, but I do as he says, sitting forward and tipping my face up, enjoying the way the breeze feels tousling my hair. It's beautiful out here. Aphelion starts to recede in the distance, the golden domes and spires of the city glinting in the failing light.

I look at Nadir, who's watching me with a satisfied smile.

"When do I get to find out?" I ask.

"Soon." He pulls out a narrow strip of fabric from his pocket. "First, you have to put this on."

I eye it dubiously. "You're blindfolding me?"

Leaning in, he wraps the fabric over my eyes and whispers in my ear. "Just trust me."

"I do," I say, making my words firm. "You know that, right? I do."

He pauses as he ties a knot at the back of my head, growing quiet.

"I know that, Lor," he finally says after a moment. "And I'll never give you any reason to do otherwise."

"I know that, too."

He kisses the shell of my ear and again folds me into his embrace. The simple black dress I'm wearing leaves my arms and legs exposed, and the cool breeze makes me shiver. His hand lands on my knee, caressing the skin as he protects me with his warmth.

"We're almost there."

I feel the rock of the boat as we roll over the gentle waves and a soft bump as we come to a stop.

Nadir takes my hand and pulls me up. "Come on," he says, leading me off the ferry and onto what feels like hard-packed sand.

"Don't let me fall," I say as I feel blindly in front of me.

I'm beyond curious about what's going on, but I'm allowing myself to sink into this moment and just enjoy it. Whatever Nadir has planned will be something I like. I'm sure of it.

"Never," he says with such rawness in his voice that I swallow the thick knot that grows in my throat. I squeeze his hand as we continue walking.

"Careful, there's a step here," he says, lifting me by the waist and then settling me on a surface that feels like grass.

"Are we almost there?"

"Almost," he says, and I can hear the amusement in his voice.

"This had better be good."

"Only the best for you," he replies, and finally we come to a stop. He stands behind me, and I feel him untying the knot at the back of my head.

"Ready?"

"Yes! How much longer are you going to make me wait?"

There's a chorus of laughter before Nadir slips the blindfold off. I gasp as I take in our surroundings. We're on a small island, the water stretching out in every direction.

In the center of a small clearing is . . . everyone.

Tristan and Willow and Amya and Mael, Hylene, and Etienne. They're surrounding a long wooden table that's covered in food, enclosed by trees strung with hundreds of little white lights. Circling above everyone is a cloud of golden lightning bugs.

"What?" I ask in disbelief.

"Happy birthday!" they shout as Amya and Nadir each lift a hand, sending out ribbons of magic that twist and bend to spell out the words against the darkening sky.

"I . . ." Willow and Tristan run for me, squeezing me into a tight hug as a tear slips down my cheek.

"What is all this?"

Nadir wraps an arm around me from behind, his large hand spreading across my stomach. "Your brother and sister let it slip that it's your birthday tomorrow. Something you failed to mention to me." He arches a brow, and I laugh.

"Sorry. With everything going on, it just didn't seem important," I say, absolutely overcome with this gesture.

"Lor, you're always important to us," Willow says. "It's been so many years since we could celebrate properly. When Nadir suggested we do something special, we didn't hesitate."

I look up at Nadir. "You did all this?"

He tips a crooked smile. "I had some help."

"We have some special visitors," Willow says, and that's when I notice three more figures that bring a huge grin to my face.

"Halo! Marici!" I squeal, running over and wrapping them into another hug. "What are you doing here?" Behind them stands Callias with his hands stuffed into his pockets.

"We heard a rumor you were in the city, and convinced Gabriel to send a note."

"Convinced?" I ask.

"Badgered until he had no choice," Halo says, and I laugh before I look back at Nadir.

"Our notes actually passed one another," he says. "You said you wanted to see Callias, and when I heard your friends were asking about you, I knew you'd want to see them. I figured there wouldn't be much harm if we set up a meeting away from the house."

"We would never tell Atlas," Halo says. "You know that, Lor."

"I do know that." I hug her again.

Callias also wraps me in a hug and then pulls back, searching my face. "So you want me to deal with this?" he asks, and I nod.

"I think so."

"What's going on?" Willow asks. "Deal with what?"

"My scar."

Neither of my siblings says anything for a moment, their gazes meeting and then pulling away. "Did either of you know? Who really caused it?"

Tristan lets out a long breath.

"Lor, you'd convinced yourself it was the result of helping Willow, and that seemed to bring you comfort, so we didn't correct you." He exchanges another worried glance with my sister. "I hope you'll understand we thought it was the best thing to do."

My lips clamp together as I nod. It was. I can't blame them for trying to shield me from the shadow of those memories.

"I understand why you did it," I say, and they both visibly relax. "But now that I know, I want it gone."

"Of course," Willow says. "No one ever expected you to keep it."

"Okay," I whisper.

"Should we eat first or do it now?" Callias asks. "I've brought my supplies, and we can work on it right here. Since it's the product of magic, it might require a few sessions to erase it completely, but for today, we can make a significant improvement. How does that sound?"

"Perfect. But . . . food first."

"I like the sound of that," he declares, and then Halo and Marici surround me again.

"I'm so glad you're here. I've been dying to see you. You have to tell me everything you've been up to since the Trials," I tell them.

We all take a seat at the table, passing around food and wine. Callias, Marici, and Halo sit across from where I'm sandwiched between Nadir and Willow as they share everything happening in the palace. Mainly, that Apricia continues to be insufferable, especially when Atlas kept delaying the bonding.

"Her hair is completely blonde now," Halo snorts into her glass.

"I've been working full-time trying to make her look like the 'proper glowing Sun Queen' while she hurls insults like poisoned arrows," Callias says, rolling his eyes. "As if the color of her hair is what makes a queen."

"How about you two?" I ask Halo and Marici. "I'm sorry I couldn't do anything to help you with Atlas in the end."

Marici waves a hand. "Atlas has absolutely no interest in any of us. We're doing just fine."

My shoulders slump in relief. "I'm so glad. I know it's not ideal."

"It's the best we can hope for, given the circumstances," Halo says, and I smile.

"Can you tell us where you've been?" Marici asks. "What happened at the end of the Trials?"

I let out a breath. "I don't think that would be a good idea," I say. "I know you mean well, but the fewer people who know, the better. You might not have a choice but to reveal information if Atlas finds out."

Halo nods. "Of course. We understand. You were never really an Umbra rat, were you?"

I snort at that. "Well, I was never from The Umbra, but the rat part is probably true."

"Somehow, I doubt that," Marici says, her blue eyes brimming with kindness.

"A toast!" Mael cries from the end of the table, drawing all our attention to him. "To Lor on her birthday. To my boy Nadir, who finally found himself not only love but a fucking mate. And to stirring up some shit in Aphelion!"

Everyone agrees and raises their glass as we all continue eating. As I stare around the table, I'm seized with the warmest feeling of hope. We're attempting to break into the Sun Palace in two days and praying for the best. Our odds aren't great, and there's a more than likely chance Atlas will get his hands on me, but at least I had this moment. It will have to be enough.

When we've all had our fill to eat, Callias leans across the table. "Whenever you're ready."

"Okay," I nod. "Let's do it."

"Do you need me to come?" Nadir asks, taking my hand.

I shake my head. "I think I'll do this alone," I say. This is a moment to cut away a piece of a past I was clinging to, and I think this is something I need to do by myself.

Nadir leans down and whispers in my ear, "When you're finished, come and see me on the beach. I have something for you."

"Okay," I say.

Callias stands and rounds the table, holding out a hand.

"Let's go, Final Tribute."

About thirty minutes later, I traipse through the trees. The joyful sounds from the others follow my route, wrapping me in honeyed warmth. Despite everything, I am so grateful for everything good that's happened.

As I approach the beach, I spy Nadir seated on a patch of grass, facing the water, his knees up and his arms wrapped around them. I take the opportunity to watch him, wishing I could see his face in this unguarded moment.

A moment later, I drop down next to him.

"Hi," I say, and he peers over and frowns as he studies my face.

"It looks the same. Did Callias have trouble with it?"

I shake my head. "I changed my mind." He arches an eyebrow as I continue to explain. "I realized the meaning behind this mark is what I choose. That just because *he* was responsible for it, it doesn't make it any less a symbol of the things I'd do to protect the people I love." I fall silent. "Maybe that's foolish, but it's how I feel."

Nadir's face is a mixture of raw heartbreak and overflowing pride. "It's not foolish at all."

"I did do something, though," I say, pulling the neck of my dress aside to reveal my left shoulder. I didn't ask Callias to remove my scar, but I did ask him to remove the black brand charred into my skin from Nostraza.

Nadir lifts his fingers and gently touches my now unblemished skin. I'm guessing he's not much of a crier, what with the whole dark prince persona, but I swear I see a hint of silver lining his eyes.

"Excellent choice, Heart Queen." He leans down and presses a kiss to the spot, his warm lips lingering on my skin.

In the distance, the chatter of the others reaches us, and I bask in the radiance of their laughter and their joy. Across the water sits the Sun Palace, glowing in the moonlight. I wonder what's happening inside right now. What's Gabriel up to? What will we encounter when we attempt to get inside?

"It's going to be okay," Nadir says, his gaze following mine.

"You can't promise that."

He reaches into his pocket and pulls out a small box.

"No, but I can give you this. A birthday present."

I take it from him and crack open the lid. Inside is a beautiful ring with a deep red stone.

"What's this for?" I ask, pulling it out.

"It's my promise to you," he says. "To keep you safe. To love and protect you for as long as there's breath in my body."

I look at him. "It's beautiful."

"And red, of course, because you are the Heart Queen, and what other color could it be?"

I smile at that. "How about the color of the northern lights?"

He shakes his head. "You are Heart through your soul, Lor. That is your legacy and your home. No matter what happens going forward, always remember that. No matter what's happened in my life, I've always held on by remembering what I was fighting for."

He stops and then takes the ring from me. "Wear this, if you choose, as a reminder that whatever demons we face, I will follow you until the very end. Into the fires of the Underworld if I must."

My throat grows tight, and I find myself unable to speak as I nod and hold out my hand. Nadir slides the ring onto my finger and then stares at me.

"What do you want, Lor? For your future. What do you want more than anything?"

"This," I say immediately. "You. A life where we can live together and be happy and free. It's all I've ever wanted."

He tips his head and smiles. "No more revenge?"

"Oh yes. I still want that. After we finish that part." He laughs.

"That's my girl."

"But when it's all done. If we win. Then that's what I want."

He nods as the corner of his mouth twists up. "Then I want to give you that."

Nadir leans over and kisses me, his mouth hungry as our tongues slick together.

"I want you," he says, his voice rough. "Here under the sky."

"Everyone is right there," I say, and he doesn't hesitate, his hand lifting as beams of light sprout from his fingers and close around us, forming an iridescent dome hiding us from the outside world. Lightning bugs slip through small cracks, gathering at the peak, making this seem like the most magical spot to have ever existed.

"Now they can't see or hear anything."

"They're going to know exactly why you just did that," I laugh, and his eyes go dark.

"Good, then hopefully, they stay the fuck away."

He pulls me towards him and kisses me long and deep with a hand cupped around the back of my neck as he eases me onto the grass. We continue kissing as his hand slides down my ribs and then up, cupping my breast before his fingers roll my nipple. We continue kissing, taking our time, allowing it to stretch and bend as we dive and roll and *languish* in this moment.

His hand travels over my stomach and then under the hem of my skirt, where he finds my stomach, smoothing over my skin, tracing slow circles around my navel.

Slowly, I pull apart the buttons on his shirt, exposing brown skin and the swirl of his bright tattoos. He watches me, holding still as I open the last one and then run my hands down his chest and over his back, loving the flex and bunch of his muscle and his silken warmth.

"You're incredible," he murmurs against me as his hand drifts lower, under the waistband of my underwear, directly to the needy wet ache between my thighs. He groans as his finger slips against me. "Always ready for me."

I gasp as he touches me, circling my clit with his finger before he dips into me. I fumble for the button on his pants, pulling them open and feeling for the hard evidence of his cock straining against his underwear.

As he continues to alternate between fucking me with his fingers and rubbing my clit, I slip under the fabric and take him in my hand, stroking him as he moans into my mouth. We continue pleasuring each other for several indulgent minutes, our short breaths and panting gasps filling the quiet night.

He pulls away and then tugs off my underwear, yanking them off before he crawls on top of me, nudging my entrance. Slowly, he eases into me, and I cling to his shoulders as I whimper at the pure, exquisite sensation.

"I love you," he whispers, pulling out and then sliding in with agonizing slowness. He thrusts hard and deep, filling every empty corner of my heart. "From now until the Evanescence takes us, Lor."

"I'll love you longer than that," I say as he rocks into me. "Until the world turns to ash."

He sighs and tips his forehead to mine as he continues churning his hips. My magic sparks, pale wisps of lightning twinning with his. We climb the peak and climax together, shuddering against each other's mouths.

When we've finished, we lie in the grass, watching the lightning bugs dance and twirl. I'm so content and happy, and I feel like I could just lie here forever. A burst of laughter from the table summons our attention, and our gazes meet.

"You should go back and spend some time with your friends," he says.

"Thank you for this. All of it."

"You know you don't need to thank me."

"Yes. I do." I kiss him again before we retrieve our discarded clothing and try to look somewhat like we didn't just have sex. Well, at least I do. Nadir obviously doesn't care, since he leaves his shirt hanging open and does nothing to fix his mussed hair.

He takes my hand, and we approach the table.

"Ah!" yells Mael. "They're done fucking. Come have a drink!"

I roll my eyes and shake my head, but I accept the glass he's holding out, briefly considering dumping it on his head.

"I know what you're thinking," he says with a grin that does its best to charm me. "And I really wouldn't blame you."

At that, I burst out laughing.

Chapter Forty-Four

Gabriel

The Sun Palace

The palace is the site of pure, unfiltered chaos. I've never seen it like this. Every corner is stuffed with so many people and flowers and rolls of fabric, I can barely walk without bumping into something or someone.

It's claustrophobic. It's drowning me. I fantasize about a tiny island floating in the middle of the ocean where I have to catch fish with my bare hands and collect rainwater in coconut shells and my only company is the sweet bliss of silence.

While Apricia screams at everyone, Atlas hides in his study, summoning me daily to ask if I have news of Lor's whereabouts. I've made up a thousand lies and rumors. Sightings of her on the other side of Ouranos, potential leads that all conveniently end in nothing. But I'm running out of time. *She's* running out of time.

Atlas is losing his patience, and I feel the increasing strain of deceiving him. Pressure squeezes around my organs, and my tendons stretch like they've been wrenched over a loom. I consider asking Tyr to alter his orders so I can work around them, just enough so I can breathe. The few times I've done it in the past, I've always had to be careful so as not to arouse Atlas's suspicions. I've become a master of operating just outside the rigid circle of my parameters without drawing too much attention to myself. I, too, am a master of illusion of a different sort.

But even if I could convince Tyr to loosen Atlas's hold on me, the effort is wasted. He's stopped speaking entirely, and nothing I do has been able to coax out a word in weeks.

Today we're all stuck inside the future queen's massive entertaining salon. The official presentation, when the citizens of Aphelion will gather at the gates to kneel before their king and queen, is tomorrow, and Apricia is throwing a party today. The other nine warders and I, along with half the fucking castle, have been summoned on the pretense of celebrating, but this is all the most pathetic facade.

Atlas and Apricia lounge on a pile of cushions at the front of the room, taking in well wishes and greetings from guests floating through. The fallen Tributes are also in attendance, and Apricia is sure to remind them at every opportunity that they could have been in her place had they been "better."

Even I can see the relief on their faces. I'm reasonably sure not a single one regrets failing the Trials right now. I wonder if Halo and Marici have seen Lor. It would be just like her to risk her neck to get a moment with her friends. I also wonder why Nadir asked for Callias, but I'm keeping myself on a need-to-know basis.

Atlas is tense. I can tell from across the room where I stand with my hands behind my back. Apricia likes how the warders appear—our white wings are unique and a source of curiosity to everyone we meet.

Admittedly, the ten of us cut striking figures in our golden armor, but she doesn't allow us to speak. We've been positioned on opposite walls of the room, five on each side, where we've been ordered to stand with our wings stretched like we're fucking marble statues.

At first, Atlas tried to defend us, but Apricia shut him down instantly. He didn't try very hard to object, and I'm sure it's because he's angry I haven't found Lor. The irony being that I *could* be using this time to find her instead of standing here like I'm furniture.

But Atlas is mostly angry with me, and the others don't even know they're being punished for my lies. I've kept this knowledge from them, not because I don't trust them with my life, but because the less they know, the safer everyone will be.

But the strain is starting to wear on me. Because the order isn't direct, the effect is more gradual. A few aches and pains here and there. An uncomfortable but manageable tightness in my chest. But it's starting to get worse, and I'm not sure how much longer I can or should hold out.

At this point, I'd gladly let myself die to keep this secret.

Not necessarily out of loyalty to Lor, but because I'm so fucking angry with Atlas.

I look over, feeling eyes on me, and notice Atlas watching. I keep my expression neutral—I am nothing but a servant clad in golden armor who knows how to keep his mouth shut—but I worry that he can sense what I'm hiding.

I inhale a sharp breath at a stabbing twinge below my ribs, and resist the urge to bend over. Fuck, that hurts. I hope that whatever Nadir and Lor are planning, they get on with it soon. A bomb is ticking over all of our heads.

For the next two hours, I stand on the sidelines, shifting from foot to foot as I grow increasingly miserable. It's hot in here, and the air stirs with a toxic residue of bodies and alcohol and noble snobbery.

Another couple enters the room, and I tense, recognizing Hylene, the woman who was with Lor. She's stunning with her long red hair and that body of luscious curves. If I were a freer man, I'd fantasize about all the things I'd like to do with her bent over a table.

What is she doing here? I think I recognize the Fae she's with as Apricia's brother; her arm is looped through his as she pretends he's the most fascinating man she's ever seen. At least, it seems like she's pretending. Her smile doesn't reach her eyes, and her laugh sounds a little forced, but her date seems oblivious.

Either they're in a relationship, or she's here to spy for Nadir. I'd bet money it's the latter, and the twist in my stomach intensifies. How many more secrets can I keep before I collapse under their weight?

Hylene and her companion sidle up to Atlas and Apricia, kissing cheeks and uttering bland platitudes typical of these gatherings. When they're done, they find themselves refreshments and mingle with the crowd.

I blow out a breath and roll my neck, wondering how much longer I have to stand here. I wonder if I threw myself from the window, whether I'd survive the drop to the rocks below. I'd probably break a few bones, but at least that would get me out of this.

Finally, after what feels like a hundred years, the guests start to slowly drift away, returning to their respective rooms to sleep off their inevitable day-drinking-induced hangovers. It's moving towards evening, and everyone will want to get some rest before the presentation begins tomorrow. I'm dreading it already.

Eventually, Apricia stands, and Atlas follows. They toss out a few more goodbyes and then retreat further into the queen's apartments.

To everyone else, it will look like Atlas plans to spend the night with Apricia in her room, but I know he has no intentions of doing so.

I've never quite figured out if it's because Apricia holds no attraction for him or if he's too consumed with his schemes to consider such matters right now. Atlas has never been one to shy away from female company, but I don't think anyone has truly held his attention in years.

Once Atlas and Apricia disappear, I catch the eyes of my brothers. Not waiting another moment, we all duck out of the room, heading towards Atlas's apartments. He'll use one of the palace's many hidden corridors to make it back to his study, where he'll be expecting us.

We arrive at his wing, and the door to his study flies open a second later.

"Gabe!" he barks. "Enter."

I exchange a look with the others but do as I'm told, closing the door behind me.

Atlas paces the room, and it's obvious I'm not the only one feeling the physical effects of current events. Atlas looks tired and worn in a way I've never seen him before.

"Any news?" he asks.

"I'm sorry, no," I say, and then tamp down my wince at the pain that shoots up my spine. He stops pacing and looks at me carefully. I try to keep my face bland, hoping he can't read my lie.

"Atlas," I say, hoping to distract him and finally learn what's going on. Maybe if I understand what he wants from Lor, then I'll feel less guilty when I'm forced to reveal her. Maybe it's not that bad. "Please. For the thousandth time, tell me why. What do you want her for? Your bonding is in two days, and I don't think you're going to find her in time." I carefully use the word "you" and not "we," hoping that's enough of a half-truth.

Atlas spins on me. "You think I don't know it's in two days!" he shouts, his face turning red. He's shaking with fury, his hair wild and his eyes wilder.

"This is all going to fall apart if I have to bond to that . . . woman!"

"What is?" I ask, taking a step closer. I'm no stranger to Atlas's outbursts, and more often than not, he's all bark and no bite. "What is going to fall apart?"

"I'm going to bond to Lor, Gabriel," he says, and only part of that surprises me. There was a reason she was in the Trials, and after what she told me, I understand he wanted access to her power as a Primary.

What I don't understand is how Atlas plans to make any of this happen.

"I don't follow," I say, pretending I don't know who or what Lor is.

He looks over with a patronizing smile. "No, you wouldn't."

"Atlas, please," I say. "I've spent a century holding my tongue. Years wondering how you've managed any of this. Why has the Mirror allowed you to keep up this charade?"

The words hang in the air. These kinds of sentiments have always been forbidden, but there is no hiding from this anymore.

The corner of Atlas's mouth curls up.

"Destiny has offered me the means to fix the mistake that was made, so don't presume to stand there with that look on your face, judging me, Gabriel."

"I'm not judging," I lie. "I'm just trying to understand."

Atlas looks me over, the corner of his mouth twisting up into a cruel smile.

"Lor is going to help me find an object that will allow me to bond with her," he says, and I get the sense he's been dying to say these words out loud.

Atlas has lived alone with his lies and his murky version of the truth for so long that he needs someone else to become a part of his narrative just to ease his isolation. Despite living in a golden palace surrounded by hundreds of servants and advisors and courtiers, the Sun King is a lonely, lonely man.

"What is it?" I ask, furrowing my brow.

"It's an amplifier that will allow me to reverse the Mirror's decision and seize the power I've been denied."

"What?" A cold dread slithers through my veins.

"When I get Lor back, I will make her find it and use it to bond with her, and I'll finally be the true king of Aphelion."

I do my best not to react. Internally I'm screaming. What is going on here? Is anything he's saying true? Has he lost his mind?

"How do you know about this?"

Atlas gives me a patronizing smile, but I don't miss the touch of wildness that's entered his eyes. He's been slipping away for months, and now I wonder about the real monster living under his skin.

"It doesn't matter," he says. "All you need to know is that we must find Lor, and then everything will finally be as it should."

I step back because several things are clicking together.

"What do you mean, '*true* king of Aphelion'?" I finally ask, my voice raw. "What about Tyr?"

Atlas tips his head, peering at me with an expression that makes my blood turn cold. He walks over to the window and peers out.

"That's another benefit of this plan. I will finally be rid of him."

"No." The word slips out without my meaning to, and then

Atlas turns to me with a patient smile that feels as honest as a thief with stolen jewels tucked under his floorboards.

"Oh, Gabe," Atlas says. "I know you've always hoped you'd get your precious Tyr back and you two might get another chance to be happy. But I assure you that getting rid of him has always been in my plans."

I take another step. No. I can't let this happen.

"Do you still love him?" Atlas asks, approaching me now. "After all this time, does your light burn for him the way it once did? Do you still pine for a king who is nothing more than bones and skin? A hollow shell of a man? Do you think he remembers how he feels?"

My forehead breaks out in panicked sweat as he stalks closer.

"Why are you doing this?" I ask, the words coming out as a whisper.

Atlas knows he's picking at all my fears and worst anxieties. My feelings for Tyr that I've tried to push down for so long. In spite of everything, a small part of me hoped he'd break free of this cage and return to himself one day. Deep down, I have always known Atlas would find a way to get rid of him. But still, hearing it confirmed chips out a permanent piece of my heart.

"You can't do that," I hear myself saying, and Atlas doesn't even bother to correct me, because we both know I have no power here.

"Where is she, Gabriel?"

I swallow hard, trying to bury my response.

The strain of my lies cinches a band around my chest, and

it's the slightest movement. The slightest squeezing of my eyes and the barest hitch in my breath, but Atlas sees it.

Atlas, who sees almost nothing, finally sees this.

"Where is she, *Gabriel*?" he asks again, approaching me now, his gaze scanning me from head to toe, shredding me apart bit by bit.

"I don't know," I whisper, but I can barely get the words out. They come out garbled and feeble, like the blatant lie they are. A stab through the meat of my stomach causes my nostrils to flare as I clamp down on a scream.

"You're lying to me," Atlas hisses. "You've been lying to me." I shake my head, but another pain shoots behind my eye, and I bend over, clutching my face, agony burning over my scalp.

"You're lying!" Atlas roars. He yanks me back up by the collar, his nose inches from mine. "Tell me the truth! Where is she? Have you seen her?!"

I press my mouth together, the words attempting to fly out of me like a cannon shot. I've never wanted to betray Lor, but now that I know Tyr's life is on the line, the stakes have changed. Whom do I betray?

Atlas shoves me against the wall, his fist pressing into my throat with such force, I grow lightheaded.

"Where. Is. She?" Atlas demands, his teeth bared. The flash of mania in his eyes says he wants to kill me right now. I can't answer as a fist closes under my ribs, and my mouth gapes open.

He lets out a sound of frustration and tugs me against him. Then with his hand gripped in my collar, he wrenches open the door. All the warders still wait outside with expectant expressions. Atlas shoves me into Jareth, who catches me as I stumble towards him.

"This traitor is lying," Atlas says. "Are the rest of you holding out on me too?"

They all exchange wary glances. I'm so glad I kept this information to myself.

"Answer me!" Atlas screams, and another warder answers.

"I'm sorry, we don't know what you're talking about," Rhyle says, which makes Atlas roar. There are no other servants in the passage, but someone must hear this commotion.

"Come with me," Atlas spits, already storming away. "All of you."

The ten of us exchange another look, but we do as our king asks and follow him through the palace. I already know where we're headed, and I try to run ahead, hoping to stave off whatever is coming next.

"Atlas," I say, but he cuts me off.

"Don't speak to me. Don't ever fucking speak to me again, Gabriel. You've been lying to me all this time. After everything I've done for you, this is how you repay me?"

I nearly bite through my tongue. Done for me? The only thing I've ever been is his punching bag and his fucking slave.

We arrive at the tower door, and another warder unlocks it before we all ascend the stairs. I don't want to follow, but I'm terrified of what Atlas will do to Tyr without my intervention.

Atlas strides over to his brother, who lies on his stomach, and grabs him by a fistful of hair, dragging Tyr to his knees. My heart clenches at the confusion in his expression.

"Order them to tell me where Lor is hiding," he says. "Directly. And then tell them they're to retrieve her immediately."

Tyr's gaze flicks between Atlas and me. He hasn't said a word in weeks.

"Atlas," I say. "He stopped speaking. You know that."

Atlas shakes his head.

"Oh no, you fucking don't, big brother."

Before I have a chance to react, Atlas is on me. He circles an arm around my chest and holds a dagger to my neck. The other warders cry out in anger, but Atlas hisses, "If any of you come near me, I'll kill him." He presses the blade to my skin— it's so sharp that I feel a warm trickle of blood seep down the line of my throat.

Then he glares at Tyr. "If you do not give the order, I will spill his blood all over your fucking bed and force you to sleep in it. Do you understand me?"

Atlas's voice has risen to a fever pitch, taking on a frantic edge. I sense his control slipping away. I try not to struggle, genuinely worried Atlas might nick an artery.

He presses the blade in harder, and I feel another trickle of blood ooze down my neck. Everyone in the room leans forward as Atlas backs us into the corner.

"I mean it," he says. "Tyr!"

Tyr holds out his hands and levers himself off the bed, making slow, deliberate movements. I watch him, my heart breaking in two. He's been a shell of a man for so very long, but watching him like this, so frail and broken, while we all stand in this room with a fake king who's losing his mind grinds a piece of me down forever.

"Don't!" I try to gasp, but Atlas grips me harder, cutting off my air.

If Tyr gives the order and I'm forced to reveal Lor, then Tyr's life will be forfeit. If I'd known this was the potential outcome, I would have told her to run and hide forever.

"Shut up," Atlas snarls. "I should have done this a long time ago."

He points the blade at his brother. "Say it! None of your bullshit, Tyr. Say it."

Tyr opens his mouth, and I try to object again, but it's no use.

"You will tell them where the girl is," Tyr says, his voice soft but steady. "And you will find her and bring her here."

The words fall over the room, landing on each of us like a noose coated in acid.

Finally, Atlas lets me go, shoving me so hard I stumble and trip, landing on the hard stone. Several warders go to help me, but Atlas stops them.

"No," he says, and they freeze into stillness. "Leave him to squirm on the floor like the worm he is."

Atlas approaches and crouches down on his haunches. "Where is she, Gabriel?"

The pressure of my tether cinches around my heart, forcing me to give an answer.

"In Aphelion," I say, and every single person in the room reacts.

"Where in Aphelion?" Atlas asks with a feverish light of triumph in his eyes.

"In the Eighth," I say. "Staying in the house of some High Fae."

He furrows his brows and cocks his head. "Who is she with?"

Fuck. I was really hoping he wouldn't ask that.

"With her brother and sister," I say, praying he'll leave it at that. Keeping Nadir's presence a secret feels like giving them a chance.

"She got them out of Nostraza?" he asks.

Lor said Nadir helped liberate her family, but I don't technically know who got them out, so I nod, hoping that's close enough to the truth. But pain wrenches against my ribs, causing me to gasp.

"Who else is with her?" Atlas says, picking up on my discomfort.

"The Aurora Prince," I choke out, and that answer definitely confuses Atlas. Thankfully he doesn't ask me why, but then I recall my conversation with Nadir in the café.

If he's in a relationship with Lor and Atlas thinks he's going to take her, then this will turn into a bloodbath before this is over. The Aurora Prince doesn't take kindly to anyone interfering with what's his. Will it be enough to protect her, though?

Atlas leans in, baring his teeth. "You're going to go and retrieve her right now. All of you. Is that understood? If you have to kill the others, then do so. I don't care."

My shoulders sag. I have no choice anymore. Even if I resist, the others can't. Even if they could, they don't understand what's at stake.

"I don't know why you've been lying to me, Gabriel," Atlas

says as I struggle to my feet. "But understand there will be consequences for this." I nod as our gazes meet. I know what those consequences will be. What they've always been.

"Go," Atlas orders, and then we file out of the room. I look back, hating the idea of leaving Tyr alone with Atlas, but for now, the true king is safe. If we return with Lor, then I don't know what happens next.

When we emerge at the base of the tower, the warders turn to me. They won't begrudge me for my lies. They won't judge me. They understand enough to know why I had to do it. They, too, find ways to work around their leashes. I'm just not sure any of them has ever had this much to lose.

I pass through the line of them, saying nothing as I march through the palace before we spill into the crowded streets.

My brothers march behind me silently, passing a line of wagons carting in supplies for the ceremony. We've probably scraped half the countryside clean of food and alcohol and everything else needed to pull off this sham of a bonding.

There are people in every direction we walk, celebrating and drinking without a care in the world. I want to scream at their obliviousness.

The noise swells around us as we walk, ten silent specters passing through the boisterous crowd. Some people stop to gawk, but most are too drunk or having too much fun to care that we travel in their midst.

My jaw clenches tightly as we wind our way to the Eighth District. When I catch sight of the house where Lor and the others are staying, I come to a halt. The other warders stop next to me, casting uneasy glances my way.

With my lies exposed, pain has released from my body, and I am once again free. Sort of.

"Let's go," I say. There's no point in lingering here any longer. It's time to do this.

"There," I say, pointing in the distance. "She's in there."

They nod, and we approach, surrounding the house. I'm not sure if the ten of us can fight off Nadir, Amya, and Mael together, but I'm hoping it won't come to that.

When did I get so fucking optimistic?

I stand at the front door and take a deep breath before I kick it down. We file into the house, and I enter the living room, then grind to a halt.

It's empty.

Not because there's no one here, but because literally everything is gone. The furniture, the rugs, the art on the walls. The only things left are the curtains hanging on the windows.

The rest of the warders file in, casting dubious looks my way, and I'm not sure what they're thinking. Am I still lying? Do they care?

"This was where I found her," I say, feeling the need to explain something.

"It looks like they left," Jareth says.

"Spread out and search the whole house," another warder says, and they all stir into action.

I'm . . . relieved. I can breathe again, but where did she go? Is she still in Aphelion? Did they do what they needed to do? How will Atlas react when I return and tell him she's gone? He won't stop. His actions today told me that even if this is a setback, he will never stop. He's waited almost a hundred years, and he wants to be a king, free and clear of the shadow close to consuming us all.

I listen to the thump of footsteps over my head as the others search through every room, and then I know what I must do. It's what I should have done years ago, but some hopeful part of me always thought maybe there would be another way.

But Atlas showed me there isn't. Atlas has only ever had one goal, and now he's closer to achieving it than ever. Even if he doesn't have Lor now, he's going to see this plan through one way or another.

I let out a sharp huff and then spin on my heel, storming out of the house and making my way through the streets with only one destination in mind.

This ends now. I'm done with his lies.

Finally. It's time for a fucking reckoning.

CHAPTER FORTY-FIVE

LOR

After my birthday celebration, Nadir surprises everyone by telling us we won't be returning to Nerissa's in the Eighth. Instead, he's arranged lodging closer to the palace in the Twenty-Third District. Not only will it be more convenient, but he's worried about Gabriel knowing our location. It isn't that Nadir doesn't trust Gabriel to keep his word, but we all understand he might not have a choice, and we've pushed almost to the limit of his timeline.

Aphelion has become a seething mass of people arriving from other parts of Ouranos, drawn to the city for the festivities. Throughout the twenty-four districts, there is entertainment and merriment. Acrobats performing in the streets, and musicians stringing notes around every corner. Food stalls and wine stands pop up everywhere, sustenance flowing as fireworks fill the night sky, and people dance until the sun comes up.

If we weren't about to embark on what is sure to be an increasingly dangerous task, I might find joy in this.

Of course, very few understand this is all a ruse. Under the smokescreen of celebration is the salient fact that Atlas has no interest in bonding to Apricia.

Gabriel's warnings still ring in my head. He's supposed to be looking for me, and he's running out of time. I don't blame him for choosing himself over me either. I understand what it's like to be trapped between difficult choices, and we all do what we must to survive.

Nerissa sits in the middle of a spread of books all over the living room floor of our new flat. She's been reading nonstop, trying to learn more about the arks.

"Whatever Cloris told you seems partly true," Nerissa says. Her long brown hair is tied up in a messy bun with a pencil stuck in it. Tristan sits next to her with his legs crossed, also flipping through pages.

I don't miss the way she keeps laying a hand on my brother's arm to ask him to pass her a book, and I certainly don't miss the look in his eyes every time he steals a glance her way. I think he's trying to be subtle, but he's failing miserably.

Nadir catches my eye, and we share a knowing smile at Tristan's expense.

It would bring me so much joy to see my brother find someone he could fall in love with.

"It says here that at the Beginning of Days, when the

Artefacts were formed, other objects of power were also created," Nerissa reads. "Each was intended to pair with an Artefact and could be used both to amplify and channel the magic of its realm."

"That has never been a part of the origin stories of Ouranos," Nadir says.

Nerissa shakes her head. "Because it seems like they were purposely hidden."

"What do you mean?" Nadir asks. "Why?"

"From what I can tell, Zerra's priestesses were actually created to retrieve them from each realm. When they tortured and killed in her name, they were trying to get their hands on the arks."

Nadir folds his hands under his chin. "For Zerra?"

"So one might assume," Nerissa answers. "It was all so long ago, but I suppose when the rulers realized she was after them, they hid them away well enough that they were mostly forgotten."

"Is there anything that says where they might be now?" I ask.

"Nothing that is clear," Nerissa says. "There are passing references to small rectangular objects, each carved with a woman bearing its corresponding Artefact."

"An ark is like a chest or a box, right?" I ask.

"Yes, or sometimes a coffin."

That answer sets the hairs standing on the back of my neck.

"So they're big?"

"No. I think they are fairly small. More like an art piece you'd keep on a shelf. The way the books talk about carrying them would suggest they're manageable. I suppose in the case of some of the larger and more unwieldy Artefacts, they were useful in channeling their power. They were created from a material mined in the Beltza Mountains."

"What material?" Nadir asks.

"That I don't know. But it also held magical properties."

"Anything else?" Nadir asks with a frown. I suspect it's taking everything in his power not to run home to find out what he can about The Aurora's ark.

Nerissa shakes her head. "Eventually, the histories just stop mentioning them at all. Like everyone collectively forgot."

"What about what Cloris said about the land reacting? Are all these incidents connected?"

Nerissa nods. "I think she might have been telling the truth about that."

She holds up a book. A standard text on the history of Ouranos. Even I recognize it with my limited reading experience.

"This is the story we all know about the Beginning of Days. The one in which Zerra brought all the rulers together and bestowed the gift of magic and the Artefacts she'd created on each of them."

"Right?" Nadir asks, leaning forward and clasping his hands between his knees.

"Well, I found this," Nerissa says, holding up another book. "It talks of an alternate history. This suggests that what we know as the story of the creation of the Second Age of Ouranos isn't entirely the truth.

"Zerra didn't create the magic, she just became a caretaker."

"What do you mean?" I ask.

"Magic was always here, but before the Beginning of Days, it—for a lack of a better way to describe it—began to spill over. The land could no longer contain it, and that's when it was granted to Ouranos's human inhabitants before they were ascended to High Fae."

"Granted by who?"

Nerissa's finger slides along the page. "Some higher authority. The author doesn't seem clear on who or what actually made the Artefacts."

"If that's true, then why do we give the credit to Zerra?" Nadir asks.

"Perhaps it was just propaganda to make her seem more powerful and used to lure in followers," Nerissa says. "The author does seem to think the Artefacts are more sentient than we normally give them credit for."

"So they're alive?" Tristan asks, and Nerissa shrugs.

"That's why they talk to you," Nadir says.

I nod. It had always been unnerving to understand how much they knew each time I spoke with them. "Maybe."

"That doesn't answer *why* they talk to Lor, though," Tristan says.

Nadir's gaze falls to me as though he's trying to see through me. He shakes his head.

"I know."

"Do you think it matters?" I ask. "Maybe it has something to do with my grandmother."

"Perhaps," Nadir says. "I think, for now, it's just important we get to the Mirror and figure out what it has for you. If it's the ark, then the next question will be what we do with it. If it falls into Cloris's hands, what could *she* do with it?"

I shake my head. There's something about this knowledge that's bothering me. It feels like there's a thread I'm missing, but it's written behind a thick sheet of fogged glass.

Whatever the case, Nadir is right. We need to focus on the task at hand. One step at a time. One revelation at a time. Just like when we were in The Aurora, I sense there are still many parts of this story yet to be told.

A moment later, the back door to the house bangs open, and Mael and Etienne stride into the room.

"We received a note from Hylene," Mael says. "She talked to Willow, and it isn't good news."

Mael hands the note to Nadir, who scans the missive as we all watch.

"What is it?" I ask after a moment.

"Hylene has confirmed the presentation will take place in the palace courtyard tomorrow morning as planned," Nadir says. "But there will be a party for the VIP guests *inside* the throne room."

"No," I reply. "But that was our chance."

"It says the party was supposed to take place in one of the back gardens, but they moved it inside at the last minute because they're expecting rain tomorrow."

"So what do we do?" I ask.

"We need a diversion," Etienne says. "Something to draw everyone away."

"What would be big enough to convince them all to leave?

And even then, the guards will be trained to stay put," Mael counters. "They know not to abandon their posts."

"So we do away with the guards," Nadir says. "And create a big enough disturbance to call the guests and the majority of the palace soldiers to the front, where everyone else will already be gathered."

"The throne room is suspended over a cliff," Amya says, her expression thoughtful. "What if part of it were to, say... collapse? I know the layout well enough. We could destroy the southern window without touching the Mirror. Everyone would be climbing over one another to escape."

Everyone seems to consider this idea, but I say, "No. We aren't killing off a bunch of innocent people who are there attending the bonding."

Nadir pins me with a glare. "Those people aren't innocent, Lor. They all stood by and watched you compete in those Trials, cheering for every moment of your suffering. They're complicit in how Atlas treats the low fae, and while a handful might object in theory, none of them have ever lifted a finger to join the resistance."

"And you have?" Tristan asks Nadir. While the two of them are starting to warm up to one another, it's clear there's a divide yet to cross.

"I've never claimed to be better than them," Nadir growls. "But I'm the one who wants to help your sister, so right now, mine is the worthier cause. Agree?"

Tristan grunts but nods his head.

"That still doesn't mean they deserve to be murdered in cold blood," I say.

"Do you have a better idea then, Heart Queen?"

"Not yet," I say. "I'm thinking."

"We drug the guards' food and water," Mael says, and before I can object to that, he raises a hand to silence me. "Just enough to knock them out, not to kill them. Okay?"

I close my mouth and nod. Okay. I can live with that.

"Do you think Willow can access the guards' kitchen?" Etienne asks. "I have something she can use. It won't affect everyone, but if we hit them at breakfast, it should knock out enough at the right time."

"What about your magic?" I ask Etienne. "Could you shift us inside? Or get in and poison the food yourself?"

He shakes his head. "There are safeguards against that," he says. "Otherwise, anyone with similar magic could slip in and out. It would be too dangerous without wards in place. Every stronghold in Ouranos is protected similarly."

I knew that would be too easy.

"What else does the letter say?" Tristan asks.

Nadir continues reading, and I notice his shoulders tense.

"Father is here," he says to Amya before he looks at me.

"What is he doing here?" she asks, echoing everyone's confusion. "Atlas invited him? I thought we were all banished."

"Are they working together?" I ask. Cloris spilled our secrets to both kings. Have they found some common ground?

Nadir shakes his head. "If they are, then Father must plan to double-cross him. If we know Atlas wants to bond with you, then how would my father use you? He's not going to share you."

"Father can't bond to Lor," Amya says.

"No," Nadir replies. "Not only because it's impossible but because I'd destroy him."

"Is it possible for *Atlas* to bond to Lor now?" Tristan asks. "What with the whole mate thing?"

Nadir shakes his head, a wicked grin sliding onto his face.

"No, he cannot."

I'm not sure why that answer surprises me so much, but it makes sense. The Mirror refused to allow me to become queen of Aphelion, because it claimed I had another destiny to fulfill, but what if it was about more than being the heir to Heart?

"Your father," I say, grabbing Nadir's arm as a flash of clarity finally coalesces in my head. Ever since Cloris mentioned the arks, it's been nagging me.

"What?" he asks.

"He's looking for the ark too."

Our gazes meet, and his head shakes imperceptibly.

"What are you talking about?"

"Our last night in the Keep when I was talking to Vale. He said he'd been tasked with searching for an object of great power. He called it an ark."

The entire room goes silent enough to hear a pin tumble to the ground.

Nadir groans and rubs his face. "You're sure that's what he said?"

I nod. "I dismissed it at the time because I was so sure he was going to tell me about the Crown. And then with everything else that's happened, I forgot about it."

"Fuck," Nadir says.

"This is bad," Amya adds.

"So now what?" Tristan asks. "Does this change anything?"

"No," I say. "If the Aurora King is also after it, then it's more imperative than ever we don't let it fall into the wrong hands."

I can tell Nadir wants to object.

You know I'm right, I say to Nadir, who glowers with all the subtlety of a hive of killer bees.

This just got more dangerous.

It was always dangerous. We don't have another choice.

Everyone in the room is looking at us during our silent exchange.

"That is so weird," Mael says.

Nadir exhales a resigned sigh. "Fine. The plan is the same. We get in, we talk to the Mirror, and we get out without either king getting his hands on Lor."

I nod, though I don't like any of this. The Aurora King's presence makes this all feel a lot more precarious, but who knows what kind of catastrophe awaits if Rion gets the ark?

Nadir tosses the letter on the table in front of him, and I go to pick it up, scanning the words he's already confirmed.

"Drugging the guards helps us only if we can lure everyone from the throne room," Nadir says, returning to the details of our plan. This has to be our focus. "And we require at least a few minutes. I'm not sure how long Lor is going to need with the Mirror."

"There are rumors the low fae resistance is planning something tomorrow," Etienne says, his arms folded across his chest, from where he leans in the corner, as quiet as a shadow.

"Can we use that?" Nadir asks.

Etienne shakes his head. "I'm not sure, but it seems a risky thing to rely on. What if the rumors have been planted to direct attention from somewhere else? They might hit a completely different part of the city. We'd need to confirm."

Nadir looks at me and purses his lips.

"Lor, if this isn't the diversion we need, then we have to consider Amya's plan."

I rub a hand down my face. "Fine. But only as a last resort."

He dips his chin. "Then let's go pay a visit to Erevan."

We all share a look around the room. We know this is a long shot. Our chances of dying or getting caught are nearly a hundred percent.

But we're out of time, and this is the only choice we have.

Chapter Forty-Six

Nadir

The Umbra

The streets of Aphelion are alive with activity with the celebrations for the bonding well underway.

"Do you think he'll meet with us?" Lor asks as we weave through the crowds a few hours later. It took a little bribery, but I managed to uncover the location of Erevan's headquarters without too much fuss. It's hard to predict how he'll react when we arrive, but I'm taking a leap of faith that he won't run to Atlas as soon as he lays eyes on Lor.

A riot is the diversion we might need to get inside the palace. People will get hurt, but that is inevitable. None of this can be stopped.

Ducking down a narrow alley, we approach a plain black door. It's the entrance to a gambling den that runs around the clock. I'm told Erevan runs his activities from the basement, and I hope the information I've received is correct.

I knock on the door in a series of quick taps as I was instructed, and we wait.

Lor squeezes my hand, her gaze darting down the alleyway, and I smile at her, trying to ease her worries.

A cold dread slithered through my blood when I heard my father was in Aphelion. His presence is an ominous sign, but with any luck, we'll be in and out of the palace before he knows we're here. *Why* is he looking for the ark too?

The stress in my shoulders pulls so tight I'm on the verge of snapping right in half.

After we wait for what seems far too long, the door pops open. A low fae elf stands in the doorway, blinking at us.

"We're here to see Erevan," I say, and the elf sniffs as though he's stepped in horse droppings.

"And who the fuck are you?"

"You can let him know the Aurora Prince is here to see him. I have a proposal for him."

The elf narrows his eyes and gives me a once-over as if trying to validate my claim. To support my point, I allow the swirl of my magic to filter out, wrapping me in the tendrils of light that prove my heritage. I don't know if this elf understands what he sees, but it's enough to make his eyes widen.

"Fine. I'll go see if he's willing to talk to you."

Then without another word, he slams the door in our faces.

"Rude," Lor says. I can tell she's trying to make a joke, but she's so tense that it comes out wrong. She shakes her head, and I pull her towards me, wrapping my arms around her as she buries her face into the crook of my shoulder.

We stand there, and I can't get over how right this feels. How perfect she feels. How much I want to protect and hold her like this forever and ever. Her entire body relaxes as she melts against me.

"Lor, I'm not going to let anything happen to you," I say.

"It's not me I'm worried about," she replies.

"Or your siblings or anyone else."

She sighs and clings to me tighter. "I know you believe that," she says, looking up at me. "I know that's what you want, but even you won't be able to watch over everyone once we're inside. Anything could happen."

"I know," I say, running a hand down the back of her head. "I'm just trying to be comforting. Work with me here—I'm not used to this."

She snorts out a small laugh and cracks a tiny smile in spite of herself. I remember when I vowed to be the one to make her smile every day, and I still hope that's a promise I'm able to keep.

Finally, the door opens again, and the same elf gestures to us.

"Come on," he says, stepping aside to let us enter the dim hallway before he closes and locks the door firmly. "This way."

We head down a set of narrow stairs where we're forced to walk in a single line before we turn down another hallway.

We enter a tunnel interspersed with cobwebbed torches.

"Where are we going?" I ask, a sense of foreboding creeping down the back of my neck.

"To see Erevan," the elf replies in an almost bored tone. "I thought that's why you came."

I resist the urge to make a pithy remark, because it would serve no purpose. It hardly seems like this elf's plan is to drag us down here and clobber us to death.

Eventually, we emerge through the tunnel into a large chamber carved into stone that forms a dome over our heads.

The space might be cold and unwelcoming, except that a large fire burns in a hearth carved into the far end while thick woven carpets muffle our steps. In the center is an arrangement of brown leather chairs and sofas, with a low wooden table in front.

Erevan sits on a sofa, reading through a stack of papers. At our entrance, he looks up and then rearranges the pile before he flips the entire thing over, ensuring we won't be able to read anything on the page. A signal that while he agreed to see us, he doesn't trust us.

He stands up and holds out a hand.

"Prince Nadir," he says, his tone polite but neutral. "I admit I was rather surprised to hear you were asking to see me. And that you're in Aphelion at all."

I shake his hand, and he looks at Lor.

"And you are?"

"I'm Lor," she says, and he narrows his gaze.

"Why do you look familiar? Have we met?"

She presses her lips together. "You might have seen me during the Trials."

It takes Erevan a moment, but when he puts it together, his eyes go wide.

"The Final Tribute."

Lor nods.

"What on earth are you doing here? I thought you disappeared."

"Well, it's a long story, and that's part of the reason we're here today."

Erevan hesitates for a moment, but whatever he sees in Lor's face must convince him that she's telling the truth and, more importantly, that she's worth hearing out.

"Have a seat then," he says. "Can I get you a drink?"

"No thanks," Lor says, settling into the spot where Erevan directs us.

I drop down next to her, and Erevan sits down and waits.

Lor exchanges a look with me, and once again, she launches into a loose version of the truth that recounts the events of the past few months, keeping Erevan on a need-to-know basis when it comes to divulging all the facts.

When she's finished talking, Erevan perches on the edge of his seat, his legs wide and his hands clasped between his knees, hanging on her every word.

"So, you need to get to the Mirror without being seen," Erevan says when she finishes talking.

"We need a diversion," I say. "Something big enough to draw everyone's attention away from the palace and out of the throne room."

"And you want me to do that?" he asks, looking between us.

"We heard a rumor that you plan to start a riot during the presentation festivities tomorrow," I say, and his eyes darken.

"You expect me to put my people in danger so you can get inside the Sun Palace? Why would I do that?"

"I'll offer whatever I can," I say. "Money to fund your cause. Whatever resources you need."

"End slavery in The Aurora's mines," he says immediately, and I knew this would be his ask.

"Done. As soon as it's in my power to do so. I would have done that anyway, though, so I'd still owe you another favor at some point."

He studies me as if reading the truth in my words.

"That could still be centuries from now," he says, and I nod.

"It could be," I say with a smirk. "But one doesn't get a no-strings-attached favor from a future king every day."

Erevan tips his head in a gesture that seems to say *Good point.*

"If we get what I think the Mirror might have, then it won't be centuries," Lor says. "The only thing I've ever wanted is to destroy the Aurora King. We have many reasons to ensure he's gone much sooner than that."

Her gaze slides to me, and I know that, along with everything else, she's thinking about my mother and the way she's trapped inside her empty existence. I squeeze her hand.

"How? Why?" Erevan asks, and these are very good questions.

"I can't tell you everything," Lor says. "But you'll have to trust me. No one hates that man more than I do. Well, except for maybe him."

She looks at me with a sad smile, and I tip my chin.

"Guilty," I add.

Erevan blows out a long breath, considering our words. He runs a hand through his blond hair.

"The truth is we *were* planning to start a riot, but I'm not sure that will be enough to do what you're asking. It's not like we haven't tried this before. I've been hoping for some way to make this one more definitive than the others, but so far, nothing of significance has materialized. There are too many guards, and Atlas has them all on alert. You aren't the first to hear of the rumors."

"You want a diversion that Atlas will notice?" A voice comes from the door, and all three of us look over to find Gabriel. He storms into the room and stops. There's a wild light in his eyes, and his jaw is set hard enough to crack through marble. "You wanted something that would embarrass Atlas and tarnish his name? I know a secret that not only will get everyone's attention but will change Aphelion forever."

And then he clutches his chest with a grunt and collapses to the floor.

Chapter Forty-Seven

King Herric

THE EVANESCENCE: THE SECOND AGE

"Can I get you a drink?" Zerra asked from where she lounged across the room, her elbow propped up on the back of her chair and her tanned legs bared by the slit in her dress. She rubbed her thighs together and licked her lips as she stared at Herric. "Why are you all the way over there?"

Herric pushed himself from the pillar where he was leaning, ran a hand through his hair, and strode over, settling into a closer seat. She reached over and adjusted the collar of his shirt.

"Hmm?" she prompted, and he nodded. "Anything, my dear?"

"Some water would be good."

It had been years of capitulating to Zerra's invitations, arriving to service her with his head or his hips between her thighs. While he hadn't minded at first—he'd even enjoyed it for a time—he was growing weary of this mundane relationship. If that's what one could call it. There was no passion here, only duty and necessity.

One of Zerra's servants arrived with the promised drink balanced on a silver tray. She bent low, giving him an eyeful of cleavage.

That's all this place was. Sex and drinking masquerading as this sham of the divine. Zerra was meant to be ruling over Ouranos, not partaking in the same vacuous entertainment she'd indulged as a mortal. For the millionth time, Herric wondered what the Empyrium had been thinking when they'd chosen her.

Soon, he hoped, it wouldn't matter.

Today, he would test the theory he'd been working on for years.

Around his finger he swirled a ring made of the same glittering black stone his workers had mined from the mountain. The same enchanted material recovered after the collapse.

He'd spent countless hours testing its properties, and it hadn't taken long to realize he could channel magic through it. Not only that, he could use it to amplify and control the gifts he'd received when he ascended to High Fae.

He had his crews working around the clock as they pulled up more of the material. Herric had built an entire castle from it, confident in the protection of the stone that surrounded him, which he had dubbed *virulence*.

On one of his visits to the Evanescence, he'd channeled a thread of magic through his ring, and shortly after, Zerra had complained of a headache. She'd then taken to her bed for the rest of his visit.

At first, he'd thought nothing of it. But then he began to notice a pattern. Anytime he made use of the stone while visiting the heavens, Zerra would take ill. Over time, he worked with the theory that somehow, it was affecting her.

"You're quiet today," Zerra said, dragging a hand down his chest, before she fisted her hand in his shirt and dragged him closer. Her touch was starting to make his skin crawl, but he would endure this for as long as it took. Today, he would verify his hypothesis with a larger surge of magic channeled through his ring.

"Just tired," he said with a tight smile as he took a sip of his water.

"Poor baby," she cooed as she slid off her velvet lounger and dropped to her knees, peering up at him with a coy flutter of her lashes. "Maybe I can help."

She undid his belt, then the button on his waistband as he tried his best not to tense up. He'd loved this once—she was very skilled, and he'd never put much stock into love or feelings—but he was over it. She was pathetic and desperate, and he was mentally done with her and this entire place.

This all belonged to him, and he intended to take it.

He stopped her from proceeding, snagging her chin in the cup of his hand as she gave him a quizzical look. He channeled his magic out, spiraling colorful whirls of light as Zerra's smile stretched.

488   NISHA J. TULI

"Your magic is so lovely, Herric," she said.

"I'm glad you like it."

Then he forced it through his ring as she continued to watch the patterns he sketched. It took several moments before Zerra sighed, pressing her hand to her forehead as she sat back.

"I'm suddenly not feeling well," she said as he funneled more magic into the ring.

"Why don't you lie down?" he asked, helping her back to her seat. "Close your eyes."

She nodded as her lids drifted shut, and he used the opportunity to filter out a stronger thread of magic. He stood over her as she lay oblivious, more and more magic surging into his ring.

Gods, how he loathed her. He wanted to kill her. He wanted to end her.

He would destroy her and make sure everyone knew what a wastrel she'd been.

But this wasn't working. While it was causing her plenty of discomfort, this wasn't killing her.

He sliced off the source of his magic and watched her, his chest heaving with the effort of expending so much power. The sound of his serrated breaths roused her from her stupor, and whatever she saw in his eyes caused her expression to pale.

"Herric?" she asked, sitting up as she tried to scramble back. "What's wrong?"

"Zerra," he snarled, his hands balling into fists.

"Get out," she said, her voice wavering as she tumbled over the back of her divan. "Get out!"

She clung to the furniture, screaming at him to back away. Terror rolled in her eyes.

He realized he'd made a mistake. He'd been too impatient. Pushed too far and revealed his hand.

A moment later, he found himself once again on the surface, standing alone in the middle of the wind-whipped mountains under the dark Aurora sky.

"Zerra!" he screamed at the stars, and he wasn't surprised when no answer came.

She couldn't reach him down here, but neither could he return to the heavens without her invitation.

But that was okay.

It was obvious he couldn't kill her himself.

This needed more strength than he possessed on his own.

But now . . . he had a plan.

Chapter Forty-Eight

LOR

Present Day

With my hood pulled up, I wait in the bustling crowd with Nadir at my side. We all agreed he would escort me into the palace because he's in the best position to protect me, given my still inconstant grasp on my magic.

And quite frankly, I thought he might kill anyone who suggested otherwise.

Not even Tristan tried to argue, and neither did I, for that matter. I want Nadir with me because I know there's no one I'll be safer with. I look over, catching the flash of his dark eyes under his own hood, smiling to myself in spite of everything.

My mate. My heart. The man I fell in love with despite the

rivers we had to cross to get here. The hurts and the betrayals we had to overcome.

What? You okay? he asks through our bond.

I nod and lean against him, tilting my face up for a kiss. He holds my chin between his thumb and finger and bends his head, touching his soft lips to mine.

Our kiss is slow and unhurried, tongues slicking together and soft moans rumbling in my throat. I forget the press of bodies around us as I melt into him, savoring the smell and taste of arctic wind, cold winter nights, and the sweetness of what it feels like to finally be where you belong.

I can't believe I thought I understood what a kiss was before I met him. Everything that came before was a dusting of dandelion seeds versus being doused under a mountain of velvety rose petals.

We kiss a bit longer before we break apart. The lust in his eyes matches my own, and I wish we could lose ourselves in each other, but everything is moving and shifting, and our time is compressed into something hard and immovable. I want to know everything. About his days as a boy growing up in The Aurora—even the ugly parts with his father. I want to know about that tiny scar on his eyebrow and the one on the back of his hand. I want to know where his name came from. I've never even asked him what his tattoos mean. At least we had the night of my birthday, and I could have lain there forever under the stars, saying absolutely nothing, and been the happiest woman alive.

After he pulls away, the corner of his mouth crooks up into a smile before he touches his forehead to mine.

"Lor, I need you to know that no matter what happens

in there, I'm with you. For now, and until the end. Through death if I have to."

I nod my head. "I know." My hands slip under his cloak, finding his waist, where I grip the armor he wears underneath. "I know. The same goes for me."

"You are not dying today. If this all goes to shit, then you save yourself. Do you understand?"

I scoff at his words. "Absolutely not. Have you learned nothing about me at all?"

"I know you far too well, Lightning Bug, but you need to survive this. I'm sure you're part of something bigger than any of us understand, and I *need* you to live. As long as I know you're okay, I don't care what happens to me."

My hands twist in his cloak.

I left this scar in place because I wanted it to represent everything I'd do to protect the ones I love. That meant you too, Nadir. I will never leave you behind.

He stares into my eyes with that intensity that is so very him. It's overwhelming to be the focus of it. To be the very object of his love and his longing and his desire. It makes me feel like the sun and the moon being circled by a galaxy of stars.

"Please, Lor. I can't take you in there unless you promise me this."

I raise an eyebrow. "What happened to being with me through to the end?"

He huffs out a breath.

Please.

I find myself nodding at the earnestness in his tone.

Fine.

But if he thinks I'd ever abandon him, he still doesn't truly understand what he means to me. Once this is over, I'll find a way to prove it.

Good girl.

He draws me close, kissing me again.

After we pull apart, I face our surroundings while he keeps an arm banded around my waist. I spy Mael, Etienne, and Tristan in the crowd, their hoods also up as they slowly weave through the masses.

Tristan and Mael are to get close to the king and assist with whatever distraction Gabriel has planned. He'd said he would need backup of the steel and brawn variety.

I wish we knew what we were waiting for, but Gabriel refused to disclose his secret, only saying that he promised it would have every eye in Aphelion pointed away from the throne room and squarely on Atlas.

Etienne's job was to get the drugs to Willow that she used to tamper with the guards' food. We still can't risk that any of them will remain behind in the palace even when Gabriel reveals what's up his sleeve.

After he blacked out at Erevan's, it took several minutes to revive him, and he struggled to compose himself. He was too pale, and a sheen of sweat coated his skin. He kept wincing and clutching his stomach like he was on the verge of collapsing.

He'd told us to be near the gates when it all goes down, and he'd ensure someone is there to let me and Nadir in. He didn't say who, and I got the sense he didn't know yet either. None of this is instilling me with much confidence.

During that discussion, I also learned Erevan is Atlas's

cousin, which surprised me in more ways than one. To be openly rebelling against his flesh and blood is a dangerous game, and I'm shocked Atlas hasn't tried harder to kill him. Perhaps the Sun King has some decency in him after all. Or maybe he's just biding his time.

"What do you think's going to happen?" I ask, stretching up on my tiptoes to see over the crowd.

"I have no clue," Nadir says. "But stay alert. When the coast seems clear, we head for the gates."

I nod, and then my gaze drifts to where Atlas and Apricia sit in matching golden thrones, taking a moment to really look at them for the first time since we arrived. They're both trussed up in gilded finery, their clothes so stiff their movements appear stilted. A gold tent provides shade from the beating sun, though I can see clouds rolling in the distance. Dozens of guards surround them, their hands on their swords and their eyes scanning the crowd for threats.

I suspect Atlas must be nervous sitting out in the open with the rumors of Erevan and the low fae planning to riot whispered in every corner of the city. Gabriel said his big reveal would also support their cause, though the words were so difficult for him to articulate, he began coughing hard enough to bring up blood. I wonder if this has something to do with what's in the mysterious tower Willow caught him sneaking in and out of.

Atlas has aged since I last saw him, thanks to the dark circles under his eyes, and I swear he's lost weight. He appears on edge, his knee bouncing and his jaw clenching, while he scans the crowd as if looking for something. I sort through my thoughts about seeing him again. I've thought so much about the lies he

told me. Those half-truths he led me to believe. The way he manipulated and tricked me. There was a time when I trusted him and
believed in everything he told me. A time when I thought it might
be me sitting there next to him, preparing to become a queen.

But he got me out of Nostraza, and whatever his ulterior
motives, his scheming is responsible for me standing here right
now next to the man I love. A man who's about to embark on
potentially the stupidest and most dangerous errand of my life.

Apricia is all beaming smiles as she welcomes another citizen of Aphelion who kneels at her feet and bows their head.
But I can see how the smile doesn't completely reach her eyes
and the tight lines that frame her mouth.

After hearing what Halo and Marici said, it seems like the
fairy tale in her head was just that—a vision built on nothing that has failed to materialize in the most spectacular way.
I wonder what will happen if we manage to get out of here
without Atlas noticing. The bonding is tomorrow. Will he be
forced to go through with it?

Another person moves down the line, and I scan the crowd
again, wondering where Gabriel and Erevan are.

Behind the dais is a small group of upper nobles, along with
the fallen Tributes. I spy Tesni, along with Halo and Marici.
Instead of being surrounded by a crush of bodies, they move
freely between servants passing food and wine from golden
trays. Hylene confirmed this morning the others are still
gathering in the throne room, and as I peer up, I note the sky
is growing darker with the promised threat of rain. Atlas and
Apricia will be protected enough under the tent—it's only the
gathering crowd that will get wet.

I'm nervous, I think to Nadir, looking up over my shoulder at him. He leans down and nudges my hood aside, pressing his mouth to the curve of my throat.

I know. Not much longer, I'm sure.

I shift, feeling a bead of sweat run down the side of my face, both from the ballooning humidity and from the nerves twisting in my stomach. I'm not sure I've ever been so scared in my life.

A hush falls over the plaza, and my gaze meets Nadir's. This is it.

We maneuver our way through the crowd and closer to the gate. Nadir lifts me up onto a stone barricade, allowing me a view over everyone's heads.

At the end of the long golden rug stand three figures. Gabriel and Erevan flank a third High Fae male I've never seen before. Around them, the other nine warders fan out, forming a circle of protection. Beyond that Tristan, Mael, and Etienne bring up their rear.

The crowd suspends into perplexed stillness as Gabriel and the others approach the dais where Atlas and Apricia sit.

The stranger between Gabriel and Erevan is wearing a pair of glowing cuffs around his neck and wrists. He's thin and frail, his gait shuffling and his shoulders rounded, though there's a purpose in his expression that speaks to something noble. Like a once-grand castle where you can still hear music playing through its halls, but that has been abandoned to the decay of time and loneliness.

Who is that? I ask Nadir, who's studying the third man and blinking rapidly like he's seen a ghost materialize from the ether.

Gabriel, Erevan, and the warders all shuffle down the carpet as murmurs ripple through the gathering. There are gasps and small cries of surprise as people start dropping to their knees, their foreheads pressing to the ground in supplication.

Just as many are as confused as I am, looking around and seeking an explanation for what in Ouranos is going on.

"Nadir," I whisper out loud this time. "Do you know who that is?"

Finally, he leans over and whispers in my ear.

"It's Tyr," he says, his tone uncertain. "At least, I think that's him. It's been so many years since I've seen him, and he looks different, but I think..."

He trails off, and I wonder if this is the first time the Aurora Prince has ever been at a loss for words.

"Who is Tyr?" I ask, but don't get an answer, because Gabriel starts speaking.

"People of Aphelion!" he bellows, his voice carrying over the stunned crowd. "This king has been lying to you all for over a century! He is an impostor!"

Gabriel is having trouble speaking, just like he did earlier with Erevan. Sweat pours down his temples, and he clutches his chest, pain carved into every line of his features.

But he isn't to be deterred.

"He forced us to lock up the true Sun King. He told you he died of the Withering, but it was all designed to deceive you. Atlas stripped him of his power and tricked you all into believing his lies."

Atlas, who is slowly rising from his seat, stands frozen in place by the accusations Gabriel hurls his way. I see him flinch as each one lands and explodes against his chest.

Gabriel takes another lurching step towards Atlas, the warders surrounding him, all of their expressions hard. Each of them was forced into silence. I don't know the limits of their tethers, but it seems they're all struggling too, their breathing labored and their complexions sallow. But they stay by Gabriel's side, and it's clear Atlas doesn't know what to do in the face of their mutiny, because he's gone as white as a sheet.

"Gabriel," Atlas says, his voice softer than I was expecting, like he can't believe his friend would betray him this way.

"You made me do this," Gabriel hisses at Atlas, flinging a finger at Tyr, who stands with his shoulders sagging and his hair in his face. "You've been killing him, and you made me do this!" Gabriel screams so loud that his voice cracks, and I feel the pain and anguish in it. Of everything he must have suffered under the grinding thumb of his king.

Gods, this explains so much about Gabriel.

Nadir's grip tightens on my arm, and I look up to find him transfixed on the scene before us.

"People of Aphelion!" Gabriel shouts, rallying himself despite the way he's laboring under this stress. "This king is a liar and an impostor. He's been deceiving for years. Tyr is and always was your true king!"

Dark clouds roll in the sky and his words echo against a crack of thunder, like a curse sent from the heavens.

Words that can never be undone.

Words that can never be put back.

And then all hell breaks loose.

Chapter Forty-Nine

As the realization of what we're all witnessing sinks in, everyone loses their minds.

Atlas has been lying to *everyone*.

Nadir and I are shoved left and right, and I stumble against a large body. Pushing myself away, I try not to trample anyone, but we're surrounded by chaos like we've been dropped into the middle of a churning, roiling ocean teeming with hungry sharks.

"Now's our chance," Nadir growls in my ear, his arm still banded around me. "Let's go."

We elbow through the crowd hand in hand, jostled from every side. People surge towards the center of the plaza, where Gabriel stands with Tyr, as the Sun King's guards attempt to hold them back. I catch sight of Tristan and Mael moving in with their weapons poised.

The energy around us paces into a feverish swell of emotion.

People are angry and shocked and confused. But most of all I taste it, because it's a flavor I know so well—the sour bite of betrayal from a king with bright blue eyes and a honeyed smile who was lying to their faces the whole fucking time.

It seems to take forever to make it through the press of bodies, but finally, we squeeze through, emerging at a less densely crowded spot.

I scan our surroundings, noticing the guards lining the palace have all moved in to help quell the uprising.

As we continue to muscle our way to the gate, I worry about Gabriel—he was clearly about to collapse from the weight of revealing Atlas's lies. This is the price he's been forced to pay all these years.

Tyr is alive, and Atlas was never the true king of Aphelion. All of the warders must have known. All of them forced to be complicit in this crime. No wonder Gabriel is always such a dick. Now I understand why he didn't run to Atlas the moment he spotted me. How long has he been working against his false king?

"Lor!" Nadir calls. "This way."

My chest expands with relief when I spy Halo and Marici beckoning us towards them. Gabriel came through for us. In spite of everything, he delivered what he promised.

I fling off my cloak as we approach, revealing the gold palace livery beneath, as well as the bag strapped to my chest containing the Heart Crown. Willow managed to sneak us two sets of clothing to help us blend in, but Nadir absolutely refused to wear it, opting for his usual black and arguing that he could easily conceal himself with magic if needed.

I didn't press the issue too hard this morning when we were dressing, but I did call him a drama queen before he started tickling me, and we both ended up wearing nothing as I rode him on the floor of my bedroom. *Our* bedroom. It wasn't something we discussed when we decided we'd be sleeping next to one another every night, but it's been that way since we returned from The Woodlands.

With our hands clasped and heads down, Halo and Marici flank us as we walk-run towards the palace. No one acknowledges us, too consumed by Tyr's appearance to pay us any mind.

Inside, we come face-to-face with Hylene, who's dressed like a proper Sun Palace courtier in gold from head to toe.

"Is it empty?" Nadir asks, and she nods.

"There are a handful of guards outside, but everyone ran to see what's going on. What exactly *is* going on?"

"I'll fill you in as we walk. Lead the way."

Hylene nods, and the five of us skulk through the palace. We pass the occasional servant, who barely glances at us as they head for the eye of the storm.

"This way." Halo gestures as we slink around corners, checking for guards. We pass a few lying asleep against walls where they've fallen. *Good job, Willow,* I think to myself.

The rest have abandoned their posts, and I'm sure Mael was right about their training, but I don't think anyone anticipated news of this caliber coming in to sweep away all of their preconceived notions.

We turn a few more corners, and I'm reminded of those first days after I woke up in Aphelion and didn't understand what I was doing there. Everything was so beautiful and luxurious, and it felt like I was living a dream. Until it started to become a nightmare.

Finally, we come upon a familiar hallway and slow to a stop.

Nadir peers around the corner while I huddle with the other three women behind him.

"Two guards at the doors. I can easily handle them," he says.

I nod as he turns to Halo and Marici. "You two should return to the courtyard. If anyone notices you're missing, it'll arouse suspicion. Atlas might punish you if he discovers you've been helping Lor."

I can tell they want to do what he's asking. They probably have a thousand questions about the return of Tyr as well. This is their home, and Atlas was lying to them, too.

"Thank you," I say, wrapping them both in a hug. "For everything."

"Good luck," Halo says. "I hope you find what you need here." She glances at Nadir and then back to me, and I see the softening in her eyes. "And I hope we see you again, but whatever happens, know that we want the best for you and you'll always have friends here."

We study each other for a long moment, and I get the sense Halo understands something big is about to happen. I know she wants to ask. I see the questions on her face, but I can't offer her the explanation she seeks. Maybe someday we'll have that chance.

"I hope so too," I say, and after another hug, they both scurry off, disappearing around a corner.

"Hylene, keep an eye out," Nadir says. "If anyone comes this way, distract them."

Hylene tips her chin. "Of course."

Then Nadir takes my hand.

"Are you ready for this?"

"As I'll ever be."

He nods and then uses his magic, sending several tendrils of light towards the guards. The assault is nearly on them before they notice, but it's already too late.

His ribbons of light cinch tightly around their chests, forcing them to drop their weapons, while more tendrils snake around their throats until they follow their swords, collapsing to the marble floors. He uses another sweep of magic to pull open a door and drag them inside the room, lest anyone passing notice two unconscious guards.

When Nadir is finished, he takes my hand, and we enter the room, being sure to close the door behind us.

The Mirror stands at the far end of the room, covered by a thick velvet sheet.

When I stood in this place last time, everything was so different. Now I've returned, and nothing will ever be the same.

My steps echo in the cavernous space as I approach.

Nadir waits next to me as we stare up at it. It seems bigger than I remember.

"What do I do?" I ask.

"You're the one who's been here before," he says. "What did you do last time?"

"I just had to stand in front of it."

We exchange a glance.

"Then start there."

I nod and take a step towards it, overcome by the magnitude of this moment. I've been running towards this place for weeks, and now that I'm here, I'm not ready.

A bang at the door has us both spinning around.

"They're in here!" comes a muffled voice.

It seems I have no choice. It's now or never.

"Nadir," I say.

"Go. I'll handle them."

The doors burst open, and I catch the flash of his magic before I turn to face the Mirror. Soldiers are pouring into the room, and Nadir fends them off as best he can, but they stream in, dozens of them. How did they find us so quickly? What happened to Hylene?

A guard wearing black fights his way towards me, snatching me in his arms.

"Gotcha," he sneers in my ear, but a moment later, he's gone, lying on the ground choking on the noose of green light slicing off his air.

"Lor! Go!" Nadir calls as his magic bounces around the room.

I waste no more time and run for the Mirror, skidding to a stop as my hands slam into the surface. I tug on the heavy velvet cover with all of my strength, and it slides over the top, pooling at my feet like a funeral shroud.

"I'm here!" I scream. "I found it. I have the Crown!"

I pull the bag with the Crown over my head and hold it

up like an offering. It remains still and silent. I bang my fist against the glass as flashes of colorful light gleam in its surface. I see Nadir in the reflection as more guards stream in.

"Hello! Can you hear me?"

I lean against it, pounding again, willing it to notice me.

"I'm here! I have it!" I shout over and over.

Then something clicks.

Heart Queen.

The disembodied words enter my head, and I breathe a sigh of relief as I sag against the Mirror.

"Yes! I'm here."

You've come back to me. You have the Crown?

"Yes. It's here in my bag. Do you need it?"

Oh no. I don't need it. That was for you.

"You said you'd have something for me when I found it."

The Mirror falls silent, and I stare at it, dimly aware of the fighting going on behind me.

"Hello?" I call.

I place my hand against it, my fingertips pressing into the cool, smooth surface. I lean my forehead against it and breathe out and in. I'm here. I did what it asked. Was this not enough?

The sounds of fighting have tapered off, and I look back to find Nadir finishing off with the last of the guards, at least for now.

"Please," I say, pressing my forehead to the Mirror. "Please."

I have something, it finally replies. *I have something for you, Heart Queen.*

"What is it?" I look up.

It laughs then. The sound is low and dark.

When your grandmother broke the world, we held on to this for safekeeping.

We? The Artefacts. It's then I know. I'm sure. There can be only one thing it has for me.

Back up, Heart Queen. It is time for you to go home.

The surface of the Mirror begins to glow with silvery light, and I do as it asks, jogging in reverse, peering over my shoulder at Nadir, who waits in the middle of the room.

He takes my hand and squeezes it as we watch the Mirror glow brighter and brighter.

The surface liquefies into a molten whirlpool before an object comes hurtling towards me.

Everything slows down, the world holding its breath as the object flips end over end, curving through the air.

"Nadir," I say as my magic lurches under my skin with the force of a tidal wave. "Get down."

Sparks dance along my fingertips. My arms, my torso. I feel them crackle in my head.

He needs to get out of the way.

"Get down!" I scream as my bag tumbles from my grip, and my hands reach for the object, the cool dark stone imprinting my fingertips with the caress of magic.

It's the ark—an oblong cameo with a woman wearing the Heart Crown carved into its surface, just like Nerissa said.

My fingers curl around it, feeling the ridges and grooves sculpted into that black sparkling rock that I suddenly realize I know so well. That glitter-flecked black stone I stared upon from my hole in the Hollow when I vowed to tear the Aurora King and his Keep apart bit by bit.

I have only a moment to register the incongruity of that fact.

And then I explode.

Red lightning erupts from my hands as the sealed door in my chest finally slams open, releasing waves and waves of power through my blood and my limbs, stirring in my cells and my nerves. It spears out of me in long, jagged streaks, spreading out like I'm a magnificent tree unfurling its branches.

Hundreds of flashes twirl in my gaze. Thousands upon thousands of them as the room spins and turns. We're standing inside a beating heart—pulsing rivers of crimson feed my organs, expanding in my lungs, allowing me to finally *breathe*.

I feel Nadir clinging to my waist, keeping me in place while I shake, as magic, so much fucking *magic*, ripples through me until the glass-domed ceiling blasts apart, detonating in a spray of sparkling shards. The sound roars against my raw scream as my power flows and flows, finally unleashed.

For every day it was locked up, for every moment I was forced to hide it away, it flows out of me in angry, righteous waves.

This is who I am.

This is who they tried to cage.

And *this* is who they will now fear.

My arms spread wide, and my head tips up.

Today, I am the fucking Heart Queen.

Finally, it stops, and the room falls silent. Rain cascades over us, and it takes me a moment to realize I'm drenched. The promised thunderstorm flashes overhead, white lightning streaking across the sky as if calling to the ruby sparks circling my arms and legs.

Nadir climbs up my body and cups my face in his hands, kissing my cheeks and my lips and my forehead.

"You did it," he whispers over and over as I shake.

"You did it," he says. "What did it give you?"

"The ark," I say. "It was the ark."

I realize I'm no longer holding it. It must have flown from my grip.

Then the unbearable clink of stone against marble echoes in the quiet room, drawing our attention.

We both spin around.

The ark of Heart lies on its side near the doorway next to the toe of a polished black boot.

A boot that belongs to the Aurora King.

Chapter Fifty

I hear every thump of my heart vibrating in the silence of the room.

My mouth opens in horrified stasis as Rion smirks and then bends down, picking up the ark and testing the weight in his hand with the casualness of an apple at a fruit stand. I want to lurch for it, but I know it would be futile.

"Nadir," Rion drawls. "Thank you so much for telling me where I'd find her."

Those words ping in my brain as I take a moment to process them.

I look at Nadir, whose face has gone ashen.

I shake my head and take a step back, one hand stretched out in front of me. My magic hums in my veins, traces of lightning circling my arms and sparking from my fingertips.

The door is open, and I finally have my full strength, but is it enough to go against the Aurora King?

Rion tosses the ark in his hand and catches it, a slow smile spreading over his mouth. He knows what it is and has been searching for it all along. Was this what he wanted from me?

That's when I exchange another glance with Nadir.

"Lor. Run," he says, and then we both spin and bolt for the door on the opposite end of the room.

I don't have the presence of mind to fully sort through what Rion just said to Nadir as I fling out a blast of magic behind me, hoping to inflict damage. I must have misheard or misunderstood. He wouldn't ... He couldn't ...

My magic collides with the king's, sinking into it like it's clay, soft and malleable, expanding and contracting. It's different from Nadir's. While his magic feels like silk, this reminds me more of quicksand.

We run, crashing through the door on the far side, where we're met with a spiraling staircase that winds down and down to a bottom that disappears into darkness. We both leap onto the railing, and Nadir pulls me against him, wrapping an arm around my waist before we plummet as my stomach claws up my throat.

Just before we hit the floor, he uses a translucent cloud of blue and green to slow our descent, floating us harmlessly to the ground. Another door deposits us into a quiet hallway somewhere in the lower levels of the palace. We've mapped out this route thanks to Willow's drawings, but every plan we made has been shoved out of my head.

Thank you so much for telling me where I'd find her.

"This way," Nadir says, and I follow him through the twisting maze of corridors.

"Which way?" I ask. "Are we lost?"

I try to imagine the drawing we studied before we left. I'm sure this isn't the way we were supposed to go.

Thank you so much for telling me where I'd find her.

"No," Nadir says with conviction.

In the next breath, a blast of colorful light shoots between us, hitting the end of the hall and sending shards of rock and marble arrowing towards us. I duck, covering my head, peering over my shoulder to find the Aurora King with the ark of Heart clutched in his hand.

"This way!" Nadir calls, grabbing my wrist and yanking me down another corridor. Rion chases us. More of his magic ricochets off walls and the ceiling, and falling debris and stone strike me on the back and shoulders. I'm not sure if his plan is to kill me or simply capture me, but whatever it is, I can't take either chance.

We wind through the corridors, flinging magic at each other. I feel the sharp burn of a violet blast of light as it grazes my arm, singeing the fabric and drawing a trickle of blood. I cry out, firing more red lightning. I don't have any control over it, but at least it doesn't feel like I'm pulling out my veins to call it up.

So I fire blindly, hoping I can make up for my lack of precision with raw, brute force.

Rion's light clashes with our magic, raining chaos over our heads.

We're destroying Atlas's palace, but I'm having a hard time feeling too much guilt about that.

We round another corner and then another before we come to a door. Nadir crashes into it, but it refuses to budge. I turn around, planning to face Rion, but the other end of the corridor is silent.

"Did we lose him?" I ask.

"I doubt it," Nadir grunts as he flings himself at the door again. This time it gives way under his weight, revealing another staircase that spirals up. "Let's go."

I'm *sure* this isn't the way we planned to come.

Nadir is dragging me by the hand as we take the stairs two at a time. A bang comes from below, but we don't temper our pace. We lost the ark. *I* lost the ark. The Mirror gave it to me for a reason, and now it's in Rion's hands. Then I remember I dropped the Crown in the throne room too. I choke back a sob, spiraling with the knowledge of just how much I fucked this all up.

The air around us starts to darken like someone is layering gauze over a window. I'm shaking my head, trying to clear it, when a puff of black smoke surrounds me, slithering against my skin. It fills my mouth and crawls down my throat as I sputter and cough. But it's not smoke. It feels denser, like fingers scraping the insides of my lungs.

"Nadir," I try to choke out, and then we both fall through another door, collapsing on the marble, both of us hacking until the darkness finally clears. For a moment, I stare up at the ceiling, trying to catch my breath. We're on one of the main levels again, surrounded by the gilded brightness of the Sun Palace.

"We have to keep moving," Nadir says, standing up and hauling me to my feet. "Are you okay?"

"I think so."

We've ended up in a large open space with wide arched doorways leading in multiple directions. Above us, a clear dome reveals the grey thundering sky. Again, Nadir takes my hand, and we make a run for it, heading towards the furthest opening, when a figure steps out in front of us.

The Aurora King is now bordered by guards, and we skid to a halt in the middle of the room, realizing they've closed in around us, and every single one of them holds a bow aiming for our hearts.

Rolling with panic, I spin around, seeing we're completely outnumbered. There are at least a hundred crossbows trained on us, and I know that even with the full force of my magic, I'm not fast enough to take them all out.

Nadir and I stand back-to-back as Rion chuckles, sauntering closer.

He still holds the ark in his hand, and I turn to face him.

"What do you want?" I ask, and his face stretches into a slow, catlike smile.

"So many things," he says, tipping his head. "And you're going to help me get them, Heart Queen."

The way he says the last two words forces bile into my throat. Rion holds up the ark, and I fire at him, but he blocks my magic with the sparkling black stone. The ark absorbs my lightning, making it glow with a red aura.

I take a step back in horror. This couldn't have all gone more wrong.

"Seize them," Rion says with a lazy flick of his hand as that dark smoke surrounds us again.

Nadir is yelling something I can't make out as mist fills my eyes and nose and lungs, while rough hands grab me before someone cinches my wrists behind my back.

Then we're dragged from the Sun Palace as every hope and every dream I've been carrying for the last twelve years filters out of my heart and circles down, down, down the drain.

CHAPTER FIFTY-ONE

GABRIEL

I clutch my chest, my breath stuttering in short, painful gasps. My body bends in half as I reach for Tyr. A surge of pandemonium surrounds us, but the noise is distant and muffled against the ringing in my ears. I can't focus as my vision blends with a smear of color from the pulsating crowd.

"Release us," I beg, twisting my fingers in the fabric of his tunic. "Give the order. Free us from this."

Tyr looks down at me, hesitation flickering in his eyes.

Atlas is now storming towards us, his expression speaking of ruin and vengeance and war. A clap of thunder echoes with enough force to shake the ground. People scream, though I can't discern the specific source of their terror.

The guards are doing their best to keep the rioting mob

from consuming us at its center. The beating heart of Aphelion is slowing, its pulse turning sluggish. With me, I bring a new heart. One that hasn't been blackened by treasonous blood covering his hands.

Apricia trails behind Atlas with her eyes wide, and even she's been stunned into shutting up for a few seconds of bliss.

"Tyr!" I gasp through strangled lungs that are slowly closing off.

"Don't you dare!" Atlas hisses, understanding my goal. "If you do it, I swear these will be his last moments on this earth." He points to me, his meaning clear.

Again, Tyr hesitates as I fall to my knees grasping my stomach and my chest as my organs turn themselves inside out. My fellow warders fare no better as they, too, stand in solidarity with their true king, their brows sweating and their insides twisting.

But I am the greatest betrayer of them all.

I brought this upon us.

"It doesn't matter," I wheeze out. "I'm dead anyway. Tyr. Please. Do it for yourself. Do it for your kingdom."

I witness the conflict in his eyes. The dull grey hue that once burned so bright. Atlas has abused him and traumatized him for so many years. The man I once knew is a broken, hollow tomb. He's been beaten and damaged until his confidence has been ground down to motes of dust.

Atlas seizes Tyr's collar. They used to be matched in size, but now Tyr appears like a child next to his younger brother.

"You will regret it," Atlas hisses. His face is twisted with venom, and in all our turbulent years, I've truly never seen the false golden Sun King look so ugly. Another crack of thunder booms over our heads as thick grey clouds tumble over one another.

"Tyr," I whisper again as my vision starts to turn black. I need him to say it. Not for my sake, but because if I die now, then it will be only Atlas and Tyr, with no one left to protect the man I once swore my heart to.

Still, Tyr says nothing, and I realize he won't. Atlas has him so thoroughly under his spell that he can't fight his way out. As much as I battled all these years, hoping there would be a happy ending for any of us, I understand the end has finally come.

I will die and Atlas will find Lor, and he will do whatever is necessary to rid himself of Tyr to take the crown he's coveted for so very long. I'm not sure how the people of Aphelion will forgive him after learning his secret, but Atlas has always been a master of persuasion. He'll figure something out.

I drop to my hands and knees, willing myself not to pass out. I don't know what I'm holding on to, but I struggle against the final whispers of death crowding in my ears.

"Tyr," I gasp one last time before I collapse to the ground.

"I release them," comes a soft but steady voice a moment later, and I wonder if I've imagined it. I look up, watching Atlas's face transform from fury to horror.

For the first time in decades, Tyr's eyes light with that spark I recall only in the deepest layers of my memories. His shoulders stretch back, and he pins his brother with a look that guts my heart as it leaks through my ribs.

"I release them from the vow to protect you and your secrets, Atlas."

And that's when the sky opens up and the rain starts to fall.

The vise around my chest releases instantly, and I let out a heaving breath as air floods my lungs. I lie on the ground panting, and it takes me a moment before I push myself up.

"Guards!" Atlas yells as chaos swells around us. He retreats, backing away. "Guards! Arrest them!"

He points to me and the other warders, who now all have their swords out and pointed at their false king. The rain pummels our heads, drenching through clothing and armor.

"Arrest him! These are lies!"

I'm not sure whom Atlas thinks he's fooling when the evidence stands here in front of everyone. He stumbles back, crashing into Apricia. She screeches as he tramples her foot, and that seems to release her tongue.

"What's going on?!" she shrieks, her makeup running down her face and her fancy hairdo as flat as a wet pancake. "I demand to know!"

"Guards!" I shout, finally able to breathe again, as I pull my own sword from my back and step in front of Tyr.

"Gabriel!" Atlas shouts. "You would do this to me?"

Those words snap something loose inside me, and I storm towards him, swinging a left hook that crashes into Atlas's cheek. I feel the collapse of cartilage under my knuckles, and then I'm whaling on him, raining down blows on his face and body as he thrashes under me. I've never been so fucking angry in my life.

"You monster!" I scream, feeling the hot rush of tears that mixes with the rain coating my face. "I'll never forgive you for any of this! You tormented us! You held us prisoner! You fucking piece of shit! I will destroy you if it's the last thing I fucking do!"

I punch him in the nose so hard I hear the crunch of bone, before blood gushes down his face in a river of crimson, stained with all of our sins.

"You'll pay for this," Atlas hisses through a mouthful of blood. "You're going to regret this, Gabriel."

Even now, he thinks he can control me.

"You think I care? What do I have left to lose, Atlas?"

Finally, I'm hauled off him by two other warders, who have to restrain me from attacking again.

"Arrest him!" I shout. "He's a traitor to Aphelion!"

The guards circle him as Atlas scrambles back, fear finally settling in his eyes.

Apricia is still screeching, and the crowd has lost control. Dimly, I become aware of the scent of burning, the haze of smoke hovering in the air. Worlds collapsing and screams echoing as the rain continues to punish us from the skies.

I wonder briefly where Lor and Nadir are. Did all of this provide the distraction they needed?

My thoughts are cut off when a resounding shatter blasts through the crowd. The entire roof of the Sun Palace explodes, glass flying in every direction. I realize it's the dome over the throne room. The sky fills with forks of bright crimson lightning, mixing with the white jagged streaks of the storm. It crackles and dances, and the sight is so staggering that it stills everyone into silence.

As I watch more lightning crackle overhead, I understand this must be Lor.

I've heard stories of the Heart Queen's magic.

And here she is, returned after almost three hundred years.

I'm not sure why that brings me as much comfort as it does.

My throat knots up. Lor did what she needed. I'm weirdly proud of her.

The lightning cuts off a moment later, and it takes several seconds for everyone to come back to themselves.

Atlas's gaze drifts from the sky and over to me. He lies on the ground where I knocked him down, blood covering the front of his golden jacket.

"Gabe," he says, his eyes filling with tears, but he will not manipulate me this time. I'm done swallowing the prickled fruit of his lies.

I stand over him, and his expression crumples with resignation.

"This is over, Atlas," I say, touching the tip of my sword to his throat.

"Long live the true king."

Chapter Fifty-Two

LOR

"Lor." A voice whispers to me, and my eyes peel open. The light is bright yet soft, like it's being filtered through frosted windowpanes. "Lor. Wake up."

I groan as I shift, my body tight and achy. I'm lying on a hard floor, and my eyes shift up as someone enters my view and a soft hand gently touches my cheek.

I try to focus, but whoever it is flickers in and out, shifting from the form of a woman with dark hair and pale skin to become a man with a shaved head and an olive complexion. It's too many people all blurring together, and my head spins as my axis tips sideways.

"It's so nice to finally meet you," the figure says with a

voice that ripples in a dozen octaves—high and low, soft and strong. "Let us help you up."

They take my arm and tow me into a seated position.

"Who are you? Where am I?"

"You are in the Evanescence," they say, and that fires off every alarm bell in my head.

"Am I . . . dead?"

The last thing I remember is that putrid black smoke filling my lungs, Nadir yelling, and then Rion's soldiers tying me up.

"No, you're not dead," the figure says. "We are the Empyrium."

I must've hit my head, or Rion gave me hallucinogenic drugs to shut me up, and now I'm dreaming I'm in the Evanescence with some weird ghost or whatever this is.

"Um . . . okay?"

They smile patiently and then push up to stand, holding out a hand. "Come. We have things to show you."

My nose wrinkles as I stare at their outstretched fingers, watching them transform from one hand to another's. "Is this real?"

They nod. "This is real, Lor."

Corralling my disbelief, I reach out and take their hand before they help pull me up.

We're standing inside a circular room, the walls and floor covered with pale grey and white marble. Arched windows surround us, glowing with soft sunlight.

Seven people stand in a circle facing one another. I study them, noticing some bear a resemblance to people I've met before.

"What's going on?" I ask. Something tells me this isn't a dream.

"You are witnessing the Beginning of Days," says the Empyrium at my side. "Who you see here are the human kings and queens who ruled over Ouranos at the end of the First Age."

I wait for the Empyrium to continue explaining as they gesture for me to watch.

"Your lands were suffering," they say. "Curses and plagues. Illnesses without explanation. They all tried to fight for the health of their people, but it was no use."

I recall the story Nerissa recounted in the living room yesterday about magic going wild. At least, I think it was yesterday. It's a little hard to tell right now.

"Because the magic was overflowing?" I ask.

The Empyrium nods. "Exactly. It had become too much, so we gathered the seven of them together."

"And you are?"

"We are your gods," they say.

"But isn't Zerra our god?"

They shake their head. "Not exactly. No."

I wait with my mouth open for more, but the Empyrium stares ahead.

"Look, I'm going to need something more here. What am I doing here? What's going on? This is all very mysterious, but the last thing I remember is being kidnapped by my mortal enemy, and if I'm not dead, then I really need to get back and deal with that shi—stuff."

I'm not sure why cursing next to these gods feels wrong, but I correct myself at the last moment.

Their gaze slides to me, and I swear they're trying not to laugh.

"Understood," they say. "We assure you that your visit here will be worth your time, Lor. Zerra is not a god in the way your people believe. She became our emissary. Your world is governed by us. We oversee hundreds of continents and worlds and galaxies beyond your wildest imaginings."

They take my hand to pull me closer as I puzzle at those words. I guess they make sense? I've never heard of such a thing, but that doesn't mean it isn't common knowledge. What I know about the history of Ouranos could fit into a thimble, and that's even after learning everything I have in the past few months.

"No, the people of Ouranos do not know who we are," they say.

"Can you read my mind?"

"No. Not entirely, but we can glean echoes of what you're thinking."

"That's a little creepy."

Again, they seem to be trying to contain a smile.

"Oh, you will do well, Lor."

"Do well at what?"

Instead of answering my question, they sweep out a hand. "When we gathered the kings and queens here, we gave each of them a gift. Of course, you are familiar with them. Seven Artefacts used to tether Ouranos to the magic so it could come under their control and would no longer consume them."

"That's what they do?"

"Amongst a few other things, but their main function was to bind the humans to the magic and ascend them to High Fae, and that has been their main role for generations."

"So then what?"

"For the magic to transfer, each ruler was asked to bind themselves to their Artefact. Their life would become one with it, and when they passed on, they would remain with it forever."

I allow that thought to settle. "That's why they talk to me. They're alive."

They tip their head, the movement feline in its elegance.

"In a manner of speaking. Their bodies are long gone, but their minds remain."

"That sounds . . . uncomfortable."

They shrug. "We wouldn't know."

"So, who is everyone?" I glance around the circle, noting a woman in gold underwear with bronzed skin. "She's from Aphelion?"

They nod. "She was. They were experiencing a heat wave of unprecedented proportions when she was taken and brought here."

"What about the others? What about Heart?" I ask just as seven objects appear above their heads spinning slowly. A woman with dark hair, wearing a red gown, stands under the Heart Crown.

"Queen Amara's people were plagued by a disease they called the Sleepness. People would fall into a deep sleep and never wake up."

"That's horrible."

"It was," they agree.

"So she's who lives inside my Crown?"

This is getting weirder and weirder.

"In essence," the Empyrium says, "though their memories are not of their mortal lives."

"Now what's happening?" I ask.

"One of them was asked to lead. We requested that someone volunteer to remain in the Evanescence and become the symbol of divine worship for Ouranos and its people, living here for an indefinite time that would stretch beyond memory. The others would be free to return home with their objects of power and enjoy their lives until their natural ends.

"As you can imagine, few jumped at the chance to become the sacrifice. They were being offered near immortality and magic not only for themselves but for their people. And no one wanted to abandon their homes."

I watch the seven rulers standing around the circle. They're alternately eyeing one another and staring at the Empyrium, who stands in the center of the circle. I can't hear anything, but I get the sense this was the moment the Empyrium asked one of them to sacrifice themselves.

Even without the benefit of sound, I feel the tension reaching between them.

Finally, one of the men steps forward and lifts his hand. He's wearing a long black cloak and has dark hair and eyes that are so achingly familiar a burr of emotion sticks in my chest.

"King Herric of The Aurora," the Empyrium whispers. "He was drawn to the power. The promise of what it would mean to be worshipped as a god, even if he wasn't technically one."

We watch as everyone listens to Herric speak, his mouth moving with voiceless sound.

"But we rejected him," they say.

"Why?" I ask, keeping my gaze focused on the seven rulers.

"He was needed on the surface." The Empyrium pauses. "And we did not think he was suitable for the role."

"Why not?"

"His heart was . . . dark."

I recall the Aurora Torch told me the same thing about Rion.

I watch as rage flashes over Herric's expression—visceral with anger. He looks around the circle, but no one can meet his accusing stare. He storms back to his place and then spins around to face the room as a shiver rolls down my back. I see the promise of war in the depths of his eyes.

Everyone goes back to staring at one another, when finally, the queen from Aphelion slowly raises her hand. It's clear she's unsure of herself, her shoulders rounded and her arm covering her stomach in a posture of self-consciousness.

I watch the relief on everyone else's faces as she quickly drops her arm again, but Herric stares at her with that same promise of bloodshed in his eyes.

The woman speaks to the Empyrium, her spine straightening as I watch her find her confidence.

"Is that Zerra?" I ask. "Zerra was from Aphelion?"

The Empyrium nods.

"Why her and not King Herric?"

The Empyrium pauses, debating what to say next.

"She was not a good queen. When the other rulers laid down everything to help their lands, Zerra turned away, preferring to indulge in only her wants and needs."

"So why would you want someone like that leading everyone?"

"We sensed she wanted to be better, and we saw in her the ability to rise to the challenge. Besides, like Herric, the others were needed at home. Her queendom would not miss her.

528   NISHA J. TULI

Another was assigned in Zerra's stead, and King Cyrus went on to rule for many years."

I pinch the bridge of my nose, having trouble absorbing everything I'm hearing. This is how it all went down?

"The rulers were sent away, and Herric returned home, but he was not to be content with the hand he'd been dealt. And so he set out to counter the magic of the Artefacts by creating objects of opposing power. After years of research and hunting, he found a material that he called virulence."

"What's virulence?"

"It is the antithesis of the magic in the realms. If your magic is the light, then it is the dark."

"That's the black stone?" I ask.

They nod. "Indeed. He made six arks in Zerra's image, such was his loathing of her. He dug into the deepest recesses of the mountains to retrieve it, pushing his workers to death, his kingdom nearly to ruin. It twisted him, made him into something other.

"And so, he fell, inadvertently trapping himself in a world of shadow and ash, where he rules over his lonely, empty dominion. He sought the power of a god but was reduced to nothing but a caretaker of the souls of the damned. Those of you on the surface refer to him as the Lord of the Underworld."

I gape at the Empyrium, struggling to arrange these pieces of knowledge.

"But the arks were left behind—he had sent one to each of the rulers, claiming they would help control and amplify the magic of their homes. In the early days, they'd had trouble containing it. The magic was wild and untethered, and things got worse before they got better. So they reached for this lifeline, using the arks with impunity. Six coffins made to contain the effigy of Zerra's form. And every time the rulers channeled their magic through the arks, they would slowly kill her."

"Six arks," I say, recalling Nerissa's research. "Not seven."

"Herric had no need of one for himself," they say. "He had mountains of virulence at his disposal."

I nod and then ask, "But why didn't you do something about this?"

"By then, we'd moved on. We had other things to attend to, and you are only a mere speck of dust in the vastness of our existence."

I make a sound of derision. "Oh, how nice."

They almost smile again.

"So then what?" I ask, hanging on every word.

"So Zerra sought to find and destroy them. It became her singular focus. She was interested only in saving herself. We had misjudged her desire to do better. Never underestimate how hard old habits die.

"When she realized she couldn't get to the arks herself, she selected a group of High Fae to help find them."

"The priestesses," I say.

"Yes. She created the sisterhood in her image, giving them a form of magic that would help them seek out the arks." Their mouth presses together. "But she manipulated their devotion, and they quickly spun out of control in their quest. She'd given them too much power, and it poisoned their minds."

I remember the stories Nadir told me about how the priestesses had carried out horrific acts in her name.

"Oh," I say.

"She made so many mistakes," the Empyrium says with a disappointed tone.

"You kind of forced her into this, though, didn't you?"

That earns me a side-eye, but no further comment.

"And now? Why are you telling me all this?"

"Her time in this role has passed. She has proven herself unworthy and is no longer strong enough to keep the magic under control."

"So someone else needs to become Zerra?" I ask.

The Empyrium tips their head. "Well, they'd be free to use their own name."

"Who?" I ask, a sense of foreboding prickling in the abyss of my subconscious.

They turn to face me, and I see the depths of an entire universe in their shifting eyes. The years and worlds and lifetimes beyond this moment.

They are infinite, and *I* am only a speck of dust tossing about the cosmos.

"Someone with a better heart than hers. Someone who would have fought for her people and who would fight for Ouranos and against the evil that roots deep in its darkest corners. Someone with only the shadow of a crown, long since tarnished by the sins of their ancestors."

They pause, and the air stills around me, coalescing into a vague destiny that gathers like billows of dark smoke, as they give me a sad smile.

"Perhaps . . . a queen without a queendom."

CHAPTER FIFTY-THREE

The sway of movement rouses me from unconsciousness. The first indication that something is wrong is the pinch in my shoulders. My hands are tied behind my back, and I'm lying in a way that sends pain radiating down my side.

I blink in rapid succession, trying to dislodge the cobwebs muffling my thoughts.

Where was I? Was that all a dream? Did I really speak with the gods of Ouranos?

Another lurch drags me back to the present. I'm lying in a cart. The sky is blue, and the rain has stopped. Where are we? How long have I been out? Does anyone realize we're missing?

I wonder what's happening in Aphelion. How are Willow and Tristan? What happened with Gabriel and the king? *Where* is Nadir?

I can't let all of these questions derail my focus right now. I have to get out of here. Then I can sort through the events of that strange encounter in the Evanescence, though I can't be sure any of it was real.

Slowly, I peel my eyes open to slits, hoping no one notices I'm awake. Soldiers march beside me on horses, the top halves of their bodies visible over the edge.

I'm surrounded on all sides by the Aurora King's guard.

Is Nadir also tied up or riding next to his father as they cart me back to The Aurora yet again? Rion's words ring through my head.

Thank you so much for telling me where I'd find her.

More words come back to me with the damning clarity of a silver bell.

That way lies only heartbreak.

I twist my hands, but my bindings hold tight—they're made of a cold, hard material that chafes against my skin. A surge of magic shoots through my limbs, calling up a sigh of relief, though I know I will forever live in terror of having my magic locked away again.

I wish I could gauge how many people surround us. How far does this line go? If I use my magic on those in my immediate perimeter, will I be met with more soldiers? Where is Rion? Is he traveling close to me or far away?

None of this really matters. All I know is I have to try. I can't let them take me up the road we're traveling. Only bloodshed waits for me at the end.

I pray no one is looking too closely as I focus on the spark inside my chest, preparing to blast out my power. It already feels like an old friend. Will the restraints prevent me from accessing it? I have no idea how to do this without using my hands.

I squeeze my eyes shut, sure that I have only one chance.

I *cannot* let Rion take me back to The Aurora.

My magic stirs inside me like a pot of boiling water. I feel it fizzing against my skin, the sensation so different from what I'm used to. It's alive and electric and bubbling under the surface. Bright, loud sparks that sing and hum. I don't have to try anymore.

Why did Rion leave me like this? Does he still think me harmless? He had to have seen what I did in the throne room.

"Hey!" comes a voice, and something hard pokes me in the back. "Shut up, bitch! Alert His Majesty! She's awake!"

I don't think. I just react.

Magic erupts from my hands, blowing apart my bindings as it pours out of me. I can't control it. I don't try to. I want them all to bleed. As it courses through me, I remember how I felt in the throne room, invincible and capable of tearing apart the sky.

It surges and pulses, destroying everything around me. I struggle to stand and then stop, curling my magic back into my hands, surveying the spoils of my victory. That same dome of lightning I used on the Aurora King in the Heart Castle surrounds us, only now it's at least ten times larger. And this time, I didn't just cage them—this time I destroyed them.

The air crackles with static, and my hair floats off my face from currents of sparking electricity. Bodies surround me. Soldiers in uniform. These bastards who thought they'd keep me caged. I taste blood and cold satisfaction, doused in the pitch-black fantasies of my revenge.

At my feet lie the pieces of a glowing blue material I presume were the tethers binding my arms. I pick one up, studying it, recalling that Tyr wore the same thing around his wrists and throat.

But I toss it away when I spy a familiar body lying in the charred grass. The outlines of his achingly beautiful profile unmistakable across the distance. I'd know that face from a million miles and buried in a thousand layers of brick and stone.

I'm already moving. I jump down from the cart and sprint, skidding to my knees in the dirt.

"Nadir!" I scream, grabbing him by the shoulders, pressing my ear to his chest, registering only the faintest heartbeat.

Gods, what have I done? There's no wound that I can see. No blood. Nothing that I can heal.

I shake him by the shoulders. His hands are bound behind his back with cuffs made of the same glowing blue stone, forcing him to lie at an awkward angle.

"Nadir, wake up!" I scream, tears slipping off the tip of my nose. "Wake up!"

He doesn't move. He doesn't speak. If I press my cheek to his mouth, he barely breathes.

What have I done?

I scan the clearing, noting heaps of bodies, all of them seemingly unharmed but for the fact that none is moving.

I did this.

Is the king among them? I can't worry about that. I have to get Nadir out of here and to safety. I have to fix this.

He didn't betray me. He wouldn't. The king was lying. Attempting to drive a wedge between us. Trying to destroy any slice of happiness his only son tried to carve out for himself. I believe that. I know in my heart of hearts that Nadir didn't sell me out.

Even if he had, I wouldn't let him die. Even if he was forced to betray me because he had no other choice to save his mother or his sister, I wouldn't let him die. If all we had together were these moments, then I'll be content to let that be enough. This changes nothing about my feelings for him. There have never been any easy choices for us.

I've always known I was never destined for a happily ever after.

Heartbreak. Ruin.

I stand up and hook my hands under his armpits and heave. I expect him to be too heavy to move, but with some effort, I manage to shift him several feet. That's when I realize I'm also in my Fae form. Whatever happened in the throne room must have unlocked that too. Finally, I catch a break.

I lurch again, relieved to discover I'm capable of moving his heavy body, though it's not without some effort. The dome that surrounds us is massive, and it takes me several minutes to drag him across the clearing.

Every few steps, I stop to take a break, dropping my ear to his chest and checking for his heartbeat. It continues pulsing, but it's faint, and I try to convince myself it isn't growing weaker.

When we reach the wall of the dome, I'm not sure what to do. I don't want to remove it, even if I knew how, since it will contain Rion and his guards, giving us a chance to escape.

I reach out and touch it, and my hand passes through unharmed. Interesting. It makes sense my own magic wouldn't hurt me, but I surely can't say the same for Nadir.

I wonder if I can make a door or an opening, but I don't know how to do that, and I'm running out of time. I touch the lightning again, trying to do something with it, but it remains in the same state, flickering and crackling.

I'm acutely aware of how long this is taking. Someone is going to wake up soon.

What if I just cover his body with mine?

This is, no doubt, the worst plan anyone has ever conceived, but it's all I've got.

Dropping to my knees, I roll Nadir to the edge of the dome before I shield as much of him as I can and then maneuver us through, rolling him under me. It's awkward and hard, and when I catch the scent of burning flesh, I have no choice but to press on.

When we finally reach the other side, I tumble off him and onto the grass, panting with the effort. After a moment, I note that I allowed his feet to touch the lightning where my shorter frame left them exposed. There are singes all over his clothing, but the worst of it is confined below his knees, where his boots and the fabric of his pants have melted away, leaving behind angry red patches of skin.

Once again, I listen for his heartbeat, the sound so faint that my vision turns black. I must keep moving, one foot in front of the other. I can't think about it. I need to find us somewhere to hide out of sight.

I drag him off the road and into the trees, wincing because if he were awake, this would probably hurt like hell.

"Nadir," I sob. "Wake up. Wake up."

I continue dragging him further and further until we're deep in the forest. I wonder how long the dome of my magic will remain in place. Rion escaped last time, and I have to believe he can do it again.

Finally, I spy a small outcropping of rock to hide us from view. Sweat runs into my eyes, and my heart thrashes against my ribs. I lean over Nadir, once again searching for his heartbeat and his breath as wild panic swirls in my gut.

"Nadir," I whisper. "Wake up."

With my hands pressed to his chest, I let out a tendril of my healing magic, forcing my lightning to the side with no small amount of effort. It winds out in a blood-red satin ribbon, curling around his heart as I concentrate on trying to feed magic into it, hoping it will wake him up.

I whisper his name over and over as tears slide off my chin, landing on my hands and soaking his chest. "Nadir. Please. I love you."

My ribbon wraps around his heart, and I try to fill it with as much love as I can. With everything I feel for him. With everything I have to give him. With every smile and wish and moment we've shared together. With everything I want for our future.

The beat slows, shuddering to a sluggish pace.

Thump.

Thump.

thump.

thu...

My magic slides against a dense knot of tissue and blood, then...I feel his heart stop.

...

Silence, horrible unbearable infinite silence, shatters in my ears.

The ribbon falls away, and I imagine it, suspended in the slow death of time, twirling to the floor, limp and lifeless as it collapses into a weightless curl.

My ribcage cracks, my heart imploding and leaking out on a crimson flood of all my mistakes.

I collapse on top of Nadir, pressing my cheek to his chest, my hands fisting in his shirt, as the forest echoes with the agony of my broken, never-ending scream.

ACKNOWLEDGMENTS

I have so many people to thank, I barely know where to begin. I barely know how to put into words just how wild 2023 was for me. It was the most incredible and astonishing year of my life, and the best part is that it feels like only the beginning.

To my agent, Lauren Spieller. The moment I met you, I knew you would be the one. You understood me and my vision from the very first call, and I could just feel your enthusiasm through the screen. I was looking for someone to keep up with me, and now I can hardly keep up with you. You brought my wildest dreams to life, and I'm so grateful.

To my editor, Madeleine Colavita, at Forever. Thank you for believing in me again. It's crazy to think just how much we've been through together and yet, this will be the very first book we officially publish together. I look forward to so many stories we're going to create over the next few years. A big thank-you to Grace Fischetti as well for managing all the details.

To my UK editor, Nadia Saward. The way you were always a dream editor on my list ever since the day you posted you wanted more spice in romantasy on the site that shall not be named. I'm honored to be working with you and so grateful to have your insights.

To Estelle Hallick and Dana Cuadrado, my publicists at Forever. You're amazing and I love your enthusiasm. Thank you for putting up with my endless ideas and questions and "what abouts." I'm aware I have zero chill. Thank you for bringing me to New York and to Comic Con. Did that really happen? I'm still pinching myself.

To everyone else at Forever and Grand Central Publishing (including my favorite Constance), thank you for supporting these books like you have. I'll never get over seeing them in Target (well, not technically since I live in Canada, and we don't have Target, but someday I will—in the meantime, the photos are enough).

To the whole team at Orbit UK, thank you so much for going a thousand miles for me. The necklace is incredible. I hang it over my desk, where I get to admire it every day.

To everyone at Folio Lit, especially the foreign rights team, Chiara and Melissa. Wow. You promised and you delivered. I'm so excited to see Lor and her friends popping up all around the world.

To the entire BookTok and Bookstagram community for sharing my books with such enthusiasm. I couldn't have done this without you (with an extra big shoutout to Rachel Skye 'cause she knows what she did).

To every single one of my readers. I am so, so grateful for your support.

To every beta reader and critique partner, especially CM Levya, who's become the alpha reader of my dreams. Your comments and insights made this book a hundred times better. To the rest of my betas: Shaylin, Bria, Ashyle, Priscilla, Elayna, Ann, Raidah, Manuia, Rachel, and Liz. Thank you so much. This process would be impossible without you.

To my assistant, Margie. Your help has been a godsend. I'm sorry for my chaos.

To my family—Matt, Alice, and Nicky. I love you all so much. Seriously, thank you for putting up with me and my insane work schedule and for being the proudest ones of all.

ALSO BY NISHA J. TULI

About the Author

Nisha is a Canadian fantasy romance author, whose books feature kick-ass heroines, swoony love interests, and slow burns with plenty of heat. She loves to draw upon her Indian heritage and her love of fantasy to bring her stories to life, weaving together vibrant and compelling characters, settings, and plotlines. When she's not writing or exploring, Nisha can be found enjoying travel, food, and camping with her partner, two kids, and their fluffy Samoyed.

Follow Along for More
Website and newsletter: https://nishajtuli.com
Instagram and Tiktok: @nishajtwrites